a Novel

TAMMY BARLEY

WHITAKER
HOUSE

Love's Rescue proves chivalry is not dead in an action-packed Western romance between two hurting people. In her fiction debut, author Tammy Barley pulls you in with her true-to-life characterization and tender message of finding hope in the midst of devastating loss.

—Vickie McDonough, award-winning author
of sixteen books and novellas

Set in the Nevada Territory during the War Between the States, Tammy Barley's debut novel tells an unforgettable story of love and loyalty, hatred and healing, and the true meaning of family and friendship. Like the blanket the heroine weaves, *Love's Rescue* blends fascinating details of Paiute culture, well-placed moments of humor, and heart-pounding drama to create a beautiful portrayal of a woman's struggle to survive after tragedy.

—Amanda Cabot, author, *Paper Roses*

In *Love's Rescue*, Tammy Barley writes a Western historical romance with great heart backed by solid research and packed with surprising twists and turns. Her setting is one that has seldom been used during the Civil War but which nonetheless was deeply affected by it. It was a pleasure to read from start to finish.

—Laurie Kingery, author,
The Outlaw's Lady and *Hill Country Christmas*

Unless otherwise indicated, all Scripture quotations are taken from the King James Version of the Holy Bible. Scripture quotations marked (NIV) are from the *Holy Bible, New International Version*®, NIV®, © 1973, 1978, 1984 by the International Bible Society. Used by permission of Zondervan. All rights reserved.

LOVE'S RESCUE
Book One in The Sierra Chronicles

Tammy Barley
www.tammybarley.com

ISBN: 978-1-60374-108-8
Printed in the United States of America
© 2009 by Tammy Barley

Whitaker House
1030 Hunt Valley Circle
New Kensington, PA 15068
www.whitakerhouse.com

Library of Congress Cataloging-in-Publication Data

Barley, Tammy, 1969–
  Love's rescue / by Tammy Barley.
    p. cm. — (The Sierra chronicles ; 1)

  Summary: "When Jessica Hale loses her family in a fire set to their home by Unionists targeting Southern sympathizers, she struggles to heal and rebuild her life with the help and protection of Jake Bennett, a godly ranch owner, and by the grace of God"—Provided by publisher.
  ISBN 978-1-60374-108-8 (trade pbk. : alk. paper)   1. United States—History—Civil War, 1861–1865—Fiction. I. Title.
  PS3602.A77557L68 2009
  813'.6—dc22
                              2009008856

2 3 4 5 6 7 8 9 10 11 12 **W** 16 15 14 13 12 11 10 09

Dedication

To the memory of my dear friend, the sister of my heart, Lynette Moll. I wish you could have seen what you inspired.

And to my parents, family, and friends, especially Connor, Reece, and McKenna, the joys of my life. I couldn't have done this without you.

Acknowledgments

My deep appreciation goes to...

Kurt Holman, Manager of Perryville Battlefield State Historic Site in Perryville, Kentucky—never have I met anyone so generous with his time and knowledge.

ACFW critiquers and friends Flavia Crowner, Lisa Lickel, Beth Shriver, and John Otte—you all are answers to prayers that I haven't told you about.

My tireless literary agent, Terry Burns, who probably likes my writing because I write a little like he does.

The talented, talented editors and cover artists at Whitaker House. You all are a blessing to many.

Tim and Iris Gosselin, my parents, who inspired my love of history, horses, and nature, and who encouraged and believed in me.

My Lord and Savior, for whispering in my ear that I should be a writer.

My dear readers—I pray you are entertained, inspired, and drawn closer to God, who loves you always.

Prologue

Carson City, Nevada Territory
April 1860

She was going to lose him. With trembling fingers, Jessica Hale pushed back the brown tendrils of hair the wind was whipping into her eyes. Further down the road, her brother handed the last of his cases to the driver on top of the stagecoach, then tossed his hat through the window onto a seat with an air of resolve. He turned and strode toward her.

His wavy, wind-tossed hair gleamed brightly in the morning sun, its sandy hue like gold coins dulled intermittently by shifting dust. His sky-blue eyes—eyes that gleamed with subtle mockery or shone with patient understanding—now attempted to disguise unspoken regret. He smoothed a hand over each of the sorrel coach horses and calmly took in the young town he was leaving behind. Jessica knew better. He was going to miss this—the town, their parents. But his heart called him home. Ambrose was every inch a Kentucky gentleman. He always had been. Her throat tightened.

"Jessica?"

She couldn't help but smile. *Jessica.* Like always, he spoke her name with that deep, flowing timbre that made her think of the brook they had often played in as children.

"Now what is that smile for?"

"I'll miss the sound of your voice. It's so pleasant."

The L*ord* *said,*
"Go out and stand on the mountain
in the presence of the L*ord,*
for the L*ord* *is about to pass by."*
Then a great and powerful wind tore
the mountains apart and shattered
the rocks before the L*ord,*
but the L*ord* *was not in the wind.*
After the wind there was an earthquake,
but the L*ord* *was not in the earthquake.*
After the earthquake came a fire,
but the L*ord* *was not in the fire.*

And after the fire came a gentle whisper.

—1 Kings 19:11–12 (N*iv*)

"It is?" Ambrose's eyes sparkled at her in amusement. "You never told me that before."

"Well, now you know." She loved the Southern lilt of it, the quiet honor he wore just as naturally as his greatcoat. She took a deep breath to steady herself. "Are your bags loaded, then?"

"They are. The driver was kind enough to strap them down. With the rough going, I'll get bounced out long before they will."

Her smile faded. "Perhaps you should stay."

"Jess..." Ambrose patiently drew her hand through the crook of his arm and tipped his head toward the road. "We have a few minutes left before the stage leaves. Let's walk for a bit."

Jess sighed in frustration but complied, letting her head fall against his shoulder as they walked. At the edge of town, she looked back at Carson City's wide streets, lazy with the long, morning shadows of tall buildings and newly built frames that smelled of sawn wood. One by one, other pedestrians appeared, striding briskly; then came rattling wagons, kicking up trails of dust this way and that. The wind whipped at Jess's skirt and Ambrose's coat, cavorting among the silvery green desert sage leaves that fluttered around them. The sights and sensations that usually intrigued her had amalgamated into one frolicking, singing fool, playing cruelly to her burdened heart.

Jess's gaze followed the road out of town, then lifted to rest on the peaks that rose high above. The Mexican people called these mountains the Sierra Nevadas—the snowy mountains. When she had come West with her family a year before, Jess had thought them magnificent. In a wild, untamed way, they reminded her of the Kentucky homeland they had left behind. Instead of the rolling green hills and broadleaf forests she had always known, the Sierras jutted boldly from the desert like a rare stone half buried in sand. Depending on the angle of the sun, their terrain was a glorious red or gold.

For a moment, Jess merely breathed, drawing in the fresh scent of the pinyon pines that dotted the distant slopes and mingled with the earthy aroma of sage. Only a few months ago, winter had prevailed, and so had the glittering snows on the Sierras.

Ambrose, dear Ambrose, had understood her need to be outdoors. He'd convinced their father a time or two to excuse him from work, then had taken her riding amid the stark beauty of the mountains.

Their father.

Jess frowned, pushing back strands of hair that had torn from their heavy twist and were stinging her eyes. A brusque but shrewd businessman and horse breeder from Lexington, their father had brought the family West to escape the growing turbulence in the South, and here, his import business thrived. With the recent discovery of untold millions of dollars in gold and silver buried in the land, the eager-to-be-rich swarmed to the Comstock from every major seaport in the world. Those fortunate enough to strike a vein of the mother lode scrambled to Hale Imports to stake their claims in society by acquiring French wines, Venetian glassware, Turkish carpets, and handcrafted furnishings made of dark German wood.

A golden dream for many, perhaps, but not for Jess. Her family had considerable wealth, but possessions beyond life's basic comforts didn't matter to her. What did matter were her father, her mother, and her brother, Ambrose, and the strength they had always given one another in face of the threat of war between North and South.

And the threat had become considerable.

Jess tightened her grip on Ambrose's arm. He patted her hand reassuringly.

Worse, her family hadn't left war fever behind as her father had hoped they would. Its effects were sweeping across the country like the unstoppable waves of the sea. Miners and other men in town chose sides as the conflict loomed nearer. Heated political discussions often erupted into fistfights in the streets. In the same way, tension had escalated within the Hale family as their loyalties divided. And now, Ambrose was about to return to Lexington—against his father's will—to rejoin his militia unit. It was predicted that war would break out within a year. Two days earlier, when Ambrose had announced to Jess and their parents his intent to fight to protect Lexington, Jess had stood strong—stunned but unflinching. The announcement was followed by two days of her father and brother yelling and her mother pleading. A lifetime of paternal love was burning to cinders.

Their father was still so angry about his son's decision that he had refused to see him to the stage stop, coldly disallowing all but the briefest of good-byes between mother and son.

Jess finally broke the silence. "I thought this place would be the answer, Ambrose. I thought here we would be safe from the war." She stopped walking and tossed him a valiant smile. "What will I do without you?"

Ambrose considered her soberly. She'd hoped he would tease her gently. Not this time. "You're seventeen now, Jess. At seventeen, most ladies stop concerning themselves with their families and set their eyes on marriage."

"Marriage? Marriage! How could you suggest that?" She flung aside her earlier self-promise to remain calm. "*This* particular subject has never come up before, but since it has, let me tell you, Ambrose, I don't need a husband to manage my life and order me about."

"Jess—"

"I know you want to protect me, and I love you for it. But the South and its marrying traditions are a great distance away. Here, women are strong and independent"—she fought

11

to control the anger in her voice—"and so am I. I've seen too many wives' hopes destroyed by their husbands' selfish wants and ambitions. I could never live my life under some man's boot heel. I'll make my way on my own."

Ambrose gave her a reluctant smile. "All right. There's no talking you into an idea your mind is set against. Keep yourself busy, then. Tell Father you want to keep books at Hale Imports. You've been schooled the same as I have. You'll do well."

Jess's legs nearly gave out. "Keeping his accounts is your job!" Ambrose wasn't coming back at all—not even after the war. She really was going to lose him.

"No, Jess. Not anymore." He shifted his gaze to the territory around them. "This place has never fit me the way it has you. That house in Kentucky is our house. Its lands are Hale lands. I was born and raised at Greenbriar, and so were you. That's my home, Jess." He faced her squarely. "When the war comes, I'll defend it, whether the invading army is from the North or the South."

Jess's throat ached to beg him to stay. Their friendship was special, rare, in spite of growing up together amid talk of secession and war. Or perhaps because of it. She wanted to keep her brother close—and safe. Yet she forced down the urge to give words to her feelings. Ambrose's blood flowed for Greenbriar, for Lexington. A year away hadn't changed that. Yes, she loved him. Enough to understand that. Enough to let him go.

"I guess I always knew you'd go back," she admitted, "and I understand, I really do. I just hate knowing that you'll be right in the middle of the fighting." She raised a hand. "And I hate that Father's turned his back on you when you need him most! How could he do that to you? How could he do that to Mother?" All at once, she knew. "He's doing this because of Broderick, isn't he?"

Broderick had died as a baby, when Jess was only five. Even

now, she could clearly remember holding her little brother as his fever raged, could remember how helpless she had felt when she'd lain awake at night listening to his pathetic coughs in the nursery down the hall. Jess had been devastated when he died, but their mother...their mother had never been the same. Her joy and laughter Jess knew about only because Ambrose had told her of the way she had once been.

Ambrose acknowledged the fact. "Father doesn't think Mother could bear to lose another son."

Jess nodded slowly. "Then you'd best stay alive."

The corner of his sandy mustache lifted. "You're a Hale, that's for certain. Idealistic and stubborn, through and through."

"Hopefully stubborn enough to get through to Father. You know I can't let things remain the way they are between the two of you."

"Jess, I'd like to warn you against—"

"That would be pointless." At his gentle frown of censure, she ordered her thoughts and explained. "For as long as I can remember, you were the one who held our family together. Not Father, even when he was home. It was not Mother or anyone else, but you. You reasoned with Father when business made him unreasonable, you were a constant comfort to Mother, and you sat by my bed at night when storms and thunder threatened to shake the house apart."

"You just wanted company while you were awake." He lightly tugged a lock of her hair in a teasing way. "You never feared storms or anything else."

"For the past few years, I've feared the coming war." She lifted her chin and, with a mental step forward that she would never retrace, left the remnants of her childhood behind. "You won't be here to keep us together. Now I'll take your place and do what you've always done, and rely on solid Hale determination to see me through. Ambrose, don't worry about

Mother, or about Father's anger at your decision to go. I'll hold our family together, and I'll do all I can to change his heart."

Gratitude battled concern in his face as he studied his sister, but Jess knew that he also understood firsthand the inborn loyalty that drove her. "Just be careful you don't jeopardize your relationship with him on my account," he said.

"I will be careful."

There was a movement near the stagecoach. A mailbag was slung aboard.

Jess's heart lurched. It was almost time for him to go.

Ambrose patted her hand and looked intently into her eyes. "I don't know when I'll see you again. We'd better say good-bye."

"No!" She shook her head, fighting sudden tears. "I won't say good-bye."

"Jess, I don't want to frighten you, but if the war comes—"

"Then the war will end! Ambrose, if we say good-bye, it's as if we won't see each other again. I can't do that. I have to believe—I have to know—that one day you'll come back."

"Believe it," he said, his gaze firm beneath his brows, "because I intend to."

She tightened her grip until it pained her. "Then we don't say good-bye?"

He hesitated, then shook his head to assure her. "We don't say good-bye."

Suddenly, Jess recalled what she had wanted to do. With a quick tug, she untied the green satin ribbon of the pendant necklace she wore, slipped the ribbon free, and pressed it into his hand. "I'll want that back one day," she said. "Until then, keep the best memories of us all close to your heart."

Ambrose smiled and tucked the ribbon into his shirt pocket with a little pat. "I can't think of a better place to put them."

Another movement drew her gaze. The coach driver climbed into his seat.

"Ambrose?"

"Pray for me, Jess. I'll write to you as often as I can, I promise."

Ambrose hurried toward the stage, Jess's hand tucked in his. At the door, he pulled her into his arms and hugged her warmly.

"Will you write to me?"

Jess buried her face into the gray cloth of his coat. "Just try to stop me."

He kissed the top of her head, briefly hugged her tighter, and then stepped away.

After Ambrose had swung aboard the coach, he turned and leaned out the window. His blue eyes shone. "The Lord has a plan, Jess!" he called. "Remember that!"

The driver cracked the reins and the six-in-hand pulled the stage away from Carson City, away from her. Jess watched until the coach disappeared through a pass in the mountains.

Keep him safe, Lord, she prayed. *Whatever lies ahead, please keep him safe.*

It was all she could do not to run for her horse and go after him.

Near Perryville, Kentucky
October 1862

His boots firm in the stirrups, Ambrose leaned over the heaving neck of the mare as he charged into the sunlit field. Well-muscled and dappled gray, the mare tore up stones with her thrashing hooves while Ambrose's cotton shirt ballooned behind him and snapped in the blowing heat. His fear for General Bragg's paltry command of sixteen thousand burned like liquid fire in his belly, and with heartrending despair, he recalled Mr. Lincoln's reputed strong conviction that "to lose Kentucky is nearly the same as to lose the whole game."

His colonel's rapidly scrawled reconnaissance report was secured in a leather pouch tucked into his waistband. It was the only warning Bragg would have that the Yankee advance at Frankfort was merely a diversion, and that the whole of General Buell's Union army was, in fact, moving toward Bragg's position. Buell meant to take Kentucky.

The enemy was fifty-five thousand strong.

Sixteen thousand up against fifty-five. Ambrose whipped a sleeve across his forehead to blot the sweat seeping from underneath his hat. If he didn't reach Bragg in time for the general to pull back and regroup, Kentucky would fall to the Federals—and to their torches. Ambrose tilted his head to hear the distant *pum, pum* of cannon fire.

Fields dotted with white and blue wildflowers blurred by. This was his home, his land, and now, Greenbriar was his, too. Ambrose frowned as he recalled the letter written by his stiff-necked, outraged father—the sole one he'd sent—in which he had given him Greenbriar. His father intended the house as an accusatory monument to the heritage he believed his son had betrayed by ultimately fighting for the South. But to Ambrose, if Greenbriar survived the war, it would again become his home, his livelihood, and the place his old bones would be laid. He yearned to fall in love there, to marry there, to raise children amid all its gurgling streams and grassy paddocks. Children who would love it as he always had, and as Jess had.

Memories intruded—memories of the day Jess was born and the moment he first held her. He had been seven, and the tiny, warm bundle that stared up at him with curious green eyes had captivated his heart. As she grew, it was to him that she had come for comfort and advice; with him, she shared her inmost thoughts. He had taught her more about the person she could become than their parents ever had, and she had matched his strength and dedication toward those whom she loved.

Now Jess was his proponent and confidante. She wrote to him as often as he wrote to her, discreetly hiding his letters from their father. He knew many of their letters never made it through enemy lines since, in letters he did receive, Jess frequently referred to events he was unaware of, as well as to war news he had previously penned. Even so, they both persisted in sending them. As promised, she patiently worked to sway their father's heart toward his son.

And she remained firm in her belief that her brother would survive the war.

His mind turned to the letter he had written to her only a few hours ago. He imagined her reading it at night by candlelight, the flame's glow illuminating her casually knotted hair, highlighting the loose strands she rarely bothered with. He could almost hear the smooth flow of her Southern voice as if she were reading it aloud.

> *My dearest Jessica,*
> *Like others here, I often look ahead to the end of the war and dream of what I will do after.*
> *For me, it has never been a question. The day I muster out, I will come without hesitation to all of you there, to make up lost years of brothering for you and baby Emma, and to find a way to repair the damage between Father and me. I will remain until Mother's worries for me have gone, and she sees her family healed. Until then, Jessica, you must continue to convey to her news of my well-being,*

and tell her of my unflagging determination to return to you all.

Then, as Grandfather would have wished for me to do, I will come back home to Greenbriar and rebuild what the war has ruined. I'll fill its paddocks again with the prized horseflesh that has always graced its lands.

I yearn to walk again the brick path leading to the porch, to step into the downstairs hall and feel it welcome me home...

Startled, Ambrose entered a town huddled beneath a haze of smoke. Perryville! The mare was slick with sweat and foam, but she had a bold heart, the likes of which he'd rarely seen in an animal. Spying a cluster of saddled mounts, Ambrose halted before a red brick house. The gray tugged at the reins while he listened to a soldier's instructions on how to find General Bragg.

Ambrose immediately headed northwest on the river road. The roar of battle grew deafening. Yankee wounded and dead lay scattered over the hills.

He topped a rise. Below, gray-clad soldiers swarmed through thick smoke into the enemy, several falling beside their comrades. All around, cannon shells burst in sprays of jagged metal and earth.

"Lord in heaven," Ambrose murmured, "help us all."

Urging the mare along a path behind the lines, Ambrose ducked the whizzing cannon fire. He pulled out his leather pouch and withdrew the message.

...to throw open the nursery doors where we played, and step into the sunshine flowing through the window glass. Do you remember how we watched from that high

window the newborn foals bounding about? And the way
you were ever leaning over the sill for a better look, know-
ing that I would hold you safe? After the war I must find
myself a young lady, and convince her that we should fill
the room anew with children's laughter....

A cannon shell exploded, and a terrible pressure struck his chest. The mare screamed. Groaning through his teeth, Ambrose clung to her neck. To the west, rifles barked flashes of orange as men in blue and gray surged into their enemies.

Ambrose pressed forward, searching the high ridges for the familiar starred collar and white-streaked beard of General Bragg.

...Lastly, I admit to looking ahead to sharing my life with
someone who, like you, will write to me when I must be
away, who will hold warm thoughts of me in my absence.
I pray she may ever keep hope alive for our children that
I will return to them, just as you, my sister, have done for
our family. You have kept me alive through this war, Jess,
for I know one by whom I will always be loved, always be
remembered fondly, and always be welcomed home....

Ambrose kicked the gray forward with all the strength he had. Fortunately, she lunged in response, not wavering at the unsteady weight on her back. Ambrose fought through the thickening fog in his mind and gripped the dispatch tighter.

A sudden burning burst along his thigh, and the smoky daylight and soldiers' movements began to dim. Beneath him, the mare pulled ahead, pitching like a rocking chair. He imagined the stern face of General Bragg turning in surprise as he approached.

…I keep your ribbon in my pocket and frequently feel it there. When I think of you, as I often do, the single thought that comes is this: I cannot wait to see you again.…

He felt himself reaching out to her, to Jess. Wanting to see her one more time, to tell her how dear she was to him, had always been. He was fading. The message. He couldn't feel it. Did the general receive the message?

Ambrose no longer knew what direction the mare took but threaded his fingers through her mane, imagining he was weaving hands with Jess.

…Your ever loving brother,…

No sky fell under his eyes; he saw only a lone field of dappled gray, oddly crossed with streams of red.

"Jess…," he rasped.

Ambrose.

Chapter One

Carson City, Nevada Territory
February 1863

J essica moved another impatient step forward in the slow line, her frustration mounting. Near the corner stove, opinionated miners in wrinkled, unwashed clothes passed around the first bottle of the day and growled about the dry winter, Indian attacks, and war news as it came in over the wire. A dapper man at the front of the line relayed his message to the telegraph operator, and the two began to argue over the phrasing of the telegram.

Jess withheld a scathing suggestion and glanced around the room. An attendant shoveled more coal into the stove and raised the wicks of the oil lamps against the predawn darkness. Inwardly, she was growing annoyed with her plan to send a telegram to the States. With the clear pro-Union sympathies among the patrons, she didn't expect the clerk would much care what happened to her brother.

Her brother.

Jess's head dropped back restlessly, her temples throbbing with pains of worry. Ambrose had written frequently over the past three years, and though an occasional letter had been lost, she'd received word from him nearly every month since he had left for the war.

The last letter he'd sent was dated almost four months ago.

Jess stared angrily at the coattails of the man in front of her. She hated herself for waiting this long, for hoping for word. Something had happened to Ambrose. She knew it had. She knew it right down to her boots.

When his letters had stopped, she had written to his commanding officer, but her letter was neither responded to nor returned. For weeks, she had pored over newspapers and casualty lists until long into the night, but she never saw his name. Now few options remained. This telegram had to work. She had to know what had happened to Ambrose. She had to know what to tell their mother.

Three or four of the miners chuckled over another man's jest, and the line moved slowly forward. Jess pulled her cloak tighter around her. Ambrose, were he nearby, would remind her that the Lord was with her, even in this place. Jess tried to believe that He was, and she took another step closer to the chatter of clicks and beeps coming in over the wire.

꧁ঞ౿꧂

Jake Bennett lifted the saddle from his horse and laid it over the top rail of the corral fence beside him. The winter morning was still dark, the corral and barn wall dimly discernible in the starlight, and the livery stable had yet to open for business that day. No matter. During the previous day's ride from the ranch, his men, seldom known to interrupt a good silence with talk, hadn't passed a mile without one of them commenting on a new hat or saddle he wanted to see in Carson City. All four had been content to break camp before sunrise, and, when they'd arrived, to look through shop windows until proprietors unlocked their doors.

Resting a gloved hand on his stallion's back, Jake leaned over to swipe the road dust from its flank. Almost four years had come and gone since he had built his ranch up near Honey Lake in '59, and he and his men now supplied horses and fresh beef to settlers in gold and silver mining towns that hadn't existed then. Even Carson City, though a fledgling compared to long-established urban areas, was a far cry from the open stretch of wilderness it had been only a few years ago. Board buildings and adobes stood in the valley where the easternmost Sierras parted. When Jake had ridden in a short while earlier, they had seemed to rise out of the desert, the silhouette of a growing town beneath star-rimmed mountains.

With a hearty pat on his horse's neck, Jake straightened. Hurried citizens bustled past, bundled in coats and scarves. A small man scuttled along the storefront toward him, head bowed low against the wind. He stepped off the boardwalk, glanced up in surprise at the huge black horse he had nearly collided with, and lifted his eyes higher to Jake's. The man blinked, murmured an apology, and eased around the stallion, gasping when it flicked its tail warily. Jake watched the fellow's hat pass beneath him as he slipped by, then shifted his regard to the telegraph office across the road, where he had seen a young woman enter a few minutes earlier. Even by lantern light, the woman had appeared agitated about some matter, yet she'd held her head high as she strode through the door with unmistakable boldness, like a cat he had once watched tree a bear. He hadn't seen such beauty and fortitude in a townswoman in quite some time. It was a refreshing sight.

Jake returned his attention to his horse. He reached into

his pocket for a comb, which he used to pull tiny burrs off its flank.

Jess stepped up to the counter. The thin man in shirtsleeves standing behind it grabbed a blank form, barely giving her a glance. "What's your message?"

She steadied herself with a long, deep breath. "To Dr. J. S. Newberry, Secretary for the Western Department of the Sanitary Commission, Louisville, Kentucky."

At the sound of her voice, the man's pencil stopped. Conversations in the room tapered off. The telegrapher's eyes flicked over her in disgust. "Kentucky?"

Jess bristled at his subtle insult. "Yes," she said evenly. "Kentucky."

Gradually, the other men in the room resumed their discussions. The telegrapher rubbed his chin thoughtfully. "Sanitary Commission, huh? All right, go ahead."

Jess waited until he had completed the address. "Dear Sir: I must ask your assistance in locating my brother, as I have no one else to turn to. His last known location was Versailles on October eighth of last year."

The pencil scratched across the page. "Go on."

"He is Lieutenant Ambrose Hale, Second Kentucky Cavalry, Company A"—Jess hesitated only briefly—"Army of the Mississippi."

The discussion behind her ceased abruptly.

Jess felt several pairs of eyes turn toward her.

Jake looked up as the door of the telegraph office burst open. A mob of angry men was dragging someone, thrashing and bucking, down the steps and into the street.

That someone was wearing a skirt.

Jake jerked the lead free of the fence rail. Grasping a handful of mane, he swung himself onto his horse and whistled sharply to the already moving animal.

~⊙⋘⊙~

Jess stared into a sea of snarling faces and rage-reddened eyes. She shrieked as a burly, pockmarked man grabbed a fistful of her hair.

"Confederate trash gets hung in Federal territory," he roared into her face. He was nearly ripping the hair from her head. Jess swatted desperately at his hands. "I lost two cousins at Shiloh," he spat. "Two cousins!"

"You can hardly accuse me—" Jess gasped as she was shoved into the arms of one of his companions, arms that held tight against her ribs, though she fought to wriggle loose. All around, faces leered at her, moving closer: a skeletal, balding man with sunken cheeks. Another with long, white-blond hair. Tobacco-stained teeth. A twisted, broken nose. Others, pressing against her skirt. Rough fingers clamped onto her throat.

Jess was finally flung free as a huge black stallion reared up beside her, massive hooves thrashing. Her attackers stumbled back to a more respectful distance. The horse came down, and the big man astride it speared her attackers with a glare.

"Start walking," he said.

Swiftly recovering their wits, her aggressors glanced around at one another, silently assessing this intruder's ability to hold his own against a large group. Then their eyes shifted to four other men who had stepped into the street and were lining up behind Jess and the horseman.

Jess's heart hammered in her chest. The threat from both sides hung in the air. The four who had joined them— friends of her rescuer, judging by their dress—looked more than ready to take on two times their number, along with anything else that might get in their way. In the lightening gray of the sky, their faces were little more than shadows and gleaming eyes beneath their hat brims. Yet, menacing as they were, none of their scowls could match that of their leader.

A cold blast of wintry air pelted her. The men drew back their heavy coats, hands hovering near the guns at their hips. Jess's breath came in intermittent puffs of vapor. A small crowd had gathered on the boardwalk, and their suspense was mounting tangibly.

Finally, Jess saw the burly man's eyes narrow and his stance relax; it seemed he had decided to let the matter be. With a jerk of his hand, he signaled his companions, who started to back away.

Jess watched them retreat until they disappeared from sight, the last man piercing her with a hate-filled glare. She counted. There had been nine of them. Her stomach felt as if a mule had kicked it. Twice. In the window of the telegraph office, the thin man in shirtsleeves pointedly flipped the OPEN sign to CLOSED.

"That went well," she muttered sarcastically.

"You seemed to be holding your own," a deep voice behind her said.

Jess started. The big man stood an arm's length away, his stallion nuzzling the broad shoulder of his sheepskin coat. He was so tall that she had to lift her head to meet his gaze, and she calculated his intimidating height as six feet—and that was not counting the cowboy boots and hat. Beneath the brim, his brown eyes were calm yet keenly alert, his nose slightly hooked—Indian blood, perhaps?—and his rectangular face was undeniably handsome, dusted with a trace of whiskers. He seemed familiar, and she struggled to place him.

"I think those fellows were fortunate we came along when we did," he said. "You looked mad enough to shred their hides."

Jess stared up at him, recognition dawning. "Mr. Bennett?" She recalled him as a rancher who had come into her father's store a number of times. He had once joined them for dinner when her father was considering investing in cattle of his own.

"That's right." His dark eyes studied her face. "You're Isaac Hale's daughter."

"Jessica," she said. "I was mad. Frightened, too, but mostly mad." With her fingers, she combed back the hair that had come free in the struggle and winced at the tenderness of her scalp. "I'm grateful you came along when you did."

"We'd best move aside," Jake said, seeing that the onlookers were going about their business and usual traffic had resumed. As they crossed the road toward the livery stable, Jess began to shiver. The wind was about as genial as a blanket of ice. Her eyes darted back to the place on the road where the men had dragged her, but her cloak wasn't there. No doubt, she had lost it in the telegraph office. So be it. She wasn't about to go back for it.

Bennett tied his horse to the corral fence. The four cattlemen stood lookout near their horses at the hitching rail, and Jess paused by them, intending to thank them for their help. "Do you have another wrap?" Jake asked her.

Jess looked at him in surprise.

His brown hat tipped toward the telegraph office. "You went in with one," he said.

And the Yankee-loving telegrapher likely had it in hand, and was just waiting for her to slink back in and beg him for it. "I'll be fine until I get home."

Without preamble, the rancher shrugged out of his thick sheepskin coat. "There's more to consider than your pride, Miss Hale," he murmured as he swung it over her shoulders. "Influenza can be a hard lesson."

The coat was heavy and tremendously warm. Jess extended her arms in the sleeves and buttoned it rapidly, nodding in thanks.

The thinnest of the ranch hands, a young, wiry man, pulled his ragged, woolen scarf from around his neck and passed it to her. Jess wrapped it over her freezing head and ears and knotted it under her chin. She flashed him a look of gratitude, but he had already lowered his blushing cheeks into his upturned collar and resumed his survey of the street.

Another of the four handed her a pair of man's gloves. He was stout, with fiery orange hair and a bushy mustache and beard to match. An Irishman, no doubt—her grandfather had had the same flame-red hair and fair skin. This man had a look of joviality about him, though he evidently restrained it in favor of remaining vigilant about any who might return to do them harm.

At her questioning look, Jake introduced her to the Irishman. "Miss Hale, this is Taggart." One bright-blue eye winked. "The boy is Reese." Jake then turned to a big, black man who was nearly as tall as he. "This is Doyle, and the Spaniard there is Diaz."

Doyle barely glanced at her, but Diaz gave her a jaunty salute with the knife he had drawn to carve a piece of wood. He was a contrast of brown skin, black mustache, and grinning white teeth. "*Señorita*," he said with a slight bow.

"I'm grateful to you all for your help with those men," Jess said. "I knew there might be trouble, but I didn't anticipate violence."

Though she was tall for a woman, she still found herself at eye level with either coat buttons or bandanas. She had to lift her gaze to see even the youngest, Reese. Jess glanced at Jake, knowing she could trust him with the truth. "I was trying to wire a high-ranking doctor in the States. My brother—" Her voice caught. She tried again. "My brother, Ambrose, is missing in the war. I wanted the doctor to help me find him. Those men became offended when they heard that Ambrose is fighting for the South." She attempted a smile. "I don't expect they cared much for my accent, either."

Having said the words, Jess felt the weight of her failed efforts and of the tension that awaited her at home. Writing to Ambrose's commander had availed nothing, and her attempt to obtain assistance via the telegraph had failed. She could try to wire from another town, but she strongly suspected the response there would be the same. Given her accent and the fact that half a continent separated her from her brother, she felt as trapped as a wild bird in a cage. And the urge to break free nearly choked her.

Jake briefly considered her, then strode toward his horse. He lifted the blanket and saddle from the fence rail and settled them on its muscular black. As he buckled the cinch, he glanced at the other horses tied nearby, then at her. "Is yours the Appaloosa, Miss Hale?"

"The Appaloosa, yes. And please call me Jess. I—how did you know?"

"The stirrups. They'd be a bit short for a man." He pulled a leather coat over his blue flannel shirt and vest and buttoned it. "I want to take you riding for a while."

"*Riding?*" Jess hadn't expected that. "Why?"

"A couple of those Unionist boys are back. They're keeping

to the shadows near the end of the road, but they're watching. If you leave for a while, I expect they'll get bored and move on." He added, "I also think a run on a horse might do you some good."

As his words set in, Jess gazed at the long stretch of desert beyond the town. She started to shake her head but almost immediately changed her mind. If she didn't get away from the city for a few hours, she would go crazy. In the next instant, she was moving to untie her horse. "I'd be grateful if I could borrow your coat until mid-morning," she called over her shoulder. "I'll leave it for you at my father's store."

"You can borrow it," he said, "but I'm going with you."

"I don't need a guide, Mr. Bennett."

"Jake, please. Aside from those two looking on," he said patiently, "seven other men who took issue with you a short time ago are still in town. The boys and I can make certain they don't follow. Not to mention the prospectors all over this territory who are wary of trespassers—they pan gold with one hand and hold loaded rifles in the other." Behind him, Doyle, Diaz, Taggart, and Reese readied their horses. "There are outlaws, too, Jess."

At the concern in his voice, she searched his eyes. Their depths held a glint of something, a meaning he did not choose to share with her.

Five cattlemen stood waiting.

Jess grunted with impatience. "You must have more important matters to see to than playing nursemaid to me."

"No," Jake answered. "We came to contract with buyers for the autumn roundup, but it can wait till later. We have time."

"Your horses—"

"Our horses are rested. We broke camp only an hour ago, and they're going to spend the rest of the day at the livery stable."

Desperate to get away, with or without them, Jess gathered her reins and stepped up into her saddle.

Ten minutes later, Carson City had disappeared behind her. She raced south, heart soaring, the angles and edges of the red-earthed Sierras flying past as the sky slowly lightened. She didn't bother to look back. Bennett was there, she knew, keeping pace easily on the black, and the other cattlemen trailed behind him, watching out for her. She felt safe—safer than she had since the day Ambrose returned home to Lexington, perhaps even since the day they left Kentucky.

Why did Jake come, and the others with him? she wondered. A hawk glided on reddish-brown wings over the endless desert ahead, almost daring her to follow as far as it would go. She gave in to the urge to chase after it and wondered no more.

Sometime later, Jake appeared beside her and took the lead. They turned west, then followed a trail into the mountains that led up toward Lake Tahoe. The valley fell away below them.

Jess gave the mare her heels, her eyes almost tearing with the invigorating feel of the wind on her face.

༺⚔༻

Half an hour later, Jess and the cattlemen dismounted on a ridge. They tied their horses to clusters of juniper, then stretched their legs.

Jess wandered for several yards, peering warily through the pine trees to the road they had taken. Far below, miles of valley stretched out in all directions. Peaks loomed all around and wisps of pink clouds floated above. Jake came and stood beside her. "Did any of those men follow us?" she asked him.

"No one followed."

"Good."

Cozy as a kitten in Jake's coat, Jess momentarily let go of her worries. She had forgotten how awed she had been by this mountain range when she'd first arrived from the East. For months, she'd seen little more than the buildings and crowds of Carson City. And now she stood near the top of the world. Below her feet lay green pine forest, the Sierra foothills, and the dark-red valley beyond.

She didn't realize she was smiling until Jake spoke again. "Beautiful, isn't it?"

"Yes. It almost doesn't seem real."

"The Almighty sure knows how to say good morning."

She glanced at him, studying the relaxed, open expression beneath his hat brim. "Is that what He's doing?"

"I think He is. Look." In the east, streaks of pink, orange, and gold lit the sky.

All at once, a sliver of blazing sun burst over the curve of the earth. Jess squinted at its brilliance, shifting her eyes to glory in the hues above.

"That's the Almighty reminding us that He's with us each day," Jake said. "Kind of like a present every morning, without the paper wrapping."

"A subtle reminder, perhaps," Jess said, "but there are times I wish He would just tell us He's with us." She sighed. "I do love the isolation and the wildness of this place."

Beside her, Jake looked over the miles of red desert and mountains. "I know what you mean."

Jess felt the rising sun's energy flow through her, renewing and refreshing her. Ambrose was out there somewhere—and alive. Though he was far away and fighting in a war, they were still connected—the same sun was shining down on them both.

When the horses had rested, Jess and the cattlemen remounted and started back down the mountain. They were riding roughly in pairs now—Taggart and Reese in front, Doyle and Diaz after, with Jake and Jess following behind. The five men had said very little; it was as though talking would be an offense to the stillness. She understood. Since they'd ridden away from Carson City, she'd been too contented to even think, though she hadn't been able to do much else as of late. And she needed to. She still had to find Ambrose.

"You don't believe he's dead," Jake said.

Jess glanced at him, surprised by his perceptiveness. "You're right, I don't, but I know something happened. Ambrose's last letter came in autumn. I did all I could to find him, then I tried to send the telegram."

"In autumn?" Jake reined the stallion thoughtfully. "With the frequent movements of armies in the States and Indian attacks on the mail stages out here, I expect some folks in this territory haven't received letters from the East in a year or more."

"We've had letters lost, as well, but I've still received one nearly every month." Jess gazed at the trail ahead. "I'll have to try wiring the doctor from another town."

"And if that fails?"

Jess glanced over somberly. "If that fails, I'll take the first stage east and track him down myself."

Jake considered that. "Shouldn't your pa be trying to find him?"

"Yes, he should, only my father has disowned Ambrose as a traitor—to his family, as well as to his country—even though Ambrose enlisted only to defend our home near Lexington. Ambrose finds slavery as cold-blooded as my father and I do." She shifted in her saddle, battling feelings of resentment toward their father. "In truth, my father's done it to protect my mother. You saw how frail she was when you came to dinner months ago. She lost a son, Broderick, when he was only a baby. She never really recovered, and now she's terrified she'll lose Ambrose. My father doesn't believe Ambrose will survive the war. He behaves as though he is dead already so that, if the worst happens, it won't destroy my mother. At least that's what makes sense to him." A glance at Jake told her he was listening. "He's forbidden me to even write to him."

"That hasn't stopped you," he observed.

"It hasn't," she agreed. "Nor will it. I keep his letters hidden and respond to them in secrecy." She asked, "Do you know Edmund Van Dorn? He and my father co-own the import business."

"Sure, I've met Edmund."

"When Ambrose's letters arrive, Edmund slips them to me with the mail, or he leaves them in an office safe that only he and I use."

"And he and your father are friends," Jake said. "A tough situation all around."

"They're the best of friends, and have been all their lives. Edmund is all heart. He's loyal to my father, but he also sees what's happening to my mother." Though Bennett was little more than a stranger, he was a man who listened, and Jess was relieved to talk to him. "We have a new baby sister whom Ambrose has never seen. He writes how he longs to meet her when the war is over. I *have* to write to Ambrose. And Edmund… Edmund does what he thinks is best for each of us."

Jake said, "I have a friend, Tom Rawlins. He's a captain over at Fort Churchill. I plan to see him tomorrow to talk him into buying some of my horses. There's a telegraph office at the fort. I'll ask him to do what he can to find your brother."

Jess stopped her horse, sudden dampness pricking her eyes. "He'll do this?"

"Search for a Confederate soldier? No, but if he were to search for news of his missing *cousin*," he grinned a little, "now that's a different matter. As long as Tom wires only the North—hospitals and prisons and such—he shouldn't raise too many eyebrows."

Jess wasn't sure whether to shout or cry with joy. The urge to do both swelled to what felt like a fist-sized lump in her throat.

"Of course, Tom will have to wire his findings to Carson City," Jake went on. "I have other sales to arrange, so I'll be in the area until the end of the week. Tom can send the telegram to me." He nodded in the direction of town. "We'll let the Unionists throw me out on the street, if they can."

Jess laughed. Jake Bennett was such a strong, solid man that it would take several lesser men to budge him. She glanced at him again and her laughter died down. The man was muscular and ruggedly handsome. She liked how the corners of his whiskey-brown eyes crinkled when he laughed, how his cheeks showed crooked creases when he grinned, and the fact that he smelled of horses, leather, and the outdoors...

Before her thoughts could go too far in that direction, she forced her mind to easier matters: the sun-dappled trail, the cold, refreshing wind, and what Jake had said in Carson City—that a run on a horse might do her some good. He'd suggested the ride to give her attackers time to move on, yes, but it seemed that he'd had other intentions—to talk to her about the captain and to offer to speak to him on her behalf, and without the risk of being overheard. She was sure of it.

He intended to help her find Ambrose.

Jess forced herself to shift thoughts again before she could tear up and embarrass herself in front of the ranchmen.

Captain Rawlins...what kind of a man was he? He was a Federal officer at a fort that had been established, in part, to put down any Southern uprisings in the territory, and yet Bennett trusted him. Either the captain sympathized with the Confederacy or he was simply a good-hearted man.

As they reached the valley floor and continued toward Carson City, Jess thought back over what she'd told Jake—that she didn't believe Ambrose was dead. She didn't believe it. She couldn't. After all, she had asked the Lord to keep him safe. *Besides,* Jess thought to herself with a smile, *Ambrose is too stubborn to die.*

After a time, Jess found her musings drawn again to the man riding beside her.

Jake Bennett amazed her. For as long as she could remember, she'd not met a man interested neither in selfish gain nor in seeking some advantage from a meeting with a woman. Jake was simply doing a kindness for her, with no other motive than doing what was right.

Jess made several attempts to engage the rancher in conversation. He wouldn't say much about his past but was inclined to discuss his work instead. So, in a lighter vein, they talked about his cattle—the breeds he kept, their particular habits, the trouble they were...and how there was no better life than working horses and cattle.

"Do you sell them this far south?" Jess asked. She recalled that his ranch was some distance away, in the northern Sierras.

"Cattle? Now and then, but mostly horses around here."

"For the settlers, you mean."

"And for the Overland, the Pony Express while it ran. They need strong mountain horses. I breed a good stock of Morgans and Indian ponies; mustangs, when they're about. They're good horses," he said. "I've never seen better."

Jess patted her mare, Meg, and gazed out over the valley. The sun was fully up, chasing away the shadows. "You should bring in Thoroughbreds."

Bennett shook his head. "Thoroughbreds are racehorses— good for short distances but lacking in long-term stamina."

"Not to sell," Jess clarified, "to breed. They're fast, so their endurance doesn't matter." She looked at him thoughtfully. "If you cross them with your Morgans, the Morgan will give you the endurance, while the Thoroughbred will give you pure speed. That's what could be out there running the mail."

A look of amusement came over his face. "What is it you do, Miss Jessica Hale?"

"I keep account books for my father. Why?"

"You keep books," he echoed in disbelief. His brown eyes shone with gold flecks. "As a point of fact, I've considered crossbreeding myself, but good breeding Thoroughbreds are hard to come by out here. A man would have to go back east for them, and the only time a ranching man might have free would be winter. Then there's too much snow to cross the Rockies."

"Yes, I suppose that's so," she said.

As they entered Carson City, Jake and the others watched for the men who had attacked her, but no one was standing in the shadows, and no one on the streets paid them any notice. More at ease, and feeling more hopeful than when they had left, Jess dismounted beside Jake a few blocks from the Hale house. The white two-story was visible on a distant corner, but Jess was far enough away that, if her mother were to glance out a window, she wouldn't see her daughter with a group of unknown horsemen. If she did, she would fear that some tragedy had struck, a trauma Jess meant to avoid.

"I didn't see any of those men," she said. "Did you?"

Jake looped the stallion's reins around a hitching rail. "No. They seem to have moved on, but you should walk or ride with your pa or Edmund from now on when you have matters to attend to in Carson. A Southern woman alone on the streets is no longer safe."

Jess decided that Jake was part mother hen. Before now, her Southern origin had sparked anger, but not violence—and she didn't expect it to do so again. The men who'd attacked her had been drinking and discussing unpleasant war news. They were angry, but they'd only wanted to frighten her. There was nothing more to it than that, she was certain. Jess knelt down to check Meg's hooves for stones.

"Ye know horses," a voice with a brogue boomed above Jess, "near as well as a cat knows its whiskers, by the look of things."

Jess pulled herself to her feet with a smile. "My family used to raise horses in Kentucky. Thoroughbreds and saddlebreds, mostly."

Taggart's merry eyes looked her over. "Ye appear as though the boss's coat, those gloves, and yer own skirts have swallowed ye!" he said. "Are ye in there somewhere?"

She grinned. "I am, and I'm not coming out!" When Taggart's gaze shifted, Jess's trailed after it. Three women bustled past, each of them glaring at Jess as if at something loathsome.

"And that on account of yer accent?" Taggart asked softly.

"I suppose." Jess watched them go, telling herself their rudeness didn't matter. And yet her cheeks burned.

Jake approached. "Jess?"

She strove to shrug off the brief encounter. "It's nothing." Then to change the subject, she said, "I need to give you information about my brother."

From the pocket of his vest, Jake pulled out a small notebook and a pencil. Jess gave him her brother's full name, rank, and unit, along with the name of his commanding officer. Jake glanced up when he heard the name of the renowned colonel, John Hunt Morgan, and Ambrose's last known location. While he tucked away the notebook and pencil, Jess walked over to the cattlemen. The four removed their hats.

"I appreciate all you've done for me," Jess told them. "Taggart, your gloves." She returned them, then smiled up at Reese. "My ears thank you for the loan of your scarf." She pulled off the warm length of wool and gave it back to him.

"It's been our pleasure," Taggart said.

The Spaniard's mustache curved in a grin as he shook her hand. "Señorita."

Jess grinned herself, never having been addressed as such before today, and shook hands with each of them. When she turned to Doyle, the large man stared down at her for a moment before taking her hand reluctantly.

"Ma'am."

His manner was icy, like the three women's had been. Jess smiled and thanked him again, just as she had the others. Jake had already gathered Meg's reins. She joined him, and together they began the walk home. "Bennett?"

"Hmm?"

"Few would have stepped into a fight the way you and your men did today, and even fewer would have bothered to look after a stranger once the immediate threat was past." She met his eyes. He was listening to her with a directness that almost startled her. He nodded for her to go on. "That's what I was to them—a stranger. Why did they watch out for me?"

Jake came to a stop. "Look at the ranchmen, Jess. Go ahead."

The four had tied their horses and were talking among themselves. They were rugged and strong from hard work, and more than one passing townsperson carefully kept his distance, not knowing the good these intimidating men were capable of.

"Those men respect women, Jess. Other men claim to, but, all too often, their words and their actions don't match up. Cattlemen live far from settled towns, seeing nothing but dust and cows for months on end." His voice softened. "When they finally catch sight of a woman, it's like finding a diamond in the desert. That beautiful thing is so precious to them, and they're so awestruck by it, all they can do is stare. And rather than use it in some manner for their own gain, they're likely to keep watch over it, as if the Almighty had entrusted its care to them. They're likely to protect it, preventing anyone or anything from bringing it harm." Jake searched her face. "Something rare is treasured, but there are those who have come to treasure the call of gold and silver above human worth."

Jess slowly nodded, astounded at the depth of the man. Up till now, he'd revealed so little about himself that if she hadn't gone riding with him, she never would have guessed the kinds of thoughts he entertained. Though he hadn't used the exact words, Jake had defined what he found honorable, what he saw as his duty to his fellow man. In a way, he reminded her of Ambrose.

They continued walking.

"You'll talk to this Captain Rawlins, then?"

"The boys and I will leave for Fort Churchill as soon as I've seen you home. Telegrams should be going east before dinnertime."

"But that will alter your plans."

"I'll be back in Carson City in a day or two. I'll see to the contracts then. Besides, other men from my ranch will be meeting me here with supply wagons at the end of the week. I need to be here to stock up on some things before we head back north."

"I want to thank you again."

"There's no need," he said, and she could tell he meant it.

They stopped across the road from the Hales' house. Jake noticed that a white fence now enclosed the yard. It had been added since his visit the year before, and it helped the formal house look more like a home. "I'll find you here or at Hale Imports, then?"

"Every day except Sunday."

Jess shrugged out of his coat. She was slender yet sturdy, her eyes green and her lips dark red, as though God had formed her from the gray-green sage and red earth of the desert. Jake recalled how she'd stepped into her saddle, here in Carson City, then in the mountains, and the way she'd ridden—boldly, with heart, but also with the well-being of her horse in mind. Rare was the honorable man who took such care with his animals. Among women, the quality was rarer still. He admired that.

Jess took the reins. With no assistance, she gained her saddle in a swirl of underskirts and boots, then loped toward the carriage house, equally at ease in the saddle as he.

Jake watched her natural, effortless movements until she disappeared from sight. Taggart came up beside him. He, too, looked in the direction she had gone. Jake shared a single thought with the man before they rejoined the others. "That woman," he said, "belongs on a horse."

Chapter Two

As the days passed, Jess alternately hoped for and dreaded news from Jake. By the evening of the yearly ball given by Edmund Van Dorn's wife, Miriam, Jess had gone three days without sleep. She worked long hours at the import store, hoping that another letter from Ambrose would arrive in the mail and that Edmund would slip it to her.

No letter came.

When she climbed the stairs to her bedroom late Saturday afternoon, she knew the strain had begun to show. The servants were discreetly helping her to shelter Mrs. Hale from events or news that might distress her, and, knowing that Jess was carrying a heavy burden, they were doing all they could to keep her spirits up.

At the top of the stairs, Jess saw the door to the nursery standing ajar. Warm air, giggles, and sounds of water splashing greeted her from within. Jess stood just outside the door and watched.

"Ooof!" A young woman's laughter filled the room. "The bath was meant for you, little one."

The nursemaid, Elsie Scheuer, knelt among a string of puddles, laughing as she pushed her dripping blonde hair from her face. The carpet had been rolled back to accommodate both the small, round, galvanized tub and the tidal waves of bathwater that plunged over its sides. Inside the tub, a very wet Emma Hale flailed happily in the bathwater, then paused in surprise to blink the unexpected deluge from her eyes.

"See, that's what happens when you hit the water," Elsie chided with a laugh. Emma smiled up at her nanny, her sweet blue eyes bright.

Elsie had been hired ten months earlier, when Emma was born. Coming from a large family herself, she had proven invaluable to Mrs. Hale. As soon as they'd met, Jess and Elsie had become close friends. Elsie was a cheerful young woman a few years older than she, with eyes so pale in color that one had to look very closely to see that they were blue. She wore her soft, blonde hair rolled in an easy knot atop her head, but a few loose strands now hung, dripping wet, around her face.

Jess opened the door a few inches and poked her head in. "Should I bring you a raincoat, Elsie?" she said softly, with a smile.

Her German friend looked up and grinned, her face and eyelashes glistening with tiny water droplets. The red calico dress she wore was soaked—clear through to her skin, from the looks of it.

"A bit too late for that, Jessie, but I think I'd like your help," she laughed. "I'm afraid there are no dry places, though. Only puddles." She turned adoring eyes to her charge. "Emma," she exclaimed, "look who has come to see us!"

Emma's eyes grew round as she looked up from the water and squealed as Jess made her way across the room, smiling warmly at her sister. "I missed you today!" She settled herself down on the floor beside Elsie, who freed the sponge in the tub for Emma to play with. Sitting back, Elsie raised her delicate brow at her friend in visible concern. "Jessie, you have a ball to go to tonight. You should rest. You won't net a husband with circles under your eyes."

"A husband?" Jess managed a laugh, though she wanted to growl in frustration. "Is that all you ever think about?" Unexpectedly, an image of Jake Bennett sharing the sunrise with her filled her mind. True, qualities about the rancher attracted her to him, but they hardly knew each other, and Jess had no intention of being distracted by thoughts of him. She had plenty to keep her busy, holding her family together as the war raged on. "You sound like my father," she teased.

"*Ja*, but you're twenty years old now. Surely, you want a husband."

Instead of responding, Jess smoothly shifted the focus to her friend. "Do you want to marry?"

"Oh, Jessie, I do. I am happy here now with Mr. and Mrs. Hale and Emma and you, but one day, I want my own home to take care of, and a husband to share my life with." She ducked a spray of water, her eyes shining. "Then you can visit me when I have my own children to bathe, *ja*?"

"Of course I will."

"Truly, Jess? Even if I move away?"

Jess attempted an imitation of Elsie's accent. "Ja," she said, "even then. Dat's vat goot friends do."

With a soft laugh, Elsie unfolded a fluffy towel and held it open to Emma. "Are you finished bathing us all, *liebling*?" she asked gently.

Jess lifted her baby sister and held her over the tub for a moment to let the water run off her body. Then she handed her to Elsie, who enfolded her in the towel and pulled her into her lap. Glowing, Elsie patted Emma dry, then dusted the towel over her delicate golden hair until it stood crazily on end "like Mr. Hale's." Jess and Elsie shared a smile. "I want twelve children just like her," Elsie confessed.

"How can I visit, then?" Jess teased. "There won't be any place for me to sleep."

"You'll visit," Elsie predicted, "and I will always have room for you, Jessie." The nanny gathered up the child in her arms. "Go and rest now. You need your strength. You can spend the day with your Emma tomorrow."

Gratefully, Jess kissed her sister's forehead. With Elsie's help, Emma waved good night, and Jess went to her own room.

Her mother's maid, Maureen, was in a rush to press Mrs. Hale's ball gown, so she had Jess out of her day dress in minutes.

"It's all right, Maureen. I'll finish on my own," Jess assured her, leaving the maid to hurry out and close the door.

Alone at last. Jess pushed her petticoats and hoop cage to the floor and crawled into bed.

It seemed her head had scarcely touched the pillow when Maureen came back and gently shook her awake. "Jess? Your mother wants you to dress now."

"Thank you." Jess forced her eyes open. The dim light of sunset shone through the window, but Maureen pulled the drapes and lit a lamp. Resolved to make the best of the evening, Jess sat up and rubbed her eyes.

"You look better," the maid commented. "Elsie said you were tired."

"I was. How long did I sleep?"

"Forty-five minutes. Are you ready to dress?"

She told her she was. What was more, Jess found that, though her fatigue remained, she was at least ready to face a night of dancing and visiting with friends. For the duration of the evening, her Southern accent wouldn't matter. Just for one night, there would be no war.

When Jess stepped out into the upper hall, her ball gown swished around her like a silken cloud—the only benefit of being bundled in the heavy thing. She had chosen a dress of midnight blue, a hue that set off the brightness of her face and eyes. Wearing her widest hoops, she felt like she was pulling an ocean of fabric from her waist, but she wore it anyway to please her mother and to appease Miriam Van Dorn's sense of decorum. Getting out of it later, she mused, would be like trying to find the center of an onion.

Jess stopped at her mother's door and knocked. After a brief moment, her mother opened it.

Georgeanne McKinney Hale's green eyes and chestnut hair may have once resembled her own, but the luster of both had faded. She still possessed a motherly gentleness, but she also bore the uncertainty of a troubled soul who little dared to hope that better times would come. With the loss of Broderick, followed by two miscarriages, she had good reason to be sad, but Jess rued how the past three years of worry over Ambrose had made her frail. The vibrant, copper-hued gown she wore, which once had won her lavish praise, now emphasized how pale and thin she had become.

Refusing to allow her own concern for Ambrose to show, Jess walked in with the air of a young woman about to enjoy a ball, and, for her mother's benefit, she held a brilliant smile.

"You look beautiful, Jessie."

"So do you," she said in earnest. Fragile, but beautiful still. "Maureen said you wanted to see me."

"Yes, I do." She beckoned Jess further into the room, then appraised her daughter with tearful eyes. She looked upward from Jess's smoothly pressed overskirt to the long, fitted sleeves and scooped bodice, ending at the mass of curls secured over her shoulder with an inlaid rose-and-vine-patterned comb. Her mother gazed at the emerald pendant Jess wore, the one Ambrose had given her, now suspended from a gold chain instead of the satin ribbon that Ambrose carried. Her eyes rested on her own emerald teardrops surrounded by blazing diamonds, which danced below Jess's earlobes. Finally, her mother sighed through her tears.

"Was there something you wanted, Mother?" Jess asked gently.

"No, I just wanted to see you before we go. Once we arrive, I won't get another chance to see you until we leave. You and your friends are always anxious to go off somewhere and visit." She laughed a little as she said it, but Jess glimpsed an uneasiness in her that pulled at her heart.

"Am I as awful as that?" she asked. Jess took her mother's hand. "I promise I'll make sure to find you often and let you know how I'm faring."

Her mother nodded. "Yes, I would like that."

"Are you ready to go?"

"Yes, dear, but we still have nearly an hour before we need to leave. Why don't you ask Ho Chen to fix you something to eat? You know how late Miriam serves dinner."

Jess wasn't hungry, but she said, "I will. Shall I bring you something?"

"No, thank you, dear. I'll go visit Emma for a while. Elsie should be getting her ready for bed."

After a brief embrace, Jess returned to her room, desperately needing a few minutes to herself.

What was taking Captain Rawlins so long? She pressed her fists to her brow, exhausted and frustrated. She'd already waited four days. More than that—she had waited four months! Four months of not knowing what had happened to Ambrose, four months of empty assurances for her mother!

Why are things getting worse? Jess asked the Lord. *You said You wouldn't give us more difficulties than we can bear, but I'm at my wit's end! Please, I need to know that Ambrose is well. I need to hear from him. And I need to know that You are with me, Lord. I can't get through this by myself. Sometimes...sometimes You just seem so far away.*

She'd been raised to pray that the Lord's will be done, but

she couldn't anymore. She was too afraid of what His will might be.

Maureen came to retrieve Jess's cloak and then carried it downstairs for her. Jess composed herself and followed behind. In the front hall, she passed several minutes chatting pleasantly with the butler, Malcolm, while waiting for her parents. Finally, she heard sharp footsteps clatter on the stairs above. Her father, Isaac, hurried down in handsome black trousers and sweeping tails, consulting his golden pocket watch on its intricate, gleaming chain.

At fifty-two, her father was brawny as an ox and sometimes as surly—his thinning, feathery white hair often stood on end like a madman's. Ever the businessman, he had a quick, shrewd mind, ready at a moment's notice to woo a mammoth investment from an unsuspecting banker.

He reached the bottom of the stairs, his white hair already disheveled beyond hope. "Your mother will make us late, for sure," he grumbled. At her questioning look, he explained, "Emma was having some trouble getting to sleep, so she's giving Elsie a hand until she's settled." He gave Jess a closer look, then added, "You look good enough to marry off."

She smiled vaguely at his colorless jest. Aside from their occasionally heated disagreements over Ambrose, they exchanged lighthearted banter over her unwed state. "Thank you, Father. Since we have time, perhaps Ho Chen will make us something warm to drink while we wait for Mother."

"That's fine," he said. "Only you drink and I'll pace."

In a relatively good humor, she and her father started toward the back of the house. Someone rapped on the front door, and a heavy, dark sense of foreboding descended over Jess when Malcolm opened it. Feeling as though she was moving underwater, she turned and took in the familiar boots, greatcoat, and hat of the man who stepped inside. Jake Bennett lifted unreadable eyes to hers.

"Jake Bennett!" Isaac strode forward to greet their unexpected guest. "Good evening! Come inside, have a drink with us."

"Thanks, Isaac," he said quietly. "Actually I came to talk to Jess. Would you mind if she took a walk with me?"

Jess couldn't breathe.

If Isaac was surprised at the request, he didn't let on. "Not at all. We have time, anyway." Isaac shook Jake's hand to take his leave. "Dinner tomorrow?"

"Thanks, but I can't. The boys and I need to load up supplies in the morning and head home."

"Then we'll see you the next time you pass through." With a brief glance at Jess and the rancher beside her, Isaac headed off toward the kitchen, the butler trailing after him.

Jake said nothing as he helped her into her cloak. Jess fastened the closures at her throat and searched his eyes. She had to know.

"Ambrose?"

Jake's gaze shifted to the direction Isaac had taken, then back to her. "Let's talk outside."

Her heart pounded in her chest. She pulled her hood over her head and let Jake lead her outside. The night closed in around them.

A sharp wind wailed and snatched at their clothes as Jake led her past dark yards lined with low fences. Jess curled into her cloak as if the fabric would protect her from the news and the cold alike.

When they were several houses away, Jake slowed to a stop.

Jess's suspense slowly shattered as he slid his hat from his head.

Her eyes fell closed. It was over. The waiting, the wondering—all of it—was over.

A terrible heaviness settled within her. She breathed deeply for several moments, willing herself to calm. Finally, her eyes met Jake's. Their glimmering depths mirrored the regret he must have felt since he received the telegram. He had known the pain that would follow.

"Tell me."

"Tom wasn't able to learn anything from the Federals," he said gently, "but a telegraph operator, a Confederate, tapped into one of his transmissions and decided to make inquiries on his own. He learned that your brother carried a message into a battle in Kentucky. There were thousands of casualties on both sides, and few doctors." Jake turned the hat in his hands. "Those who are still missing have been presumed dead."

Hope flickered as Jess clung to that lovely, indefinite word, *missing*. "That doesn't mean anything. Ambrose could have been wounded, and maybe he's recovering in a hospital somewhere, or in someone's home."

"No, Jess. Your brother's colonel relayed Ambrose's description to the telegrapher. Confederate artillerymen confirmed that he was the courier they saw in battle. They said they saw him riding hard just before being hit by exploding cannon shells." Jess's hopeful conviction wavered. "Those same soldiers found a dispatch on the ground some time later. Colonel Morgan's signature was on it, and he confirmed it was the one he sent with Ambrose. Ambrose...Ambrose was never seen again."

Her bravado began to fail, but Jess lifted her chin. She would not fall apart in front of this man. "He's a Hale. Hales are too stubborn to die."

Jake didn't comment on that. "The Confederates headed out to join other forces while the Federals gave chase. They weren't able to see to the wounded or—"

"Was he buried?" She knew she sounded angry, but she didn't care.

"Nearby farmers buried all the dead. Union and Confederate dead, some in mass graves, but most of them where they fell."

Farmers, not soldiers, did the burying? "So we don't know for sure—"

"Jess." His voice was calm, final.

Jess walked a few paces, feeling wooden. Not many people were about, she thought absently, what with the hour and the cold. Yet inside the saloons down the road, hundreds of people were milling about, even now. Suddenly, it all seemed so empty—the city, the mountains, all of it. The land was empty and her heart was empty. Empty because Ambrose was no longer alive to fill them.

The smell of smoke drew her uncaring gaze to a neighbor's chimney. She let her head fall back. It met with Jake's solid chest. His comforting presence was her undoing.

The stars above blurred. Jake's words swam in her ears, more nightmarish than real. *Thousands of casualties...mass graves... farmers buried the dead.* Jake gripped her arms in sympathy. How was she supposed to continue on without her beloved brother? And Emma...Emma would never know her brother, and her mother... Jess dug her fingers into her hair. How could she sit her mother down and tell her she had lost another son? The months after little Broderick died remained painfully clear in her memory. Icy fear stabbed her. Would her mother survive this? And their father...

Jess cried for them all. Between Ambrose and their father, there would be no amends. No penitence expressed, no forgiveness granted—no peace. Isaac Hale would not have another chance. None of them would.

"It's such a waste!" she hissed through her sobs.

"Hang on, Jess!" Jake urged. "You're strong. You'll get through this!"

She shook her head stubbornly.

51

Jake turned her and pulled her against him.

Welcoming the embrace, Jess curled her hands around two fistfuls of sheepskin, pressing her head against the flannel where it parted. His chest was warm…and remarkably solid. His arms tightened around her. Jess felt as though he was taking her concerns into himself and leaving in their place his own quiet assurance. She breathed in his pleasant smell of horses and leather.

All at once, he felt too close to her. Jess pushed mightily to get away. She jerked free, confused by her own actions. Jake didn't object but thoughtfully pulled a handkerchief from his pocket and handed it to her. Jess snatched it from him, muttered "thank you," and swiped at her tears.

At the far end of the road her house lights were still on, but the carriage had not been pulled around to the front. Mercifully, her parents were not yet ready to go. Jess dried the tears as they came, silently demanding they cease. They persisted. "I can't stop crying," she moaned.

"I know," Jake said.

"But I have to! I can't let my father and mother see me like this."

"You only have to hold it together until your folks leave."

"Jake, I have to 'hold it together,' as you put it, for the rest of the night."

He frowned. "You mean you're still going out tonight?"

"What did you think I would do? Claim to have a headache and hide in my room? I have to go. I have to continue on as though everything is normal until I can decide how I'm going to handle this." She shook her head and winced with grief.

"You're not going to tell your parents?"

"My mother's been ill from worry, and her mind is fragile, at best. I can't tell her. She wouldn't survive. I'm sure of it. She wouldn't want to, not even for the sake of my baby sister."

"And what about you?"

"I'm strong, Jake. I'll get through it," Jess said, echoing his words with subtle humor. Gradually, she took control of her ragged breathing, and her eyes dried. Outwardly, she would be presentable; inwardly, however, she felt barren, as though she had no more vitality than someone in an old, faded painting, with nothing left to give, no substance behind her pleasant façade. And yet she had to. She'd promised Ambrose that she would hold their family together. It was a promise she would keep. Especially now. "Will you walk me back?"

Jake nodded. "Of course, I'll walk you."

She walked slowly, and Jake patiently matched his steps to hers. Jess thought back over the long months she'd waited for word from Ambrose—the letters she had written, the anxiety she had felt, everything she had gone through to find him. She smiled sadly, knowing that Ambrose would have done the same for her. He would have...

"The boys and I will be heading home in the morning," Jake softly reminded her, setting his hat on his head.

"You've gotten all your supplies, then?"

"Most of them. We have a few more things to pick up tonight, the rest at first light. The boys will meet up with me soon."

Jess was reluctant to see him go. She liked that when they talked, he listened to her—really listened, as if blocking out every other sight, sound, and thought so that he could absorb every word she spoke. Maybe he did.

Jess lifted her face to let the wind cool her cheeks. A far-off, shadowy male figure was out walking along the road, hair tossing wildly about in the wind. He lifted a hand. Seeing him, Jake returned the wave. "Isaac won't be back for a few minutes yet," he observed.

"Good." She was regaining her composure. "I'll have time to put myself back together."

The way Jake's eyes touched on the black velvet hood and her face warmed her. "You do look beautiful, Jess," he said, "in spite of your tears."

They shared a hint of a smile.

All was calm for several paces. Suddenly, an odd brightness flickered up ahead. When Jess saw where it had risen from, she gasped in horror. Dizzying blackness enfolded her. Jake's hand clamped fiercely on her arm, and he commanded her, "Stay here!"

"Fire," she breathed.

Flames burst across the front of the Hale house. When Jake was almost to the front gate, Jess defied his firm order. She picked up her skirts and started to run in the same direction. From down the road, her father was scrambling furiously toward the house.

Jess hesitated at the gate, eyes wide in terror. Jake was already in the yard, turning in a circle to look for any of the servants or family members who might have escaped through the front door. He sprinted left and right to scan the side yards.

Like the face of the house, the sides were walls of fire. The blaze illumined the neighboring houses, its orange flames mirrored in squares of window glass. Above the house, dense smoke rolled upward with the force of the wind.

Jess's hood kept the worst of the heat from her face, but nothing could block out the predatory roar of the fire. Jake ran to her and pulled her back several steps. "I'm going around the house to see if anyone has made it out," he yelled in her ear. "Stay here!"

Instead of turning away, Jake glanced over her head, then lunged for the walkway.

Jess was immobilized by a howl of pure rage. Her father had cleared the fence and was furiously striking Jake as the younger man fought to keep him away from the house. Jess shook her head, tears streaming down her face. Why wouldn't Jake let him go in? Her father had called her mother and Emma's names. Jake *knew* they were in the house. Surely, there was still time to save them! Her father yelled something, swinging at Jake like a madman. Jake struggled to hold him, yelling something in response. Flaming boards were falling to the yard from the rooftop high above. Isaac broke free of Jake's hold and bolted for the front door. Jess ran after him. If her father couldn't get to her family, she would! A long timber dropped from the edge of the roof and hit the ground, spreading flames as it tumbled toward her. She screamed and leapt aside, and it crashed into the fence behind her, instantly igniting her mother's withered roses.

Jess's head snapped up. Mother! Emma! Already, one precious minute had flown by. Emma's nursery window revealed angry spears of flame and billows of smoke within. Above, fast-multiplying flames stabbed through the roof, which shrieked and groaned as it was consumed. Unconsciously, Jess reached up toward her mother, who was dying right this moment, burning. She knew it. In her mind, she could see her trapped upstairs, twisting away from the fire that rolled over her. Rolled over her, devoured, and won.

Jake threw a thick arm around Isaac's throat, fighting to drag him back from the inferno. Isaac broke free again and thrust a boot against the front door, scattering blackened boards and flames onto the already burning carpet and stairs.

A gale screamed past, scattering white-hot embers into the yard and spreading them to other homes, driving the blaze onward. Somewhere above Jess, a window burst. It was too late. Jess ran forward again, this time to stop her father. Then she froze. Her father drove an elbow into Jake's gut, which loosened the rancher's hold on his throat. He wrenched free, then faced Jake at arm's length and shouted at him once more.

This time, unbelievably, Jake stepped back and let him go. *He let him go.*

For one clear moment, her father faced her with apologetic desperation in his eyes, his cheeks black with soot, the once-elegant black trousers and coat burned in a dozen places. Then he spun and ran into the burning house.

Sparks fell between Jess and Jake in a shower of embers. The roofline sagged. The front wall near Jess began to give way.

Her eyes drifted, as if in a dream, to Jake. He darted off the porch and ran toward her as more timbers descended, crashing in a sea of flame that separated them. He came to a stop, then waved his arm in a wordless command to someone on the road. Jess turned her face to the glowing window of her father's study, a sick dread engulfing her as she accepted the fact that her family was gone. The war had killed her brother, and a fire had claimed her mother, her father, and her sweet sister. From within the house sounded cracks like gunfire and a long, groaning wail as the main staircase gave way.

Suddenly, a strangely comforting sound came to Jess. It was the thrumming of horse hooves somewhere in the night. Blinding light filled her eyes, and she closed heavy eyelids. *All of them gone,* she thought, in rhythm with the hoofbeats. *All of them gone.*

She was tired, so tired. A shrill whinny came from a distance that sounded miles away. Darkness and indifference descended as something caught her around her waist and she was swept like a rag doll from her feet.

Chapter Three

The darkness in her mind was a deep haven of peace—a haven she rose from unwillingly as she was tugged toward dreaded consciousness. Jess hovered below the surface, fighting against the need to break through, even though she couldn't quite recall why she did not want to do so.

She felt as though she were rising and then falling over ocean waves, gliding from one crest to the next. With the swelling movement came a familiar, rhythmic beat, and she realized she was being carried on a horse.

Jess opened her eyes and fixed them on the night stars above. One ear was pressed against something firm and warm, but the rest of her face, exposed by her hood, caught the cold desert wind. She turned her eyes toward the warmth to see that she was being held by an Indian man wrapped in fur. His face was hard, and his eyes stared straight ahead.

Jess grunted, trying to move. The Indian's dark eyes, looking concerned, connected with hers. He pulled her higher against him, and she felt the pressure of twisted crinoline and hoops. Jess passed her fingertips over the smooth silk of her ball gown. The searing pain of recent memories rushed over her, flooding her mind with terrible pictures—Ambrose lying among hundreds of dead on a battlefield. Jake releasing her father as flames curled around the doorframe. The last look her father gave her before disappearing into an inferno of smoke and flame.

The reality of these images rapidly drove her back toward

the escape of unconsciousness, while, beneath her, an unfamiliar Indian man kept her safe and carried her, on horseback, to a place unknown.

~❦~

A low murmur of masculine voices reached Jess's ears. She felt hard ground beneath her and warm furs swathing her from chin to feet. With great effort, she shifted her tired legs among the layers of her petticoats. A steady hand brushed over her hair, and she was impressed again with the image of the hard-faced Indian.

Unable to resist the welcome current that dragged her under, she gave in to it and let it take her away again.

~❦~

Eventually, both gliding stride and blowing cold ended. Jess became aware of the dense curves of a cotton-filled bed beneath her. Her body seemed weighted, and her heart felt heavy with a dull ache as she finally passed from hopeful dreams to grim reality. Hearing movement beside her, Jess opened her eyes.

A lovely young Indian woman in a doeskin dress turned to her in surprise, a pitcher and basin suspended in her hands. Her black hair was cut chin-length—a sign of mourning, Jess recalled—but warm, dark eyes shone from a caring, brown face.

"It is good you have awakened," she said softly. "The burns are not bad, but we must bathe and dress your arm."

Jess struggled to shake the cobweb of confusion from her mind. "I didn't know I had any burns."

"We will put a salve on them. They will heal soon." The woman set down the basin and began to fill it with water.

From somewhere near the bed, a lantern scattered meager

golden light. Jess lay in a small room constructed of thick pine logs. The walls to both sides were angled, the slanting, timbered ceiling only a few feet above her head where the roofline sloped down. Across the room rose a high log wall, its uppermost tiers nearly lost in shadows. In the far corner to her right was a door, and to her left was a window. No curtains covered it, and Jess was able to see that the sky outside was a deep gray—the hour was either after dusk or approaching dawn. She surmised that she was on the second floor, for the sky was all she could see.

Where she was, she couldn't guess. This was a place she had never been before, and, like the Indian man, this woman was a stranger.

Reluctant to continue lying as though helpless, Jess rolled on one side and braced her hand against the mattress to sit up. She gasped as a sudden burning sensation raked her right arm.

"Please, you must keep still," the woman urged her. "The burns will hurt more if you use your arm. If you wish to sit," she offered, "I will help."

Dazed, Jess allowed the kind woman to help her sit up. She took great care with Jess's stinging arm, then placed a folded Indian blanket at her back for support.

"I am called Red Deer," the woman said, dipping a ladle in the water basin. "The one who brought you is my husband, Lone Wolf. Here, drink."

Jess complied eagerly, then thanked the woman. Finally, her mind was beginning to clear. With considerably slower movements, Jess took in her soot-blackened hands and the wide blotches of angry red skin along her arm. The burning sensation extended up her right arm and halfway across her chest. She was clothed in her linen chemise, which was good, she decided—she wouldn't want to ruin a borrowed garment with greasy salves.

With a sigh, Jess carefully shook back her long, tangled

hair. She felt neither the weight nor the motion of her mother's earrings. Her hand flew to her throat. The necklace was gone, too. Her jewelry! Jess scanned the dark room. To her right, her damaged cloak and gown hung on wall pegs. Her corset, petticoats, and pantalettes were folded neatly atop a dressing table. Beside them, twinkling in the pale lamplight, lay her rose and vine inlaid comb, her mother's emerald and diamond earrings, and the emerald pendant Ambrose had given her. They were all she had left of the family she loved. From her garments drifted the bitter smell of smoke.

Red Deer caught her gaze. "I will wash your clothing," she assured Jess, "but I will tend to you first." With a kind smile, Red Deer wrung a cloth soaked in water and handed it to her. Little shells that fringed her doeskin dress made gentle clinking sounds. "Do you know where you are?"

Jess frowned as she carefully applied the cloth to her face and hands. "No, I don't. I remember a long journey...sleeping on the ground." The murmuring. "Men's voices."

"The voices were those of the cattlemen who helped to bring you. This is the house of Jake Bennett—his ranch."

Jess narrowed her eyes sharply. Jake had waved his arm to someone—he must have been signaling Red Deer's husband, Lone Wolf, to take her away. The last she'd seen Jake, he'd been standing before the blazing façade of her home, or what was left of it—right after he had let her father perish.

"Is Bennett here?" she asked coldly.

Red Deer frowned in confusion. "The ranchmen said he will not return for many days, but you need not worry. He will let you stay."

"Forgive me, Red Deer," she countered, "but I don't intend to stay."

Jake had let her family die. He should have allowed her father to try to get to her mother and Emma. He should have helped him. Instead, he held him back when they yet had a chance, and then, when it was too late to save them, he let her father die. He let them all die.

The feelings of friendship she'd had for Jake had vanished as smoke. All she felt for him now was hatred. She would stay in Carson City with the Van Dorns until she could support herself, or she'd stay in the cramped upper room of Hale Imports, if she had to—but she would not remain at Jake's ranch.

Jess shoved aside the covers with her left arm and dropped her legs over the edge of the bunk. She ground her teeth against the burning in her right arm and chest, moving in spite of it.

In alarm, Red Deer helped Jess to her feet, not certain what she was intending to do. "Do you wish to bathe now?"

A cold sweat broke out along Jess's skin. She felt physically ill from the burns, and she began to shake. A white haze clouded her vision. She knew she was in shock.

"You should not do much yet," Red Deer said in a soothing voice. "I will help you to wash and put more salve on the burns, but then you must rest. I think a terrible thing has happened to you. Sleep will help your body and your heart to heal."

Jess nodded weakly, unable to do anything else. Red Deer helped her lower herself into a chair. Jess noted again how her black hair was cut just a few inches above her shoulders. She, too, had lost a loved one. And recently. With all the strife between the Indians and the settlers, perhaps she knew suffering all too well. Though Jess couldn't stop the deluge of sorrow and reminiscence, she regretted her own surly attitude. She did not want to cause this woman further sadness. "I appreciate what you've done for me, Red Deer. Forgive me if I was unkind."

Red Deer reassured her with a gracious smile, then asked, "You lost someone?"

"Yes, my family." *And any servants who didn't make it to safety,* she realized. What *had* happened to Elsie, Maureen, Malcolm, and Ho Chen? Were they safe?

Red Deer's black eyes shone in empathy. Her face was round

with a softly flared nose, characteristic of the Paiute people. "I saw the way you looked at your ruined dress and ornaments," she said. "You are one who will remember your dead with the strength of great love, Miss Hale."

"Please, call me Jess," she said.

As she carefully sponged her burns, Red Deer rinsed the cloth. "Jessica...I heard the cattlemen call you by this name. Does it have a meaning?" she asked. "I have learned that not all white names have meanings."

Jess shook her head, too exhausted to elaborate. She remained quiet while Red Deer applied a salve and wrapped her arm in clean strips of cloth.

When she had finished, Red Deer said she would prepare a bath, but Jess held up a hand. "If you wouldn't mind, I think I'll rest again. I can bathe later, if it isn't too much trouble."

"Yes, Jessica. The rest will be good. I will bring food later."

Gratefully accepting assistance, Jess slipped under the covers once again. Quietly, Red Deer left. Alone again, Jess cried as the hours came and went until, at last, the comforting arms of sleep embraced her.

❦

In the days that followed, Red Deer left trays of food for Jess, which she discovered each time she awoke. She would eat a little, and then, grieving, drift back to sleep.

While she slept, nightmares tormented her—her family dying horribly around her, sometimes along with Maureen, Malcolm, or one of the others. She would bolt upright, initially flooded with relief that it had been only a dream. In the next instant, though, reality would assault her, and she suffered anew the pain of her loss. Then she would cry herself to sleep again, only to have the brutal cycle repeat itself as the sun rose and set.

One morning, just before daybreak, Jess woke from a mercifully dreamless sleep, and, for once, tears didn't come. Rolling her pillow more comfortably beneath her head, she finally felt clear of mind.

What was she to do now? Jess thoughtfully searched the shadows above. First, she had to find out if the servants had survived. She had to make certain they were well, and, once she did, she would help find them new places to work. After that... her father's share of the import store was hers now. She could support herself by helping Edmund to run it.

Edmund...and Miriam. Jess pressed a hand to her eyes. The Van Dorns had been her parents' closest friends since before she was born, and none of the Hales had arrived for the ball that night. The Van Dorns must have been devastated to learn of the fire.

No, she couldn't let herself think of all that again. She had to focus on the months ahead. Jess dropped her hand from her eyes. Her father's bank accounts would fall to her, and though she knew little about his investments, she would learn to manage them wisely.

The uncertainty lay in what people's reactions would be to her, a woman, co-owning a "man's business." She'd had conflicts aplenty while working discreetly as a bookkeeper in an unobtrusive corner of the showroom. Every situation imaginable had arisen, from women snubbing her as something less than a beggar to men who wanted her job making threats. None of these reactions had troubled her then, but now her income would depend on people accepting her new position.

Jess frowned. When she was young, she had paid close attention while her father taught Ambrose the strategies of playing poker. He had frequently lifted his thick, gray eyebrows and warned Ambrose, "Never bet money if you're holding less than two pair." She could still hear his voice. What would he tell her to do? The way she saw it, she was holding a slim two pair—and an objectionable Southern accent, to boot. Hardly decent odds. At the same time, she had no other means by which to support herself.

And there was also Kentucky. Bittersweet tears trickled onto the pillow. They had all gifted her with one remaining bequest. Greenbriar. It was hers now, hers to hold dear—but also hers to maintain for those who followed after, if it survived the war.

Jess began to envision the possibilities. Perhaps, if she sold the Hale property in Carson City, worked hard, and lived meagerly, she could sell Edmund her half of Hale Imports when the war ended and go back home to rebuild. She would have her father's investment money, and she would find some way to prosper in Kentucky. In the meantime, she needed to regain her strength and wait out the war. Jess wiped her eyes and sat up carefully.

Besides, other Southerners live in the territory and occasionally come into the store, she thought. *I might succeed or even excel in Carson City—who's to know?* Time would tell. She hoped it would also heal.

Someone knocked softly on the door. Red Deer entered silently, her steps muted by the moccasins on her feet. She carried a tray with two bowls and a steaming teacup, which she placed on the chair beside the bed. "You look rested," she observed. "This is good. When the heart is sick, the body suffers, also."

Jess nodded sympathetically at Red Deer and fingered her own hair. "You've known sadness too, Red Deer."

"Yes. I lost my sister, Blue Bird. Two summers ago, she traveled with her husband and son to the mountains. They wanted to live far from white men," she said with an apologetic look, then specified, "the white men who kill our game until we starve and who hunt our people like dogs."

Jess understood and nodded for her to go on.

"This winter has been very cold. Even in her dwelling, fire and blankets could not keep out the terrible wind. Each night, Blue Bird slept holding her son against her to warm him. But one morning, he crawled from her arms and spoke to waken his mother. She did not answer. He touched her, but she was dead."

Jess's heart sank in regret. "She had frozen?"

"Yes. Now my husband and I take care of my sister's son. His father lives in the north, protecting our people. Blue Bird is gone only one month. It is difficult to speak of her."

Only one month. Jess didn't believe a hundred months would lessen the pain either of them felt. "How long will you mourn?"

Red Deer lifted the tray and set it before Jess. "My people mourn until our hair again reaches the length it was before our loved ones died. I know my dear sister is with the Great Spirit Father, but always she stays close in my heart. This is why my people also bury the possessions of one who dies, that we will not see what was theirs and feel pain from the reminder." Red Deer smiled softly. "But we always remember them, yes? And when we die, we live on in someone's heart, also."

"I suppose so," Jess murmured, clenching the bedcovers to fight off fresh tears. She now lived in a country where death was becoming as common as life, and she couldn't bear to hear another tragic thing. Red Deer had lost family, and she'd watched her people die. Jess didn't know how she had survived it. She didn't know how she would survive it. She only knew that if she had to remain in bed much longer, she might go mad.

For both their sakes, Red Deer sought to disperse the gloom. "But now we must talk of better things." She paused expectantly, and Jess appeased her by taking a few bites from a bowl of dried peaches and steaming porridge. "Your food, it is good?"

"It is very good," she agreed, taking a sip of hot tea. Red Deer chatted quietly about simpler matters, and Jess realized she was quite hungry, eating the soft oats by the spoonful until they were gone.

Jess was curious about the reed tray on her lap, and Red Deer described to her the plant baskets, bowls, and trays the Paiute women made, which were not only prized for their beauty, but also woven so tightly that not a drop of water could seep through. Jess listened, eager to hear about anything tangible that anchored her to life, and she marveled at the skill—and cuts and blisters—required for such skillful construction.

Glancing at her clothes, which were hanging to the side, Jess saw that Red Deer had laundered them, as promised. By the time she finished her meal, she resented the soot and dirt that remained on her skin, and she couldn't bear that her hair still smelled of smoke.

"Red Deer, how long have I been here?"

Red Deer stood up and removed the tray from her lap. "Today is your third day."

"Three days!"

Red Deer gazed at Jess in alarm. "Do you wish to sleep again?"

"No, but how long was I on the horse?"

Cautiously, she answered, "One day and one night."

Jess pushed herself upright. The pain of the burns had dulled. "I have been gone four days?" She shoved her covers aside and gained her feet beside the dressing table. "Four days? Red Deer, I need to bury my family! I need somebody to take me to Carson City." With short, fitful movements, Jess flipped through her undergarments in search of her corset. "Will your husband take me? If not," Jess muttered, "I can saddle a horse and go myself. The horses belong to Bennett, don't they? He owes me, anyhow." She tossed the corset and her pantalettes onto the bed. "Carson is to the south; I can find my own way." Jess read hurt and confusion in Red Deer's face, and she quickly curbed her harshness. "Could you tell me where water is to wash with? I don't wish to trouble you any further." A glance out the window told her the sun had risen.

"Jessica, I will get you water, but are you sure you should do this? You are not strong yet, and a woman traveling alone is not safe."

"I have to bury my family," Jess insisted, desperately yearning to be near them. She struggled with a knot in the drawstring of her petticoat.

"I understand, but you have been ill. You are not ready for this journey. Look how thin you are, and how you shake!" Her voice softened. "Jessica, days have passed. Friends will have buried your family. You would be wise to stay here."

The Van Dorns again. Yes, Edmund would have seen to it they were buried. Dear Edmund. He had done so much for them all.

"Is Bennett still gone?" Jess asked.

"Yes. When he leaves, he is often away for many days."

She recalled that Jake had said he needed to purchase other supplies for the ranch. "Then I will stay, Red Deer," Jess said with resignation. "If you don't mind, I would like to help with a few chores so that I can regain my strength."

"A little work may be good. But now I will bring up water. In the trunk are dresses that may fit you." Red Deer left with the tray.

Aside from the bed, chairs, and dressing table, the trunk

holding the lantern was the only other furnishing in the room. Jess rounded the bed to the trunk, pushing past her fatigue and drawing on a need to escape the four walls. She set the lamp on the floor and knelt down to open the lid.

Inside were three gowns: two of yellow calico and one of dark red wool. Beneath them lay a belt of braided leather. *Jake keeps full sets of women's clothes at his ranch?* Jess thought with disgust. Whether he gave them as payment or as replacements, she didn't care to contemplate. Thinking of the man only infuriated her. She didn't want to think about him, much less see him. To be certain of avoiding him, she determined to leave the ranch before he returned. Two days. She'd give herself two days to regain her strength. Then she would leave.

Jess lifted a bundle of yellow out of the trunk and pushed herself to her feet. All three dresses had essentially the same pattern: button fronts, full sleeves, and yards of skirt. They were in good condition, no matter what kind of woman they were intended for, and would serve well for the remainder of her brief stay.

Red Deer returned with a child-sized bathing tub balanced on one hip; in her free hand, she carried a large bucket of steaming water. Unprepared to reflect on bittersweet reminders of Emma, Jess directed her gaze to the items inside the tub—a towel, a soaping cloth, a hunk of oddly shaped soap, a hairbrush, and a pair of fur-lined Indian boots. While Red Deer arranged these items on the plank floor and dressing table, Jess glanced curiously through the half-opened door. She saw a short hallway and a stick-and-branch railing, which opened to reveal a set of stairs leading to a lower room. Beyond it, the opposite side of the timbered roofline sloped down.

Jess stopped the smile of pleasure that was forming on her lips. This cozy home was Jake's, she reminded herself.

Red Deer set the bucket and towel within Jess's reach, then left her alone.

Above the trunk, a small mirror hung on the wall. Jess studied her reflection for the first time since the night of the fire. Her chestnut hair and green eyes resembled those of the woman Isaac Hale had fallen in love with and married more than a quarter of a century ago. Her mother's earrings and the emerald pendant Ambrose had given her lay, as before, on the dressing table. Jess was thankful that her own culture didn't bury these precious reminders of those dearest to the heart. She would cherish these heirlooms and remember her family for a long time to come, and she was glad of it. There was nothing she wanted to forget. Except for the pain, now inextricably wound with the pleasant memories.

∼◦⊰⊱◦∼

The hot bath greatly revived Jess's spirits. She applied herself to scrubbing away the soot and smoke from her skin, and she found herself drawn to the scents and sensations of the present. For a time, she was able to set the recent past aside.

Only after Jess had scrubbed her hair and rinsed it twice did the smoky tinge fade to her satisfaction. The room began to smell less like ashes and more like rosewater and pine.

She pulled the dress on and buttoned it, no longer needing wraps since her burns had begun to heal. With none of the fashionable set around to impress, her corset held her to a more comfortable degree of confinement than she was used to, and Jess breathed deeply for no reason other than she was able to. The gown fit a bit loosely in the middle, even with the slackened corset, so she simply let the waist fall to the top of her hips and drew in the braided leather belt. With their fur linings, the Indian boots were warm and comfortable.

She needed to rest occasionally as she bathed and dressed, but the exercise gradually restored a portion of her strength.

When Jess had finished weaving her hair into a thick braid that hung to her waist, Red Deer brought her a more substantial, meaty soup to eat, and the nourishment helped strengthen her even more.

Alone again, Jess used the corner of a towel to rub her teeth with a sprinkling of salt from a jar in the dressing table in order to clean them. Next, she used a needle and thread from a small sewing kit to secure her jewelry among the layers of her petticoats for safekeeping. Her gaze shifted frequently with renewed interest to the door. Finally, she hung her towels over the chairs to dry, deciding she would return later to put away the tub. She wanted to explore the ranch house and slake her curiosity about her new surroundings.

When she opened the door, the cheery sound of a crackling fire greeted her from below, and she stepped out onto what was more of a short balcony than a hallway. Jess opened the door next to hers. It was similar to her own in size and shape and was currently being used for storage. She continued on. At the top of the stairs was a third bedroom. This one was filled with a man's belongings.

Bennett's.

Jess approached the open doorway, catching pleasant whiffs of leather from within the room. From wall pegs hung long trousers, a few woven vests, and an old set of spurs. On the floor beneath them lay strips of cowhide partially braided into a whip-thin rope. Helplessly drawn by the belongings that were so masculine—so *Bennett*—Jess moved into the room. She trailed her fingers over the brightly colored Indian blanket that overlay the large bed and added warmth to the room. Beside the bed stood a tall chest of drawers topped with a lamp. On the peg wall was a washstand, a furnishing her room lacked.

Jess paused beside it to gaze out the window. Less than a mile to the south rose the pine-dotted slopes of the Sierra Nevadas, and, quite near the house, sat the outhouse. Jess lifted a brow. Until now, she had been using a chamber pot. She would forgo that amenity in favor of an excuse to go outside.

Stabs of guilt for intruding on his space pricked her conscience. Disgusted with herself that she even cared, Jess spun about—and froze.

Jake was standing in the doorway, watching her quietly. Her heart leapt to see his whiskey-brown eyes gazing steadily into hers. She recalled the pleasant ride they had shared into the mountains, and the way he had held her against him that last night in Carson City. Though he looked tired, his face was handsome with two days' whiskers roughing his jaw. He wore another flannel shirt, this one dark red to match the bandana around his neck. His sturdy frame practically filled the doorway, made more impressive still by a new sheepskin coat.

Jess swiftly recalled where she was and what had happened during her last night in Carson City—everything she had lost—and squared her chin. She refused to allow this man she had begun to care for to step any further into her life.

"Hello, Jess."

The timbre of his voice made her heart race at a panicked speed. By an effort of will, she slowed it by dwelling on her discontent. Moving toward him, she ignored his gentlemanly gesture of removing his hat, and she concentrated instead on images of when she had seen him last—when he had abandoned her father to the flames.

Rage swelled inside her, and she pushed past him forcefully. "Stay away from me!" she said firmly, then ran from the room and rushed down the stairs.

Below the stairs to the left, a low table, sofa, and two chairs faced the hearth. Nearly hidden from view by a column of chimney stones was the door.

Jess heard Jake descending behind her, gaining rapidly.

She'd never make it to the door before he reached her. At the fireplace, she whirled around to face him.

Jake paused before her, hat back on his head, ready to continue his pursuit.

"I'm going, Bennett."

"Going where?"

"To Carson City."

"You can't, Jess. It isn't safe."

Jess spun around and strode with singular purpose to the door.

"Your parents are gone," he softly reminded her.

The plank door blurred. She reached for the latch.

"Jess, there's something you need to know."

His tone held a solid warning. Her hand stilled on the curved iron latch as she awaited the news.

"A flag was left near the ashes."

The significance of the word slowly set in. Jess turned to face him. "Left?"

"That's right. A Confederate flag, staked in the yard."

"But we didn't own a Confederate flag. Why ever would—?" Jess listened to the Southern tones of her own voice. "The men from the street?"

Jake nodded. "Maybe. I also found an empty kerosene can in the bushes behind the stable."

Stunned, Jess leaned her head against the door. "The fire wasn't an accident?"

It had spread so fast, she recalled. More than just wayward embers from a neighbor's chimney had prompted the fire. Those Unionist fanatics had purposefully doused the sides of her home with kerosene and struck a match.

She barely noticed when Jake approached her from the hearth. Her eyes trailed up the stone chimney to where it disappeared through the ceiling high above. "What about the servants?"

She pictured Elsie, Maureen, Ho Chen, and Malcolm, almost afraid now to hope that they had survived.

A few feet away, Jake bent to gather logs from the woodpile. He fed them to the fire, and the dry wood crackled. "They're as well as can be expected. Edmund gave them references to find new employment."

Jess let out her breath. They were safe.

∼❧✠❧∼

Jake silently asked the Lord's forgiveness for keeping the full truth about the servants from Jess. Only minutes before, Red Deer had told him that Jess had been unable to do anything but cry and sleep for days. He couldn't burden Jess further—not now, especially when there was something else he had to tell her, a matter that couldn't be put off.

He took a seat in one of the two leather chairs by the hearth, hoping she'd be encouraged to do the same. "There's more."

She shook her head. "I don't want to hear it."

"You're trembling, Jess. You'd best come sit down."

"No, I'm going to the Van Dorns'."

"If you go to Carson City now, you'll be putting the Van Dorns in danger. Except for Edmund, everyone in that town thinks you're dead."

At this, her eyes focused and cut to him. "And just who put such a notion into their heads? You, Bennett?"

Jake studied her. He had expected a degree of resentment for having her taken from Carson City without her consent, but he hadn't expected her rage or the hunted look in her eyes. Maybe he could appeal to the grief he believed lay beneath her angry exterior. "Jess, it's hard for you to see now, but the Lord has a purpose for everything, even for this."

"The Lord?" she spat bitterly. "Ambrose and my parents

73

and Emma were dying, and where was He then? Where is He now?" Jess dismissed Him with a flick of her wrist. "I don't want to hear any more about the Lord!" She moved toward Jake like a panther stalking its prey. "And perhaps it hasn't occurred to you that I will have a need for an income, and that my father's share of the store now belongs to me. I also have friends in Carson City!"

Apparently faith matters would have to wait. "And enemies."

She stared at him.

"The men who wanted you dead now believe you are. If you show up, you'll be in danger, as will the Van Dorns, if you're seen with them. Jess, right now Edmund is known only as the business associate of a Southerner. If those men had questioned Edmund's loyalties, they would have burned his house, too. For now, his family is safe."

Her green eyes blazed. "You mean safe as long as they aren't harboring any Johnny Rebs?" she demanded. "They're acceptable now that they're no longer associating with traitors? Go ahead, Bennett, you can say it!"

"Jess, none of the Hales was a traitor. From what you said, your brother was fighting to defend his home, not to support some political cause. Most people know that honest people stand on both sides of the conflict, and that the worst trouble comes from fanatics." He rested his hands on his knees and sighed. Every conversation attempted on the wrong side of a Hale was like holding a torch to a barrel of gunpowder, and it was about to get worse. "Jess, for your own safety, you need to stay here until the sheriff figures this out."

"No, I have to go and run my father's store. It's the only means of income I have left. Besides, murderers don't wait around to be caught. Those men must have gone," she insisted, retracing her steps to the door.

Jake rose. "You don't know that. You could be in danger, Jess," he warned. "Worse things than fire can happen."

Jess threw open the door and stepped out onto a covered porch and into a frigid blast of winter air. A rust-colored cat scurried in.

In the room behind her, Jake said, "In Carson City, you would be a woman alone with no one to watch out for you."

Several cattlemen glanced up from various tasks in the ranch yard. Jess swept her gaze over three large corrals, various outbuildings, the barn...the stable. Ignoring the cold as best she could, she descended the two rough steps and marched past the men, her attention fixed on the stable.

Jake caught up with her and walked at her side. "You'd put yourself at risk? Your father wouldn't want that, Jess. He'd want you to live."

How dare he speak to her about her father! "The risk is minimal. My father would want me to support myself honorably. I can hardly stay here." Several ranchmen had gathered in front of the stable.

"There's good, honest work here, Jess. That scent you're breathing in is clean mountain air and fresh pine. There's nothing above you but sky, nothing walling you in but sunrise and sunset."

"The pay is insufficient and I find the company detestable."

"It's a good way to get past hard times, Jess."

Jess was growing more frustrated every moment. What he had said about a Confederate flag and kerosene whirled viciously in her head, and she choked with the need to be alone to scream at the injustice of it all. "You haven't heard me, Bennett—I'm leaving."

She came up short before a wall of chests. A line of perhaps a dozen ranchmen stretched shoulder to shoulder across her path, blocking the entrance to the stable. Impatiently, Jess pushed back her wind-whipped hair, her body shivering in the cold. Trail-hardened and leather-tough, the cattlemen gazed at her as one, obviously regretting such treatment of a lady but equally resolved to keep her from accessing the horses—her means of escape.

"What are they doing, Bennett?"

"I gave them orders that you're not to leave."

Outraged, she spun around to face him. "You instructed them before you spoke to me?"

"I thought you might not see things my way." Though he'd been right, he neither chuckled nor grinned. Jake's gaze held only…understanding. *Understanding?* She'd have to figure that out some other time. "You'll have the freedom of the ranch, Jess," he said, "and you'll be safe. It's only until the arsonists are found."

"That could take months," she growled, "or perhaps they'll never be found. They could be in another territory or even on their way across the continent by now. And if a lawman is looking to arrest someone for ridding the place of Confederate sympathizers, he likely won't be looking too hard!"

"I've asked Tom Rawlins to investigate."

"How dear of you."

None of the men gave any sign of backing down. At the same time, Jess instinctively knew that none of them would harm her. She began to walk around them, but they moved in order to bar her way.

"I can't let you go, Jess." Jake's voice was apologetic but final.

Jess neither refused nor agreed to stay. She shot the men a glare, then marched back the way she had come. She went straight past the house, heading toward the creek and the scattered cottonwoods in the distance.

The men returned to work. A few whacked Jake on the back in good-humored sympathy, and Jake thanked them for their help in staying Jess. Every one of them looked relieved, almost eager, for the changes in their relatively static existence that Jess's presence would surely bring.

When the other men had gone, Lone Wolf silently came up beside him. Jake scanned the foothills that stretched out to the west. The day was young, and the men could see to what little work there was.

"I'm going to see her, Lone Wolf. For a little while, at least. I've been away too long."

"You have made this journey for more than a year, my friend," Lone Wolf said quietly. "A journey that will not change how things are." When Jake did not respond, Lone Wolf let the matter be. "I will look after the girl until you return."

Jake gave him a nod of thanks, then walked to the rear of the stable. With a small knife, he took two cuttings from the spindly bush that stood there. Not long after, he was riding toward the mountains, two cuttings in his hand.

Chapter Four

J ess had watched Jake saddle his horse, but she had
stubbornly kept her back to him when he passed her.

A small cluster of trees near the bank of the creek
gave her a measure of the privacy she sought. She was shaking
from cold but was too frustrated to care.

In Carson City, she had worked in a dark, cramped corner
of her father's store. She hadn't liked it, but it had been her
choice. Being brought here had *not* been her choice, and she
had no intention of staying. She knew she wouldn't have much
of a house left in Carson City, but the town provided a means of
income, and she desperately needed to be near her family, even
if they were...deceased. But more than anything, she wanted
the men who had murdered her family to be found and hanged.
The sheriff and Captain Rawlins had only Jake's description of
the men who attacked her on the street. *If* the killers remained
in Carson City and she returned, she would know them the
instant she sighted them, and they could be swiftly captured.
Moreover, her presence in Carson City would ensure that the
sheriff pursued his investigation—and the hanging—with
diligence. She would see to that.

Jess's throat ached with the need to vent her anger at Jake
for keeping her at his ranch, especially after everything else
he'd done to her. Instead, she set her shoulders. She was her
own woman now. Nobody was going to tell her where to live.
She would leave the first chance she had.

At that thought, Jess finally surveyed her surroundings.
The Sierras towered behind her to the south, as she had

discovered by glancing through Jake's bedroom window. Honey Lake, she knew, lay in the broad plain to the west. Beyond the purling creek, an immense grassy valley stretched away to the north, and to the east of the valley huddled distant groups of mountains. All around the ranch, the sage plains lay open and flat, uninterrupted except for the creek and the cottonwoods. Leaving wouldn't be easy. There wouldn't be many places to conceal her while she rode away. Waiting for the right moment would take time and patience. She had neither. Her family's killers might have already left the territory. If she were to have any hope of finding them, she would first need to get free.

In the ranch compound east of her, a hammer banged on a rooftop, and she saw a tall ladder braced against the barn. The building looked like a toy miniature from where she stood, and two men were working on the roof. Down in the yard, another man led a spirited horse to one of the corrals. Two more loaded a buckboard wagon at the near end, their movements partially hidden by one of the buildings. One of them casually lifted a sun-weathered face in her direction, then returned to his work. Jake—may he rot—clearly had ordered them all to watch her.

For more than an hour, she seethed in silence. Eventually, Jake rode in. He returned his horse to the stable, then emerged again. Jess stared into the creek, her eyes focusing on nothing in particular. From the cluster of buildings, sounds of hammering persisted. She rolled her eyes.

Refusing to while away the hours when everyone else was busy, Jess strode back toward the barn. Perhaps she could find a way to lend a hand over the next few days, as she had suggested to Red Deer. At the same time, she would study the workings of the ranch and thereby determine the best means and moment of escape.

Jess studied the compound as she approached. To the right, between her and the two-story log ranch house, sat a long plank structure she suspected was the bunkhouse. The cookhouse stood to her immediate left, smoke rising from its chimney. Beyond it was the smithy, its giant doors open. Inside, she could see Doyle moving about in a leather apron. He was working a hammer and red-hot tongs. Finally, she spied Jake, leaning over the side of the buckboard wagon, between the bunkhouse and the nearest corral. Though she resented the man, he was the one who could direct her toward a duty she could undertake, as well as answer the question burning inside her. The other two men who had been loading the conveyance each heaved in a grain sack, then headed for the barn.

Jake looked up and saw her walking over. With slow movements, he reached his arm over the side of the wagon, grabbed an oddly shaped bundle, and eased it out again just as carefully.

Jess was unable to get a word in before Jake surprised her by unrolling a thick, woolen overcoat like those the ranch hands wore.

"No point in coming down ill, Jess," he said. "It may not look like much, but it's new and it's warm. There're also mittens." He held out a pair to her.

She didn't take them. They were undoubtedly part of the goods he'd purchased in Carson City. "Keep your woolens, Bennett. I'll freeze before I'll accept so much as a thread from you."

"There's another month or two of winter left," Jake said, undaunted. "This was made to fit a man, so it's certain to keep you warm as a spud in an oven, clear to your knees. The men swear by them."

"Not all my possessions were lost in the fire, Bennett. I have my cloak to wear, should I choose to fetch it. Save your charity for somebody else."

"Charity?" He gazed at her as if trying to solve a puzzle.

"We're out in the wild here, Jess. There are no towns nearby, no stores around the corner. Out here, folks help one another. I don't refuse a passing man a meal or a bed if he has a need, and neither does anyone else. Ranch folks figure they may be traveling themselves someday, and they appreciate a sack of biscuits or a pair of mittens if someone has them to spare. This is a way of living that you might not be used to, but in these parts, it's how things are."

Since her most urgent need was to be away from him, Jess grabbed the coat and stuffed her arms into it, then snatched the mittens and pulled them on. "Why do you want to keep me here?"

"The ranch is remote, so you won't be discovered, and from what Isaac said, you don't have any other relatives you can stay with," he said. "Or do you?"

"I don't, but that's not what I meant. I meant, why *you*? Why are *you* keeping me here? Because it's honorable?" She scoffed at the word.

"Should there be a better reason?"

Certain that challenging the point would be akin to running in circles, Jess tilted her head toward the ranch. "Where can I lend a hand?"

"Red Deer's in the cookhouse. I'm sure she'd be glad for your help."

With that, he turned and started across the yard. His pace was slower than usual, almost lumbering. Jess briefly recalled the way he'd reached into the wagon, how he'd avoided stretching his shoulder and back. Reluctantly, her gaze followed his progress until he disappeared into the stable. She wondered how he'd injured himself, frustrated by the fact that she even cared.

Jess closed the door of the cookhouse behind her, the tension draining from her as her icy limbs tingled and thawed in the room's steamy heat.

"Jessica!" Red Deer greeted from somewhere in the kitchen. "Come! There is hot tea."

Jess glanced around the simple, welcoming room. Six rough-hewn tables with benches were arranged in two long rows, with plenty of space in between them to accommodate the ranchmen. The walls were plastered white, the one nearest the door studded with coat pegs. The hearty warmth of the room, combined with her willingness to forget about Jake for a time, lightened her mood. "I'll be along in a moment," she called, breathing deep. Meaty, spicy aromas permeated the place.

She hung the coat and mittens on pegs, then made her way to the kitchen. The plank floor bore hundreds of dents and scratches from the ranchmen's boot heels and spurs. A man's domain it was.

An enormous, custom-made sideboard separated the kitchen from the mess hall. Jess rounded it wonderingly. Beneath it, open-fronted shelves were divided into cubbyholes that stored a wide assortment of goods: boxes of teas, jars of spices, iron trivets—fashioned by Doyle, perhaps?—old ammunition boxes heaped with forks and spoons, a medical kit, and an oft-used coffee mill, judging by the thick coating of dark powder that covered it.

Huge barrels flanked the sideboard. Jess lifted their lids to discover stores of flour, salt pork, beans, salt, oats, coffee, and sugar. Large, cloth-covered baskets on a long table held dried fruits, jerky, pale nutmeats she didn't recognize, and an assortment of drying herbs she suspected had been cultivated by the Indians. Ubiquitous braids of onions, garlic, and chili peppers dangled from the low ceiling beams, and shelves were stacked with clean pans, iron kettles, and enough tin plates to feed an army of cattlemen. Beside a massive stone fireplace, a low bunk hugged the wall.

Red Deer turned from the fireplace, grinning at Jess's evident amazement. "There is truly much food here," she said. She pointed to a second door, partially hidden behind a water barrel in the corner. "Outside is a small corral the men have built for the pigs, and a fence of wires for the chickens. Nowhere else have I seen such a thing—a fence made of wires! Here the ranchmen and my people have plenty. We all work hard, and there is enough for all."

She smiled and returned to stirring a huge pot suspended over the fire. In it, Jess glimpsed a steaming broth brimming with cubes of meat.

Jess retrieved a clean mug from a shelf, then filled it from the kettle on the hearth. "May I help?"

"Help?" Red Deer looked at her curiously. "You wish to work beside me, an Indian woman?"

"Does that trouble you?"

"It is not common for whites to treat Indians as equals."

"I'm not someone who puts myself above others because of the color of their skin. Or the sound of their voice," she added. "My grandfather came to America from Ireland. As a girl, my mother was treated cruelly by other children because of her Irish blood. When she had children, she taught us that every person matters, that everyone has a special purpose, no matter who he is."

"The stew will need onions, if you would like to cut them," Red Deer said.

Jess spied a thick braid of the bulbous onions overhead. Locating a stool, she reached up and took them down from their nail. She began to separate the bulbs on a cutting board. "Do you always cook for the men, Red Deer?" she asked.

"Not always. We had a cook, but he left before winter.

The men say Mr. Bennett hired a new man. He sent him to get supplies from Sacramento City." Red Deer pointed to the onions. "You can put the skins into the fire. The ends we will put into that pail with other trimmings to feed the pigs."

Jess chopped the onions neatly, gratified that she had begged her mother's cooks to teach her the basics of their art. "Jake thought I could help with the cookhouse chores during my time here."

"I am glad for the help, Jessica. I often work here alone." Jess thought she would say nothing more, but then she continued. "The women of my village do not like to be near white men, though they know the white men of this ranch are good. The work they do near their homes is still helpful to the ranchmen." She scooped up the diced onions and added them to the pot.

"Helpful in what way?"

"The women prepare fresh cowhides for the ranchmen. Then they cut the hides into strips for the men to braid into lassos, or they sew them into chaps to go over the men's pants. The men pay them fairly."

Jess took a sip of warm tea, which was flavored with bits of dried apple. She found it delightful. "What kind of nuts are these in the basket, Red Deer?"

Red Deer borrowed the stool and broke three red chilies from their stalks. She followed Jess's gaze. "They are the nuts we pick from the pinyon pine."

"How do you pick so many nuts this small?" Jess asked, stirring them with a finger. She was curious to know, but she was also glad to have someone to talk to, someone to distract her thoughts.

"My people traveled in these mountains gathering pine nuts for food long before the white men came. Sometimes, we still do, but there are not as many now. I once hated the white men who cut down the pinyon pines to build their houses," she admitted. "They could have cut down other trees. They could have lived elsewhere." Red Deer paused reflectively, then worked to regain her cheerfulness. "We use forked sticks when we pick them from the trees." She laid the peppers on the cutting board for Jess and began filling a large bowl with handfuls of beans from a barrel.

Forked sticks? That was it? Jess doubted that even Miriam Van Dorn could make this woman keep talking. She recalled seeing brown-skinned children in the distance, and gave the conversation another try. "How do the children help?"

Red Deer laughed at the question, surprising Jess. "The boys like to climb the trees to pick them, and their bodies turn black with sap. Then they roll in pine needles until many stick to them, and they chase one another, laughing and growling as if they were bears."

Jess smiled at the thought. She took another sip of tea. "What are the gatherings like?"

"We pick the cones before they open, in the cool of the fall. We fill all the largest baskets with them."

"With the pinecones?"

"At first; then, with the nuts. We break out the nuts in the mountains, for there are too many cones for the people to carry away." Red Deer's slender shoulders relaxed a little, and she finally seemed more comfortable sharing the experience with Jess. "All the people who come are family and dear friends. Some stay near camp to dig out a large pit and to build a fire. All people—men and women, young and old—work together, and the gathering is very happy, for months have passed since we have seen one another."

"It sounds like hard work."

"It is hard work, but it is also good." With her free hand, she tucked her short hair behind her ears. "Some people pick, and others carry baskets of cones to the fire. There the green cones are roasted to dry them and to open them."

"The heat makes them open?"

"Yes, and they sound like many eggs frying in a skillet. When they are cool enough to touch, we lay the cones on large, flat rocks, and then we strike them with smaller stones to break out the seeds. The children like to do this because they sneak bites when they think nobody sees them, but they do not know that we also did this when we were children."

Jess shared a laugh with Red Deer and began to slice the chilies.

Red Deer poured the dried beans into the cooking pot. Briefly, she considered the broth, then used tongs to lift a large rock out of the fire. With great care, she lowered the rock into the stew, the liquid around it sizzling as bubbles burst on the surface. When she had released it, she withdrew the tongs and added more logs to the fire.

At Jess's look of wonder, Red Deer explained, "It is stone boiling. In this way my people often cook food, by heating the stew from the inside. We often cook in vessels made only of animal skins, and those we cannot cook over a fire like iron pots."

"I suppose not," Jess agreed, watching Red Deer stir the fragrant dinner.

"When I cook for the men, I must prepare much food. By stone boiling, it does not take so long. Would you like to taste a pine nut?"

Gamely, Jess selected one of the seed-like nuts. It had a soft crunch and a mild flavor. "It's wonderful. Do you eat these by themselves?"

"The nuts we eat in many ways. If there is a good hunt, we mix them whole with flavorful leaves and berries and cook them with rabbit or antelope. We also grind them into flour and boil them in soups like white man's porridge. In winter, we sometimes let the porridge get very cold, adding sugar if we have it. I once tasted ice cream—it is much like this, but nutty. The children love to eat it this way."

An hour or more passed amiably. The stew would simmer until that night's supper, Red Deer explained, and they needed to make dinner now, for the men would be coming in soon. Together, they prepared ham steaks and beans, which they arranged on the sideboard, along with pans heaped with corn bread that Red Deer had made that morning. Added to the meal were pots of hot coffee and crocks of fresh, sweet butter for the bread. Jess had just finished setting plates and flatware on the sideboard for serving when the ranchmen started pouring in the door.

The men said little, which surprised Jess. They helped themselves from the serving platters, and as they filled their plates, many of them nodded to Jess, treating her as respectfully as they treated Red Deer. *At least Bennett's order to watch me hasn't caused them to treat me like a detestable miscreant,* she mused. They were frugal with their words, but they seemed to accept her presence easily enough. A woman looking to escape couldn't hope for better.

Jess glanced out a window at the empty compound. Nearly all the men came to eat at once. Yet, she realized, meals were too short to provide sufficient time for her to slip away.

Bennett didn't come in for dinner, she noticed; neither did Doyle nor Diaz, two of the men she was familiar with and had expected to see. She began to hear the distant *tink-tink* of Doyle's hammer, the sound wending through the cookhouse wall, dull but continuous. After the ranch hands had finished and returned to work, Jess fixed three plates of food to take over to the smithy. Working men needed to eat.

The sharp banging became considerably louder as she entered, and the heat in the small building was intense. Jess pushed several tools aside and set the plates on a dusty table, then waited for Doyle to pause so she could tell him she'd brought dinner. Apparently, Jake and Diaz were elsewhere.

After a long moment, Doyle glanced up, seeing her and then noticing the steaming plates.

"For you and Bennett and Diaz," she explained.

He gave her a brief, appraising look, then nodded his thanks and continued his work.

After Jess and Red Deer had eaten, they washed all the dishes and wiped down the tables. With dinner complete, they turned again to their preparations for supper. Red Deer set Jess to grinding coffee for the men's supper while she selected herbs to add to the stew.

"Where did you learn English, Red Deer?"

"A missionary came to teach us, and to tell us about the Son of the Great Spirit Father, the one they call Jesus. My sister and I learned this language, as did many of my people. We speak it to the whites, but to one another, we speak mostly the Paiute language." Her face hardened slightly, like a flower petal frozen from cold. "The missionary told us it is wrong to hate, and wrong to kill the white men for harming us. He said that Jesus forgave the people who killed him, and we should do the same. I still struggle to forgive." She lowered her eyes to the herbs she had been chopping. "It is often because of white settlers that my people suffer. We have learned that many of our Shoshoni neighbors have been killed because of whites in Idaho Territory. Yet we know that your God sees us as His children, also." She glanced up with a small smile. "The Bible says that many of those who followed Jesus were fishermen, like the Paiute, though we also hunt antelope and gather seeds and berries. All this land near Honey Lake Valley used to be our home, but now it belongs to ranchers. For hundreds of years, Paiute women have gathered the reeds and grasses for making baskets that we need. The lake and creek held food for us, and with branches from the trees our people made their homes. Now the white men say, 'This land is ours. You can no longer come here.' We do not understand such a thing, taking land and keeping for one what had belonged to all. My people have been very angry at the settlers, and there have been many battles, fought by Paiutes who did not want to leave."

Red Deer scattered the dried herbs into the bubbling pot, then wiped her hands on a cloth. "But Mr. Bennett is different. He is a good man."

Unless danger threatens, Jess thought.

"He lets us live here so that other white men do not trouble us, and he speaks peacefully to all people. The Paiute men work and are paid the same as the white men. Always there is food for us and for our old people and our children."

Jess was ready for Red Deer to stop talking now, but she continued, oblivious to Jess's animosity toward Jake.

"Among the Paiutes, he is known as Many Horses, and he is respected. On this ranch, our people can hunt when they wish, and they catch fish. Our elders teach our children the ways of the people, and they also teach them to honor the Spirit Father and to send their prayers to Him."

She sighed in acceptance—no, contentment, Jess realized.

"I know that my family will survive here. While I cook, they are nearby in our village. They, too, work and teach and learn the old ways, and when Lone Wolf and I walk home each night, we know that our place here is good."

Red Deer looked up. Jessica was sitting as far from the coffee grinder as she could while dutifully turning the crank. The Indian woman laughed softly.

"You do not like coffee, Jessica? I will grind; you may stir the soup."

Later that afternoon, when they began to set up for the evening meal, Red Deer took the stack of plates from Jess. "You are moving slower. You are not well yet. Why not get some rest? When you feel strong, you may help again."

True, Jess was utterly exhausted. She had done little physical work, but invading images of battles and fires had begun to trouble her and wear down her mind and, by extension, her body. With a word of gratitude, Jess put on her coat and mittens, then crossed the yard to the big house. The wagon had not been moved, though a canvas covering had been pulled over its bulging load.

Winter's early darkness encroached, turning the wind cold, and she was chilled and shaking when she pushed the heavy timber door closed. Inside felt blessedly warm, like the cookhouse. The hearth blazed invitingly, and Jess moved toward it, still huddled in her coat. Evidently, someone had kept the fire going just for her, since she didn't think that Jake spent much time here other than at night, to sleep. She gave the matter no further thought than that. She was far too tired.

Gradually, she warmed up. Red Deer's words came back to her—how her people lived on the ranch, how she could go home to her family and find comfort with them. Aching with memories and loss, Jess hung the coat and mittens on a peg near the door. She made her way to the staircase and climbed the steps to the privacy of her room.

The towels were dry, so she folded them, then set all the bath items on the floor. She removed all but her chemise and climbed into bed.

Through it all, she harbored a heavy, hardened heart toward Jake. She couldn't forgive him—couldn't begin to— though she'd been brought up knowing the wrongness of such an attitude. She fell asleep in the dark silence of the house, wondering where she and her family would be at that moment if all of them had survived.

∼❦∽

Jake came in for the night and closed the door behind him, his eyes pausing on the woolen coat Jess had finally accepted. Well, that was one battle won. He slowly removed his hat and clapped it on its peg, satisfied with the day's other accomplishments.

He worked his way out of his new sheepskin coat and hung it beside Jess's. His old one hadn't survived the fire, but it had kept the worst of the falling embers from him when the house had collapsed. He had the Lord to thank that Lone Wolf, Taggart, and the others had rushed to the Hales' house when they saw the flames. Lone Wolf had saved Jess's life. Jake wouldn't have reached her in time.

Attempting to draw his thoughts back to the present, Jake sat down to weigh his plans for Taggart for the following days. The wagon was loaded and ready to be driven to the winter line camps come morning. He pulled out the notes he'd made and went over the list of supplies Taggart would take, making certain that nothing had been forgotten.

But images of the Hale house lingered in his mind.

Edmund Van Dorn had arrived, greatly alarmed, only minutes after the ranchmen had ridden off with Jess. He had seen the blaze from his house. Jake knew that folks must have seen the flames and smoke from all over the city. When Jake had told him the fate of the Hales, Edmund had wailed hopelessly for them while howling flames consumed the rest of the house.

The wind had blown cinders to neighboring houses, and the night had become a frenzy of bucket lines and people with wet blankets beating out fires.

By morning, several other homes had suffered smoke damage, and a few rooftops had been burned, but the only house that had been leveled was the Hales'. After dozens of people spent a sleepless night battling the inferno, the sun rose to reveal black ribbons of smoke rising from the ashes. Jake and Edmund had picked their ways through the residual heat and brittle ruins to locate the bodies of the Hales. After the remains had been covered and taken away for burial, Edmund had collected himself well enough to invite Jake to his home to clean up and get some rest. He didn't sleep much, though.

Later that afternoon, Edmund went to ask the Hales' pastor to perform the funeral service. Jake purchased a new set of clothes for himself to replace the scorched ones. With a list of the Hales' full names—including Jessica's—in his pocket, he arranged for a burial plot and ordered a tombstone. Isaac had been their mutual friend, and, during dinner that night at the Van Dorns', Jake, Edmund, and Miriam exchanged quiet and sometimes lighthearted reminiscences of the man and his family, none of them wanting to dwell on the funeral service to come. Later that night, in the privacy of Edmund's study, Jake told him that Jess alone survived and expressed his concern about the Confederate flag and the kerosene. Together, they had made plans, and Edmund had agreed that Jess should remain in safety at Jake's ranch until the arsonists were found.

Jake rubbed his eyes with his thumb and forefinger, trying to decide what to do about Jess. Jess fought helplessness with anger; he'd seen her do it before, but she had chosen to direct her anger over her loss at him. The moment he had arrived at the ranch this morning, she'd set out to leave. He couldn't let her. Not with men out there who wanted her dead. Not when everyone in Carson City believed she was dead. Here, she was safe. Besides, working around the ranch, as she'd asked to do, would be to her benefit. At best, it would give her the chance to tell him what was on her mind, if she chose. At least…well, she'd be out in wide, open places, closer to the Almighty, and she just might be reminded of His nearness amid the beauty of the land and mountains.

He knew firsthand how that could help when nothing else could. There were days when being in the wilderness— witnessing its natural, untainted beauty—had been all that had gotten him through. Gut-busting work had helped him through the rest. Yes, he'd try to get Jess to talk to him over the following days. He'd seen hatred toward him in her eyes earlier. He hoped to find out what had put it there.

That settled, Jake lighted a lamp with a stick of wood from the fire and climbed the stairs to his room. He placed the lamp on the chest of drawers, and then, with painstaking movements, eased out of his clothes. His naked back was reflected in the window glass. A wide crescent of burned flesh extended from his shoulder blade to his ribs, caused by the roof collapsing above him when he had tried to go in after the Hales.

Chapter Five

After breakfast the next morning, Red Deer asked Jess if she would see to dinner and supper for the men. A friend's child had become ill, Red Deer explained, and since she had healing skills, she had been asked to help. Jess assured her she would take care of the meals.

Once she was alone in the cookhouse, Jess noticed the heartache of past days gradually fading as she busied herself. She prepared ham, biscuits, and sweetened apples for dinner, then potato soup and corn bread for the evening meal. It was perhaps seven at night, to her estimation, when she finished drying the last of the supper dishes. As she was hanging up a dishcloth, she looked up to see Jake and a ranch hand stroll into the cookhouse. Both hung up their coats but kept their hats on their heads, as if hats didn't belong anywhere else. Jess smiled a little. Cattlemen must be born with hats on. Jake nodded pleasantly to her as he came over, then gestured to his companion.

"Jess, this young man is Seth Griffin. Seth, this is Miss Jessica Hale, who's staying with us for a time."

Young man was right. Wide, brown eyes stared down in amazement at her from beneath his tan hat, and below his boyish face, his Adam's apple bobbed. Jess was willing to bet he had yet to need a shaving, though he stood with confidence, and something about him told her he could make good use of the gun at his hip if he needed to.

Respectfully, he touched his fingers to his hat. "Ma'a—" His voice caught. He cleared his throat and tried again. "Ma'am."

Jess concealed her surprise at his admiration of her. She still wasn't used to the way cattlemen, by nature, put women on a pedestal. "Good evening," she said. She couldn't bring herself to acknowledge Jake. "Are you newly hired, Seth? I don't believe we've met."

"Oh, no, ma'am. I've been working out at one of the line camps—small stations set at the borders of the ranch," he explained when he saw her confusion. "The big ranches in Texas and the plains do the same. We look after the cows until spring, make sure they have food and water and such." Looking pleased with her attentiveness, he went on. "When there's a hard winter with lots of snow, we have to dig to find them food and chop holes in the ice to water them, but mostly we search for strays and bring them back, and keep an eye out for rustlers. Since there are few neighbors to the west and none to the east, there're lots of places the cattle can wander off to, and there's a lot of thievin'." He briefly turned his attention to Jake. "Taggart's keeping an eye on things until I get back tomorrow. He said that with the mare nearing her time, I'd best bring her back here to foal."

For a moment, the two discussed which horse Seth would take when he rode out in the morning. While they did, Jess realized he must not have eaten yet. She waited until they quieted.

"Seth, would you care for supper?"

"Oh yes, ma'am, I surely would."

Jake went to put more wood on the fire. "Is there any coffee, Jess?"

She reached for a clean plate and shuddered at the word *coffee*. Jake saw it. The corner of his mouth lifted in a smile.

"No, there isn't," she said. "Red Deer made enough this morning to last the day, but the others finished it a short while ago."

"No matter," Seth said cheerily. "I brought a kettle of coffee along to keep me warm during the ride. I'll go get it."

When the door closed behind him, Jess glanced at Jake, having no choice but to discuss a matter that concerned her. "Bennett, I can't stay at the ranch house...sleep there."

"There are two extra rooms, plenty of space. Besides, I'm hardly ever there."

"It's bad enough for an unmarried woman to stay one night in the same house as a man, but to live together for days on end, it...it just isn't done!" Her current feelings toward him had nothing to do with this. She had been raised a proper, genteel Southern lady with a corresponding sense of decorum!

He rested his hands on his hips and bowed his head in thought.

"Jess, I wasn't brought up knowing all the social dos and don'ts you were taught, but my pa did raise my brothers and me not only to act honorably, but to be honorable. I will bring you no shame, Jess—not here, and not anywhere else. The folks around here know that." He lifted his eyes to her. "None of my men has shown you any disrespect, right?"

She thought of the harmless four who'd ridden with them when they'd seen the sunrise together and the many more she'd met over the past few days. "No, none has," she conceded.

"They won't, either. I've never known a man who has higher regard for a woman than a cattleman. That's just how the breed is made."

After mulling his words, she nodded, then added warm apples to the plate for Seth.

"This is a good place to be, Jess," Jake said softly. "The land is good and the work is good. Some folks even believe it's easier to see the Almighty out here where there's no city or crowds to block your view."

Resenting the reminder of the God who had abandoned her, Jess didn't answer.

When Seth returned with the kettle, he set it in the flames to heat it. Jake grabbed a biscuit and sat down with him. Several minutes passed before Seth paused from eating to make a compliment. "Those are the best apples and biscuits I've had in a long time."

Jess waved a hand toward the barrels and sacks. "All the makings were right here."

"Someone like me don't much know what to do with them, though. This kind of work can make a man thin."

Jess didn't understand. "You mean ranch work?"

"He means duty at line camp," Jake explained in his deep voice.

"Yes, ma'am, that's what I meant. The food here at the ranch is real good. It has to be, or else the men'll move on to better. I can't cook none myself, but some of the linemen do just fine."

Jess nearly laughed until she saw the boy was serious. She took a seat near him on the bench, pushing aside her aversion to Jake to talk with the boy, who seemed hungry for company. "Men will leave to work at a ranch with a better cook?"

"Yes, ma'am. Cattlemen will stay to finish a job if they give their word, or if they feel beholden to a rancher, or if there's a pretty girl to look at." He grinned, surprising her and apparently himself, as well, with the comment. He was quick to recover. "But they also move on when they want, for their own reasons, or for no reason at all. One night, a man's here; the next morning, his bunk is empty and he's gone. Working cows at one ranch is pretty much the same as working cows at another, so nobody stays long if the food is bad."

"It happens," Jake affirmed. "So I employ the best cook to be found, and then I have my pick of good working men. Most have been at the ranch since the beginning."

Seth scraped his plate until it was spotless. "But I heard that the last Cookie went and got himself married."

Jake finished his biscuit. "I found a replacement."

Seth glanced at him. "Oh, yeah? Who? I hope it's old Cracker Jack from the Bar Seven."

"I wouldn't hire him. He drinks too much." Jake sidestepped the question. "Red Deer's running the kitchen while he and a couple of the men are off getting the supplies I couldn't find in Carson City."

Seth brushed crumbs from his hands. "Miss Hale, I think the boss should fire the new dough roller and just hire you."

Jess smiled at his enthusiasm but inwardly cringed at the thought of being stuck inside a cookhouse from sunup till sundown. She was still recoiling from the notion of spending months on end inside a small room when she realized that this was exactly what Seth and the other men on line duty were doing. She shook her head, wondering how the men could survive it, and she found herself respecting the strength and forbearance of the cattlemen. Seth interrupted her thoughts when he placed three mugs of steaming coffee on the table, two within easy reach of her and Jake.

He sat down again and took a sip from his mug, looking over the rim at the amusement in Jake's eyes and what must have been obvious revulsion in hers. He lowered his mug. Jess's mind scurried for a way to avoid hurting Seth's feelings.

"It isn't all that bad, Jess," Jake said.

Jess hesitated. Then, glimpsing Seth's understanding grin, she quietly muttered, "It smells like a pot of something left on the stove too long." She added, "I'm sorry, Seth."

"That's just fine, ma'am."

Jake raised an eyebrow. "Have you ever tasted coffee, Jess?"

"Taste something that smells like that? Why punish myself?"

Seth chuckled at her disgust.

"It's just roasted beans and water," Jake said.

"An adulteration of perfectly good water."

"When you're cold, it'll thaw you clear to your toes," Seth cut in.

"I've heard men claim it puts hair on your chest."

Seth nearly spewed out a mouthful of coffee, laughing. Jake smiled and glanced pointedly at her braid. "Don't worry, Jess. The worst it does to women is make their hair curl."

Jess carefully lowered her gaze away from Jake's handsome face to peer doubtfully at the inky brew inside her cup. Grounds were floating on the surface. It wasn't like any coffee she'd ever seen. Cautiously, she asked the boy, "How do you make it?"

He shrugged. "Same way most cattlemen do, I reckon. You fill a pot with water and throw in a handful of roasted, ground-up beans. It cooks a while and then you drink it. Of course, the pot gets low by nightfall, so the next morning, you add water and throw in more beans."

Jess bit back a smile as Seth sobered importantly and continued his instructions in the fine art of coffee making.

"After a week or better, I find I need to toss out the old beans and start again with new, or else it gets too thick to pour." He frowned. "That's a shame, too. Right about then, the grounds quit floating, and you can drink it without swallowing any bits."

Jess felt Jake's eyes shift to her. By strength of will, she didn't shudder, but neither did she ask the boy how old this particular batch was. She merely lifted her cup and, with all the resolution of a martyr, took a sip.

Seth waited anxiously for her reaction. Her eyes watering, Jess set down the mug. She looked at the two men in disbelief, all at once laughing at the absurdity of the situation.

"It tastes like liquid coal!" she declared. "How can you drink this?"

Jake chuckled and Seth shrugged good-naturedly. "Nothing's better on a brisk winter night."

Feeling its heat spreading within her, Jess silently agreed and, from then on, sipped the brew with declining repulsion.

"Do you know how to read an' write, Miss Hale?"

The question surprised her. "I do. Would you like me to write a letter for you?"

"Well, ma'am, I'll be returning to the line camp come morning, and I haven't sent a letter home since fall. I'd sure appreciate it if you could."

"Gladly. We'll do that as soon as I've washed the dishes."

While she finished in the kitchen, Seth relayed to Jake the number of cows lost through the winter due to freezing, thieves, and predators. When Jess sat down again, Seth handed her a piece of paper and a pencil, then started dictating his letter.

Jake busied himself logging notes in the small book he kept with him. As she wrote, Jess considered him from the corner of her eye. He seemed to sit slightly leaning to one side. He was tired, maybe, but overall he appeared contented with the homey quiet, as if, by stepping away from the busyness of Carson City, he had become one with the mountain wilderness, and she, the men, and the ranch had melded into it with him.

After Seth had provided his family's address and Jess had penned it, she folded the letter away with a promise to send it with the first man who went to town. Seth thanked her heartily, then glanced over at Jake.

"I have a dozen pelts, boss."

"A dozen?"

Curious, Jess looked up.

Jake turned a page in his book and made a new notation. "A dozen is a good catch for one season," he said.

"I'll bring them to you when I come back next month."

Jake eyed him. "I pay you a dollar a head to bring them down. The pelts are yours to keep, like I told you last fall."

Grinning, Seth pulled a deck of cards from his vest pocket.

"In that case, I'll sell them and buy me a fancy new pair of boots. They'll be even fancier than those ones Diaz wears."

Jess frowned back and forth between the two. "What kind of pelts?"

Jake made one more notation, then closed his book. "Wolf. They attack the cows, and sometimes people, if they're hungry enough."

Jess sat a little straighter. "There are wolves out here?"

Seth's grin widened. "Well, there's a good twelve fewer than there might have been. Poker?"

After Jess had returned to the house and Seth had turned in, Jake remained behind in the cookhouse to bank the coals. He nudged bits of wood aside with a fire iron, reliving a moment minutes earlier when Jess had shrugged into her coat for the walk across the compound. He had stood, looking down at her, and something had shifted inside his chest at the shining brown hair that hung to her hip in a thick braid. She'd tugged her collar close under her chin, and he knew that if she had lifted her face, he would have seen eyes the color of summer sage. Suddenly, Jake realized the path of his thoughts and swiftly changed the focus of his contemplation.

Well, he mused, *she has taken to Seth well enough.* He chuckled, the sound echoing across the empty room. Whatever her troubles were, he knew poker wasn't one of them. Companion-starved, Seth had challenged her to game after game of cards. She couldn't bluff, but she had a good head for odds. She won more than she lost.

Jake's attitude sobered. He set aside the fire iron and leaned a hand on the mantle, sifting through other reflections of the past two days. Although Jess had warmed to many of the cattlemen, she had held him at a distance, confirming his belief that her vexation was with him alone. But that didn't trouble him beyond his concern for her. She had laughed at Seth's coffee-making lecture, and it was good she'd made that small step away from the weight of recent memories. Thinking too long about such things could tear someone up inside.

Jake doused the lamp, gathered up his coat, and left the cookhouse. The night sky glittered above him, and he paused to appreciate the awesome beauty of it. Yes, it was good out here. This place had a way of taking a body's mind off those troubles that just won't let go.

In her room, Jess lay on the bed and settled under the covers. She had been at the ranch just a short time, yet she was quickly coming to love a kind of people she had never known existed. Like young Seth, many of the linemen would likely keep the pelts to sell for additional income, and she fully expected there to be a swarm of new hats and silver-ornamented hatbands and flashy spurs, as well as heavily decorated boots, strutting about the ranch come spring. She grinned in the darkness. A few of the men had spoken as though the world held no finer goods, and perhaps, to them, it didn't. She was beginning to understand that others would refuse any additional payment to the dollar for each animal they had originally agreed upon, firmly believing that if the wolves were on Jake's property, the pelts were his. The cattlemen's code of ethics was like nothing Jess had ever experienced before—men hardly older than boys neither taking anything they believed they didn't earn nor standing in obligation to remain at a ranch if wanderlust beckoned.

Jess realized she felt no differently. She would stay at the ranch until she had worked off the cost of her food and clothing, along with the horse she would take. Perhaps, by then, the sheriff or Captain Rawlins would have news. When she left, she would have no reason to feel guilt or further compulsion to repay Jake Bennett. She would owe him nothing.

⚜

Jake hurried up a staircase flooded with morning sunshine to retrieve a pair of chaps from his room. With Jess spending her days at the cookhouse, the place was empty, silent. His gaze traveled across his room as he buckled the chaps on, recalling that first morning when he had found her there, looking out his window. On a thought, Jake crossed the short hall to stand in her doorway. Her bed was neatly made; the sparse furnishings were dusted and arranged along one wall. None of her own things was out, he saw. She must have placed her cloak and ball gown in the trunk. On the dressing table stood a basin and pitcher.

With one last look around the room, Jake strode out.

Late that night, after all but the watch had turned in, night sounds drifted in through the partly open door of the workshop. Inside, Jake patiently worked over a whirring lathe, turning a spindle to carve away peels of fresh wood. Beside him, a sturdy, uncut plank and three more shapeless spindles waited.

Chapter Six

The days passed with Jess gradually taking on more responsibilities, sharing with Red Deer the tasks involved in caring for a ranchful of men. Jake and most of the men, she'd learned, rode out each morning before sunrise to see to the cattle, while half a dozen or so stayed behind. The air had lost its wintry chill. As soon as new grass appeared, the linemen would return, then the ranch yard would be full of working men…and attentive eyes.

During the second week of March, Jess decided she'd worked off her debt to Jake. She began watching for an opportunity to ride away.

One morning, she undertook the task of scrubbing the floors of the main house. When she carried out the last pan of dirty water and emptied it away from the buildings, the sun felt warm on her face and arms—the warmest it had felt since autumn. Letting the pan dangle from her hand, she turned to take in the view around her. Horses had been freed in the corrals, and suddenly she was filled with pleasant memories of Kentucky. The horses tossed their heads and frisked about, seeming to welcome the oncoming spring.

Across the yard, one of the cattlemen raised a hand in greeting, and she surprised herself by waving back. The man went on about his work, and Jess strolled aimlessly in the sunshine, ending up, by happenstance, at the stable. *The stable.* Suddenly, her mind was alive with possibilities. With an air of innocence, she leaned the pan against the outer wall and breezed inside.

Searching furtively for any observers who might stop her, Jess wandered down the long central aisle. If she were a ranch hand, she mused, this would be the outfit where she would want to be. The stable was well organized, and it snapped with newness. The men kept it freshly bedded with straw, and they also took great care of their mounts and tack. If her father had been there, he would have made some remark about telling a good man by his way with horses. She smiled sadly at the bittersweet musing as she made her way to the far end of the building.

Aside from the remaining horses and herself, the stable was empty. With Jake gone working cattle, this was her best opportunity to leave. Walking back the way she had come, she lifted a bridle from its peg, slid open a gate, and entered a stall.

The sleek horse within eyed her warily, her ears pricked up. "Whoa, girl. Here now, have a sniff of me." She moved slowly, allowing the palomino to see her. The mare stretched out her muzzle, her nostrils taking in Jess's scent. Jess reached up gently to stroke the animal, smoothing her hand over her forehead and cheek. "Yes, you're a sweet girl," she murmured warmly. "How would you like to chase the wind with me?"

The horse nudged her shoulder for more petting. Jess obliged, then drew on the bridle and buckled it in place. As she slipped the reins over the horse's head, her hands began to tremble.

Jess listened for anyone returning to the barn, peering about as she led the tan beauty toward the waiting saddles. There were four of them, and Jess found the one that would best fit the mare. She laid a thick blanket over the mare's back, then set the saddle on top. Ducking under the mare's neck, she lowered the cinch and a stirrup, then slipped under again to retrieve the cinch strap and secure it. With the threat of discovery, she decided that the current lengths of the stirrups would have to suffice—there was no time to adjust them. She swung herself up into the saddle and eased the horse out into the sunshine. Taking one last look about, she gave the horse her heels.

The mare was solid, and she stretched out with remarkable speed. Behind them, the cluster of buildings faded away rapidly. None of the men was in sight. No one shouted after her. Jess took a long, deep breath of spring air. She was free. Laughter bubbled in her throat with the joy of it, but she held it in. Eventually, someone would discover she was missing. She needed to keep her wits about her.

Red Deer had said that the ranch was a day and a night's ride from Carson City. Jess knew that if she followed the general flow of the creek, there would be food and water for the horse, and she could manage without food until they reached the city.

As they raced southeast, Jess kept her distance from the occasional settlement, but she was compromising speed in order to avoid being seen. Finally, she searched out a rough road that wended south, and she pressed the horse to her limit.

The sun was high overhead when she slowed the mare to a trot to give her a rest, wiping sweat from her own forehead as the sun poured out the warmth that it had long held back. She passed opposite the tent of a prospector, who was placer mining near the creek. Once he was out of sight, she rode to the creek's edge, intending to water the horse.

Jess glanced back the way she had come…and froze. A huge black horse and rider were charging straight for her, closing the mile between them with unnerving speed. Recognizing the familiar bulk and brown hat of the rider, Jess spun the mare around and kicked her into a run.

With her horse already worn from the morning's pace, Jess knew she wouldn't be able to outrun Jake for long, but she had gained a fair distance—as well as an overwhelming need for vengeance—and devised a way to unhorse him.

A stand of oak trees appeared near a spur of the mountain. She rode straight toward it, scanning the ground ahead for a stick large enough to suit her purposes. There! She jerked the horse to a stop and swung to the ground. She hefted the branch that had fallen, swiftly regained her saddle, then forged ahead in a clatter of hooves.

For a moment, Jake lost sight of Jess. When he passed a grove of oaks, he caught a glimpse of her again—a flash of sun-gilded braid glinting through the dust. He maintained a steady pace, watching for a place to overtake her.

Jess rode the way he remembered, as bold and confident as the horse that carried her. He intentionally gave her a lead, watching her ride as any man observing a thing of beauty. She was not suited for household chores and domestic tasks alone, he realized. She was too much like he was—she needed the outdoors, wind, and freedom. As soon as he was able, he would find work for her alongside the men, even if it meant that she would have to be watched more closely. It was necessary for her to stay, and stay she would.

Jake was familiar with the scattered hills they were approaching. He would use the terrain to trap her and to put an end to the chase. As soon as she disappeared around a bend, he cut sharply to the opposite side of the hill and loosed the reins. The stallion bolted forward, sniffing intently for the scent of the mare.

Jake rounded the curve, then leaned abruptly on his reins. Jess was flying at him head-on, viciously swinging a branch at his midsection. The jagged end of the limb ripped his vest as it passed. He shouted his rage, more from surprise than from pain.

He whipped the stallion around, tore his lasso from the saddle, and shot after her.

Jess glanced back. When he was nearly alongside her, she flung the branch at him.

Jake knocked it aside. He let out a piercing whistle and smacked her horse's rump with the rawhide.

Panicked, the mare thrashed and bucked to fight off her unknown attacker. Unable to keep her seat, Jess tumbled to the dry desert ground.

Instinctively, she rolled away from the hooves of the pitching horse, but Jake was already waving the frightened horse back. The mare's eyes rolled white, and she bolted away riderless, thrusting warning kicks behind. The mare, he determined, wasn't the only one who needed the sting of a rope applied to her backside.

Jake dismounted with rope in hand. Jess's face flushed with anger as she scrambled to her feet. Jake braced himself as he approached, his hat pulled low, the lasso gripped threateningly in his hand.

Jess's attention flicked to the gun on his hip, where her gaze lingered an instant too long.

"Forget it, Jess. I wouldn't want either of us to take home a foot full of lead."

"I usually hit what I aim for, Bennett, and I've never yet hit a polecat in the foot!" she seethed.

Jake ignored her threat. "Would you care to explain why you tried to break me in two with that branch?"

"Not in the least." She glanced in the direction her horse had fled, and then, on second thought, eyed the stallion. "I've told you enough—I'm not staying."

"Yes, you are."

Her attention snapped to Jake. He began to uncoil the lasso, and for the first time she appeared uncertain.

"You think to tie me?"

"If I thought you'd ride back without trying to knock me from my skin, I wouldn't have to tie you."

She raised her chin, stepping back. "I am not riding with you."

Instead of insisting, he studied her quietly. "What's this all about, Jess? Carson City? A cramped store and men who attack you in the streets? That's not why you were leaving."

Jess didn't answer. She radiated stubbornness.

"Perhaps you'll tell me when you're ready. I'd best get you back."

"I said, I'm not going!" Her yell must have carried halfway back to the ranch.

"You know I can't let you just walk away."

Jess spun and stalked off in the direction of Carson City.

Jake wasn't a man to let things go. In two steps, he'd caught up with her, and he clamped a warning hand on her arm.

In the next instant, Jess lunged at him, shoulder first, attempting to knock him off balance, no doubt so she could make a grab for the horse.

Using her momentum, Jake spun around and took her down like a yearling calf.

Pinned facedown in the dust, Jess kicked furiously, trying to wriggle away. Jake grasped her wrists behind her and bound them in a heartbeat, his knee planted firmly yet gently across her back to hold her in place.

Jess screamed. Jake ignored her. He flipped her onto her back and roped her arms to her sides. In the next moment, he snared her feet together and whipped a double coil around her ankles. She was secured. He hefted her in his arms and made for his horse.

Jess pulled at the ropes in desperation but was unable to budge them. Her green eyes blazed as they bore into his.

Feeling unusually lighthearted, Jake set her in the saddle, then mounted up behind her. Jess turned her face away, refusing to acknowledge him. She didn't see the way he smiled behind her and shook his head slowly, amazed by this fearless spitfire who had stepped into his life.

They rode back to the ranch at an easy pace—Jake had run the stallion at top speed to catch up with Jess, and now he was burdening it with the weight of an extra body. He kept his silence, knowing that anything he said would only fuel Jess's anger. He also figured she still needed time to sort things out in her mind. He used the ride to do the same.

He wasn't entirely sure what to do with Jess over the coming months, but she certainly wouldn't be safe in Carson City. If the murderers didn't succeed a second time, anyone who had believed her to be dead would grow suspicious. When the war ended, perhaps she'd want to go home to Kentucky. If so, he would see she got there safe.

That thought didn't sit well with him. Isaac had once said that everyone the Hales knew there was gone. A beautiful woman by herself was easy prey. No, he wouldn't allow Jess to come to harm, not in the States and not in the West. But in forcing her to stay, he was inviting a battle of a whole other kind.

Lowering his gaze, he took in the smooth line of her jaw, the shine in her chestnut hair as a cool breeze ruffled it. It smelled of flowers, and she was soft and warm against him.

His gut clenched at his own betrayal. Recalling the beauty

of the one he loved, he put his admiration for Jess from his mind. He was honor-bound to protect Jess, but he belonged to another, and he wouldn't betray his lady's love.

∾◦⊱◈⊰◦∾

Having calmed down as they rode, Jess suffered regret, of all things, that she was responsible for the loss of one of Jake's horses. The mare had been affectionate and had a lot of heart, and there was little chance that whoever would find her would treat her as well as Jake's men had. She had run off toward the northeast, away from the nearest water source. Jess ached with the need to apologize, but she doubted she could manage civility if she tried. So, she asked about another matter instead. "Have you received word about the search for the men who set the fire?"

"Not yet. If I don't hear from the sheriff or Tom Rawlins in another week, I'll send a man to find out what they've learned."

Another week! Six weeks had already passed since the fire. Soon, the sheriff would give up the hunt and move on to other duties, if he hadn't already done so. It made no difference. Jess would keep watch for those responsible for the rest of her life. When they surfaced, she'd see justice done. On that thought, she asked another question.

"Did you see anyone the night of the fire, Bennett?"

"See anyone?"

"Yes. You and your men were in front of the house, and the servants must have escaped out the back. Did any of you see the arsonists run from the house?"

"No one saw anyone unusual that night, not even the neighbors. I asked around."

"Don't you think it odd? After all, nine men attacked me in the street."

"Nine attacked you, but likely only one or two started the fire. A group of men couldn't have slipped away unnoticed."

"I suppose."

It was late afternoon before she recognized the terrain, and only then did she realize how far she had gone. The air grew cooler, though it seemed unlikely night would bring the bitter cold of months gone by. She wondered what the land would look like come spring, then mentally reproached herself for thinking of any future here.

Unexpectedly, Jake reined in the horse and dismounted, leaving Jess to balance herself. He began untying the ropes.

"What are you doing?"

"I tied you because I had to, but we're almost back. I don't want to show you disgrace, especially in front of the men."

She stared at him blankly. What was she to make of that? When her wrists were free, she rubbed them, then realized there was no need. He had secured her soundly but not harshly, and the ropes had barely chafed the skin.

"But I'll tell you right now that I plan to give orders to my men to hog-tie you if you ever try to run again."

Jess closed her mouth against the gratitude she had nearly conveyed. Too bad they hadn't stopped by the creek. She'd have lifted her boot and kicked him straight into it.

With a few quick movements, he coiled and secured the rope, then swung up into the saddle behind her and pulled her securely to him. But before he could stir the horse, Jess stopped him with a hand on his arm, then turned her head to face him. "It's my fault she left, Jake."

He drew back, shaken. "What?"

"The mare," Jess said, her cheeks warming. "It's my fault she ran off. I'm sorry she's gone."

Jake let out his breath and passed his dark eyes over the hills. "She knows her way home. I'd like to think she's there already." This he said with a tone of added significance, and for the rest of their journey, Jess wondered what else he had been thinking.

When they reached the compound, Jake stiffly handed her down, then rode off without a word. She watched him go— not into the stable but behind it. After several moments, he reappeared, then galloped away, heading west. Jess stood puzzling over a new curiosity—she thought she had spied two slender cuttings in his hand. Around her, a few of the ranchmen silently exchanged glances. She entered the house to change, all the while mulling over what all this had meant.

Chapter Seven

What part of the ranch do you live on, Red Deer?" Jess knew that Lone Wolf and Red Deer lived nearby with their clan, but she hadn't seen their dwellings. She lightly slapped the lines to the hindquarters of the gentle palomino mare—the mare had returned, as Jake had predicted—and the two of them rocked about in the wagon seat as they made their way to the creek. Behind them in the wagon bed were two huge barrels and a dozen buckets with rope handles. She and Red Deer needed to draw water to soak and launder everyone's clothes. Red Deer had no trouble convincing her that gathering water from the creek would be more refreshing than straining at the pump handle.

"Our village is on the eastern part of the ranch. Our wigwams are near the creek. When there are no rabbits or antelope for our men to hunt, they catch fish." She glanced at Jess. "There has been no game for a very long time, but since the Paiute men work at the ranch, we have meat to eat." Red Deer smiled demurely. "But my husband and I will fast from all meat for one month in late summer, for then I will have a son."

Jess gasped in surprise, sharing the other woman's happiness. "How wonderful, Red Deer!"

"Yes, my husband will have a son to teach and to ride with, and I will be glad to bring him such happiness. Fasting from meat is one way we show we will be responsible parents who will go without food, if necessary, to see that our child is cared for."

Jess stopped the wagon near the creek. "You're certain the child will be a boy?"

"In my heart, I know it." Red Deer beamed at the churning ripples, at the land, at the sky. "So I work hard, that my son will be born strong, like his father." She stepped down carefully from the wagon and went around to the back to lift out several wooden buckets. Jess tied off the reins and joined her, and together they carried them to the water's edge.

Jess kicked off the new hide moccasins Red Deer had given her. She tucked the back hem of her gown up into the front of her belt and waded into the creek.

"You have skin like a white lily flower," Red Deer said from the shore.

Dipping a bucket into the water, Jess smiled at the comparison. She handed the heavy vessel to Red Deer. "This is the first my legs have seen daylight since I waded in rivers as a child." She filled another bucket. "White mothers teach their daughters not to expose any part of their legs, not even their ankles, especially to men."

Red Deer carried the brimming buckets to the wagon and set them down on the ground. "Yes, I once had a white woman friend who told me this also."

"Oh? And who was this white friend?" Jess passed another bucket to her, looking up inquiringly when Red Deer didn't take it from her. "Red Deer?"

"I am sorry, Jessica. I cannot speak of her." Red Deer took the bucket. After a long moment, her cheerfulness resurfaced. "The Great Spirit Father has given me another white woman friend, and this makes me happy."

Jess lowered her eyes as she worked. Red Deer saw her as a friend, and for that, she felt honored, but she also intended to leave as soon as she could. Instead of looking at the kindly brown face, Jess turned to consider the ranch yard and the busy tasks that filled it.

The men from the line camps had returned with their cattle, and roundup had begun. They rode in, leading cows that had been injured or that were too sickly to survive without help. Others rushed to take the cows into the barn, where they could be fed and cared for. The previous summer had been long and hard; one of the men told Jess that many cows had died in the heat. Most of them had survived, but the terrible cold of the recent winter had weakened them. Jess observed the men closely. Each one knew his job, and each worked steadily as a fluid part of a whole. They were like spokes on a wheel, and, for a time, she was one of them. Part of her would miss that when she was gone.

She plunged the last bucket under the water. Cool ripples swirled over its edge, dampening the wood and giving off an earthy smell. Once the bucket was filled, Jess carried it to the bank, where Red Deer pulled down the back gate of the wagon and climbed in. As Jess passed the heavy buckets up to her, Red Deer emptied them into the giant barrels, then handed the buckets back down to Jess. When they had finished, they returned to the creek to refill them.

Finally, Jess spoke again. "I've never thanked you for helping me when I first came to the ranch. Not just with the burns, but seeing to it that I ate and regained my strength. When I was a child, my infant brother, Broderick, died. I did the same then as when I arrived here—I cried and slept for days."

"It is nothing to be sorry for, Jessica. My people cry, too, when someone passes to the Spirit Land—the missionaries call that place 'heaven.' We feel better when we cry for them, because crying relieves our pain. I was glad to help you, and also I see that I am your friend because you tell me this."

Jess sighed. She'd only wanted to thank the woman before she left, not make it harder for Red Deer when she was gone. But Red Deer didn't seem to notice. She continued to work, singing a cheery song in her own language. Again, they poured water into the huge barrels, Jess growing more curious about her companion.

"You once asked me about the meaning of my name. Why are you called Red Deer? Most deer are brown."

"I am named for a flower, not a doe. Paiute girls named for a flower are called flower-girls. Others we call rock-girls because they are named for rocks, or else they are named for something they like. I am named for a flower."

"Aren't deer flowers yellow?"

"I was born with very red skin, so the Paiutes called me Red Deer." All at once, the dreaminess left her face. Her eyes cooled. "I am glad I will have a son, because it is no longer safe to have a daughter. Many white men are coyotes, very bad men," she explained, "and we must always protect our daughters from them, even when they are very young."

Jess shuddered. For these people, it seemed good always came with bad and happiness with sorrow...and she understood a little of how Red Deer felt.

"That's why you don't live on the reservation—because of the white men who run it?"

"Many of the white agents hurt our people. The Great White Father in Washington promised to give us supplies as long as we remain peaceful, but they gave us clothes and food only once, then no more. So our friend Jake Bennett told our men we could stay here and he would pay the men to work at the ranch. So we live here. He is an honorable man. All my people know this."

Jess didn't know what to say to that, so she asked to know more about flower-girls. Red Deer's face brightened again.

"Oh, we all used to watch for spring to come with such eagerness! We looked for our flower to bloom, then, when we saw it, all the young women would walk out into the hills with the handsome young men and show them the flowers we were named for. We would make up flower songs about ourselves and dream of husbands to sing our flower songs with us. All our people have great love for one another, and the old people and the children would ask us each day if our flower was in bloom. We made wreaths for girls not named for flowers so that we could all dance together and be happy. I think the young men waited for the Festival of Flowers to choose their brides. It was a wonderful time for all."

Again, *was* and *used to*. However did these people find joy among the sadness?

"I think this will be enough water." Red Deer again climbed into the wagon, filling the barrels while Jess arranged the empty buckets for the short ride back.

When they were finished, Red Deer lifted out two of the buckets with an impish smile on her lips. "Come," she said.

Curious, Jess followed, for the buckets now swung gaily from Red Deer's hands. This time, Red Deer slipped off her own moccasins and waded out into the creek, the bottom fringe of her deerskin dress swaying softly as she moved. When she bent over to wet her hair, Jess did the same. Though the air was cool, they had felt the sun, and the chilly water rinsed away the sweat of their labors.

Jess rinsed her legs, then pushed back her sleeves to wash her arms. The ache in her back faded as the bathing refreshed her. Sounds of flowing water and breeze filled her with joy and contentment.

Gazing skyward, Jess saw a broad-winged peregrine falcon riding the wind, a wild creature free to go wherever it would. Watching the falcon, her own heart floated, but instead of feeling trapped at the ranch, she felt strangely like she, too, had been freed—freed from the noise, the restrictions, and the indulgences that drove the people of the mining towns into a frenzy to discover more, get more, have more. The lot of them seemed mad, desperate to latch onto the illusion of eventual freedom. Freedom, Jess realized, wasn't to be found amid a mad frenzy, at least not for her. For her, this was freedom. The peregrine continued to glide, and Jess suddenly threw open her arms and greeted the gales.

"I've missed this, Red Deer! This is like Kentucky—home!" She spun around to face Red Deer, who was wringing out her hair. "I had forgotten. All those endless days spent in a corner with ledgers and numbers...I forgot how I was raised for this."

"You did not grow up in a town?"

"No. My family owned a kind of a ranch, but we had only horses, not cattle. I practically lived outdoors. I was schooled, of course, and taught to care for a home, but..." She lifted her hands and looked all around her. "Three years I worked in a dark corner, at a desk buried under papers. Three years, and I'd almost forgotten." She shook her head, then lifted it to take in the pine trees and the mountains. "This is not at all like Kentucky, and yet it is."

"It was even more beautiful before anyone settled here."

"This is certainly more beautiful than any city!" Jess passed her hands through the water, opening her fingers to let the cool current glide between them.

Red Deer smiled at her enthusiasm. "Where is this place that makes your face shine when you speak of it?"

"Kentucky?" Jess pointed excitedly to the east. "A decent Pony Express rider could have made it in ten or eleven days." Jess turned back to Red Deer, suddenly sheepish as she realized that her wet arm had sprayed Red Deer when she pointed.

Red Deer said nothing but smiled slyly at Jess and lifted her brimming bucket.

"Oh, Red Deer, I'm sorr—*oooof!*"

Jess sputtered and laughed as the bucketful of water ran down her hair and over her face. Tossing back the soaking strands, she dove for her bucket and, with it, showered a giggling Red Deer.

∾◌⠶⫸⠶◌∾

In a stand of cottonwoods downstream, Jake stood beside his horse, watching the two women shriek and laugh as they drenched each other. Neither of them had noticed that he was quietly checking on them to be sure they were safe.

Jess had watched the falcon and opened her arms to the sky. She had discovered for herself what he had seen in her for some time—that this was where she belonged. The mountains and desert were as much a part of her as they were of him. Neither of them was suited to a life of busy boardwalks or large crowds.

Shaking off the persistence of such thoughts, Jake led his horse away from the creek. He was right to help Jess—it was what any decent man would do—but he was getting to know her well and to understand her more than he was ready to. He needed to protect her, and to do that effectively, he needed to keep his head clear. Skilled at doing just that, he stepped up into the saddle and nudged his horse on its way.

He glanced over his shoulder at Jess. She and Red Deer were ducking and whirling as they splashed waves of water at each other, their laughter resounding through the trees.

∾◌⠶⫸⠶◌∾

Back at the ranch, behind the bunkhouse, Jess and Red Deer hung two enormous iron pots over small stacks of wood, prompting four of the ranch hands to walk over. Hiram and Nate pulled their hats from disheveled heads of hair as Jess greeted them. Reese, the shy youth who had loaned her his scarf in Carson City, followed, and the Spaniard, Diaz, approached the tan mare, which kept nudging him for a pet. If any of them noticed that she and her friend were damp from the creek, they chose to withhold any comments.

When Jess realized that the four meant to lift down the heavy water barrels, she held out an arm in protest. "Each of those barrels weighs as much as a pony. Please let Red Deer and me take the water down by bucketfuls."

Diaz grinned brightly as he patted the mare's glistening neck. "No, we take the water down, señorita. Little Luina here, she don' like the wagon much. We take the water down and unhitch her so she can run. You like to run, *verdad, querida?*" he murmured near her ear. "Eh, Sticks," he called to Reese. "Get the buckets out of the wagon, *sí?*"

A pinkening Reese climbed aboard, muttering, "Yeah, I see."

Doyle and Taggart rounded the corner in time to hear the exchange. Taggart lifted off his hat and gave the spindly lad a good-natured thwack on the shoulder. "Ha, ha! Sticks. I like that! Hand me a few of them buckets, Sticks."

Reese's eyes took on a vengeful gleam, and he began tossing the wooden buckets behind him like a dog digging up bones. One of them struck Taggart just above his ear, nearly knocking off his hat.

"Ow! Stoppit, Reese! Ye just banged my noggin!" In response, Reese sent the buckets flying faster.

Doyle shook his head and reached his powerful forearms over the side of the wagon, handing buckets out to Jess. "Never did see such foolery," he said.

Jess set the buckets down, glad that Doyle was accepting her presence. Until now it seemed he could barely tolerate her, probably due to her Southern origin, she surmised.

Doyle and Diaz climbed into the wagon and together turned each of the barrels from side to side, rocking them to the rear of the wagon. Then the other four lowered the awesome weight of each barrel to the ground.

Thinking they were finished, Jess started to thank them, but they politely nudged her aside until they had brought both barrels within a few paces of the iron cauldrons. When they had finished, Reese nabbed Taggart's hat and ran off with it. The stout Irishman hurled comical threats as he huffed after him. The others smiled in response to her thanks and then returned to their various chores. Diaz, however, cooed warmly to Luina as he led her to the barn to unhitch her.

Jess was still smiling over the man's love for the horse when she and Red Deer dipped their buckets into the barrel and began to fill the giant kettles. When that task was done, Red Deer started a fire beneath the first pot while Jess gathered up as many buckets as she could carry and crossed the yard to the stable, where they were stored.

Doyle, who had returned to the smithy, glanced up from the hoof between his knees, a large file stilled in his hands. When Jess waved, he saluted with the file, then bent over again to continue leveling the hoof. As she passed the barn, she noticed Diaz rubbing down Luina. He casually watched her pass. Yes, they had accepted her and were happy to lend her a hand, but they were also loyal to their boss. How frustrating that Jake had told the men to watch her, as if she were a child in need of so many nannies! A few others noted her passing, and her annoyance flared to a good simmer.

Jess hung up the pails, slamming them against the wall and taking fiendish pleasure in the racket they made. Her ire somewhat diminished, she smoothed her hair and crossed the yard, ignoring the eyes that kept track of her whereabouts.

At the bunkhouse, she rapped on the door, then pushed it

open when no one called out. A dank, musty odor rolled out, and she nearly gagged. The room was dim. Two dirt-crusted windows became visible at the ends, then the newspapered walls between. Thirty or more bunks stood in disarray along both sides of a fireplace where charred coffeepots were clustered around an ash-blacked hearth. Cobwebs dominated the ceiling, old boots and bits of harness leather littered the floor. There was an upended barrel stained with coffee circles to one side, sticky with flattened globs of dinners long past, around which stood chairs that had seen better days. Here and there were blankets, spurs, and stray playing cards.

"What filth!" Jess declared to no one. Her gaze dropped to the old flour sacks the men had left stuffed with their dirty clothes, and she gathered them up by the cords that secured them. With great effort, she dragged them out the door, one at a time, and dropped them in a growing pile beside Red Deer.

"Have you seen the bunkhouse?"

Red Deer sat up on her knees, having kindled a fire of already dancing flames. "Their clothing is just as bad. Look for yourself."

Grimacing, Jess lifted a pair of trousers from the top of the closest sack. She dangled them away from her, shaking them to loosen the dried mud and who-knew-what-else. "Are they all like this?" she asked Red Deer, eyes wide in alarm.

"Most are. We will soak them today and scrub them tomorrow, but they do not stay clean long. It is hard work the men do."

"I suppose. But if we soak them like this, all that water we drew will turn to mud. We really need to beat them first to get the worst of it off."

From the woodpile, Red Deer chose split logs and added them to the small fire. "Find what you need, Jessica. I will help you while the water warms."

Jess made her way through the crowded yard. Nearly two dozen ranch hands ran to care for the pitifully bawling cows that men on horseback were herding toward the barn. Apparently, the wolf pelts had sold well. New hats, spotless boots, and gleaming, jingling spurs were everywhere.

Deciding the barn seemed the best place to find lengths of rope for a clothesline, Jess entered, dodging elbows, hooves, and spurs.

The interior was clean and surprisingly organized, like the stable. She shook her head. How did the ranchmen give the animals such care while they themselves wallowed in the grime and muck of their living quarters? As she waited for several men to pass with their four-legged charges, Jess scanned the barn for rope. Some of the men glanced at her a time or two, perhaps curious about the woman they had been instructed to watch but still knew little about. She smiled sweetly to them. Finally, she spied Reese, and she asked him where she might find some rope.

Reese's cheeks reddened. He swallowed. "R-rope? H-how much are you needin', Miss Jess?"

"A good twenty yards, if you have it."

"Yes, ma'am." He led her back to the doorway of the barn and pointed, saying, "The next building there is the workshop, and between that and the stable is the supply shed." He wiped a nervous hand on his shirt. "That's where you'll find most anything you might be looking for. I'd walk you over there if I could, but..." He gestured to the moaning cows tethered about the barn.

"I understand, Reese. I'll find it just fine. Thank you."

Out in the open again, she sighed. A body could get lost in there, she decided, and no one would even notice. That thought led to another, and another, and when she finally reached the supply shed, she was certain that if she took a horse from the stable now, nobody would realize it for hours. She glanced about. Everyone was busy with the cows—a more pressing task than keeping an eye on one small woman.

She passed the shed without a glance, went around back, and hurried toward the rear of the stable. Then she came up short.

A sprawling rosebush stood before her—taller than a man and wider than her arm span. Instantly, she recalled when Jake had brought her back to the ranch the week before. He'd lowered her to the ground and headed behind the stable before riding out with two cuttings in his hand. They had been little more than stems. Now the thorny green branches were leafing out. New growth appeared at the tips, and a few tiny buds were just beginning to form. Jess's gaze dropped to the dirt where it was planted; she could tell that it had recently been turned and watered. The plant was being carefully tended—but why a rosebush, here? And what did Jake do with the cuttings?

Generating no satisfactory explanations, Jess refocused on her goal. She continued forward, entering the stable.

Near the center, she stood as she had before. Once again, she appraised the long aisle of stalls and the few remaining horses. Then her gaze shifted to the open doors at the far end. Out in the daylight, three or four distracted men were hurrying about the yard. Beyond them sat the bunkhouse, which needed a good deal of attention the men had no time to give, and although she couldn't see behind that building, Jess knew that a pregnant Red Deer was laying heavy logs over a fire, waiting for her return.

Groaning over the inner battle between her compulsion to stay and her determination to go, Jess walked back to the supply shed. She needed to help Red Deer finish the laundry, and she needed to clean out the bunkhouse. She would stay long enough to show her gratitude for the assistance and kindness of these people, but not a minute longer.

Inside the shed, Jess used a tin pail to collect various items, making plans all the while. She would stay another day to help Red Deer finish the laundry and would attack the bunkhouse the day after that. Two more days, she promised herself. Then she would go and know she had done what was right. That decided, she found a heavy coil of rope, hefted it onto her shoulder, and went to string a clothesline.

∾☙⊰⬥⊱❧∾

"What is all this?" Red Deer asked.

Jess set down the rope and pail. "I thought it would help to put up a permanent clothesline. When we're not using it, the men can hang their wet clothes and blankets on it to keep them from molding."

"They lay their blankets and bedrolls on the roof to dry them."

"Well then, we'll have to wash all the bedding, too."

"This will be much work, Jessica."

"Don't worry. I'll help until it's done."

Jess laid the rope out while Red Deer started the fire under the second pot. Eyeing her, Jess decided to refill the barrels herself after supper so they would be ready for the next wash day Red Deer undertook. If Red Deer toted the heavy water alone, she could possibly harm herself or her unborn child.

Satisfied that the rope would reach from the rear wall of the bunkhouse to a hardy cottonwood tree, Jess dragged a chair out of the bunkhouse to stand on. She retrieved tools from the pail and affixed a heavy hook to the rear corner of the building, just below the eave.

The echoes of her hammer blows drifted out across the ranch. Jess felt several pairs of curious eyes on her, but she paid them no notice. She tossed down the hammer and hung one end of the rope on the hook. Next, she dragged the chair over to the tree and stood on it, reaching for the lowest branch, but the massive limb still stretched far above her head. She set the chair aside. Coiling up a length of rope, she stood back, swung it high, and released it, trying to catch it around the branch. She missed. She gathered it up for another try. Again and again, she attempted to rope the branch. After each failure, she made another patient attempt.

To her surprise, Doyle drove up in a wagon, his expression composed as always, not giving away his intention. Six other men were seated on the two sidewalls of the wagon bed, from which a long ladder extended over the end. They looked jovial and rowdy as could be, though, when they glimpsed Jess, they reduced themselves to broad smiles, and two or three sat a little taller. Doyle set the brake and stepped down before Jess.

"If you don't mind none about some help, the boys and me can get that rope slung for you."

Jess wiped her brow, eyeing the group with a grin. The honorable Robin Hood and his Merry Men. "I'd appreciate that. The wagon is a good idea. If someone can steady the horse and a few of you can hold that ladder on the back of it…"

Amid a brief discussion and some more joking among the men, Jess got her crew organized. Soon after, the rope had been tied over the branch and secured to the tree trunk so that it was taut and suspended nearly level from bunkhouse to tree.

By the time they had finished, a full dozen additional ranchmen had assembled either to watch or to lend a hand. Eyeing the completed line, one asked, "Why didn't you just tie it to the trunk?"

Reese answered for Jess. "My mama used to tie it to the trunk, but over time, the rope would slide down." He gestured toward the setup. "She means for it to stay, that's why. You did just fine, Miss Jess." His cheeks crimson now, he left to load the ladder into the wagon.

They all stared at one another for a moment at the shy youth's unusual boldness.

Jess folded her arms across her chest. "If you gentlemen would be so kind, perhaps you wouldn't mind refilling the barrels, since your soiled clothes are going to need more than one washing." She leveled her gaze on them like a mother scolding her children.

Taggart waddled up next to Jess and pointed with mock severity at the men. "And don't ye even think o' disobeyin' her, or when your pappy gets home, she'll have 'im blister your britches good!" He plunked his hands on his knees and roared with laughter.

Jess's glare at his jest quickly faded into a grin. Despite their teasing, some of the men were gladly grabbing up buckets while others lifted the empty barrels into the wagon bed. That would mean one less backbreaking chore for her.

Like a black cloud, Jake rode up and took in the scene. A terrible combination of admiration and resentment cut through Jess at the sight of him. Whiskers shadowed his jaw, and his eyes were shaded beneath his hat brim. She couldn't read his expression, but he obviously had something on his mind.

"These men have cattle to tend to, Jess. If you could, I'd like you to get your work done on your own."

Her blood boiled. "I *was* working on my own, Bennett. Your men offered to help, and if they hadn't, I would still be trying to hang that rope!"

Glancing from Jake to Jess, Taggart rubbed his hands together in sudden cheerfulness. "Me and the lads'll fill the barrels, boss, then we'll be right over." His hands stilled.

Jake and Jess stared at each other. Jake raised a stern brow at the news.

Jess glared at him reproachfully. "Red Deer and I already filled the barrels once, Bennett. We need more water. I could refill them on my own, if you would prefer it, but Red Deer shouldn't lift heavy burdens anymore. You ought to have more regard for a woman with child."

For a moment, Jake looked as though he had turned to stone. Then, "Taggart?"

"Aye?"

"When you and the boys fill the troughs each morning, see to the barrels, as well. We'll keep them here behind the bunkhouse. Good enough, Jess?"

She nodded once, stiffly, then stormed away to find rug beaters and a washing bat. Her departure from the ranch couldn't come soon enough.

Jake watched Jess disappear into the house while his men headed for the creek. He had given her weeks to get past her anger, but apparently it hadn't subsided. If anything, it had gotten worse, and it seemed to surface only when he was near her. He had seen Jess talking happily with Red Deer in the creek, and she'd been smiling with the men when he rode up. Well, he'd been keeping his distance, but no longer. They had to live on the same ranch together, and he knew that she had it in her to be civil. He'd best find out what was behind her anger, because, somehow, she saw him as the cause of it. Tonight, he decided—they would have the matter out tonight.

He started to turn his horse, then stopped when Jess came out of the house again. When she noticed a wagon rolling into the yard, she set her washing tools against the house and started toward the newcomer. The bunkhouse stood in Jake's line of vision, so he guided the horse around it. Jess's countenance collapsed in laughter and tears when she recognized the driver.

The small Chinese man stepped down nimbly from the wagon, a broad grin across his face. As Jess hurried toward him, he bowed, his long braid of hair falling neatly down the middle of his back.

"Ho Chen?" Her cry was both sob and elation. "Ho Chen, I can't believe it's you!" She threw herself into his arms. Ho Chen had been her mother's cook and her own confidant. Through the recent years of troubles in Carson City, Ho Chen had been the only one with whom Jess had shared all her fears and worries. He had been her anchor, her friend. Now he stood beside her, thumping her warmly on the back.

"I am happy to see you alive, Miss Jessie."

"Oh, Ho Chen, I thought that you…how did you…?" She shook her head, confused. Looking on, Jake slowly dismounted and handed his reins to Doyle as Jess took Ho Chen's hand. "Did Mr. Bennett send you here after the fire?"

"Yes. After fire, I have no job, so Mr. Bennett say, 'You want job?' So I take job. Now I will cook for ranchmen."

Jess cut a glance to Jake. She asked Ho Chen, "Did you come when Lone Wolf brought me here? I don't remember much. I… wasn't myself for most of the trip."

Ho Chen chose his words carefully. "I come later, with Bennett. In Carson City, I help Mr. Bennett and neighbors put out fire. Then Mr. Edmund come. We help Mr. Bennett search rubble, and after, we bury." His brown eyelids swelled red. "Very sorry, Miss Jessie. Very sorry." He swallowed. "Mr. Bennett tell me he put Mr. Isaac in grave and Miss Georgeanne in grave, but you not in grave. I was happy you did not die. He tell me Indian take you here."

With this unwelcome revelation, Jess's shoulders rose and fell with angry breaths. She released Ho Chen's hand and turned to Jake. "You buried my family?!" At her shout, the horse Doyle was leading away spooked, and every pair of eyes turned to them. "You let everyone think I was dead?"

Jake took her arm and steered her toward the house. Ho Chen quietly went to unload his wagon.

Inside, Jess shook off Jake's grip, despising his closeness. There were so many details about the fire that she hadn't allowed herself to think about—couldn't bear to think about—until now. "You found my family? You, and not a lawman?" She blinked through tears. "Does Miriam still think I'm dead?"

"Unless Edmund's told her otherwise, Miriam thinks all the Hales were buried. Only Edmund and Ho Chen know you survived." His voice had gentled, as if trying to calm a frightened filly. "It's best that no one knows until the killers are found—not even Miriam. I don't want to risk the truth getting out, and Edmund said Miriam's inclined to gossip. If the men who attacked you in the street were evil enough to follow you home and murder your family, then they're evil enough to come after you here, should they learn that you're alive and discover where you are."

Jess trembled, not hearing him. "But how?" she asked. "You would've had to bury four Hales. I don't—" All at once, she knew. "Elsie!" Elsie had been upstairs with her mother and Emma. It had to be Elsie; after helping her dress, Maureen had gone downstairs to help in the kitchen. "You buried Elsie instead of me! Elsie worked as Emma's...oh, *noooo!*" Jess pictured the smoldering rubble, and the men picking through the ruins of her family's home to find them. To protect her, they had buried Elsie, and no one even knew to mourn the girl. Her parents lived in Germany.

"I'm sorry, Jess. On the ride here, Ho Chen told me that you and she were good friends."

"Why didn't you tell me before?" Jess growled through her teeth.

"Would you have been able to bear the news of another loss?" he asked gently.

Jess backed away, the room swimming through hot tears. "That's why you didn't tell Seth who the new cook was," she accused. "You hired Ho Chen. You hired him, then sent him away for supplies so fast that no one even knew he'd been here."

"Red Deer was here when we rode in. She said your grief had caused you to fall ill. I knew then that if you learned I'd hired Ho Chen, you would have found out about Elsie before you were ready to. Jess, people can break under the weight of so much loss."

More than ever, Jess wanted to go to her family at the cemetery, *needed* to be near them…and Elsie. And she had to find their killers. To stay away from Carson City would be impossible now. But first, she had to know what had happened. She needed to know it all. "Who else, Bennett? Who else did you bury?"

"No one else. The butler made it out the kitchen door along with Ho Chen and the maid."

Jake was saying something about Edmund taking in Malcolm and Maureen until they found employment, but all she could think of was her conversation with Elsie while Emma splashed in the tub. Elsie, sweet Elsie…she had told her about wanting to marry and have children of her own, and Jess had promised to visit her, no matter where she went. Jess's hands curled into painful fists. Elsie had shared so many dreams, had so much she had wanted to do.

All at once, a sob broke from her, rising into a scream. "How could God be so cruel?" she shrieked. "Elsie was young! Her whole life was ahead of her!"

"God is not cruel, Jess. He is a God of love! When He takes other people to heaven, their sorrows are gone forever."

"But what about us? We have to go on without them. God just takes people we love away at a whim and expects us to exist with these gaping holes in our lives. And don't you think to lecture me. You have no idea what it is to lose so much!"

Jake grasped her arms. "Isaac raised you to be a God-fearing woman, Jess. Remember Romans chapter eight, verse twenty-eight: *'And we know that all things work together for good to them that love God.'* God had a purpose in this for you, too. Trust Him. Trust Him, and let Him show you what it is."

Tears streamed down her cheeks. She shook her head.

"And in later verses, *'For I am convinced that neither death nor life will be able to separate us from the love of God that is in Christ Jesus our Lord.'* He loves them and He loves you, and in His good time, He'll bring you to heaven to be with Him. You'll see them again, Jess. You'll see all of them again."

She jerked her arms free. "Enough! All I know is that my house was on fire, and people I loved were trapped inside. My father tried to go in to save them, but you wouldn't let him. You fought to keep him away from the door, and then, when it was too late, you—" She broke off, realizing what she had nearly revealed. She would not give him a chance to excuse what he'd done.

Jake stepped closer. "I *what*, Jess?"

Jess closed her mouth. She couldn't believe she was even speaking to him. She wanted nothing to do with him. Jess turned away, shutting him out. For a moment, she allowed herself to remember the people she had loved, to recall details about them. Elsie, and the way her face brightened as she spoke of having children. The love in her mother's eyes that often shone through the sadness. Had her father gotten to her mother that final night, as he'd wanted to? Had they died together? Jess relived the times she had held Emma, curled up against her. She remembered her father's hair standing on end...and how deeply he loved his Georgeanne.

And Ambrose. Ambrose, who, since childhood, had been the

center of her life. Ambrose, who had promised to come back. Ambrose, whom she had believed was too stubborn to die.

"Where are they buried?"

"The cemetery northeast of town. I'll take you there when it's safe."

Shaking, she faced him. "I don't want you to take me there, Jake. I want to be as far from you as I can get."

"Jess!"

She marched out the door, swung the washing tools onto her shoulder like clubs, and made a straight path toward the cauldrons and the ranchmen's sacks of clothes. Behind her, the door banged shut. She whirled to face Jake, both rug beater and laundry bat ready to strike if he came close.

He didn't. With a murmured apology for causing her further pain, he headed for the barn.

Warily, Jess watched him go. With angry tears streaming from her eyes, she tightened her hold on the tools, but she had no cause to use them. Jake respected her wishes and left her alone.

Chapter Eight

J ess and Red Deer beat and boiled clothes and bedding
for two seemingly endless days. The men bunked on
the cookhouse floor each night—after dragging the
dining tables and benches outdoors with a bit of grumbling—
and stored their possessions in the barn. When the bed sacks
had dried late the second day, Jess restuffed them with fresh
straw. The next morning, she dragged bunks, chairs, and
personal belongings out of the bunkhouse until the men
surmised her intent and dutifully joined in her efforts. Then she
scrubbed furniture, windows, floors, and fireplace for several
arduous hours, pausing only twice when Ho Chen brought her
something to eat. Finally, just after sunset, the last of the odors
had vanished, and she announced that the bunkhouse would no
longer be a threat to anyone's health.

Late that evening, Jess stared at the ceiling above her
bed, not seeing it in the midnight shadows. She lay on top of
her covers, fully dressed, waiting until she could hear snores
drifting from Jake's room. A few minutes before, she had heard
his boots on the stairs. His footfall had paused, and she'd heard
the cat purr before his steps had resumed. Finally, she'd heard
his bedroom door close softly. After that, the noises had been
muffled, and she had actually blushed as she'd imagined Jake
removing his bandana and unbuttoning his shirt.

She had promised herself earlier to stay two days to see the
work done. It had taken three. Now she was ready to leave. She'd
prepared a sack of food and a canteen of water, and her jewelry

remained secure in the folds of her petticoats. She would pay her respects to her family and to Elsie, help Edmund run the store like she used to do, and follow—or demand—the sheriff's progress until the killers were caught. She'd carry a gun in town, if necessary, but she would stay there. She couldn't keep away any longer.

Finally, Jess heard deep, even breathing flow from Jake's bedroom. She lifted the sack and canteen, opened her door, and moved stealthily into the hall.

The cat was gone. Jess's hide boots were silent as she glided down the stairs. Jake's breathing never wavered.

Outside, she crept close to the house, attentive to anyone who might be about. There was no one. She tightened her hold on her provisions and ran.

The stable was silent. Instead of Luina, Jess determined to take Jake's stallion. She had seen no faster horse, and if she had a decent head start, the weight of a man on any other horse would leave him hopelessly outdistanced. The black scuffed about when he heard her, snorting when she slipped into his stall. Yet with the aid of a carrot and a little soothing, she was able to slip a rope around his neck and lead him out, keeping him calm enough to saddle him.

Minutes later, Jess thrilled at the feel of his strength as they thundered over the desert. On her last escape attempt, she had followed the creek, but now she held the black to the road, as it was the fastest path away from the ranch. The cover of night made the road a less dangerous place to be.

Less than twenty minutes had passed when the stallion swiveled his ears at a presence approaching from behind. Though she doubted the lawless would be about at this late hour, Jess urged the horse to his limit.

Unfortunately, the animal had his own agenda. Puzzled at his behavior, Jess glanced back. Diaz was coming up fast, riding Luina.

The stallion grunted as he caught the mare's scent. He turned his head and slowed against Jess's efforts to push him on, letting Diaz come up alongside him. In a last effort, Jess dug in her heels. The stallion reared.

"Whoa, Cielos! You don' want to spill the señorita. Down," Diaz's voice calmed the beast. As soon as the powerful front hooves hit earth, Diaz shot out his whirring lariat and snared Jess in a way she was quickly losing patience with.

"Diaz! Let me go!"

He stepped down from Luina, shaking his head. "I am sorry, *mariquita*." He pulled the rope snug and secured her hands as lightening-fast as Jake had. "But the boss, he say, 'You don' let her go.' So I don' let you go." He firmly lashed her hands to the saddle horn, knotting the tail end around the cinch buckle. She wasn't going anywhere without the saddle.

Jess shot him a seething glare.

In response, Diaz muttered something under his breath. Then, "The boss, he warn me about you."

Jess watched Diaz until he took the stallion by the harness, and then she stuck the beast with her heels. The stallion snapped up his head, nearly pulling the startled man over.

"*Basta!*" he snapped—whether at her or at the horse, Jess didn't know, nor did she care.

"Bennett is wrong, Diaz. He's keeping me against my will, and you're helping him. That's against the law!"

Unconcerned, he took her reins and settled onto Luina. "No matter. The law already no like me very much. Le's go, Cielos. I'm tired."

Jess twisted her hands to loose them from the pommel. "Diaz! The first rattlesnake I find, I'm going to put in your bed!"

"*No lo va a hacer,*" he said.

"What does that mean?" she demanded.

He spoke distinctly for her over his shoulder. "It means *you won't do this thing.*" He glanced at her. "You are angry now, but you are a nice señorita. I am sorry you are sad, *mariposa*, but I like you, and I keep you safe." He waved toward the mountains. "This place, it is no safe for a woman. The boss, he knows this." He rode quietly for a time while she steamed and struggled with the rope.

"There is much you do not know about the man Bennett," Diaz said, then shrugged. "*Vaqueros* all keep to themselves, mostly. But I know the boss, and he is different since you come here. He has sadness of his own, mariposa, but I see he cares for you."

Jess did not take that observation well. She fought harder than ever, and the rough loops cut into her hands.

"No, don' hurt yourself! The boss will no like it," he said, his tone soothing. "Why would you want to harm such beautiful hands?"

"Me hurt my hands? Diaz!" she snapped. "You're the one who tied this so tight!"

Diaz didn't debate the point. He said nothing further, and neither did Jess. They rode the rest of the way in silence, Cielos almost pleasant as he trotted alongside Luina.

As they approached the house, Diaz let out a shrill whistle to alert Jake, then reined in the horses near the porch. Doyle stepped out of the bunkhouse, pulling suspenders over his bare shoulders as he jogged over.

"She get away again?"

With a smile, Diaz shook his head, loosening the cinch for his mare. "No, the señorita only take Cielos for a ride." He winked up at Jess. "He wanted to chase the stars, eh, mariposa?"

"Hardly," Jess muttered with the raise of an eyebrow. "If he'd shown as much interest in the night sky as he did in Luina, I'd be waving to you from the moon." The two men smiled.

Jess was growing tired, and she waggled her fingers at Diaz, who came over to untie her. "On the bright side of things, at least I got to be lashed to this inbred mutt and dragged across the desert." Despite herself, Jess chuckled with the men at her own surly humor.

"It could have been worse," Doyle said with a grin. "You could have been tied on behind Diaz before you laundered his duds."

Jess laughed out loud, savoring the feel after having missed it for so long.

Heels pounded down the stairs inside the ranch house. Moments later, Jake flew out the door, his unbuttoned shirt stuffed into his trousers. For once, he was without a hat. Jess's levity faded.

Jake sized up the situation and spoke to Diaz. "What happened?"

Diaz unwound the rope from Jess's bruised wrists, careful not to harm her further. "*No muy mucho,* boss. I went out for a midnight ride and the lovely señorita here kindly accompanied me." He eyed her in concern when her hands were freed, but Jess smiled to let him know the pain was bearable.

Jake stepped closer. "Jess?"

She didn't answer. With his muscular arms, Doyle reached up and eased her down from the saddle. Jess nodded in appreciation.

Jake glanced at her wrists but didn't comment. "Diaz, put the horses away and get some sleep. Both of you, get some sleep. I'll keep an eye on her for the rest of the night."

Before he left, Doyle quirked a playful grin at Jess, his teeth flashing white in his dark face. "Don't you go nowhere, you hear?"

She slanted him an equally friendly glare as he strolled back to the bunkhouse.

With a grand gesture, Diaz swept his hat from his head and held it to his heart without jest. "It was a very great honor to ride with you tonight, señorita. I hope your hands are better soon."

"Good night," she said, and he led the horses away.

Jake looked down at her, his fists on his hips.

Jess strode past him. "Save the lecture, Bennett. I'm too tired."

Jake followed her and pulled the door shut behind them. "I can send someone to get Red Deer, if you like," he said. "She could help you dress for bed, and maybe put something on those cuts."

"No." Jess inspected her stinging wrists by the moonlight coming in through the window. "I don't want to wake Red Deer. I'll tend my wrists on my own."

"Hmm." Jake appeared to have his own opinion about that. He lifted a lamp from the mantel, lit it, then disappeared down the short hall between the fireplace and the stairs.

Alone, Jess collapsed on the sofa in exhaustion. The physical work she had expended that day as she'd scrubbed the bunkhouse compounded the aches she'd invited by spending two days hauling water and beating laundry. Her burning eyes fell shut. She would rest for only a minute. Fragments of odd dreams flashed through her mind. The sofa felt like a feather bed beneath her. Its pillow met her cheek, the cushions slipped under her feet. She'd rest for only a moment. For only a moment...

∾⭕⟨⟨⟩⟩⭕∾

When Jake had found what he was looking for and returned from the kitchen, Jess was asleep. Knowing she needed the rest, he didn't disturb her. He hung a small pot of water over the fire and fed a few logs to the dancing flames. As the water heated, he broke off several sage leaves from one of the dried branches Red Deer kept in the kitchen and dropped them in the water. While he waited for them to steep, he took the lamp from the mantle and set it on a table near Jess.

His gaze fell on her hair. It looked as soft as sable. Threads of it shone like copper in the firelight. In the past several weeks, her skin had turned lightly golden from the sun. Though he meant to turn back to the simmering pot, he remained, recalling the day she'd taken Luina and set out for Carson City. On the way home, he had realized that she needed to be outdoors, needed to chase the wind.

She needed the freedom to ride off her loss—and to feel close to the Almighty.

Tomorrow, he decided. Tomorrow, he would take her with him when he and the cattlemen went to round up the nearby cattle. She had finished helping Red Deer with the laundry, and Ho Chen was here to cook. Jess would have no reason to stay behind. He would take her along tomorrow, and any day after, when he could.

Jake returned to the hearth to check the medicinal brew. The water had begun to resemble tea. A few minutes later, the sage remedy had darkened to a greenish brown, and he lowered two strips of white cotton cloth into the pot—a healing method of the Paiutes. He fetched another bowl of water from the kitchen, along with a pair of soft towels, which he set on the table near the lamp. He pulled the steaming pot from the flames and set it on the hearth to cool. Finally, he lowered his body to the edge of the sofa where Jess lay. Her breathing was even and deep.

"You go ahead and rest," he murmured. "I'm going to have a look at those hands."

He lifted one from where it lay among her skirts and studied the wrist, turning it over. There were a few cuts, and she would certainly develop bruises. Jess stirred, pulling her arm back, and Jake let her. After she had slept a few minutes longer, he lifted her hand again. Reaching to the side, he dampened a towel in the bowl of clean water, squeezed it gently, and touched it lightly to her wounds. Diaz was a good man with a rope, probably the best he'd ever seen, and Jake knew that he hadn't done this. Jess had done it, trying to get away. He didn't want to hurt her, but he would not allow her to throw herself into greater danger. So, short of allowing his men to be jousted from their saddles or otherwise find themselves at her mercy, there was no choice but to let them snare her like a rabbit when they caught her in flight. She might be less inclined to leave, however, once she was given the freedom to ride with the men.

Jake's eyes shifted between her wrist and her face as he painstakingly tended her cuts. He swabbed away every speck of dried blood on both hands. That done, he got up to search for the softest cotton fabric he could find. He decided on a calico tablecloth with a rose blossom print. If Olivia were here, she'd willingly part with it to help someone else. To muffle the sound, he carried the cloth into the kitchen to tear off two makeshift bandages.

He scooped up the pot of sage brew and sat beside Jess once again. The tea was warm but no longer hot. He wrung all but a moderate dampness from the white cotton cloth, now lightly stained with tea. Then, careful to remove the sage leaves, he wrapped a healing strip around each of her wrists. Afterward, he wound the strips of rose calico around each of the two damp cloths and knotted them to keep them in place.

When he had finished, he put away the bowls, then returned to stare thoughtfully down at her again. He debated taking her to her room, but in the end, he spread a heavy quilt over her and left her to sleep where she was.

Jake turned down the lamp and went up to his room for the night.

He awoke before dawn and left without making a sound. When the sun lifted its face over the edge of the earth, he was on Cielos, headed west, two tiny yellow roses clutched in his hand.

∞⟨⟩∞

Jess awoke to a great brightness in the room. Given how refreshed she felt, she guessed she had slept half the morning away. Wanting it to last just a little longer, she rested with her eyes closed and let the details of her surroundings come to her as they would.

She was on Jake's sofa with a heavy blanket draped over her. She stretched and relished the warmth of the coverlet as cool air brushed her face. There was a deep, wonderful quiet and stillness, with none of the rattling and shouting that rose from the streets of Carson City. She sat up, certain that, with a renewed heart such as she had, she would undoubtedly find much to enjoy that day.

Jake's wide front window sparkled with sunshine, and through it, she could see the men going about their usual tasks near the corrals and barn. The fireplace crackled and flickered, and from the kitchen came sounds of someone moving about. By the lightness of the steps, she assumed it was Red Deer. Jess blinked away the last traces of sleep.

An unlit lamp sat on the low table beside her, and near the far end of the table dangled two small feet wearing child-sized moccasins. Jess smiled and turned her eyes to Jake's chair to see a little Indian boy with a sweet grin slap a hand over his mouth and giggle. He wasn't at all distrustful like Red Deer and some of the other Paiutes had been at first. Laughing to herself, Jess pushed the large quilt aside and swung her feet to the floor.

"Good morning, young sir," she greeted the boy softly.

He dropped his hand and tilted his head to the side. He was perhaps five or so, with a round face, slightly flared nose, and black eyes like Red Deer's—by the bobbed hair, she knew this must be the son of Red Deer's dead sister.

He scooted to the front edge of the chair, slowly raised his hands, and spread his fingers. When Jess smiled in confusion, he pointed to her hands. She lifted them, noticing the bandages of floral calico wrapped around her wrists. *Bennett.* Bennett must have wrapped her cuts. The boy grinned and nodded. Jess grinned back, thinking that he admired her fancy bandages.

"He tells you his name, Jessica," said Red Deer, poking in her head from the kitchen. She spoke in Paiute to the boy, and he held up his hands again to show Jess. "We call him Two Hands. He likes to count things on his hands." The boy spoke to Red Deer, and she answered him kindly. The only word Jess could understand was her name.

"Jessica," said Two Hands, and he left his chair to stand before her. He raised his small hands to her cheeks.

"He hasn't seen many white people, Jessica," Red Deer explained. "He sees the ranchmen, but they are brown from working in the sun."

Two Hands looked closely at Jess's forehead and slowly rubbed his thumbs against her much lighter skin. The boy frowned in bewilderment at his dark thumbs. The white didn't come off. Red Deer smiled and returned to the kitchen, and Two Hands leaned close to inspect the white woman's unusual green eyes.

Just then, Jake strode in through the door. He glanced at Jess and Two Hands, then lifted a coffeepot and filled one of the mugs on the hearth, motioning an inquiry to Jess. In reply, she made a disgusted face. Beside her, Two Hands made the same face, and he and Jess shared a laugh.

To her surprise, Jake spoke to Two Hands in the Paiute language. Two Hands commented to Jake, then Jake translated for Jess. "He says the Great Father painted your eyes like the cat's eyes." Jake's voice held unexpected warmth, and Jess lowered her gaze, turning her attention to her new little friend. Two Hands touched the floral bandages with curiosity. Jake set his mug on the mantel and took a seat by Jess.

At his nearness, her heart leapt pleasantly. She was alarmed at her reaction to him, and she wished she could move further away, but she didn't want to push the boy aside to do so.

Pulling her arm across his knee, Jake whipped a bowie knife from a sheath on his belt. He eased the blade smoothly through the top strip of calico, then replaced it in its sheath. Two Hands leaned close as Jake carefully unwound the bandage.

Jess watched Jake work out of the corner of her eye, trying not to notice how gently he cradled her arm, and how patiently he answered Two Hands's questions, allowing the child to help unwrap the bandage. Against her will, she felt grateful that he had wrapped her hands when she had been too exhausted to tend to the injuries herself. None of it went with the opinion of him that she had cultivated, for she kept seeing him exhibit qualities she respected—qualities that conflicted with the perceptions she'd had of him since the fire.

Confused, she stared out the window to avoid looking at him, but she felt his eyes on her all the same. He unwound the bandage on her other wrist. "They're not bad, Jess," came his voice, deep and mildly teasing. "It might be best, though, if you don't get yourself tied to a horse again until they heal."

She jerked her hand away. Gently but insistently, he took it again, then rewrapped each wrist with the calico.

For the sake of Red Deer's nephew, she kept her voice low. "If you hadn't given that order to your men, the future well-being of my hands would not concern you!"

Jake passed up the bait. Instead, he glanced thoughtfully—almost reflectively—at her face, as if her features had suddenly become of particular interest to him. "I'll give you a hat to wear. The days are longer now, and the sun can be harsh." After a brief moment, he added, "I'll take that as an agreement."

Jess adjusted the bandages. "Why should you?"

"Because you didn't argue. When you disagree, you're rather straightforward about it." His brown eyes twinkled. "Why don't you have someone saddle a horse for you? Or, since you seem to prefer taking matters into your own hands, see to the task yourself, if you wish."

Saddle a horse? "What? Why?"

"I thought you might like to ride with me and the men today."

"Out on the range?" She couldn't recall when last she had run a horse for the pure thrill of it. Until now, she'd run them to escape the ranch, looking anxiously over her shoulder all the while.

"It's nearly April. There'll be a lot you can do right here in the weeks ahead, but whenever you have a free day, you can lend a hand with the men. I can see you need to be out there, Jess. Horses and riding are in your blood."

She concealed her thrill at the suggestion. "You know nothing about my blood, Jake Bennett."

He gazed at her. "I know you very well. You need to live in open places, to feel the wind in your hair. You are like the Indians who don't wish to stay in one place, who won't be told where to live. The earth and sky and horses—those things are real, they make sense to you. It's who you are."

Jess stared at him in amazement. No one had ever understood that about her. Not even her mother. "How do you know that?"

"I saw you in Carson City. You were different there, sort of like a wild creature on display in a cage, but you're not like that here. Even though a part of you doesn't want to stay, the other part of you sees its possibilities."

Jess digested the truth of that, and of all he had seen in her. "What about Red Deer? She can't be allowed to do the heavy chores alone."

"You can stay here on days she needs help, or when work needs to be done. Otherwise, you can ride with me." Jake indicated her hands. "Get yourself some gloves out of the supply shed. I'll meet you in the stable." The corner of his mouth quirked. "I'm sure you know where the stable is."

"If you lag, I'll meet you in Carson City," Jess said, "and I'm fairly certain you know where that is."

With a hearty chuckle, Jake headed for the stairs. Jess followed Two Hands outdoors. She paused at the water pump for a drink and to wash her face, then she and her young companion crossed the yard. The cattlemen they passed raised a hand or tipped a hat in greeting. Jess greeted them in return, feeling as invigorated as when she had awakened. She would indeed have much to enjoy this day.

At the entrance to the stable, several men were saddling horses. Apparently, they would ride out with her and Jake. Jess retrieved a pair of gloves from the shed, then led Luina out of her stall. Two Hands expertly held the palomino horse, murmuring gently to her in his youthful, clarion voice while Jess laid a blanket over her back and settled the saddle in place. The men spoke to her as if they had expected her, and Jess felt almost giddy at the thought of flying across the range on horseback. This time, she had been invited, and she wouldn't have to cast panicked looks behind her to check for any pursuers.

To her own astonishment, she realized that she had no intention of betraying the men's trust. She was free to ride, and she planned to enjoy every moment of it. Just for today, she wouldn't give herself any reason to look back. Two Hands said something and held up four fingers. Jess turned to him and raised her eyebrows inquisitively. He pointed to all four of Luina's feet.

Jess grinned. When she was his age, numbers had come to her just as easily. She bent toward him conspiratorially. "Perhaps when I return to run my father's store, I'll take you with me to help me keep the books."

He giggled, uncertain of what she had said, but feeling complicit in some great secret, just the same.

"I'm surprised you're choosing Luina again," a deep voice said. "I'd have thought you and Cielos would be miles away by now with half the ranch after you."

The men looked up at Jake's humor, as if they had never heard such from the man.

In response, Jess drawled, "Drag Cielos away from Luina? Impossible." She passed a lightly accusing eye over him and the amused cattlemen. "Isn't that the way with males? When it comes to the gentler creatures, some of the brutes just can't be reasoned with."

Several pairs of eyes pivoted to Jake.

"Males? I recall a flighty *mare* leading an exhausting chase."

The eyes swung to Jess.

"Any mare will flee if enough burrs are thrust under the saddle," she rejoined.

Some good-natured laughter followed. Jake bowed slightly, acknowledging the wisdom of what she'd said, then handed her a light brown hat similar to his darker one.

Jess pulled it on. Glimpsing warm approval in Jake's eyes, she returned her attention to saddling Luina. She tightened the cinch strap, in spite of Luina's efforts to puff out her stomach. Jess was familiar with the ploy—the horse would release the air with the rider astride so that the strap would loosen. Despite Luina's attempts to get away with it, Jess snugged and knotted the cinch successfully. Her attention to the task gave her a moment to pull her traitorously opening heart away from Jake and to restore a cooler, more agreeable distance between them. Finally, Jess flipped the stirrup into place and patted Luina's belly. "Nice try, girl."

Jake, Jess, and the men led their animals into the sunshine and mounted up. As they rode out, Jess waved back to a smiling Two Hands. She was already looking forward to seeing the boy again.

"He's well mannered," Jake commented beside her. The other cattlemen were talking among themselves.

For her own peace of mind, Jess wouldn't spend the day in familiar conversation with Jake, but she responded, "He is. You can see he'll be good with a horse one day."

"Already is. I brought your horses back with me, and he's been helping look after them."

"My horses?"

He spoke softly. "The three from your pa's stable. The roof caught fire just after Lone Wolf and the other boys left with you." Jake paused, pulled a couple of biscuits from a pouch on his saddle, and handed them to her. "You haven't eaten yet," he said, then continued. "Ho Chen and I were able to get the horses out, but they were struck by falling timbers. Lone Wolf has been caring for them near his lodge—he's something of a healer. I'll take you to see them soon."

Jess's mind snagged on the fact that Jake had helped save her horses. Even so, she couldn't see his abandoning her crazed father in any kind of forgivable light. "Two Hands can take me," she said shortly. "You have a ranch to see to."

She gathered her reins for a run, but Jake's big glove closed over hers. "I need you to stay close, Jess."

At his tone, she looked up. For some reason, his gaze had intensified, as if warning her of an unknown danger. Frowning to herself, she recalled what Diaz had said the night before: *"This place, it is no safe for a woman. The boss, he knows this."* *What* did Jake know?

"I trust my men, and we have good neighbors. But wild animals or outlaws could do you harm. You ride with me."

Lifting his hand to signal his men, Jake split away from the group to search the distant foothills for cows, and Jess followed. He wore his revolver and, like all the other men, carried a rifle sheathed on his saddle. She thought about what he had just said, but the prospect of trouble didn't bother her for long. The glorious afternoon swiftly took her in.

Jess basked in the sunshine, and the cold of winter became a distant memory. She almost forgot they were working, and as she galloped beside Jake, she let go for a little while her concerns about returning to the city. She felt as free as the falcon she had seen gliding on the wind, and the joyous run of Luina gave her flight over the land.

Jake was drawn to the glow in Jess's face. Since the day Olivia had left the ranch the year before, he hadn't felt the passion for his work he'd once had, but now, seeing Jess ride with her heart wide open, he was reminded of himself not long ago. With a little smile he loosed the reins and let Cielos fully go. With Jess and Luina beside them, they raced along the foot of the Sierra Mountains. The thought came that he had brought Jess here for her protection, yes, but also to help heal her heart. Unexpectedly, she was helping to heal his, as well.

Chapter Nine

When a woeful bawling reached their ears, they slowed, Jake whipping his lariat at the ready. Not knowing what else to do, Jess stopped to watch. Jake approached the wary cow, keeping Cielos at a mild walk. Cielos appeared calm yet keenly aware of the cow's movements. When the bovine tried to run, Jake swiftly roped her and jumped to the ground. Cielos immediately leapt backward until the lariat tied to the saddle horn was taut, his gaze locked on the cow.

Jess looked in bewilderment from horse to cow, then back again. Never had she seen such a thing.

The immobilized cow bawled again. Jake quickly knelt beside her and began squeezing milk from her bulging udder.

"What's wrong with her, Bennett?"

"She hasn't been milked. Her calf must have died in the cold, or maybe wolves got it. I'd rather save the milk for the calves at the barn that need it, but she isn't going to wait."

Jess gazed out over the miles of sagebrush that spread out before them. "I'll have a look around. Maybe the calf is tangled in a bush or fell into a gulch nearby."

"Jess?"

She glanced at him.

"Don't wander out of earshot. I need to hear you if you run into trouble."

For once, she didn't take offense at his instruction. "I won't go far," she said, and she nudged Luina on her way.

After Jess had made a few rounds as far as she dared, she

guided Luina up a hill for a better vantage point from which to survey the area. From the top, she glimpsed a bend of the creek to the east, but she could no longer see the ranch. Far off to the north, the tiny forms of ranchmen on horseback were spreading out to herd the group of brown specks she knew must be cattle.

To the west, less than a mile off, was something odd: dozens of small rocks arranged in a rectangle on the ground. Intrigued, she lifted her hat to block the glare of the sun. A jolt shot through her as she identified the curved marker at the end of the rocks. It was a gravestone.

It was far removed from the ranch. A passing traveler must have died, perhaps long before the ranch was built. Still, seeing the grave twisted her insides. She had experienced too much death of late and had been relishing a life with few reminders.

Jess descended the hill, riding toward Jake yet circling wide, hoping to locate the calf. The more she searched for it, the more she wanted to find it and hoped it had survived. Something *had* to survive.

As she neared a shallow ravine, she spied a mob of vultures hopping about some distance ahead, and her heart plummeted. Jess knew she had probably discovered the calf, and she reluctantly guided Luina down. When she neared the ugly birds, they retreated with awkward pumps of their huge, tattered wings, revealing, as expected, a calf. It was dead.

Jake had mounted and was waiting when Jess returned. He studied her face. "You found the calf?"

"Yes, killed by wolves, I'd guess. I wouldn't have thought they'd come this close to the ranch."

"They do, especially in winter, when meals are hard to come by. Other times, though, I think they hunt for the thrill of it."

So much death. Death and no reparation. The cow stood, head drooping, at the end of the lariat. Though Jess wanted to avoid them, recollections of the fire stirred in her mind, as did another matter she'd been mulling over.

"Why do you suppose those Unionist fanatics waited four days to set the fire, Bennett? They must have followed us after we rode in from the mountains. They knew where my family lived. And when they did set the fire, why didn't they wait until we were all in bed asleep?"

"I expect a couple of them were still enraged about what happened in the street...maybe they had been drinking. They gathered up a can of kerosene and a Confederate flag, and they set the house on fire."

"As easy as that?"

"Many of the families that come west are Southerners. Confederate flags are easy to come by, and every household has kerosene."

"Perhaps," Jess allowed, "but the men couldn't have been drunk, or someone would have seen them staggering from the house."

"Then they weren't drunk," he agreed. "Now, that troubles me."

"It troubles me, as well. You know something else? I wonder why they didn't see you, my father, and me leaving the house. Even if only one man was responsible, you and I were away from the house less than ten minutes, and my father left after we did. An arsonist would have had to approach the house, douse the perimeter with kerosene, strike a match, and then run—all in five minutes, and without seeing the three of us, who remained within view. My point is, the fire took patience, forethought, planning. That doesn't sound like the result of a hot temper."

Jake chewed on her hypothesis, his expression inscrutable under the shade of his hat brim. "You think that someone else planned the fire?"

"Maybe a visitor to my father's store who hated Southerners, maybe someone else."

Thoughtful, Jake propped a gloved hand on his thigh. "If that were true, a killer would have made certain Isaac was inside the house, and, like you said, why not wait until your family was asleep? That doesn't make sense, Jess."

"It does if the man wanted to punish my father, if he wanted my father—and only my father—to survive and to watch his family die. It would also explain why all of this didn't happen the day I was attacked in the street. This man might have been around back, where he wouldn't have seen you and me leave the house. If he saw us walking, he would have thought we were just neighbors out for an evening stroll, but he must have seen my father with his unmistakable silhouette."

"Jess, the men who attacked you in Carson City openly hated Southerners. They saw where you lived, and they decided what they wanted to do about it," he said. "Unless you can think of anyone else who might have done this…"

"No," she said, "but I do see another problem."

"What's that?"

"Whoever set the fire would have watched from nearby to be sure they accomplished what they intended. If so, they were there when Lone Wolf took me away. Bennett, they saw you there. They know I'm alive."

She let that sink in, then continued, "Do you see why I have to return to Carson City?" The situation was much worse than she had thought. "I'm not the only one in danger. If I don't help the sheriff find those men, they'll come after you and the cattlemen here. Diaz, Taggart, and Reese all saw them that morning on the street, and Lone Wolf and the others were there the night of the fire. Those Unionists know there are more besides us who can identify them. They'll be looking for all of you!"

"Is that why you've been trying to leave?" he asked, incredulous. "Because you want to help the sheriff?"

"Didn't you hear the rest? The killers saw Taggart and Reese and the others. I need to help find those men before they harm anyone else!"

"Jess, one of the men brought news last night. I wanted to wait for a better time to tell you, but the sheriff has called off the search—"

"*Called off?*"

"—but Tom thinks there's something more. He's received a report of a similar fire near Lake's Crossing."

For a moment, Jess set aside her anger at the sheriff. "Another fire was set?"

"Yes. Tom will send word when he knows more, but those fanatics have apparently moved on, so there's little point in your returning to Carson City right now. I'll warn the boys. They're capable of looking out for themselves."

The thought of another fire chilled her. "The captain is still searching, then."

"Tom won't give up so long as there's a lead."

The sheriff called it off, she thought. Had she already returned to Carson City, she wouldn't have allowed the search to desist, and now her family's murderers were roaming free in Nevada Territory, possibly hurting others, while Jake held her at the ranch. Reluctantly, she admitted that although she still wanted to return to Carson City, her presence there would no longer benefit the search, since the blackguards had moved on, evidently in the general direction of the ranch.

"Bennett, what ever happened to the Confederate flag those men left behind?"

"I was angry when I found it. I threw it into the fire."

"Good. I'm glad I'll never have to see it."

When she said nothing more, Jake gathered his horse's reins.

"Are you ready to head back?" At her nod, he nudged Cielos toward home, leading the cow behind him. Jess occasionally glanced aside, but Jake remained quiet and pensive for most of the journey.

"You need a lesson in how to shoot," Jake finally said.

Shoot? Her brows drew together. "What makes you think I need a lesson in how to shoot?"

"Learning how to maneuver a gun and practicing your aim increase your chances of hitting your target," he said wryly. Then, "I'm acquainted with most of the ranch families around here, and I don't know of any in which the women don't know how to shoot."

"Perhaps I already know how—have you considered that possibility?"

"We'll see," he said with a subtle smile.

His response troubled her. Jake was patient and respectful, and he hadn't once said a cross word over the troubles she had caused since her arrival. Her anger toward him had begun to dissolve, and rising in its place was something more pleasant, followed closely by pangs of dread. She stiffened—she was beginning to like the man. When Luina suddenly sped up, Jess realized the cause and relaxed the tension in her legs. The mare slowed. Jake came up alongside her.

"Do you think to instruct me with that?" She nodded at his revolver. "Or with the rifle?"

"Both, in time. But first, you need to be able to use a revolver. They're easier to carry, whether you're on horseback or on foot."

"Don't you feel the least bit threatened?"

He chuckled at that. "No, ma'am. You might shoot a man to stop some wrong, but neither I nor my men have done you any harm." After a long silence, he spoke again. "This land is still wild, and so are all that belong to it. You've never lived in a place where you've been forced to defend your life, or the life of a neighbor or a child." His dark eyes regarded her soberly. "You're living there now."

Inside, Jess felt her former chill turn to ice. "You think the men who burned my home will come after me."

"Maybe. There are wolves about, and snakes, mountain lions, sometimes bears. But yes, if those men come after you, I want you able to defend yourself in the case that you're alone. I'll have the boys wear their guns from sack to slumber and keep their rifles close, though. Whoa." He pulled up and turned to Jess. "During the days ahead, the boys and I will bring in the cattle we find within a day's ride of the ranch. After that, we'll go on roundup out on the range, likely until the end of spring. We'll need to find the winter strays and separate our cattle from our neighbors' herds, and we'll brand the young calves and bring back mature beeves to sell."

He was leading up to something she wasn't going to like, she could tell. "And what about me?"

"I don't want you here alone while I'm gone for weeks at a time. I'm taking you along."

"And you've already decided—without discussing the matter with me."

Jake searched her face. "Wilderness," he said. "Horses. Freedom."

Jess looked out over the sage plains. They called to her, beckoned to her. "I don't much care for your high-handedness, Bennett."

"I didn't think you would," he said, a smile playing on his lips. "Let's get back. I'll take you shooting for the rest of the day."

∾ଓଈଔଈ୭ଔ

Jake and Jess rode toward a split in the mountain where Jake said he and the men often practiced their shooting. Lone

Wolf came along to keep an eye out for trouble during the lesson; it was the beginning of a heightened awareness among the ranch hands. He took up position nearby and kept scanning the horizon.

After tying their horses, Jake and Jess walked to a clearing. There, they pressed beeswax into their ears to deaden the clamor of the gun. Jake set one of the tins he had brought along as a target on a large rock.

Jess watched him, studying his muscular build and skillful movements as he reached over a large, flat rock, set the tin, pulled his arm back, and turned at the waist as he balanced it. He...

She shook her head to clear it. What was wrong with her?

Jake walked back to where she was waiting. He drew the revolver and handed it to her, barrel pointed safely away.

Jess focused her attention on the gun.

"First, I just want you to get the feel of it," Jake said.

She looked it over. "It's heavy," she mused aloud. "Long barrel."

"It's for better accuracy...less kick. Sight down your arm. Good."

She glanced at him, her arm aloft. "A lot of good aiming will do me if I'm on a moving horse."

"I'll teach you that, as well, but not today."

When her arm muscles began to ache, she lowered the gun. "I'll need to get accustomed to the weight."

"You will. Try again, and I'll help you steady it." Jake moved closer and lifted her hand in his.

Awareness of him warmed her skin where his hand and arm touched hers. Jess stood straight as an arrow, focusing her concentration on her grip of the gun. Finally, she felt comfortable with the position of the revolver, and she pulled her hand from Jake's to cock the gun. When she stretched out her arm to fire, Jake's big hand closed firmly around hers. He spoke near her ear. "It's going to kick fierce," he warned.

"Then let me try it empty first. I want to get a feel for the trigger pull."

Obligingly, Jake took the gun and uncocked it. He glanced at her as he deftly removed the load from the cylinders. "How did you know to ask that?"

Jess lifted a shoulder. "It's how my father taught Ambrose." She cocked the gun again, raised it up, and squeezed the trigger. The hammer dropped with a loud metallic snap. She readied it, then practiced firing again. "It has a heavy pull."

Jess felt his gaze on her face.

"It'll fire at about half pull," he said.

She handed the revolver back to him. "Let's see if it does."

Jess meant only to glance up at him briefly, but her eyes locked with his. Bennett, she realized, was considering her the way a man considers a woman he admires.

In the next instant, Jess was struggling to remember her anger of days gone by. She was determined not to allow her heart to get ahead of her mind, but the longer his dark eyes bore into hers, the more she felt compelled to kiss the man. Instead, she focused her attention on tangible details—the way his eyes crinkled at the corners, his slightly hooked nose, his supple lips, the handsome whiskers shading his jaw...

Abruptly, she turned away.

Jake rammed home a fresh load into the pistol. She stole a surreptitious glance. He appeared to be fighting an inner battle of his own...and winning.

"It's ready to fire," he said, in control again. He handed her the gun. They stood as before.

Jess eyed the tin, then stretched out her arm. She curled her finger over the trigger and pulled.

BOOM! A stone exploded twenty yards beyond the tin and

rained down in tiny pieces. Smoke rolled away from the gun. Jess set the hammer to fire again.

"Try easing the trigger," Jake advised, "and don't let it trouble you when it barks."

Nodding, she took aim as before, but grew uncomfortably warm and flushed with Jake's nearness. "Do you mind if I try it alone?"

"Not at all." Jake stepped back and folded his arms across his chest, eyeing the alignment of her arm and the gun.

Jess fired repeatedly, using two hands to brace herself against the recoil, until she had emptied the chambers. Then Jake reloaded the gun while she considered her progress. The tin still stood in place. She'd managed to make targets of stones that lay around it, but the tin itself hadn't a scratch.

Jake held out the gun to her. "Perhaps I should have brought a larger tin."

His humor surprised her. "Are you mocking me, Bennett?" She put her hands on her hips and eyed his handsome face with a challenge of her own. "Perhaps you should show me how to perforate a defenseless tin."

"Ma'am, that sounds like skepticism in your sweet Southern voice."

"You keep my voice out of it. If you're capable of it, defend me against that tin."

Lifting an eyebrow, Jake cocked the hammer as she moved aside. Suddenly, he crouched and fired. The tin flipped into the air, and Jake leapt to the side and fired again. It spun crazily, then fell to the ground. Jake fired again and again. Every shot ripped into the tin. Finally, he stood up and eyed his work.

Concealing her admiration, Jess walked beside him as he went to retrieve the target. When he lifted the tin, it was impossible to tell what its original shape had been. He handed it to her with boyish modesty and touched his hat. "Your outlaw, ma'am."

Jess held it up to the sky, the sunlight blazing through its torn sides and jagged edges. She looked up at him. "And just what am I to shoot at now?"

"You have a fondness for shooting rocks. There're plenty of those."

She was surprised how much she liked his teasing her.

"Then you don't think the tin is in any danger?" she baited.

They shared a smile as he holstered the gun. "Apparently not, but something else is."

He reached up behind his neck and unknotted his bandana, then proceeded to retie it beneath her braid.

"Your neck was getting too much sun," he murmured.

"Thank you." She smoothed down the fabric with her hand. "I should have thought to make one."

"No need. I have others, so you're welcome to keep it."

They returned to their firing spot, more at ease with each other. Jake began to reload the revolver, then paused with an expectant grin. "Maybe I should show you how to load it."

"Maybe I could figure it out for myself."

Jess took the proffered gun and began to load it as neatly as he had. When it was ready, she searched the desert around them. "Where is Lone Wolf? I thought he'd come and shoot with us after he saw there was no one about."

"He'll keep watch until we're done. With all this noise we're making, someone could easily come up behind us without our hearing. We'll meet up with him near sunset." At her small frown, he added, "I really don't think anyone will come after you, or he would have already. But it's best to pay attention, for now."

Jess nodded. She waited as Jake placed another tin on the rock, then turned to shoot again. The new tin remained as immobile and undamaged as before. By day's end, though, scratches webbed the surface of the rock it stood on. With a promise to resume the lesson the following afternoon, Jake put their things away in his saddlebags and gave Jess a leg up on her horse. Together, they rode to meet up with Lone Wolf.

After a brief silence, Jake said, "You hit so near the tin— many times, in fact—that I can't understand how you didn't hit it even once." He looked at her curiously. "Just what were you aiming for?"

Jess returned his gaze, her eyes wide and innocent. "Why, the tin, of course. I'm not accustomed to your gun, you know. Did you really expect me to hit so small a target with only a few hours' practice?"

Jake didn't seem to know what to make of her. "You should have been able to."

"Maybe tomorrow we should bring a larger target."

"No, you need to learn to hit a small one."

"Then, I'll just have to do my best."

He didn't reply. A few minutes later, Lone Wolf joined them, and the three rode back to the ranch.

∼᙭᠍᠍᠍᠍ᘉᐧ᙭᠍᠍᠍᠍ᘉᐧᘉ∼

That night, after supper with a ranchful of men, Jess climbed the stairs to her room, content with their good company and pleased with Jake for letting her ride that day. She closed her door and leaned against it, then peeled the calico bandages from her wrists by the orange glow of sunset coming through the window.

Her hide boots whispered on the floor as she moved toward the dressing table to toss aside the bandages. The basin and pitcher that had always been there were gone. Surprised, she glanced about. A new furnishing—a lady's washstand—stood in the corner. Jess set down the calico and walked over to

162

inspect it. The wooden surface was rectangular and elegantly beveled, its splashboard carved with scroll-like curves. On it sat the basin and pitcher, with room beside them for trinkets or towels.

In awe, she trailed her fingers over the delicate design, then sank to her knees to admire its slender legs, which had been turned on a lathe. The washstand smelled wonderfully of pine. It had been made recently, she could tell.

And this time, there wasn't a shred of displeasure in her when she mouthed his name. "Bennett."

Jake's plans to take Jess shooting in the days that followed had to be delayed when more cattle than had been expected were found within a half-day's ride. He wasn't pleased that target practice would have to wait, but Jess said it was just as well. If there was going to be a garden that year, she told him, she would have to till and plant it now.

So, Jake sent Seth to Janesville for the seeds she needed. Hiram and Nate rode to a neighboring ranch to borrow mules, a plow, and a harrow, which they used to break up and smooth the soil. Seth was scheduled to return with the seeds shortly before sunrise.

When Jake and Jess stepped out onto the porch to greet the day, Jess stopped short, surrounded by the piles of sacks the young man had left there. In the yard, Ho Chen had set up an outdoor fire pit where he could cook to keep the cattlemen fed. Taggart and several other men rode out to bring in the day's work. Others whistled and shouted as they herded calves from the nearby range to brand and castrate, rapidly filling two of the three large corrals with the young cows and the heifers that had borne them.

When two men started a fire for branding in the third corral, Jess pressed a hand to her middle. "I'd best get to work on the garden and stay away from here until the branding is done. I don't have the stomach for singed hide and all that goes with it."

"The men don't much care for it, either," Jake assured her as he stepped off the porch.

Jess began hauling the sacks of seeds to where Hiram and Nate had plowed. Red Deer soon joined her. "Good morning, Jessica."

Jess turned with a smile. "Good morning, Red Deer." Her deerskin dress was one of the two she had always worn, but now, the middle was slightly rounded from the growing child in her womb. Red Deer looked happy but tired. She laughed at the apparent surplus of seeds.

"Always it seems like too much, but we will get them planted. I will send Two Hands to bring the Paiute women. Those who are able will come today. Tomorrow, even more will help." She called to the boy, and he hurried off toward his village, safely skirting the men and cattle.

The calves bawled in fear as they were herded into the branding corral, where a man on horseback rope each struggling calf and two others wrestled the animal to the ground so that a fourth could brand it with the smoking iron in his gloved hands.

Hastily, Jess made her excuses to Red Deer and went to collect what they would need from the supply shed. On a thought, she paused at the water pump to fill a bucket in order to water the rosebush behind the stable. When she rounded the corner, bucket in hand, she saw that the ground beneath it was already damp and that several yellow blossoms had opened. She took a moment to breathe in their hypnotic fragrance, then continued on to gather shovels, rakes, and hoes.

Jess neared the porch just in time to see Red Deer hefting a bag of seeds. She set the tools aside and hurried to take the sack from her. "Not while you're carrying, my friend," Jess said. "I don't want you to lift anything heavy—not until long after your son is born. I'll move the rest." At the uncertainty in Red Deer's eyes, Jess laid a gentle hand on her arm. "Where I grew up, we always helped one another when there was a need. Isn't it the same among your people?"

Red Deer smiled. "Yes, this is so." Seeing the other Paiute women and their children approaching, she said, "Come. I want you to meet my dear Paiute friends."

For the remainder of the morning, Jess tried to get the wary women and children to warm up to her. They were more hesitant to talk to her than Red Deer had initially been. As Red Deer had said, many of them spoke at least a little English, and the few who didn't used simple gestures to communicate. Never had Jess been so conscious of her pale skin. Gradually, the Paiute women introduced their children to Jess, and by midday, they were telling her stories of their husbands and families while they worked. Some of them wore dresses of doeskin, like Red Deer; others wore long calico dresses like those of the white women. Nearly all had their hair cut below the ears in mourning, and their faces bore lines of sadness. Yet Jess was astounded at the familial love and diligent industry of the people. The children poked holes into the ground, and their mothers followed with seeds, praising their work. Jess came after with several other women, watering the seeds and laughing with them at her own bungled attempts to learn a few phrases in Paiute. It would be a day to remember.

Overhead, cottonwood branches rustled with the growth of new leaves, casting cooling shadows on those who walked beneath them. Each time Jess finished watering a row, she paused to look back over the neat line of damp earth they had just seeded. Then she would share a smile with one of the other women or look quickly around to see which child had snuck up and tugged her skirt from behind. The guilty party always hurried away with a giggle, and Jess worked on memorizing their faces so she could pay them back with playful tugs when they weren't looking.

At midday, Ho Chen summoned everyone to the fire pit for dinner. Jess set her water bucket aside and stretched out her arms, enjoying the heat of the sun mingled with the cool of the breeze. The women rounded up their children and gathered around Ho Chen, who was heaping food on small plates for the little ones. Jess called to Red Deer that she'd be along, then headed for the well, certain she could drink it dry, such was her thirst.

The cool water was ambrosial. Four dipperfuls later, she glanced toward the corrals, trying to catch her breath.

Covered in dust, Jake and Doyle were bringing down the bigger calves while Diaz plied the hissing brand. Suddenly, a man reached out a gleaming blade, and Jess spun back around to face the well pump. She had no desire to witness the castration.

Jess glimpsed Taggart, who was strolling over for a drink. She gladly worked the groaning pump as a means to cover the squealing protest of the calf.

"And how are ye farin' with God's good earth this day?"

With a grin, Jess passed him the brimming dipper and tried to mimic the rolling accent of his countrymen. "I be farin' quite well with the soil and with all the seedies we're pokin' into it." When he laughed in approval, she lifted her gaze to the brilliant blue sky. "This is as beautiful a day as I can recall."

He took a long drink, then likewise scanned the heavens. "Aye, that it is, and we've more cows that survived this winter than the last, by far." He enjoyed another helping of cool water, then sighed with relief. "Aye, it'll be a good year." Noticing that she kept her back to the corrals, Taggart replaced the dipper. "Are ye troubled by that?"

"Some." Jess glimpsed teasing in his pale blue eyes. Eager to hold it off, she asked, "What does the brand look like?"

Amiably, Taggart held out a gloved hand, on which he outlined the symbols with his other hand. "It's two Bs, flat sides down beside each other, like this. It looks a bit like four mountains together, with a creek below. The Bennett Mountain Ranch, it is, though most folks about call it the B Creek, for the short of it."

"I see." Jess chanced a quick look over her shoulder. A water barrel sat near the corrals, within easy reach of the men. Her lightly accusing eyes curved up to his. "You didn't need to come all this way to get a drink."

"Well, ma'am, the boss said different." With a friendly wink, he strolled away.

Jess wheeled toward the corrals. Jake was facing her, his eyes twinkling, apparently looking after her himself. Behind him, Lone Wolf roped a calf from his horse and dragged it to be branded. Jake broke his gaze as he turned to the calf, and then, in a deft movement, caught it off balance and took the struggling animal down.

Reminded of her own attempts to escape "captivity," Jess went to join the women for dinner, shaking her head over the calf's hopeless attempts to break free from Jake.

~✧∥✧~

Jess dug holes, planted seeds, tamped soil, and watered earth until nightfall. As twilight began to tinge the horizon, the Paiute women and children headed back to their village, but the cattlemen brought out torches and lanterns so they could continue their gruesome tasks. Jess finished planting three more rows of turnips alone. Then she propped her hoe against a tree and lowered the empty seed bag beside it.

Going to the creek, she pulled off her bandana, soaked it briefly, then dropped it over her upturned face, sighing in bliss. Life, she decided, didn't get much better than this. She wet the cloth again and wiped her neck, glad to be free of the dust and sweat of the day's work. Rolling up her sleeves, she dunked her arms in the cool current. Before she knew it, she was slipping off her moccasins and wading in. She had nearly decided it was dark enough to swim in her chemise when she saw Jake approaching, guided by moonlight. She settled for walking about in the gentle current.

"Are the men about done?" she asked.

With a sigh of satisfaction, he squatted down to be at eye level with her. "There's some cleaning up to be done, but the worst is over for today." His expression turned thoughtful. "Jess, a rider came tonight with a message from Tom. The fire near Lake's Crossing was set intentionally. The husband and wife who lived in the house escaped."

Jess stiffened, alert. "The couple is from the South?"

"Yes, from Tennessee. They saw two of the arsonists well enough for Tom to think they were the same men who attacked you in Carson City. They stole a few horses before leaving, and they haven't been sighted since."

Jess splashed water over her face, then looked up at Jake. "Then the attack against my family was only the beginning. This is more than angry drunks. They've started their own war against Southerners."

"Tom knows this. He's organized a company of cavalry to search for them."

Jess scanned the plains, half expecting an ambush.

Jake pointed to her rolled-up sleeves. "The boys brought up

extra water for washing this morning. I can fill a tub for you by the fireplace, if you like."

Jess drew her fingers through the cool water, glad he'd turned the conversation to something simpler, yet she was uncomfortable speaking about as personal a matter as what she had in mind. "Actually I—I'd prefer a dip in the creek, if I can be assured of privacy."

"I'll see to it the men keep their distance," Jake said, quick to put her at ease. He pointed to an oak about a hundred yards off. "I'll wait for you over there. Take your time, and don't worry— I'll keep an eye out for those Carson City boys, as well."

He rose to go.

"Bennett?"

"Hmm?"

She wasn't sure how to thank him for the washstand. "I...I didn't know you were a wood craftsman."

"I built the ranch house," he said simply.

Jess laughed, chagrined that the thought hadn't occurred to her. Of course he had. "And all the other buildings, as well?"

He apparently decided not to tease her. "Yes."

For some reason she couldn't explain, she didn't want to face him, so she spoke over her shoulder. "Well, I want to thank you for it. I'm glad not to have the basin in the middle of the dressing table."

"It was my pleasure."

With a soft scuffing of his boots, he left her to her privacy.

Jake stepped down from his horse and glanced at the position of the stars. It was nearly midnight. After Jess had gone to bed, he had washed off the day's dust in the creek, as she had, then had cut two roses and saddled Cielos. He stood smoothing his

169

hand over the stallion's neck in silence. Cielos had known the way. After a year of making the same trip over and over, often after dark, his horse knew it just as well as he did.

Jake briefly eyed the roses he'd brought. For him, these visits were changing…or perhaps he was changing. Raising his head, he looked over to the grave where he'd buried his Olivia and their daughter, Sadie.

For the thousandth time, he wished he had never let Olivia leave the ranch without him. Why couldn't a wagon wheel have broken before she left? Why couldn't one of the horses have gone lame? When he and Olivia had married, they were so much in love that he'd been certain nothing would ever come between them. He hadn't known that their beautiful life together would end so quickly. He hadn't known he'd have to go on without her.

And he never believed that he would have feelings for another woman again.

Jake saw that he was still standing where he'd dismounted. He tied the reins to a juniper tree and then started toward the grave. Jess was getting under his skin. It was Jess he pictured in his mind now when he woke, Jess whom he looked forward to seeing throughout the day. For the longest time, it had been only Olivia, even after she was gone.

Beside her grave, Jake slid off his hat. He cleared his throat and laid the roses on the low mound of earth.

"Hello, Olivia. I brought these for you and Sadie. Spring's here, and the rosebush is in bloom now, so I'll have more than twigs to bring you when I come." He glanced around, uncomfortable, knowing he had to talk to her about Jess. No matter what had happened during their brief marriage, they had always been able to talk openly with each other.

"I'm sorry I haven't been to see you every night. We're starting roundup, so I'm keeping busy." Jake kicked the dirt with his boot. If only he could touch Olivia's hair once more, if only he could feel the softness of her cheek pressed to his... but that wasn't meant to be. "Livvy, I've wanted you and Sadie back ever since you left. I've come here and I've brought you flowers, and I've always wished that the three of us could be as we were." He sighed, searching for words, but he couldn't tell her what he felt about Jess. He wasn't sure himself.

Instead, he talked about the goings-on at the ranch. He knew she likely couldn't hear him from heaven, but he wanted to share his thoughts with her, just the same.

Finally, Jake fell quiet. He looked up at the night, listening to the wind. Then he spoke again. "I'd best get back and get some sleep. Morning comes earlier every day." As always, it was hard to go. "Good night, Olivia. Tell Sadie Daddy loves her."

Jake turned and walked away from the grave. He pulled his hat on, thinking he should have told her about Jess. The possibility of death was something Olivia and he had never discussed, yet he wondered what she would want for him now. Would she rather he kept her memory alive? Or would she want him to continue on, maybe find someone else to love?

Jake took the reins and mounted Cielos. He lifted his hat to his lady in a solemn gesture, then made himself ride away.

For several minutes, his heart was full of Olivia.

Then, as he neared the ranch, it filled more and more with Jess.

Chapter Ten

Jess squinted in the glare of the setting sun, which also helped protect her eyes from the dust raised by the herd of cattle. Like the men, she wore her bandana over her nose and mouth so she could breathe without inhaling the thick dirt. When they had first left the ranch on roundup, she had been a good rider who knew nothing about cattle. Now, after a month of riding through mile after mile of California and Nevada Territory, sleeping under the stars, and herding cattle alongside the men, she had gained a greater knowledge of cattle than she had ever imagined. Moreover, she had stopped thinking of Kentucky as home. She was home.

One of the cows ahead of her tried to break away from the herd. Immediately, Jess tapped Luina with her heels. The horse shot forward, and with a quick wave of her lasso, Jess urged the startled cow back into place. Returning to her position as Flank, Jess glanced over to where Doyle was wrangling the remuda—the spare horses they switched with their own several times a day to keep them from being overworked. Catching her eye, Doyle lifted a hand. Jess waved back.

She had discovered that Luina was one of the best cutting horses Jake owned, and he'd set her to cutting the calves from the herds for the men to rope and brand. It was dangerous work. She'd come close to being gored by protective heifers too many times to count, but Jake had patiently shown her what needed to be done, and she had mastered it. It had been his way of keeping her as far as possible from the branding and castrating while still including her as a useful member of the group.

They had cattle to return to neighboring ranches and new calves to birth. As trail boss, Jake often rode ahead to scout water sources and grazing lands where they could gather to do their work and sleep until they moved on. Knowing Jess's experience in keeping books at her father's store, he had assigned her the task of record keeping almost as soon as they rode out. She handled the job well, and she was able to focus on the trail ahead and do the branding with the men.

He'd taught her the cutting method in the first few days, he riding Cielos, she, Luina. Several other men, mostly Doyle and Diaz, had taught her to ride Point, Swing, and Flank as they herded, and she'd even spent several days wrangling the remuda with Seth. But none of the men, with their rigid honor code, would allow her to ride Drag—the dustiest position at the rear of the herd. Jess smiled as she thought of it. Whenever they stopped at night beside a river or a hot spring, they always insisted she go in first while they respectfully remained at a distance. They gave her the place nearest the fire on cool nights, and while they rode, they frequently inquired about her well-being.

Now they were headed back to the ranch with the beeves Jake had contracted to sell. They were moving at a leisurely pace so as not to arrive with lean, wasted cows. As it was, Jake had said, he would let them graze a few weeks within sight of the ranch in order to fatten them up before the journey to market.

Jess looked up to see Jake riding toward them from the south—he had been scouting out their camp. Behind him, familiar peaks of the Sierras were visible again. They would likely be home the next day. Jake approached Lone Wolf, who was riding Point, and the two spoke briefly. Then, to her surprise, Jake thumped Cielos with his heel and trotted toward her.

She had spoken to Jake as little as possible throughout the weeks of roundup. Thankfully, all of them had been too busy during the days to do anything but work. At night, she would talk with Ho Chen near the chuck wagon or would watch the other men play poker, politely declining their invitations to join the game. As soon as the campfire began to die, she would crawl into her bedroll to sleep. It had been easier that way— easier not to invite the internal war that plagued her whenever Jake came to mind, easier not to let herself see him and then think about him constantly.

Jake pulled Cielos around beside her. "How are you holding up?"

"Just fine." She glanced up into the hot, cloudless sky. "I'm surprised we haven't seen any rain this year."

"And it's already May, so that's likely to mean trouble," he said. "We'll be back at the ranch tomorrow, late afternoon, I'm guessing."

"I thought as much."

They rode in silence for a few minutes. Then Jake broke the silence. "You've done well out here, Jess."

"Oh? Are you thanking me for not trying to escape?"

"No, I'm thanking you for your hard work. I've never seen anyone learn cutting faster."

At the compliment, Jess looked over to read sincerity in his eyes. Inwardly, she was pleased that he had recognized her efforts—more pleased than she cared to admit. She pulled her hat lower on her head and gazed studiously at the cattle. "Then you'd best start paying me like one of your ranchmen, Bennett. By now, I've earned it."

Jake considered the matter pensively, a smile playing on his lips. "Yes, Miss Hale, I guess I'd better."

Touching a spur to Cielos, Jake rode on, calling to the others to begin making camp.

Jess stood by herself and watched a glorious twilight turn the mountains into silhouettes of jagged peaks and sweeping slopes. The night was quiet except for the rhythmic chirrups of crickets and the peaceful lowing of cattle. As a warm, sage-scented wind washed over her, Jess pushed her hat from her head, letting it hang around her neck from its strings. The wind swept wisps of hair back from her face, and, loving the feel of it, she shook out her braid and let the breeze wend its way through her sun-streaked tresses.

A dull pain fanned out from her stomach. Today was the seventh. Three months ago, her life had changed forever. Three months ago, she had lost the people she never believed she could live without. Jess looked around her, taking in the countryside she had come to know as home since then. This place had taken her in. Something about it had helped her to continue on.

Not wanting to rejoin the men just yet, Jess returned briefly to camp to take a small plate of biscuits and salt pork from Ho Chen. She noticed an explosion of silence among the cattlemen when she stepped past with her long hair unbound, and she saw several unblinking eyes when she stepped past again—eyes that feasted on the play of firelight along her shining hair. The men's forks were motionless on their plates. She left as quickly as she'd come, embarrassed but not yet willing to bind her hair again.

Jess stood far from the men, as before, to eat her supper—by herself but not alone. The place filled her; the night filled her. And yet it wasn't that, but something more. She remembered what Jake had once said about feeling closer to the Almighty out here. Perhaps Jake had been right about that. Because, for the first time in a long while, it seemed He wasn't so very far away.

∾◦❈◦∾

Diaz relaxed against his bedroll, lightly scraping the point of his knife over a piece of wood that was beginning to take the shape of an antelope. Seth played a few notes on his harmonica, and Diaz glanced up.

The *vaqueros* near him had finished dinner. Now they settled down to smoke, play cards, and repair their gear. Ho Chen was scrubbing pots near the chuck wagon. Taggart headed out on horseback to circle the herd for the first watch. Jake was writing in his notebook. The señorita…she was standing by herself beneath the stars.

Seth decided on a song and began to play. With his thumb, Diaz dusted the miniature antelope before putting his knife to it again. His gaze shifted to the boss. Jake had stopped writing. He was looking beyond the camp to where Jess was standing to gaze at the stars, his notebook and pencil forgotten. A full minute passed before the boss's gaze shifted back to his immediate surroundings. When his eyes moved in Diaz's direction, he was plying his knife, carving, carving.

After a little while, Diaz contemplated the boss once more. He was writing determinedly again. With a glance at the other *vaqueros*, Diaz decided that they hadn't seen what he had.

He turned his full attention back to his whittling, hoping his mustache concealed his smile.

∾◦❈◦∾

Once they returned to the ranch, everyone resettled into his or her normal routine. The Paiute women had kept the garden while they were gone, but now Jess took over watering and caring for it so that they could see to their families and homes.

The first morning she walked out to see the crops, she was thrilled to note their progress. An ocean of green stood inches above the ground, but the creek was noticeably lower than it had been when they left. The lack of snow and rain would indeed mean trouble come summer, as Jake had said.

So, assisted by Red Deer and Two Hands, she watered and weeded each morning while the men delivered calves and foals and saw to the overall maintenance of the ranch. Often, when Jess saw a flurry of excitement near the stable or barn, the three of them would hurry over to watch a tiny, sodden calf slide from its mother or to witness a wobbly new colt or filly take its first steps. Jake was usually there, and more than once, he and Jess shared proud smiles over the heads and hats of the others who had gathered. As she and Ambrose used to do as children, she dreamed up names for the foals, now including Two Hands in her game. Many of the names they both liked best stuck.

In the afternoons, Jake took her shooting as he had before, giving her plenty of practice time as the days grew longer. Lone Wolf always rode along to be their eyes and ears while Jake and Jess focused on the use of the revolver.

By the end of the second week back at the ranch, Jess still hadn't hit the target once, though she had whittled down the rock beneath it until Jake had teasingly praised her gift for forging pebbles. She'd answered back that she'd probably have better success with a cannon, and so the evening went.

When Jake holstered the gun for the last time one Saturday night, Jess lauded her efforts. "At least I knocked down the tin once!"

"A rock chip flew up and hit it," he said dryly.

"Yes, but wasn't it exciting?"

"I'd like it a lot more," he answered with concern, "if I felt certain you could protect yourself."

At his allusion to the arsonists, Jess's levity faded fast. "I'll get along just fine, Bennett. I've always been able to take care of myself."

"How do you figure that? Since we've met, you've gotten yourself into one scrape after another. You take risks with little forethought—"

"I think things through very carefully before I take risks," she threw back. "Every one of them has been worth it!"

"Worth it?" He stepped toward her, his voice rising sharply. "You roamed the streets of a Unionist town alone, you were attacked by an angry mob, you nearly had a burning house fall on you, and you keep running away from a safe haven, determined to get killed by whoever didn't succeed the first time. Jess! Does this seem rational?"

His dismissal of the fact that she had done so out of love for her family stung bitterly. "I have no regrets," she yelled, "and don't you dare talk to me about safe havens. I had one—you were there when it burned to the ground!"

At the shout, Lone Wolf came running. He stopped, chest heaving, his bow in his fist.

"Why are you being unreasonable?" Jake pressed, staring down at her. "I wasn't the man who started the fire!"

"Unreasonable?" Angry tears ran from her eyes, and she no longer felt any desire to halt her words. "You ruined my life!" She took a deep breath.

"How did I—"

"You killed my father!" she screamed, finally freeing all that she'd caged inside. "You could have let my father save Mother and Emma, but you held him back until it was too late! And then, when the flames were everywhere, you let him go!" Lone

Wolf put a warning hand on her arm, but she shrugged it off. "It's your fault! You let him go, Bennett, and he died. He died!" she cried, glaring at him through her tears.

Jake spoke again, gently this time. "Jess, your mother and Emma…they were trapped. There was no way to save them. Isaac knew it. I think he just didn't want to live without your mother."

Hatred was thick in her voice. "So you let him die."

"You were there, Jess," he said softly. "You saw what happened. He was half crazed, and he pulled a gun."

A gun? She couldn't believe it…wouldn't let herself believe it. "Liar! There was no gun. You let him go. You did everything but push him through the door!"

"Jess!"

She envisioned that night. She knew her father carried a concealed four-barrel derringer, and she hadn't seen his gun hand when Jake had backed away. Jake was telling the truth. She'd been wrong to accuse him, to blame him, but she was too ashamed of her words and too full of pain to back down. It had felt like someone had driven a knife through her heart, but she realized now that it hadn't been Jake. "Leave me alone," she hissed. She gathered Luina's reins, gained the saddle, and whipped her into a run.

⚜

Knowing she was too upset to be reasoned with, Jake let Jess go without pursuing her. The sun had set and the sky was growing dark. He and Lone Wolf watched her ride away.

"I was there," said Lone Wolf.

"I know."

"She is wrong to say this to you, my friend."

"She's hurt and angry. I cut open old wounds tonight."

179

"You did so to understand her anger. I saw this."

"Yes, I know. Some part of her knows the truth about that night." For a moment, Jake allowed himself to relive it—the vicious struggle…Isaac's maniacal strength…the wild desperation in his eyes when he pulled the gun.

"The fire?" Lone Wolf asked. "Yes, I also believe she knows. She cares for you, my brother, but she is afraid to care too much. She fears she will lose all once more."

Jake frowned, tracking the dot on the horizon. "I know. I've known that fear myself."

Lone Wolf glanced at him. "Many seasons have passed. You must let Olivia go."

"She filled my heart, Lone Wolf."

"That was true once, but no longer. I think a green-eyed falcon fills it now, my brother."

Jake didn't answer.

"She is a wanderer, this bird. You are wise to let her fly, but do not let her become lost to you."

Inwardly acknowledging the turning of his heart, Jake untied Cielos, but Lone Wolf halted him.

"No, my friend. She will not listen to you now. I will follow and guard her. I will bring her back."

After a pause, Jake stepped into the saddle. "Jess and I need to work this out, but not tonight. Tonight I only want her safe."

"She needs to run," Lone Wolf advised.

Thinking on this, Jake nodded. "Then I'll let her. I'll bring her back when she's ready." He held out his arm to his friend, and they clasped wrists. "The Almighty has blessed you with wisdom, Lone Wolf."

"To you He has given the heart of a warrior. You will need it to save your woman."

Jake touched a spur to Cielos, knowing fully what Lone

Wolf meant by "save." He would need all the strength in his being to save Jess from her fear of love.

∾☙⬥❧∾

Jess knew Jake was right. If her mother had been able to save herself and Emma, she would have found a way. Jess knew she couldn't blame Jake for their deaths, or for her father's demise, any longer. What he'd said was true—he hadn't started the fire, and her father had likely been far enough beyond reason to shoot him. With the bandana Jake had given her, Jess wiped her cheeks, wanting more than ever before to return to Carson City, to be near her family and revisit the places that held memories of them. And though she realized he wasn't at fault, Jess hoped Jake would not follow her. She desperately needed to be away from him.

Coyotes yipped somewhere downstream, drawing her musings to the silvery water of the river and to the silhouettes of herself and Luna cast in shadows by moonlight. This night was so much like another time, years ago, near a river that curved through her Kentucky homeland.

∾☙⬥❧∾

"Are you sure we won't get caught?" she had called softly in her little girl's voice.

Young Ambrose had slowed his mount, turning to reassure her. "We aren't doing anything wrong, little butterfly," he said, "except perhaps spoiling a bit of your sleep."

"Oh, I don't mind. I'd much rather be here."

This particular summer evening, their mother and father had left them in the care of their grandparents, a doting pair who wouldn't have been surprised to learn that Ambrose and Jess were out riding by the river they loved.

"It's not much further. Are you warm enough?"

"I'm fine, but I really wanted to ride Isabelle."

"Danny is more sure-footed. I'll take you out on Isabelle in the morning."

"Promise?"

"Promise. Okay, watch out for the low branches. We're almost there."

"Do you really think we'll see them, Ambrose?"

He lowered his voice. "They're here every night. If they're shy, I'll simply tell them a beautiful butterfly has come to visit." She giggled at the tender way he spoke to her. "Shh, we stop here, Jess."

Ambrose dismounted and lifted her down from her pony. He tied their mounts to a low branch and took her hand, leading her through the woods toward a dense thicket. Unsure in the dark, Jess clung more closely to Ambrose, who squeezed her hand reassuringly.

At the edge of the brambles, he knelt down and pulled her close beside him. Not at all frightened now, she held in a squeal of excitement. His hand faintly visible in the moonlight, Ambrose eased a mantle of leafy vines to one side. Just as soundlessly, Jess gazed into the clearing beyond it. There, a doe and two young fawns were resting quietly.

Astounded by their beauty and nearness, Jess could hardly breathe. The fawns, nestled cozily against their mother, looked as sweet as new foals, only smaller. The doe licked each one on the head, and Jess decided that she was telling them good night. One laid her head down. After a moment, so did the other. The doe turned her gentle gaze toward the woods to listen and to watch. Careful not to make a sound, Jess looked up at Ambrose, and he beamed down at her.

They stayed there for several minutes, and when Ambrose noticed the doe becoming restless, he led Jess out again, much to her regret.

Her childhood memories were filled with similar adventures, nearly all of which had been shared with Ambrose. The moon hadn't changed, but the river had, and the shadow on the ground was that of a woman now. Jess missed her parents, but it was Ambrose who had always been there for her, and, especially in recent years, she had been there for him. Their closeness had been unique, precious. She remembered the letters they had exchanged since he had returned to Kentucky and how eager he had been to meet little Emma. Suddenly, tears choked her, and she cried out. For a long while, she sobbed loud and long like a child, glad no one was around to hear her bittersweet release of pain.

Unable to stop crying or to catch her breath, she pressed her face into one hand. With her other hand, she clung to the pommel of her saddle but loosed the reins. Luina wandered a little in confusion, eventually coming to stand near the creek, where she nibbled at young grasses.

Jess felt free—free of the ranch, free to cry out the agony she'd locked inside, and free to cry away the blame she'd unjustly placed on Jake. Lifting her tear-streaked face to the night sky, she yelled, "I'm sorry, God!" She shook her head and quieted. "I'm sorry…for my anger."

For a long time, she simply grieved. Then, at last, she let out her breath in a shaky sigh, feeling that a tremendous weight had left her. As the minutes passed, something else stole into its place: conviction—the conviction that she was *not* going to lose anything more and the conviction of what else she needed to do.

Jess looked around to get her bearings. Her mind was fixed: she was going to visit the place where her family was buried. Then she would pay a much needed visit to the import store, for inside the safe in its storeroom lay her last memories of Ambrose—his letters.

Jess gathered the reins and pulled them taut. "Come on, Luina. We're going to Carson City."

She started the horse at an easy lope. The air was fresh, cooler than before, and although a cover of clouds veiled the moon, enough starlight fell on the desert floor to light her way for miles.

She let Luina maintain the leisurely pace for more than an hour as she got lost in her musings. All of a sudden, Luina's head shot up.

Jess's eyes scanned the night for outlaws, for the cold blue gleam of moonlight on rifle barrels. Wary now, she listened closely. Luina's mane bristled, and she struggled against the reins in an attempt to run.

She was staring at the mountain.

Jess followed her gaze, watching for shadows of horses or men.

Whatever it was, it was not Cielos.

Jess's eyes fell on several low, dark forms twenty yards out, lunging toward them through the sage. Densely furred bodies and tails took shape, followed by long-fanged muzzles— wolves.

She stabbed her heels into Luina's sides, and the horse plunged forward and reared up. Jess grabbed her mane so as not to be tossed off. On the road before them, a wolf snapped its bared teeth. The moment Luina's hooves met the earth, a second wolf leapt up at them from the side.

Jess gasped as Luina stumbled sideways at the impact. With razor-sharp claws, the wolf raked at Luina's belly as it fell. Luina bolted—then stumbled.

In desperation, Jess whipped Luina with the reins. She ran, terrified of what might be waiting ahead.

A snarl erupted near Jess's right boot. Her eyes darted down to glimpse a flash of fangs. The wolf snarled and crouched low, a mad light shining in its eyes.

"No!" Jess shrieked.

The wolf lunged at them.

Luina swung away, her eyes rolling back, white.

Jess looked back. The wolf was keeping pace near Luina's left flank and three others were loping behind him. They were gaining speed.

From the right came a flash of gray; then there was a tug at Jess's skirt. Suddenly, a powerful weight was pulling at it, threatening to drag her from the saddle. The sharp sound of fabric tearing split the air.

The wolf fell, a patch of petticoat in its jaws.

Jess's eyes swept the night for a makeshift weapon— something she could swing at the beasts. Everything lurched as Luina kicked out behind; a wolf yelped, then tumbled away.

Two others were closing in, both attacking from the right. There was another tug at her skirt. More tearing. Then her boot was nearly wrenched from the stirrup.

"Please, Lord...," she stammered, glancing about in desperation. Two more wolves were following closely behind.

Luina leapt. Without thinking, Jess stood in the stirrups and went with the jump. A fallen tree passed beneath them. Luina hit the ground. The wolves weren't there.

Her throat tight, Jess glanced back. Immediately, she saw that the wolves' intentions had changed. No longer were they chasing for sport.

Now they were hunting.

Their heads hung low as the five raced after their prey with single-minded intent. Jess veered closer to the mountain, looking wildly for a place to go up.

There was a snap of jaws, then another. Horrible pain shredded the back of her leg. She felt the wet trickle of her own blood.

BOOM!

Jess cried out as she recognized the beautiful roar of Jake's gun. "Bennett!"

"Go right!" he shouted.

"I can't!" she screamed. "There's—"

BOOM! The wolf's cry was lost in the discharge of the gun.

Not waiting for a second command, Jess bent low and pulled right. Jake's revolver barked twice more.

Wolf carcasses tumbled to the ground. The pack was down to one.

Jess came around, heading straight for Jake. He stopped Cielos and took aim.

Several seemingly endless seconds passed. Jess glanced around frantically, looking for the last wolf. She couldn't see it.

"Why don't you shoot it?" she screamed.

"It's straight behind you!"

Unable to bear it any longer, Jess pulled Luina to a stop and ducked.

The wolf drew up alongside her. It leapt.

BOOM!

The echo of the last shot died away in the mountains. Beside her, the wolf lay dead. Jess was breathing almost as hard as Luina.

Jake holstered the gun and galloped toward them, his jaw rigid. Jess braced herself for his anger.

But he only pulled up alongside her, his dark eyes shining with concern as he leaned close to inspect her face, arms, and hands, then passed his hand over her shredded skirt. He looked at her. He was breathing hard, too.

"Did it get you?"

"Yes. My left leg. It feels like someone's holding a hot iron against it."

"We best get you back. Can you ride?"

She decided not to argue. "I can ride." She started to tremble.

Seeing this, Jake jumped down and handed her his reins. He dropped to one knee, pushed her skirt aside, and eased her foot out of the stirrup.

"There's not much left of your boot," he said.

"I'll just have to take the next one out of his hide." She laughed at her own wry humor until tears rolled down her cheeks. Jake looked up, his brow furrowed with worry.

"Are you all right?"

"I'm shaking, and I'm feeling a bit light-headed. How bad is it?"

Jake removed her boot as carefully as he could, but she hissed in pain when it rubbed against the wound.

"Three cuts. At least one of them will need stitches."

"That's nice."

Jake swiftly removed his bandana, twisting it to form a bandage. He wrapped it snugly around her lower leg and knotted it just above her calf muscle.

"Jess?"

"I don't feel very well." That was an understated version of the awful, sickly heat that was swimming through her veins.

Jake stood up. Without another word, he pulled her from her saddle and carried her toward Cielos. The reins fell from her limp hand.

"You still with me, Jess?"

"Uh-huh."

He looked grim.

In another moment, she was sitting in his saddle and trying hard to stay there.

"I have to get the reins. Can you hold on?"

She couldn't answer, but she took hold of the pommel. Everything around her swayed and pitched.

There was some movement, then Jake was behind her in the saddle. He pulled her against his warm body, and some of the swaying stilled. Her hat was lifted away. She felt his gloved hand touch her temple lightly, followed by his chin putting gentle pressure on her head.

She fought against the dizziness and pain. She was shaking, cold. "My own fault," she murmured.

Jake remained quiet.

"Please let me go to Carson City," she mumbled. "After my cuts heal."

Jake turned Cielos toward the ranch, leading Luina. After a long pause, he answered. "I want you to think about two things, Jess. One, I want you to hear—really hear—what your heart is saying about this. Two, I want you to listen to what your mind is telling you."

Jess considered his words as best she could. "My heart wants to be near them—near my memories of my family." And away from her confusing feelings for him. "It wants to go back."

"Mm-hmm. And your mind?"

Jess rubbed her forehead and sighed. "There are men between here and Carson City who might want me dead. And since the war continues on, and since townspeople have made up their minds to side with the North, I won't be able to help run a business there. I'd be burned out or run out of town. Or worse. And Edmund and Miriam could be hurt this time."

Again, Jake said nothing but left her to sort it out. She grasped a fistful of his shirt, partly to steady herself, partly entertaining the thought of strangling him. She slumped against him.

"How long, Bennett? How long before it will be safe for me to visit the cemetery?"

"I'd give it time for Tom to find those men, and to be sure folks have forgotten the Hales, so you won't be recognized. Next spring, maybe. You have a job until then. Longer, if you like."

Jess nodded, struggling to accept what she knew was right. "I'll stay, then. Until next spring."

"I'm glad to hear it, Jess."

"Bennett?" Jess thought her voice sounded sleepy.

"Hmm?"

"I'm glad you came after me. This time," she added.

Jake chuckled, his chest vibrating gently against her back.

Jess was afraid she was going to be sick. She was so hot... dizzy. She knew she was badly shaken. The wolves...they'd been so close. She could smell them on her. Could feel her blood oozing...

Darkness.

Chapter Eleven

The dark haze hadn't left her, though the surroundings had become vaguely familiar, and she realized they were nearing the ranch. All at once, Jake was no longer behind her, and then she was in his arms.

She heard the door swing open. "Hold her, my friend," Lone Wolf said. "I will move this closer to the fire." A heavy piece of furniture rumbled against the floor, and then she was lowered to the couch. "What has happened?"

"Wolves." Jake's voice was quiet, tense.

Jess heard him leave the room, and then she heard movements in the kitchen. The front door must have been open, because several pairs of boots sounded on the porch. One of the ranchmen called out, "Jake?"

"In here."

Jess tried to pull herself from the cloying haze. Jake was beside her again. Her skirts had been pushed back from her leg injuries. She heard Taggart's voice. "What's happened to her?"

A damp cloth was pressed to the back of her calf, and she grunted in pain.

"She's been bit," Jake said. "This cut is deep."

He and Lone Wolf spoke quietly as her calf first felt cold from being drenched, then burned so fiercely that her head cleared a little. "Bennett," she moaned, trying to pull away from their ministrations.

"It's whiskey, Jess. We're cleaning out the bites."

She pushed herself up on her elbows, then rolled over on her stomach to give them easier access to her wounds.

"Look at her dress." That was Reese. Jess became aware of the light of several kerosene lamps. She was facing Jake's desk.

Jake glanced up from where he knelt. "How are you doing, Jess?"

She grunted again while he poured more whiskey over her leg. "Famously."

"Wolf?" Taggart asked her.

Jess nodded, glancing up to his mop of orange hair and his blue eyes. "Five, but only one took me for mutton." She hissed when a dry cloth was pressed firmly on the wounds. Her sense of humor was fading fast.

Reese asked, "What did he look like?"

"Like a Yankee in a fur coat."

"As bad as that, Jess?" Jess didn't see Jake's smile, but she heard it in his voice.

She smiled with him. "Well, worse than some, I suppose." He released her leg, then wrapped a clean towel around it. She could feel fresh blood seeping into the cloth.

"I'll be right back," Jake assured her.

Jess glanced at the stairs. Jake took them two at time, then disappeared into the middle room upstairs. He emerged carrying a wooden box, which he set on the table when he came downstairs. Jess leaned up on both elbows, watching as he lifted off the lid and brought out scissors, needle, and thread.

Jess groaned and dropped her forehead to the arm of the sofa. When she lifted her face again, Taggart was staring into it. Without a word, he dragged Jake's big chair over and settled himself down beside her, taking her slender hand in his rough, brawny one and holding it tight. Jake tied a snug knot in the thread.

His eyes met Jess's. "This will hurt some," he warned her.

Jess faced away from him again, clenching her jaw with resolution. "Just get it over with, please."

Other boots pounded on the porch, then more ranchmen joined the group. Jess felt like a spectacle. *My fault*, she reminded herself. *My own fault.*

Lone Wolf looked down at her. "Should I get Red Deer?"

"Is she sleeping?"

"Yes."

"Then let her sleep."

Jake began the dreaded process. Jess was careful to let her injured leg lie still while he stitched it, but the other shook almost enough to break the arm of the sofa. When she started to perspire, Jake paused to let her catch her breath. She looked around to notice that Diaz and Doyle had joined the crowd of spectators.

"Doesn't anybody sleep?" she growled. Then she remembered to ask Diaz about Luina.

Jake had started stitching again.

"She is fine," Diaz assured her. "Mostly scratches like yours. The wounds are shallow. They will heal."

Finally, Jake finished. Jess had counted seven stitches— seven in, seven tugs, seven out. After he had knotted and snipped the thread, relief flooded her, followed all too quickly by the urge to expel her supper.

Jess tore her hand away from Taggart's and struggled to her feet, surprising her onlookers. She cried out when her weight came down on her foot, but it was unavoidable. She pushed past the helping hands and bolted out the door.

Her face felt flushed, damp with sweat. The outhouse was in view.

She wasn't going to make it.

She flung herself around the back corner of the house, fell to her good knee behind a clump of sage, and rapidly cleared her stomach.

To her chagrin, her audience had followed her.

That unpleasant fact was made considerably worse by their loud cheers, followed by their idiotic evaluation of her disgorging prowess.

"Is that all you got? Bring it up from the toes, girlie!"

"My granny said it helps if ye swaller tobacco juice," someone supplied.

"Nope. Flies. Dunk 'em in honey and swallow 'em wings and all."

Jess heaved again. When she could catch her breath, she sat up, fuming. A latecomer handed her a dipper of water. She rinsed out her mouth and then drank, forced to listen to the ribbing the men gave her. When she finally looked up at all the grinning, remorseless faces, she shot them a glare that said she would get even.

"All right, everyone," Jake said above her, "let's get some sleep." He grasped her arms from behind and lifted her to her feet.

The crowd broke up, still chuckling.

❧⚜☙

When Jess made her way downstairs the next morning, Red Deer told her that Jake had left the ranch.

"Oh? Where did he go?" Jess asked, surprised at the disappointment she felt.

Red Deer hung a pot of water over the fire, then carefully stretched her back. She was five months along now. "He went to sell cows from the roundup. He left this for you."

With a friendly smile, Red Deer took down a letter from the mantel and handed it to her. Then she gathered up a towel that had been hung to dry and folded it as she waddled off toward the kitchen.

Jess opened the brief note, pleased that Jake had chosen to

tell her of his plans in a personal way and hadn't just left a verbal message for someone to pass on.

The writing on the page was straightforward and bold, just like its author.

Jess,

I'll be gone a few days driving the first group of cattle to a settlement north of here. Lone Wolf is in charge until I get back. If you need anything, ask him or Doyle or Diaz.

Be good.

Jake

Reluctant to face the men after her humiliation the night before, Jess wandered about for a time, smoothing this, straightening that, and growing accustomed to the mild stinging in her leg. She had woken to find that, regrettably, little was left of her favorite yellow dress, so she had dressed in the plainer yellow instead, still buckling on the lovely, braided leather belt. Jess realized she was hiding indoors. That was the coward's way. With Two Hands at her side, she left the house to pay Luina a visit.

The mare was worse off than she had thought. Jess felt absolutely low when she entered her stall to see so many dark scratches against her fair palomino hide. Jess pulled some carrot sticks from her pocket and fed them to her. Luina didn't seem put out with her; she nibbled the carrots contentedly. Jess stroked her neck and withers, her guilt clawing deep when she saw that blood was seeping through the bandage on one of her hind legs.

"I'm sorry, girl. I surely didn't mean for you to get hurt." Two Hands entered the stall and petted Luina's nose. He looked up at Jess expectantly, and she handed him a few of the carrot sticks. He accepted them gratefully and fed them to the mare.

Thinking about the previous night, Jess decided a prayer was in order. *I suppose I haven't talked to You in some time, Lord, but I want to thank You for saving me from the wolves last night, and for helping Bennett shoot straight.* Jess smoothed a hand over Luina's back. *I don't know why You keep bringing me back here— well, in truth, I love it here, but it's impossible for me to do ranch work for the rest of my life, isn't it?* She sighed. *Lord, I want to be near where my family is buried, but it seems that You want me to stay here for now. So I'll stay. Though sometimes, I wish You would tell me why You want me here. I feel like a horse that's running with blinders on, but I suppose that's what faith is. So I'll keep running and, as much as I can, trust that You're the one holding the reins.*

When Jess looked up, Two Hands was near the entrance, watching the goings-on in the ranch yard while he waited for her. Mindful of her stitches, Jess walked slowly toward him. She squeezed the hand he placed into hers, then went to see where she could be of use.

~◌⦂⫸⫷◌~

Jess was heading toward the cookhouse to lend Ho Chen a hand when she noticed Red Deer preparing to wash the men's clothes again. She immediately changed directions, sending Two Hands to the cookhouse in her place. She lifted a bucket and began to fill one of the cauldrons. "Shouldn't you be doing lighter chores, Red Deer?"

Red Deer smiled softly, an empty bucket in her hand. "A woman once told me that if an expecting mother will not work, then she will give birth to a child who is idle."

They shared a grin. "Who said that?"

Red Deer's smile faltered. She continued filling the cauldron. "My white woman friend."

195

The way she said it told Jess that she did not wish to say anything more about it.

Several hours later, Jess was scrubbing trousers on the washboard. The soap burned her hands, and the cuts above her ankle stung, but she ignored them and kept working to relieve Red Deer of as much of the load as possible. Despite Red Deer's assurances, Jess could tell that her friend was tired. She also knew many women experienced the same increased fatigue during pregnancy. When her mother had been expecting Emma, she had slept constantly.

"Afternoon, Jess," sang out one of the passing cattlemen who had witnessed her debasement behind the house the night before. "You done any spewin' in the sage this morning?"

She scowled at him.

Another one found a reason to come over. He clapped a hand on her shoulder. "You don't have nothin' to be ashamed of, Jess. In fact, you can be proud. Why, before last night, none of us would have thought there was a woman what could retch like a mule." His eyes glinting with laughter, he started to walk away, then turned around to add, "You know, your face is gettin' red. You should put your hat on."

Jess wanted to fling a comment after him that he knew perfectly well why her face was red, but she didn't dare draw any more attention to herself. The teasing was harmless, she knew, but she only wished the skunks weren't enjoying it so much.

One by one, the others paused in their tasks to do a bit of friendly needling. Finally, Taggart made his way over. Anticipating the sort of comment he was going to make, she bent determinedly over the tub, scrubbing a pair of britches with nearly enough vigor to shred them.

"I can't tell ye how sorry I am, Jess."

She glanced up in surprise. "You're sorry?"

When his blue eyes glimmered, she knew she would regret asking. "Aye. We're all still tendin' the cows today. By the way ye were clasping the ground last eve, I thought ye'd found gold, for sure, and the lot of us could pay someone else to work." At her thankless glower, he restrained his mirth, but he still had to wipe tears from his eyes. He nodded toward the tub with a hearty compliment. "You're doin' a fine job with the britches. A fine job."

As he ambled off, her eyes hurled invisible darts at his back. She grabbed up the trousers, dashed the soap over them, and began to scrub again.

Just then, a clever grin spread over her face.

The next morning brought with it a fresh breeze, and Jess hummed merrily as she hung up the last of the clean, damp clothing and called cheery greetings to each one of the cattlemen as they passed by. Sheepish about their ruthless teasing the day before, they returned her greetings with extreme politeness, calling her "ma'am" or offering to lend a hand, should she have need of it. She responded with an outpouring of gratitude and assurances that, yes, she certainly would prevail upon their kindness, should she have a need.

The men went away, glancing at one another anxiously.

When evening came and Jess was just as charming as she had been all day, they began to relax, glad that she apparently had forgiven them. She overheard someone remind the others that they best not tease her again to the extent they had the day before. "After all, good humor does have its limits," he said.

While they ate dinner in the cookhouse, Jess remained out

behind the bunkhouse, humming again as she took down the wind-dried shirts, union suits, and pants. The sun was setting when she returned the neatly folded clothes to the men with a smile as pure as golden honey.

Jake returned at sunrise, then rode out again with twenty men. Instead of tending the cattle, they headed east to search for signs of wild mustangs, which had been seen, according to reports, near Pyramid Lake, thirty miles away. Ho Chen went along to cook the meals, following the group in the chuck wagon. Having to care for her stitches, Jess had stayed behind to clean out the stable.

When they finally dismounted at noon, Jake noticed several of the men look at one another strangely. As they walked around, their conversations grew stilted. Every one of them seemed to have an odd hitch in his step. Bemused, Jake accepted a mug of coffee from Ho Chen and leaned against the chuck wagon to observe them more closely. The men were silent now, shifting oddly in their drawers. A few reached around to check things, then all at once they exchanged horrified looks.

Jake frowned. "What's got you boys squirming in your seats?"

The men looked at him, reluctant to answer. One named Will slowly hitched forward. "I think Miss Jess done paid us back, is all."

Jake hadn't expected that. "Paid you back? For what?"

"For teasin' her about vomitin', I reckon."

Jake glanced at Ho Chen. The small man bent studiously over his cooking, seeming not to notice. "What did she do?"

Will sighed. "I think she done snipped the buttons out o' the seats of our johns."

Jake threw back his head and laughed in a way he hadn't laughed in years. He wiped his eyes as his mirth gradually subsided, and when he managed to speak again, he was able to use his tone of authority.

"I suggest you boys go apologize to the lady, then get yourselves put back together. You'll miss dinner, but I'm sure Ho Chen will keep it for your supper."

With red faces all around, they mumbled their agreement, then made their ways into their saddles with slow, precise movements.

Jake rested an arm on a wagon wheel while he watched his men ride for home. Finally, he allowed another smile to cross his face.

Ho Chen came up beside him, coffeepot in hand. "You are not unhappy with Miss Jessie?"

Jake shook his head, his smile widening. "I don't know how we ever got along without her."

❦

Jess had been laying fresh straw in the stable, and she came outside to watch the men return. She leaned on a rake as the group of humbled men reined in their horses nearby. Hats came off all around.

Jess smiled broadly at them. "What can I do for you gentlemen?"

Again, Will spoke for them. "If'n you could, Miss Jess, we'd like you to forgive us for behavin' like ill-mannered hogs, and, if it weren't too much bother, ma'am, we'd like to ask you to sew our buttons back on."

Jess leaned away from the rake and stretched. "I don't think so. Oh, I forgive you, of course, but don't you suppose you'd be more inclined to mind your manners if you sewed the buttons on yourselves?"

She gazed at them amid murmurs of "Yes, ma'am," then she bent again to sweep away the straw. "I left needles and thread for all of you in the bunkhouse," she called out. "Good day, gentlemen."

Seeing that they'd been dismissed, they reluctantly turned their horses away. The men loosed them in a corral, then shuffled to the bunkhouse.

It was nearly half an hour later when they began to trickle out. They mounted their horses and rode past her, tipping hats respectfully and mumbling appreciative words for her good kindness in laying out the needles and thread.

Jess smiled at each of them as he went by, feeling, of all things, a sense of ease and belonging that she hadn't yet felt at the ranch—hadn't felt, perhaps, since she had left Kentucky. The ranchmen had come to accept her, and she had found a place for herself. Even her rolling accent had smoothed out into the comfortable tones they used, as though it had always been that way. She swept her rake through the pile of straw, feeling wholly contented.

❧⊰⦀⊱❧

Hours later, when Jess shut herself in her room for the night, she discovered that someone had left on her bed a large bundle wrapped in brown paper, along with a small leather pouch that jingled when she picked it up. Her heart fluttered with delight. Jake had brought her something from town.

As eager as a child with a present, she slipped off the string that bound the paper wrapping and unfolded it in loud crinkles, startling the rust-colored cat, which had made a kingly bed of her pillow. Inside the paper was a new supply of yellow calico cloth—it was exactly the same pattern as that of the dress she'd liked, and which the wolves had left in tatters. Jess caressed the cotton fabric as reverently as if it were satin, her fingers finding curious bumps within its folds that she quickly found to be buttons, needles, and thread, and yards upon yards of white, machined lace.

Touched that Jake had wanted to replace the gown, Jess shifted her gaze to the leather drawstring pouch. Slipping it open, she found exactly forty dollars in coins. Her joyous laughter filled the room. It was her first month's wages for working as a ranch hand.

Chapter Twelve

Jake took a sip from his coffee mug. "I'll be going after breakfast. I won't be back until the middle of next month."

Jess sat across the table from him, the cookhouse empty now except for the two of them and Ho Chen, who was drying clean plates in the kitchen.

She looked up from her toast, feeling the same disappointment as when she'd woken to find him gone the week before. "Going to search for the mustangs again?"

"Not this time. I have to deliver the rest of the cows we brought in to Virginia City, Gold Hill, and Carson City. I'll be taking several of the men and Ho Chen, and, yes, I'll talk to Tom Rawlins to find out if he's learned anything more."

Her mind started racing. "Surely, Bennett, if I ride along, no one will recognize—"

He was already shaking his head. "No, Jess."

Jess sighed in frustration, but she let the matter be. She knew he was right. She had promised to stay at the ranch, and she intended to keep her word. She would just need to keep her mind off going back until spring.

That thought led to a request. "I'd like to have a look through the middle bedroom in the house. I saw a loom and yarns in there, and I'd like to use them, if no one else needs them."

"That's fine." The corners of his eyes crinkled. "Just when did you have a chance to see what's in that room?"

Jess shrugged and sipped her tea. "The other day, when I went in to find thread and needles for—" She broke herself off.

He was teasing her about the men's union suits. "Bennett!" She laughed and pointed a slender finger at him. "They deserved what I did, and you know it!"

"They deserved it," Jake agreed, then set down his mug. He pushed himself to his feet. "I'd like to take out those stitches, if you could spare a few minutes."

Jess lowered her eyes to her own mug. She wasn't sure how she'd fare being so close to him again. First, her wrists, then, the stitches, and now this. For some reason, it was just too... intimate.

"I can take them out, Bennett, or Red Deer can help me. You don't need to trouble yourself."

"I'd like to see to it personally, if it's all the same. I want to know you've healed well before I leave."

Jess had nothing to say to that. "All right, then."

Jake came around to her side of the table as she stood up. The cookhouse door was propped open to let the breeze in, and he respectfully paused inside it to let her go ahead of him.

Outside, Jess breathed in the warmth of the morning. With midday would come heat, but right now was heaven. As they walked, orange-breasted swallows swooped and darted through the air, their split tails elegant, their performance dazzling as they gobbled bugs and played in the sunshine.

Seeing the direction of her gaze, Jake stopped and pointed to the peak of the house above her bedroom window. "Those two are building a nest."

Jess shaded her eyes. The pair landed, clinging to the side of the house high under the eaves. They carefully pressed mud from their beaks to the nest they had started, then cartwheeled off toward the creek, dropping from view behind its bank.

"They're beautiful." Jess smiled up at him, glad to have shared the sight with him. Her smile widened when a small butterfly flitted past. It took a meandering path to a nodding stem of gray-green sage, where it alighted to rest its wings. Jess had adored butterflies ever since Ambrose had given her the nickname when she was a girl—his little butterfly.

Jake tipped his hat toward the house, and they continued on.

On the porch, he pushed open the door for her, letting her go ahead of him once again. He used a log from the woodpile to prop the door wide open, and Jess went upstairs to get the sewing box. Downstairs once more, she set the box on the table, perspiration dotting her brow.

"Summer's on its way," she commented, taking a seat in Jake's leather chair.

Jake pulled the scissors from the box, along with a pin to slip under the stitches to ease them out. He glanced up at her. "If it gets too warm, you can open the upstairs windows and the door. That cools the house pretty well."

"I will." When Jake knelt down beside her, Jess pulled off the boot she'd repaired and drew up her injured calf.

Jake took off his hat and set it on the table. With gentle fingers, he pressed around the stitches to check whether the wounds had healed. Jess lifted her gaze from the stitches to his thick brown hair, which gleamed in the morning light. He smelled pleasantly of the outdoors.

"The cuts are healing well, Jess, but it'll sting some when I pull the threads out."

She resisted the urge to finger his hair. "I'll be fine. Go ahead and take them out."

Jake expertly snipped the first thread with the scissors, then used the pin to work the thread out. When it was free, the skin where it had been bled a little. He pulled out a clean handkerchief and dabbed the dots of red to dry them. Then he moved on to the next thread.

Seven in, seven out, Jess reminded herself. Each one pulled a little and burned slightly, but Jess knew that Jake was being as gentle as he could.

"Though the men teased you," he said, glancing at her, "they admired you for taking the stitches without a fuss. They're a hardy lot," he went on, "and they accept being thrown, dragged, and kicked as part of a day's work, but they also see women as different."

"I've heard some of them talking about women who are ranchers. Those women must be as hardy as anybody."

"That they are," he agreed. Then, "I just thought you should know that the men respect that, and they respect you."

"And you?" The question was out before she knew it.

Jake glanced up at her, his voice as smooth as a caress. "I feel no different." He continued plying the pin.

Jess gazed around the room, feeling warm with the realization that she had begun to care for him. She cared, but she didn't want to. Caring led to love, and, sooner or later, love was crushed by loss. She had to see him as nothing more than a good friend. She had to. Her heart couldn't bear any more.

There was a metallic snip, and a few inches of thread dropped to the floor. Jess sighed. He was nearly done.

"You all right?"

"I'm fine."

He continued on.

There was something Jess had wanted to tell him for weeks. She felt comfortable enough to do so now. Taking a deep breath, she began, "I'm sorry I was angry at you for so long, Bennett. Angry because of the fire, because of...everything. Blaming you was unfair, but I couldn't see that then."

Jake rested his arm on his knee and looked at her again. "You had just lost someone, Jess. In fact, you'd just lost everyone. A man doesn't hold something like that against a person when she's hurting," he assured her. He bent down again to resume his task.

Jess considered his wide shoulders, her slender ankle cradled in his big hand. There was one more thing.

She found she had to clear her throat. "I'm glad you were the one who buried my family."

Jake paused without looking up, then continued tugging out the stitches.

❧❦❧

In Jake's absence, Jess kept busy in the cookhouse and garden, and the days carried her into June. Her new dress was finished. Due to the rising temperatures, she wore only one thin petticoat beneath it, relieved to be free of the others.

One Thursday, around mid-morning, Jess and Red Deer finished the breakfast dishes and then began a leisurely walk to Red Deer's village. They were going to visit the Paiute women and to finally see Jess's horses, which Jake had saved from the fire.

Red Deer's pregnancy had begun to trouble Jess. At six months along, she was far more tired than she should be, and although Jess had taken over all of the heavy chores, she could see that Red Deer's strength wasn't what it had been.

When she questioned her about her fatigue, Red Deer only smiled. "It is the same for many who are with child." She lifted a hand. "The hot days. Sharing cold winter nights with one's husband brings about hot summer days with his child."

Surprised by her suggestive comment, Jess grinned back at her. "I suppose that's so." When Red Deer's expression changed, Jess's smile began to fade.

"I am also not resting well," she admitted, "for my dreams have not been good."

Jess looked aside at her as they walked. "What kind of dreams?"

"I dream that I have my son. He is strong and handsome like my husband, and Two Hands becomes his dear brother. Then, as I look at my son, it is as if he goes away from me, and he and I cannot be together again." She rested a hand on her rounded middle. "It makes me very sad. When I speak of it to my husband, he says it is because of the death that came to the Shoshoni that I dream this."

"The Shoshoni?" Jess remembered Red Deer mentioning them that first day she had helped her in the cookhouse.

"Yes. Not long before you came here, our neighbors, the Shoshoni, were at their winter camp with their families in mountains north of the Great Salt Lake. The Shoshoni were peaceful, but they took a few cows from the settlers so their families would not starve. Soldiers attacked them for this, and many Shoshoni were killed. Husbands were killed, and mothers and children were taken away from one another." Grimacing, she used a small cloth she carried to wipe the sweat from her face and neck.

Jess stared past her, feeling sick. Jake's friend Captain Rawlins at Fort Churchill was a Federal soldier, but he was also kind to have searched for Ambrose for her. Whoever ordered the massacre of the Shoshoni wore the same uniform, but he was inhuman to have done such a thing. "Do you think Lone Wolf is right about the dreams?" Jess asked. She wasn't sure *she* would sleep well, knowing what had happened.

Red Deer lifted a shoulder. "He may be."

Jess studied her friend quietly. The knowledge that more bad times were coming for her people shone in her young eyes, yet her face remained as peaceful as always.

Softly, Jess asked, "How do you survive it, Red Deer?"

Red Deer walked a few paces, thoughtful. "When we lose someone dear to us, it is Paiute tradition to say, 'Weep not for your dead, but sing and be joyful, for the soul is happy in the

Spirit-Land.' We do weep, because it gives us relief to do so, but we also have hope. The kind missionary who taught my dear sister and me to speak your language also taught us to read. Then I read in the Bible that the Almighty Father turns bad into good for His children."

Jess nodded. Jake had once reminded her of the same passage in Romans.

Red Deer said, "I have seen this happen many times, Jessica. The loss of my sister was bad. Very bad. The good that has come is that Two Hands is safer now, and he is a joy to me and to the Paiutes here. And he is happy again. This is the good I have seen." A breeze lifted her hair, and she smoothed it behind her ears with her hands. "Jesus the Savior forgives the wrongs we do and promises life in the Spirit-Land after we die—a life of only good, where we will be with Him, where there will be no more sadness. Sometimes we can see the good that follows bad, sometimes not. But either way, we know that what comes is God's will, and we have faith that, one day, there will be only good. This is how we survive."

For a long while, they walked along the creek, now more of a brook after months without rain. Jess recalled pastors in church saying much the same about the will of the Lord. She knew it was true. She also knew that when the Lord, in His wisdom, had seen fit to take her family, she'd been angry with Him, as well as with Jake. On the night of the wolf attack, she had told God she was sorry for her anger toward Jake. Now she silently apologized for her anger toward Him, as well.

All of it had been the Lord's will—even the wolf attack. He had used it to keep her away from Carson City, perhaps even to keep her here, but she couldn't be certain. She felt as though she was wearing blinders again, but it didn't trouble her as it had before. Evidently, the Lord was teaching her to trust Him.

Red Deer brought Jess out of her reverie and back to the

present as she pointed to the creek. Along the banks, twenty or more Paiute children were kneeling contentedly in the mud, their hands busy. "Come see what the children are making, Jessica."

The children turned bright eyes toward them, and Jess recognized most of them from the days they had spent together planting the garden. Several children ran to her and spoke excitedly in a mixture of their language and hers, holding out their palms to show her the clumps of mud they had pressed and carved.

Jess's laughter at their excitement faded as amazement dawned. All around her, children were showing her the animals they had formed—animals so lifelike that they could have been the achievements of gifted sculptors. The children smiled at one another as Jess marveled at their precisely wrought creatures. There was a plump quail with each of its feathers etched in and a curving plume atop its head. A tiny, long-tailed deer mouse sat huddled with big round ears. She saw ground squirrels, a rabbit, two coyotes—one sitting, one lying—ponies, a cow, and other creatures. Jess gazed at each of the children, praising his or her carving with her eyes. She had never seen anything like this before, especially made by ones so young.

Red Deer spoke to them, undoubtedly complimenting their skills. Then the children took off toward a large group of wigwams in the distance—large, dome-shaped dwellings made of sticks—eager to show their masterpieces to more admiring eyes.

"They do not have many toys to play with," Red Deer explained, "so they make these carvings."

"The animals look so real."

"The older ones teach the younger. Sometimes, they play that the boys are hunters who bring home their kill to their young wives."

Red Deer began walking again, but she faltered, pressing a hand to her side.

Jess noticed. "Perhaps we should rest a little." To ease her friend's mind, she added, "My feet are getting hot. I'd love to dangle them in the creek."

Red Deer shook her head and laughed. "No, if I sit, I may not rise again." Jess smiled with her, but the unease she had felt earlier returned. Still, Red Deer walked on without complaint, and Jess couldn't help but respect her fortitude.

In the village, many of the women who had become Jess's friends came out to join her and Red Deer the moment they saw them. Others stayed put and waved from where they were tending small fires and iron pots; others were weaving hats or fleshing hides. The women invited Jess to see their homes and the baskets and tools they had crafted, and as she made her rounds, the morning swept by. When Jess and Red Deer continued on, they passed near a wrinkled, gray-haired man sitting with several children at his feet. He was teaching them, or perhaps telling them stories, while he repaired the broken strands of a net. When he saw Jess and Red Deer, the man's expression turned speculative, but not unfriendly.

"They all seem like one family," Jess observed.

"Our children are taught to love all people, no matter the color of their skin or their appearance."

Jess thought Red Deer seemed happier after spending time with the Paiutes. She was sure of it when Red Deer continued, "Our people do not argue often, Jessica. They talk together and listen until all agree. If a matter must be settled, we consider it for five days before we decide, so that it will be done in wisdom and not in haste. Everyone has a purpose and a place, and everyone matters." She indicated the elderly man. "The old teach the young and, in turn, are respected and loved. Many white people think we should be more like they. Some Paiutes feel they should be more like we are."

Jess thought of the ongoing battles between the Indians and the whites. "What of the settlers?"

"We teach our sons and daughters to be peaceful toward the white settlers, even when they are unkind, and we try to forgive. We love peace, Jessica; we do not love war. When white men cut down our pinyon pine trees, we find others, sometimes far away, but we will not let bad men hurt us or our children. Sometimes, we must fight." Her face softened. "We call people who are good 'father' or 'mother.' Our friends, we call 'brother' or 'sister,' and we love them as if they were our mothers' children. All this we teach our young. This makes our people strong. When I read the words of Jesus, I am glad to see that in these ways, we do as He would have us do."

Jess smiled in understanding. In the distance, several horses were grazing near the creek with two older boys watching over them. As the horses moved about, Jess's eyes fell on her father's two shiny blacks, and then her own Appaloosa, Meg.

She stopped. "They're here."

Red Deer looked at her curiously. "Yes, they are."

Jess didn't know how to explain. "I have the jewelry from my mother, but these...they're alive. Bennett told me they had survived, but seeing them..." She shook her head. "They're here. Something living survived."

Red Deer called to the boys. At her request, they led the three horses over. The animals came, their eyes bright, their manes dancing with their gaits. The blacks sniffed her and allowed themselves to be petted but soon rejoined the herd.

Meg, however, pricked up her ears when she saw Jess, and she trotted over to her like an old friend. Jess rubbed her nose, then leaned against her and ran both hands along her neck. At that, the boys grinned.

"It's wonderful to see them again," Jess told Red Deer, blinking away her tears. "Do you know if their burns are healed?"

When Red Deer spoke to the boys, the oldest passed his hand soothingly over Meg's hide and pointed to the places where bits of burning wood had fallen. There was some mild scarring, but the injuries had healed well.

Red Deer turned to Jess. "He asks if you wish to take your horses now."

Jess looked to where her father's horses mingled among the Indian ponies. As she watched, one of them dropped down on its knees and began rolling contentedly in the dust.

"I'll keep the blacks here for now. They've been carriage horses, for the most part. Bennett will have to retrain them to work the cattle when he has time. But I will take Meg with me—I can keep her in Bennett's stable."

Red Deer relayed Jess's answer to the boy, and he ran to get a halter. When he had secured it, Jess and Red Deer left, Meg's chestnut nose between them.

"Why do you call him 'Bennett'?" Red Deer asked. "The men at the ranch call him Jake."

"I don't know. He's just Bennett to me. Anything else would be too...familiar."

"Isn't he your friend?"

Jess blinked, a little startled. There wasn't a simple answer to that. Rather than answer, she made an inquiry of her own. "Diaz once told me that Bennett is...different...that he's changed since I've been here."

"It is true. He is different."

"In what way?"

"He talks more. He smiles, and he laughs. He was not this way before you came."

Jess tried to decide how she felt about that.

All at once, Red Deer sucked in her breath and grasped her stomach tightly. Jess eyed her with alarm, but after a moment, Red Deer reassured her. "He is a vigorous one, my son."

Jess was glad for the distraction from her thoughts. "Why don't you stay at the village and rest?" she suggested. "Most of the chores are done, and I can cook dinner for the men."

"I think I will stay here, Jessica. I am glad you came to my village today."

After they parted, Jess returned to the ranch. She stabled Meg, then hurried to the cookhouse to start dinner. Her mind was full from their talk about Jake, and her heart was troubled about Red Deer, yet as she cast a glance skyward, she trusted that the Lord was aware of it, and that He was somewhere looking down at His people in love.

Chapter Thirteen

On the eighteenth of June, late in the afternoon, Jake and the cattlemen rode into the ranch, more than three weeks after they'd left. At the corrals, the ranch hands stepped down from their haggard horses and began to unsaddle them while Ho Chen pushed on toward the cookhouse to unload. Jake, thinking to rid himself of the trail dust before he saw Jess, nudged Cielos toward the creek.

He reined in near the bank, his eyes passing over the fields of wild and planted grains, their tips now as high as the underbelly of a pony. A light breeze stirred them, making a pleasant, rustling sound. Apparently, Jess was holding her own, despite the prolonged lack of rain.

He saw her kneeling in the middle of the garden, her back to him. Her hat shaded her face, and her thick braid of hair dangled over her right shoulder as she worked.

Jake dismounted and leaned an arm on the saddle. The grain fields, the garden, and even the birds that chased one another overhead seemed to exist because of her. Jess had given new life to the ranch—and to him, as well. The thought of her staying with him always flowed into his mind as easily as summer follows spring.

While Cielos helped himself to a drink, Jake washed his face and arms.

◈

Kneeling among the carrots, Jess paused to rub away the soil clinging to her gloves, then continued her task of pulling weeds. Oddly enough, weeding was a chore she enjoyed. It always relaxed her.

The morning's calm had vanished rapidly just moments ago, when she looked up and saw the cattlemen returning. Several men had come into the yard, but her eyes found only Jake. Since he had been gone for nearly a month, she knew he must be worn out from the trail drive, yet he rode tall, as if he had stepped into the saddle only that morning. He showed nothing but ease in his broad shoulders and contentment in his handsome face. Unable to bear the stirring of emotions caused by his presence, she turned away from him and resumed weeding with a vengeance.

Even so, her eyes strayed to him as he stopped at the creek. He was a sight—the incomparable man beside his magnificent steed. Hadn't she dreamed of this exact scene a thousand nights when she was a girl? But now it was all wrong. After witnessing the cruel quickness of death, she would never allow love to be more than a dream.

She heard him come up behind her, but she pretended not to hear.

He seemed to be in no hurry. Perhaps he was seeing how well everything had grown. Perhaps he regretted wasting good money on fabric for the dress she was now wearing as she knelt in the dirt. Perhaps—

"Hello, Jess."

Jess hesitated. He had done nothing to invite rudeness, so she answered, "Hello, Bennett."

He was quiet for a minute. She continued uprooting the weeds.

"The garden is coming along, I see."

"A few other women and I water it at night, now. It gives the roots time to draw up the water before the sun bakes it from the ground." She sat back on her heels with a sigh and rested her spade on her knee. "Another month of this sun and the grain will be good for lining the floor of the stalls and nothing more."

"The cattle sold well, and we're contracted to deliver more in the months ahead, so we'll have the money to buy plenty for winter."

When he hesitated, Jess searched his face. "You spoke to Tom Rawlins," she said.

"Yes. He hasn't found them, and two more fires have been reported since the one at Lake's Crossing, north of there. Occasionally, they've stolen horses or a cow or two when they've needed them."

"They're coming in this direction."

"Yes, but I don't want you to worry. The soldiers will find them."

"What if the soldiers don't find them and those men show up here?"

"Things wouldn't go well for them," Jake said, "I can tell you that. The boys have been itching for a fight."

"Those men are going to come here. You know that, don't you?"

"Why would they, Jess? Four months have gone by since the fire. If they were going to come after us, they would have already. They haven't."

Jess knew he was right about that. Like a band of guerrillas, they were moving about and striking where they could. "That may be, but still…I just know we haven't seen the last of them."

"If they come, we'll be ready."

Jess realized that this was what she needed to hear. Jake was aware, so she let the matter be.

Jake lifted his gaze to the Paiute woman who was coming to help Jess. "Red Deer isn't helping?"

"I wouldn't let her. Is Ho Chen with you?"

"He's here."

Jess pushed back her hair. "Good. I'd like to be free to help with the horses in the mornings—feeding them and sweeping out their stalls."

"Why? The men can see to that."

Jess let her eyes roam the desert horizon, the distant Sierras, the ranch. In one of the corrals, mares were trotting about, their new fillies and colts frolicking beside them. "You know why, Bennett."

"Yes, I suppose I do." He indicated the new dress she wore. "You have a fine hand at sewing. I'm glad I found the same fabric. You seemed to like it well enough."

"I'm glad for it, Bennett. I should have told you that sooner." She recalled Meg and the two blacks he'd brought back for her after the fire. "Red Deer took me to see my horses. I put Meg in your stable, but I think the carriage horses will need to be retrained if they're to be of any use here."

"Now that summer's starting, I'll have time to work on that, and you'll be able to help with the horses in the mornings. But first, I have a favor to ask you."

Jess wiped her forehead with her sleeve. "What's the favor?"

"I'd like you to have a look at the ranch books, if you would. Seems a shame to have someone here with a mind for numbers," he said lightly, "and not make use of her talents."

Jess found herself smiling at the warm teasing in his voice. With effort, she tore her eyes away from his. "What about the garden? Manure needs to be turned in the soil, or it will dry out completely."

"I'll get a couple of the men to work on it. Between the spring and fall roundups, there's less work to be done, so they expect to do odd jobs." He gestured toward the house. "The books and receipts and such are on my desk. Help yourself to paper, pencils—anything you need."

The next morning, Jess enjoyed breakfast with the men, then returned to the house to start her work with the books. By mid-morning, the room was too hot to leave the door closed, so she propped it open with a log from the woodpile. The intermittent breeze was delightful.

It was nearly noon when Jake made an appearance. His clothes were covered in dust. Jess glanced up, then smiled as she returned her gaze to the pages in her hand. He had been working with her father's horses, temperamental from months of freedom. "The carriage horses giving you pains for your efforts?"

Jake grinned. "Not nearly as much as the ground is."

Jess's smile widened.

Jake nodded to the piles of paperwork. "Making any sense of that?"

"Some." Then, "I've been thinking, Bennett."

Jake leaned against the wall beside the desk and folded his brawny arms comfortably across his chest. His eyes were on her.

"I think you should use some of your income from this trip to invest in more horses. In fact, I think you should consider doubling your horse count in the coming year." She paused to gauge his reaction.

"I'm listening."

Jess leaned back in her chair, glad to be able to share what she had envisioned. "I've heard what the men have said about a government land survey of this region and about a redivision of established land claims throughout Honey Lake Valley. For you, that means you could file a preemptive claim with the land office to try to retain what's yours, or you could wait to see how the new boundaries will fall and take the matter to court, if portions of your land go up for sale."

Jake narrowed his eyes pensively, nodding for her to go on.

"Either way, with the growing number of cattle ranches in the region, and with immigrants bringing their own herds west, the demand for each rancher's cattle will almost certainly decline. What's more, if there is a rush of settlers to the region, open land for grazing will be hard to come by. To boost your profits, you might consider shifting your focus to raising horses to sell rather than cattle, something only a few ranchers have begun to do, according to your men."

She leaned forward in her chair as she locked eyes with him. "Before I left Carson City, I heard speculation that when the transcontinental railroad comes over the Sierras, it'll pass within scant miles of here, which will give you access to a vast, maybe even incalculable, market. Horses back East are being used up in the war, even those meant for farming. People will need them. In fact, as soon as the railroad nears completion, I think you should travel east before anyone else does and negotiate there with buyers. You're a good businessman, Bennett, and if the numbers you've sold are a means of measurement, people like to do business with you. Until the horses bring an income, you can continue to sell cattle. Whether or not the war ends soon, you'll be in business until you decide to hang up your spurs. You could even get by with less land, should it come to that. If you were to bring in more horses this year, you'll still have sufficient funds for winter provisions. Your profits next year are certain to pay for another large stable and your choice of men."

His gaze was inscrutable. "Anything else?"

"Actually, yes. Should the weather cooperate, you'll grow enough hay and grains to feed your stock through the winter, but you'll still have dozens of acres of land that you won't need. Why not cut the hay and sell it to hay yards in the new mining camps? Except you'll need to leave the various water plants and reeds along the creek so the Paiute women will have enough to collect to make their baskets and mats for their dwellings and such, just as they have always done."

After a lengthy silence from Jake, she added, "They're sound ideas, Bennett. I thought them through the whole time you were gone, and now the numbers have convinced me that they could work."

Jake was staring at her, but Jess decided his look was a thoughtful one. Pleased that she had likely just contributed to the prolonged success of the ranch, she leaned back in the wooden chair, stretching her arms and letting the chair rock on its back legs. The room had cooled pleasantly with the door open wide, and there was little to break the relaxing silence but an occasional voice drifting over the compound and the slow, homey creaking of the chair.

Suddenly, Jake's gaze shifted in alarm to the floor behind the chair.

Jess carefully slowed her rocking, eyes wide. Somehow, she *knew* what was there—she could sense what was coiled up on the floor behind her.

Jake's voice was low and steady as he spoke to her, still leaning against the wall, his gaze on his target. "In the bottom drawer, there's a revolver. Hand it to me, Jess, nice and easy."

Her breath trapped in her throat, Jess slowly reached down toward the drawer.

A sudden, loud rattling broke the silence.

Jess's heart nearly exploded. Her eyes flew to Jake.

"Keep going," he urged her.

Jess's breathing resumed in shallow, rapid pants. Her fingers found the drawer pull.

The rattling broke, then snapped in warning.

Shakily, she slid open the drawer and saw the holster. Slowly, slowly she lifted it out.

With a steady hand, Jake reached for it. The piece barely made a sound as Jake slid it from the holster. He cocked the gun, took aim...*BOOM!*

Jess jumped as though lightning had struck. Through the ringing in her ears, she heard the snake slump to the floor.

Ranchmen burst into the front room bearing an assortment of impromptu weapons, their manners defensive.

Jake's voice sounded muted as he told them about the snake. Jess forced herself to stand up, refusing to let the men think her fainthearted. Aware of her audience, she glanced at the snake, then turned to Jake.

"He was just a little snake, Bennett. Surely you didn't need to blow him in two."

The men chuckled. Jake eyed her as he reholstered the gun. Jess nodded slightly, silently thanking him for allowing her to save face. She was going to have nightmares for a month.

The ranchmen shuffled out. A few called back their intent to get a few supplies so they could repair the splintered floor.

Seeing Jess's fingers trembling, Taggart paused in the doorway, then came back and picked up the two large pieces of snake. With a wink to Jess, he headed out again.

"Hey, Dough Chen!" she heard him yell across the yard. "Have ye any recipes for rattlesnake?"

Her strength having gone out of her, Jess leaned her elbows on the back of the sofa and dropped her head onto her forearm. "That was exciting."

"More than that," Jake said.

As she glanced up to determine his meaning, Jake dashed upstairs. He returned moments later with a spare gun belt. Moaning again over her mishap, Jess rested her forehead in her hands while Jake lifted the holster from the desk and slipped it onto the belt.

"I think you'd best wear this from now on," he said. "I need to know that you have the means to defend yourself if there's ever a need. Keep only enough rounds chambered to hit what you're aiming for. Our shooting practice hasn't given me a lot of hope for your accuracy."

Jess's eyebrows rose in mock indignation. "Perhaps I just need a larger target."

He slid the holster along the belt. "Just how big a target were you thinking of?" His eyes were teasing.

Hers teased right back. "About the size of an irksome rancher, I think."

Jake stepped up to her, adjusting the belt in his hands. "Then I'd best work on my manners, so that you don't find me irksome."

They shared a smile.

Getting back to the matter at hand, Jake's gaze dropped to the circle of sturdy leather in his hands that was big enough for a large man, then rose doubtfully to Jess's tiny waist. She watched him with amusement as he slipped the wide leather belt around her.

Jake pulled the end through the buckle until it was snug. Enough belt was left over to go around her a second time.

As he raised his eyes to hers, his expression changed. His fist tightened on the belt.

Suddenly, he felt too close. Jess gave an abrupt half-shake of her head. "Bennett."

Jake searched her face and then slowly relaxed his grip. After a moment, he pulled the leather free of the buckle and gathered the belt in his hand.

Going over to the desk, he pulled out a knife. He swiftly cut her belt down to size, then poked a few holes through it with the point of the blade. He put away the knife, then handed her the custom-fitted belt, complete with holster and gun.

With murmured thanks, Jess drew it around her, buckled

it, and settled the heavy sidearm at her hip. "I'm going to the cookhouse," she said.

"Jess."

Wary, she hesitated.

"We're going to have to talk about this—what's between us." The deep timbre of his voice wended through her, as did the meaning of his words. Even so, she gave no indication of just how deeply her thoughts had become absorbed with him. Without giving an answer, she turned and walked out.

Jess woke before dawn and quietly dressed, anxious to begin her new job caring for the stable horses. She hadn't heard Jake's footsteps in the hall or on the stairs, so she assumed he was still asleep—for a little while longer, anyway. Jess quickly twisted her hair into the long braid she always wore, then pulled on her boots and gun belt and hurried from her room.

Jess ducked into the small kitchen to grab a biscuit from the covered bucket Ho Chen replenished each day. Taking quick bites, she slipped out the door and hurried to the stable.

A lantern had already been lit, and it hung on a square post, throwing dark shadows and pale yellow light over the stalls and ceiling high above. At the far end, the doors stood open. A wagon stacked with hay sat beyond them.

Popping the last bite of biscuit into her mouth, Jess brushed off her hands and moved down the rows of stalls, grinning like a goose. Eager foals were nursing while their mothers stood passively, their eyes drowsy, as if they were still partly asleep.

Her heart light, Jess stopped before the stall of her own horse. As soon as Meg saw her, she walked over and lowered her head to be petted. "Good morning, girl," Jess murmured, running her hands along the warm, velvety fur under her mane. "I'm sorry I haven't been to see you lately, but that'll be different now. Yes, it will," she crooned softly.

"I thought you wanted to feed the horses." Startled, Jess turned to see Jake beyond the high gate of a stall across the way, grinning in his lopsided way. "Now I see you're only going to pet them."

"I guess it's a habit I never outgrew. Pet them first, while they're still restful. There's no better way to begin a day."

"For them?"

Jess scratched Meg lightly under the chin. "And for me." As she watched Jake, she attempted to discern his mood, but she found none of the previous day's fervor there—only the calm she had come to enjoy.

Still, since they would apparently be spending a part of the morning together, she faced her single concern head-on. "Is there anything you intend to talk to me about?"

The horse behind him stretched out its muzzle and nudged Jake's shoulder. Jake took the hint and rubbed its nose. "Not today."

At his relaxed manner, Jess felt her momentary uneasiness melt away.

❧⚜❧

Lone Wolf had told Jake that he would need the heart of a warrior to save Jess from her fear of love. Jake watched her treat the Appaloosa to a nibble of grain. Jess possessed a rare and natural beauty. Most men would press after what they wanted, ignoring the needs and desires of their women. He was not like most men. If it was indeed a warrior's heart within him, then it was, above all, a heart of patience.

Jake knelt down to wrap the leg of the horse he'd been inspecting before Jess entered the stable, trying to hit upon the moment when that thrumming organ in his chest had taken charge of his will. He loved Jess. He had long known that she stirred something inside him—something more than admiration, more than caring—but until now he hadn't put a name to it. He *loved* her. Jake stilled, allowing that realization to settle in.

It was dangerous to feel so much for Jess, dangerous for him to risk losing someone again. And how was he supposed to let Olivia go? He would never forget her or their little Sadie.

As Jake continued to wrap the horse's leg, he recalled additional reasons he'd been fighting this feeling for months: Jess refused to see him as more than a friend, she was determined to leave the ranch as soon as possible, and a group of murderous fanatics wanted her dead.

Loving her certainly did complicate matters.

But then, nothing worthwhile ever came easily.

He tied off the bandage and stood up. For now he would keep his feelings to himself so that no one would question Jess's honor. He pushed open the gate of the stall and closed it behind hİm. He held out an arm, inviting Jess to go before him, and they started together toward the far side of the barn, where the hay wagon awaited them.

Shortly after Jake and Jess had begun carrying in giant forkfuls of hay, several other ranchmen entered the stable. Once the horses were fed, Jake and the cattlemen met outside the rear doors, where Jake assigned them the day's tasks. Some of them saddled up, then rode out to see to the cattle; others went to mix manure into the garden, grumbling at the indignity of it. Still others were sent to plow firebreaks—just a yearly routine, the men hurriedly explained to assure Jess. There were also minor repairs to be done to one of the corral fences, cows to be milked, troughs and water barrels to be filled, and so on.

While Jake finished speaking to the men, Jess went to fill a bucket from the pump. She returned to water the rosebush just as the group was breaking up.

Jess bent over to lift the bucket. Growing thoughtful, she tucked a loose wisp of hair behind her ear and glanced aside at Jake. He was writing notes in his little book.

"Bennett?"

"Hmm?"

"Why do you keep a rosebush?" Though Jess carefully kept her eyes on the bush, she felt him tense beside her. She knew she was breaking one of the cattlemen's unspoken rules about not prying into another's private matters, but the presence of the rosebush had gnawed at her for quite some time. She turned to him, almost wishing she hadn't brought it up, but since she had, she pressed on. "I'm sorry, Bennett, but when we were first at the ranch together, you rode off with what looked like two rose stems in your hand. Another time when you left, the stems had buds. When you go, the men behave as though you're invisible, and they treat the rosebush the same. What's more, I have the feeling you're intentionally trying to keep something from me—something that has to do with the roses." Her voice softened. "I'd just like to know what's going on, Bennett."

Jake tucked his notebook and pencil away. "Let's go for a ride," he said.

Ten minutes later, the two of them were galloping east past the Paiute village and out onto the open range. The few cattlemen they saw were far off. When they had gained a great enough distance, they reined in and stepped down.

Jake looked out over the sage plains, then finally glanced down at her, his eyes lightly guarded. He began in a roundabout way. "Has it occurred to you that maybe I like roses?"

"Is that why you brought me out here? To tell me that?"

Jake inclined his head, acknowledging her incredulity. They began to walk, leading their horses behind them. "When was the first time you saw this land?"

Jess's brow wrinkled as she thought back. "Ambrose took me riding several times before he left to go back East. Mostly, he took me into the mountains, or we'd race in the valley. Lake Tahoe was the farthest I rode."

"What about outings with your folks?"

"With all the work there was to do? No, my father rarely wasted time on leisure. That isn't a complaint," she explained. "That's just who he was."

"Sundays?"

"On Sundays, we went to church and had dinner together—Ho Chen saved his best surprises for Sunday—then my father spent the afternoons at the store. Since there was always work to be done, I'd often go with him." Sensing his disapproval, she defended herself with a deflection. "Well, it's no different here. The men don't work as hard on Sundays, but chores need to be done, the same as every other day. During roundup, there's a month of no rest at all."

"This is the life we all chose. The men work when they want, they leave when they want, and they go into town about once a month to let loose." He glanced at her, his eyes teasing. "You haven't had a break since you've been here. Do you want to go into town with them?"

"Hardly. No, I think I'll just stay here. Nate told me that Hiram once rode his horse straight into a crowded saloon, boasting to the townsmen that real men don't walk—they ride, even into an alehouse. He said the horse nearly trampled the sheriff."

Jake shook his head. "I'd nearly forgotten about that. Hiram had to work six months to repay the money it cost me to bail him out that night."

They both laughed.

The black carriage horse that Jake had ridden out suddenly snorted and danced sideways, jerking against his tether. Meg skittered away from him.

Jess figured they had been startled by a rodent or some other creature. The black's behavior reminded her to ask Jake about his progress retraining the carriage horses. She did so with a tease of her own. "You didn't appear to be wearing as much dirt to supper last night as you did to the snake-killing. Did the horses get tired of throwing you?"

"No," he said agreeably, "they just realized they couldn't breathe as well through all that dust I was raising."

Jake paused in mid-grin, his eyes snapping up to stare over her head.

Suddenly, both Meg and the black pranced uneasily. Startled, Jess scanned the desert.

Far off to the east, a wide dust cloud rose, rolling swiftly toward them. A low rumble rose with it.

Meg jerked violently against the reins. The ground beneath them trembled with the force of the hoofbeats. Jess hurried toward Meg, knowing they were in danger before Jake could voice it.

"Mustangs!"

Instantly, Jake was beside her. Without another word, he helped hoist her into her saddle. Jess whipped the reins over Meg's head. The terrified horse shot out at a run.

In moments, Jake and the black overtook them, and Jake used the ends of his own reins to whip Meg to her maximum speed.

Jess wanted to look over her shoulder to catch a glimpse of the herd of mustangs, but she didn't dare. They were close enough now to sound like thunder.

As they neared the ranch, an army of mounted cattlemen sped toward them, loaded down with extra ropes and lassos tied to every available strap on the saddle and slung over their shoulders.

Seeing Doyle approaching on Cielos, Jake pulled his mount to a rapid halt. Jess fought Meg to do the same.

"Get into the house, Jess!" Jake ordered, trading horses with Doyle in a blink. "Warn the others to bolt the doors on the barn and the stable! I'll be back as soon as I can!"

"You're going after them while they're stampeding?" she shouted, incredulous, as men shot past, their exhilarated eyes fixed on the hunt.

"They're only horses, Jess," he shouted back. "Don't worry, I promise I'll let you feed them!"

She couldn't help grinning at that. "I'll hold you to it!" she answered. When he held Cielos back for her sake, she yelled, "You'd better go get my herd, Bennett!"

"Yes, ma'am!" He flashed her a valiant smile, then spun the stallion about. In a churn of hooves, he was gone.

Jess ran Meg in the opposite direction. She rode into the yard beside Doyle but found no one left to secure the buildings. Everyone had gone after the mustangs.

At the barn, Jess leapt down. She shut the big doors and dropped the bar in place to keep them from being forced open by the frightened cattle within. Her foot barely touched the stirrup before she whirled Meg to secure the stable.

Across the compound, Doyle called out to Ho Chen, who hurried into the cookhouse.

Suddenly, Jess remembered the Paiute women...Red Deer. "No!" Jess ignored Jake's order to take shelter in the ranch house. She ran Meg all the way to the Indian village.

"Red Deer!" she called. "Two Hands!"

Red Deer hurried out of her dwelling. "What is it, Jessica?"

"Mustangs!" Jess gasped. "Wild horses," she said to Red Deer's look of confusion.

"Yes, our men went to help catch them."

"You don't understand! They're coming this way!"

Red Deer wailed something in Paiute, and the women and children hurried over in alarm. "There is a mining cave we can go to for safety!"

Red Deer instructed the others and shouted for Two Hands. He appeared, leading an old gray-haired man.

Jess prayed the cave was close, knowing they might not make it in time.

The older boys came at a run with the remaining horses and helped the old man and Red Deer to mount. Jess pulled Two Hands up behind her. He wrapped his arms tightly around her waist.

Red Deer led the way. Jess kept her gaze locked on the growing dust cloud until they reached the partially boarded-up mining tunnel. After helping everyone dismount, Jess and the older boys raced back for the young mothers and children who were farther behind.

Jess arrived at the mine with the last young woman and gave her an arm and a stirrup to help her dismount. The mustangs were coming on fast, flanked by rows of cattlemen.

They were less than a mile off, by her calculation, and galloping headlong for the ranch buildings despite the men's efforts to make them turn.

Jess spun Meg toward the compound, blocking out the warnings of the others to take shelter in the cave.

The first of the mustangs entered the yard just as Jess stopped in front of the house. Tearing her hat from her head, she leapt down and smacked Meg with it, having no choice but to send the mare running, hoping she could find her again later.

Jess bolted onto the porch. The front door flew open, and with a powerful arm, Doyle yanked her in and shut the door.

Her breath came in pants as she collapsed against the wall. "Thank you," she breathed.

Doyle stared down at her. "I thought you done lost your mind, riding off like that."

"I had to get back here. I had...to see the mustangs."

"Well, I suppose there's no sense scolding you. You weren't harmed none."

Together, they went to the front window and watched those bold, beautiful creatures of the wild thunder past, their glossy coats bright with morning sun. Their necks were stretched out, and their thick tails were streaming behind them.

"They hardly seem real," Jess whispered. "They're like a dream come to life." She pressed her hands to the window as the last few galloped by. They turned toward the creek, directed by dusty men with lassos raised.

As soon as they had passed, Jess rushed to the door, but a word from Doyle stopped her. "You best wait, Jess." For words so calmly spoken, they held sufficient warning to halt her. He hadn't moved from the window. "It'll be safer after a while."

Jess returned to his side and watched as the cattlemen whistled and waved the kicking, thrashing mustangs through the open gate of the largest corral. When Jess saw them nearly contained, she danced impatiently, bringing a grin to Doyle's face. "Like a child waitin' for Christmas," he murmured.

The instant the corral gate was closed, Jess was out the door and crossing the yard at a run, her hat flying out behind her on its strings. She leapt up onto the lowest rail of the fence, her eyes taking in the buckskins, duns, sorrels, paints...and Meg. She lifted her gaze to search out Jake.

He looked over at her from amid the boisterous backslapping of his men, and when she waved to him, he returned the greeting. In the next instant, she was drumming the top rail with her hands, giggling with unbounded pleasure. Jake separated himself from the merriment of his men, guided Cielos around the corral, and stopped beside her.

Jess smiled at his unshaven, sun-bronzed face. He gestured with a casual tip of his hat. "Your horses, ma'am."

"I wanted to come out and see them so badly, I thought Doyle was going to have to sit on me to keep me from doing it," she laughed.

"I wanted you to ride with us. You're good with horses, but I have more to teach you about the wild ones first." He surveyed the spirited herd. "Now the boys and I will have twice as much work to do with all these ponies to break to the saddle." The dark eyes met with hers. "Your plans for this place have just gotten a big nudge forward."

All at once, Jess remembered their Indian friends in the cave. "Jake, I moved Red Deer and the others to an abandoned mine until the horses passed."

"Then let's get them." He turned Cielos for her, lending her his hand and the stirrup as Jess swung up behind him. As soon as she secured her arms around him, they rode out.

"You did right," he said over his shoulder. "The ponies were headed for the village, but we were able to turn them before they overran the camp."

"They sure have minds of their own."

"Yes, indeed. This whole territory is their backyard. They probably know the terrain better than I do, and when they stretch out in open places, they go like a whirlwind, running for the thrill of it. The ranch horses, now—they do as much standing as running. They can get close to the wild horses because most of them are descended from mustangs, but they can't keep up for very long."

Jess knew the mustangs that Jake and the others had caught

were less than half of the thundercloud that had rumbled toward them.

"You cut only thirty or forty from the herd."

"We'll keep only the four- and five-year-olds. Anything younger isn't ready to train. Anything older is too stubborn, and we don't take mothers with young. But the four- and five-year-olds will do well. The Indians are especially cunning at trapping them, then lifting them out like prairie chickens."

Jess smiled behind him. "I've learned a lot from the Paiutes," he added.

As Jake and Jess approached the mine tunnel, they found the Indian women and children already on their way home. Their husbands had come to assist them.

Spotting Red Deer, Jess quickly slid down from the saddle and hurried over to tell her and the others about the magnificent horses she had seen. Red Deer related her story to Two Hands and to those who couldn't understand English well enough. Many of the women gathered excitedly around her, thanking her for coming to warn them and begging her to tell them more about the mustangs.

∽☜◈☞∽

When Jake saw the old man, Standing Bear, he dismounted and walked beside him toward the village, leading Cielos. Standing Bear's wrinkled, leathered face observed Jess laughing with the Paiutes.

He spoke in English, his voice having the tired quality of a man who has lived long and seen much. "So this is your falcon-woman. She is like a warm wind that pushes away the clouds."

Jake nodded. "That she is."

"She has no fear in her heart, this green-eyed falcon."

"She has one fear, Standing Bear, but she hides it."

Standing Bear said nothing but waited.

Jake felt a tug at his heart as Jess and the women entered the village of wigwams. Jess stood among the children and fussed over the simple toys and grass dolls they showed her. She was wearing the yellow dress she'd made, along with the cattleman's hat and bandana. The leather gun belt surrounded her slim waist, its holster lost in her skirts. "She's afraid to feel love for me." Walking Bear stopped, and Jake remained beside him. "She has love for Red Deer and Two Hands and the others, and I can see she cares for me, but she deeply cherished her family, and then she lost them. She's afraid to love like that again." He met the old eyes and spoke in Paiute. "But I am patient."

Standing Bear looked again toward the village, where a small boy was showing Jess his bow and arrow. "The fear will not win," he agreed. "It is in her to love."

When Jess lifted her gaze in their direction, Standing Bear left Jake, continuing alone into his village. Jake walked on, leading Cielos at a slow pace so Jess could catch up. She said her good-byes and ran to join him.

"Those children are remarkable," she said, breathless. "Did you know they can shape mud into animals that look real?" She held out her hand, happily displaying the perfect little song sparrow that he'd seen a young girl give to her.

Jake smiled at her delight as they strolled toward the ranch. "I wonder if the children can make tame mustangs."

"That's your job, Bennett." She grinned.

"Miss Hale, I believe that's the first time you've called me Bennett without a scowl."

"And it may be the last time," she joked. At ease, she pulled off her hat and let it swing in her hand.

Jake recalled how her hair looked the last night of the roundup—silky and unbound, shimmering in the campfire light. The sun glinted off it now in the same enchanting way. "I like it better when you say my first name," he said.

"I never say your first name," she breezed.

"No?"

She shook her head. "Uh-uh."

"Well, I'll be sure to point it out the next time you do."

"You do that, Bennett. Are you going to build a new stable for the mustangs?"

"The corral will do for now. We'll keep them in the one they're in and train them in the empty one, maybe build two more to break several at once."

"How will you be able to train them all?"

Jake looked at her to see genuine interest in her eyes. "Diaz is a fair hand at breaking. So are Lone Wolf and the Paiutes. We'll get it done. Shall we ride the rest of the way?"

Jess plunked her hand on her hip when he mounted up ahead of her, her eyes sparkling. "You're not going to let me up first?"

Jake offered a hand down. "Not a chance. If I let you up first, I'd never see you or my horse again."

She accepted his hand but looked irked at the old reminder. Once she'd settled her arms around him, Jake nudged Cielos into an easy lope.

"I said I wouldn't run again, and I haven't," Jess reminded him.

Jake glanced at her. "I was only teasing, Jess. I didn't intend any harm."

Jess's expression softened, and she smiled.

235

Jake took her past the stable, through the ranch, and all the way to the garden. She gasped in surprise when he pulled up. "How did you know I'd want to be here?"

"You spent most of yesterday on the books. I figured since you enjoyed the garden, you'd want to be here today."

"You were right."

Touched that he'd been so attentive to her interests, Jess grasped his arm and slid to the ground. Instead of releasing his arm, she continued to hold it, her eyes lifting to where his large, gloved hand still held firmly to hers.

He hadn't let go, either.

She felt as if she couldn't stop holding on to him, and for the briefest of moments, she didn't want to.

A movement beyond the creek caught her attention, and she pulled her arm away.

Jake sat upright in the saddle. Two men on horseback were passing no more than a quarter of a mile to the north. They appeared to be ordinary travelers, except that they crossed the desert instead of taking the Susanville road to the south, and they slowed as they looked in the direction of the ranch yard.

Jess watched them as they began to pick up speed, heading away. "Who are they, Bennett?"

"I don't know. They were too far away to tell. They weren't cowhands—at least not mine."

"Neighbors?"

"Maybe." He didn't sound sure.

Chapter Fourteen

In the days following, the ranchmen busted their britches. After they built the additional corrals for training, they woke each morning a full hour before dawn, needing every available moment to break the mustangs so that as many as possible would be ready to sell come autumn. A man needed nearly a week to break just one to the saddle, and when Jess woke each morning to feed the stable horses, Jake was always out in one of the corrals, already beginning his day.

Though Jess saw him little, Jake continued to look after her with subtle, thoughtful gestures—filling the woodpile near the fireplace each morning so she wouldn't have to, leaving her a pot of tea steeping on the hearth, coming and going without a whisper of sound when she was asleep so as not to waken her. The things he did for her tugged at her heart, leaving her feeling contented and cared for.

And afraid.

Fortunately, they were rarely together, and the distance kept at bay the invisible mixture of desire and dread that choked her whenever he was near.

Jess worked in the garden every morning. So far, the manure had kept the plants growing despite the drought. In the afternoons, she rode out on the range, usually with Seth or Reese. She enjoyed looking after the cattle and searching for strays, though admittedly not as much as she had when she rode with Jake.

In the evenings, she sat by her open window until the hour

was late, alleviating her heat and exhaustion with the balmy night breeze. By lantern light, she wove orange yarn on the loom into an ever growing blanket. Sometimes, she imagined the look of surprise Red Deer would have when she finally opened the gift for her newborn son. Other times, she simply wove with little thought, losing herself amid the sounds of the night.

A few weeks after the mustang catch, Jess was lying awake on her bunk late at night, too hot to sleep. She was drenched in sweat, and her chemise clung miserably to her skin. The bed sack was hot no matter how she shifted. Jess sighed. It seemed that hours rather than minutes had passed since she'd extinguished the lamp.

Through the window, the pleasant hoots of an owl and the sound of cottonwoods stirred by the breeze beckoned her. Before she knew it, she was pulling on the swim dress she'd sewn and slipping out the door with a towel.

The creek shimmered and snaked in the moonlight. Jess tossed aside the towel and wandered out into the refreshing coolness of it, then lay back until water covered all but her face. She stretched out her hands and drew them through her unbound hair, fanning it away, cooling her scalp. The mild current rinsed away her sweat and soothed her muscles. It was paradise. The fabric of her swim dress swirled gently over her legs while she held lightly to a rock to keep from drifting away.

She would rest well now, she mused, though she'd give anything if someone would just sling a hammock under her so she could sleep where she was. Jess smiled at the thought as the water purled around her. She tilted her head back to enjoy the view of stars and cottonwood branches above. There was a small, shadowy movement on a limb several feet up. As she watched, the owl that had summoned her from her bedroom roused himself. With slow, deliberate movements, he stepped to the end of his perch, then dove into the air with broad strokes of soundless wings.

Sensing another presence, Jess sat up in the water and searched the bank for the only one who might know where she would be. As the owl disappeared into the night, Jake lowered his gaze to hers. He leaned against the trunk of the cottonwood. They shared a smile at what they had witnessed while everyone else slept.

"Sometimes, I wish I didn't have to sleep," Jess confessed, feeling more comfortable with him than she had been in some time, perhaps due to the barriers of creek and night between them. "I wake each morning wondering what all I missed."

Jake crouched down at the edge of the bank, his feet bare, the top of his shirt unbuttoned. "I used to walk along the creek before sunup, when I first settled here. I'd almost forgotten about that," he murmured. "Sometimes, I'd find tracks; other times, I'd see animals still here—antelope, coyotes, raccoons—getting a meal or a drink. Panning for gold, Taggart used to say."

They shared another smile.

"They mostly stay in the mountains now, but we still see them now and again in the fall and winter."

Growing overly warm with Jake's eyes on her, Jess shifted her gaze to where the moon hovered above the Sierras. One night past full, it laid a silvery glow on the mountains, on the tree trunk...on the clean, white shirt that fit Jake's shoulders so well.

Fighting her awareness of his proximity, she pointed to where the moonlight was making tiny gold flecks glitter along the bank. "Taggart might have been right. You do have gold on your land, Bennett."

"This?" He shifted his weight, reaching with his hand to smooth a few flecks in the sand.

"And the mine I saw that day you caught the mustangs."

"There's not enough here worth panning for, and that old mine was abandoned long before I came. Whoever dug it must have thought the same and given up."

Jess's mind swiftly turned to business. "Hiring a couple of men to work it might be a worthwhile investment. The initial excavation has been done. Once it pays for your workers, everything else is profit."

Jake chuckled. "You sure have a lot going on inside that head of yours. No, I've had a look myself. There's nothing there." He leaned to rinse the sand from his fingers. "Besides, mining doesn't interest me much. I prefer being above ground. A man can't lope a horse far in a mine."

Jess smiled but continued with her train of thought. "Jake, you already own the land, so there won't be any additional expenses up front... What?" She could have seen the grin on his face from a mile away.

Suppressing his amusement, he rested his elbows on his knees. "Well, you just called me Jake again."

Her eyes widened, then narrowed in denial. "I did not!"

"Yes, ma'am, you did. You just said—"

"Never mind what I said!" With impatient strokes, Jess put a few more feet of water between them.

"Why does it bother you to say my name?" he asked softly. She paddled quietly, not looking at him. "Jess?"

Jess shook her head, lifted a shoulder. She had told Red Deer that saying his name was too personal, but it was more than that. If she started calling him Jake, she would finally see him as something more than a rancher, someone more than a friend. Simply saying that one word threatened to knock down all the barriers she'd placed between them, exposing her to love—and to loss.

Jake didn't press the matter. *Thank heavens for cattlemen's honor,* she thought.

"Are you getting cold?" he asked.

"I came out here to cool down." She peered across the water at him. "Why did you come?"

"To look out for you. I saw you go downstairs without your gun."

Jess dropped her gaze to the holster at his hip. She had become so used to seeing the men with gun belts that it hadn't seemed unusual to her that he was wearing one at so late an hour. Just then, she recalled the strangers she had seen once or twice since the first pair they'd noticed riding past the ranch. "Are you expecting trouble?" When he hesitated, she added, "I've seen the riders, Bennett."

"A couple of men have passed by, but they haven't let on about their intentions. I think it's best we stay alert, no matter what they intend. I'd like you to wear your gun at all times, same as the boys do. Even when you come down for a swim."

He spoke with relative unconcern, so Jess let the matter go.

The cat appeared and began winding herself around Jake's feet, purring softly. He picked her up, cradling her in his arm as he took a seat at the base of the tree. His expression changed, as though he was about to let her in on a surprise. "I also wanted to ask you about the Fourth of July."

"The Fourth of July?" Jess realized that was only three days away. "What about it?"

"I always put on a big shindig for the cowhands and the Paiute families. Tomorrow morning, I'll send Ho Chen and a few others to get some things we'll need. I wondered if you'd fill in for him until he gets back tomorrow night."

The idea of a party put a smile on her lips. A big smile. Nobody had done anything but work since the day she'd come. "I don't mind at all. Is there anything else I can do to help?"

Apparently, he'd been ready for that. "The men will want to look their best."

"Would you like me to fit in laundry tomorrow?"

"Do you think you can do it?"

"If I can get one or two of the other women to help me—but I don't want Red Deer to be hauling water or scrubbing."

"Ask them," Jake said simply. "Everybody will take the following day off to get ready for the Fourth."

When he fell silent, Jess's mind churned with all that would need to be done. The dance would have to be held in the cookhouse, since that building had the largest wood floor. The tables would have to be moved outside, where the men could put up a large ring of torches for light and to give the place a festive air. There should be candles for lighting the big room…

"I can see I don't have to trouble myself with planning."

Startled, Jess looked up, then humbly glided a little closer. "Jake, I didn't mean to…" She paused when she realized she'd just said his name again. Apart from an easy smile, he didn't respond. She went on. "I didn't mean to presume that I'd plan your party. I just—"

"It's everyone's party, Jess, and since I have to finish breaking in a pinto, I'm glad to leave you in charge of the planning. I'll come lend a hand as soon as I finish."

Jess couldn't have pulled the grin from her face if she'd wanted to. As Jake petted the seemingly boneless cat, she recalled what he'd said about mining not being of interest to him. She realized he was right. Mining just wasn't his passion. She thought of different times she had watched Jake when he was riding a horse, delivering a calf…when he seemed at peace with the land itself. "Did you always want to be a rancher?"

Jake's hand slowed until the cat rubbed his wrist with its head, urging him on. After a moment, he answered, his voice quiet but sure as always.

"Yes, I did. When I was little, my mother would sit in her rocking chair and read the Bible to us boys at night." He looked aside at her. "There're three of us. My younger brothers are Walt and Ty." He went on. "One time, she read in Revelation that the walls of heaven were made of all kinds of precious stones. She told us they probably sparkled like the stars did, but in colors like jewels. That really affected me—to picture what heaven would be like. That night, I thought about it so much that I couldn't sleep. So, I got up and went outside for a walk. I hadn't gone far when I found Ma walking, too, wrapped up in her shawl and watching the stars, same as I was.

"I think she knew she was sick, even then. She didn't send me back to my bed like she normally would have. Instead, we joined hands and walked together for a long while. We never said anything; just walked, looking up at stars that were shining like the walls of heaven." He paused for a moment, scratching the cat behind the ears. "My mother died a few months after. I used to go out and visit her grave at night so my father wouldn't know and be sorry for how much I missed her. I'd sit back against her headstone, and when I grew tired, I'd lay down beside the mound and sleep."

Jess bobbed quietly in the water, stricken to imagine him losing his mother as a child. She suffered fresh twinges of guilt, as well, for behaving for so long as though she was the only one of them who had ever known grief.

"A few years after—I was nine or ten—I was sitting out there one night, remembering how she used to read to us from her Bible. As I thought about it, I looked up at the stars, and I decided they really did look like jewels. I could even see bits of color now and then. So, I figured those were the walls of heaven, and that was where she was." He didn't apologize to Jess for the naïveté of his boyhood ideas, knowing she would understand.

"I wasn't as sad after that, because I couldn't imagine her

in a more beautiful place. Anyhow, I guess that's why I first thought of becoming a rancher instead of a farmer like my pa. I needed to be out on the range, where I could look up each night and feel close to the place where she was. The place where the Almighty will take me when my time here is done."

"So, you became a rancher because of your mother."

Jake sighed, then smiled the crooked smile she liked. "That and the fact that I kept trying to be a farmer on horseback. My pa said I'd best learn to tend cattle if I was never going to use my own two feet to walk."

Jess grinned. Then she grew thoughtful, lightly shaking her head at her own musings. "Jewels remind me of my mother, too." At his questioning look, she explained, "The earrings and hair comb I wore the night of the fire were hers."

"You have a few pieces of your mother's jewelry?"

"Yes. I sewed them into my petticoats when I came here," she admitted. "When I still had it in mind to leave."

"Do you have a place to keep them?"

"I keep them in the dressing table in my room."

"In a drawer?"

"No one's going to steal them—not here."

"True." Jake set the cat on its feet and rose. "I guess we'd best get some sleep if we're going to have a party in a few days." He held out a hand to help Jess from the creek.

"Oh, I...that is..." Jess indicated the towel she'd left on the bank. "I'd rather have a moment to myself."

Immediately, he put her at ease as he had done before. "I'll wait over there to walk you back."

Jess murmured her thanks. As soon as he left her, she emerged from the water, then paused on the bank to squeeze water from her hair and swim dress. That done, she wrapped herself in the towel, feeling refreshed and cooled. She held the towel close as she walked over to him, then together they continued toward the house. Deep within, near her heart, she ached with yearning.

"What all takes place at these parties of yours?" she asked, keeping her tone light.

"The boys compete in games. Horse races—rough ones," he clarified, "not like you're accustomed to. They'll race the green mustangs around the circle of ranch buildings. The Indians always make the competition fierce."

"Green mustangs?" Jess's grin was genuine. Already, she was eager to see it.

"Then there's shooting." His eyes teased her again. "I'd keep away from that, though, if I were you. We're miles from any doctor, should your aim be as it's been."

Jess tossed him a predictable glare.

His voice lowered as they rounded the bunkhouse. "Diaz taught the boys a game he grew up with—chicken pulling."

Jess winced at the sound of that. "Chicken pulling?"

Jake laughed softly. "It's as bad as it sounds. The men bury a live chicken in the ground—just up to its neck—then ride past at a gallop, leaning low in the saddle, and try to pull it from the ground by its head. When the chicken sees the hand coming, it dodges, of course, but when someone finally catches it, its neck snaps. We use a small sack stuffed with dried beans instead."

"That's good to hear." Jess shuddered at the grotesque image.

"Come nightfall, there'll be music and dancing. Don't plan to sit many out," he warned her with a smile. "A lot more men live here than women."

Jess smiled back. It sounded like an event to remember.

They were nearly to the house. Jess stopped abruptly when she noticed several dark mounds scattered about the yard. "What are those?" she whispered.

"A few of the men. In the summer, the bunkhouse gets hot,

so they sleep outdoors. I expect more will be out here tomorrow night."

"Oh," she said. Then, "You mean they'll be out here every night until September?"

"Maybe October, if it doesn't cool off."

Jess frowned and pulled the towel more tightly around her. "I guess I won't be swimming at night anymore."

"Sure you can. Just wear a towel like you are now. Jess, they're good men. They'll likely look out for you, but nothing more."

He stepped up on the porch and opened the door for her. Jess went in ahead of him, then stopped when he didn't follow her in.

"You're not tired?"

"Not enough to sleep. I'm going to straighten up the workshop. It's something I've been meaning to do."

In the darkness of her room, Jess brushed her hair while the night breezes wended pleasantly through it. When she climbed into bed, she was hardly aware of her head meeting the pillow.

∾☙⊱✦⊰❧∿

Out in the workshop, Jake settled the glass chimney over the popping, crackling flame. For a few minutes, he braced his arms on the worktable, his head bowed between them. He felt as though he were falling through the sky with no ground beneath him. It was exhilarating.

He'd had this feeling only once before, and after Olivia, he never thought to have it again. This was more than knowing in his mind, more than acknowledging the pull of his heart. To the last drop of his blood, he had fallen in love with Jess.

With a sigh of contentment, he stood upright and searched the woodpile for flat, rectangular pieces of wood.

Pulling up a stool, he sat, propped his bare heel on one of its rungs, and began to build Jess a jewelry box.

∽⊙≺⫘≻⊙∽

To Jess, the next day was a blur. She was throwing seeds at the chickens before the rooster crowed. She fed and watered the pigs, built the fire in the cookhouse kitchen, and had biscuits browning in the oven before the first cattleman in the yard rose and put away his bedroll.

While the men ate breakfast, she listened to their excited talk, atypical for them—discussions about the upcoming party and shared reminiscences of the unforgettable "Fourths" they'd been to in years past.

Jess had no sooner put away the dishes than she hashed together a hearty stew for their dinner. It would have to serve for their supper, as well, because she wouldn't have time to prepare a third meal with all the washing she had to do. Yet she knew the men would be agreeable to it, for they'd already made it be known that laundry was a priority.

Besides, they liked their buttons right where they were.

Jess had not two but three Paiute women come to help her, and together, they managed to complete the wash by nightfall.

Ho Chen returned with Reese and Doyle just after sunset, and the festive air they'd brought with them caught on throughout the ranch. Tired, hot, and dusty cattlemen freed the mustangs they'd been working in their corral, then hurried over to help unload the wagon. Torches were brought out, and Jess laughed and joked with the men as they carried barrels, sacks, and crates into the cookhouse.

Full of anticipation for the following day, when they would truly prepare for the holiday, the men cheerfully carried out the tables and benches—a task they'd grumbled about the day she'd scrubbed the filthy bunkhouse. They also arranged the additional torches in a huge ring in front of the smithy and dug fire pits. At the end of the day, Jess returned to the house exhausted, but she lay awake for nearly an hour, smiling as she listened to the sounds of laughter, howls, and splashes coming from the creek.

The morning of July third was far different from the mornings Jess had come to know. Spirits were high as dozens of cattlemen crowded into the stable, joking and jostling one another as they helped see to the horses.

Breakfast put Jess at a table crowded with clean yet disheveled men who begged her for haircuts. Moments after she had agreed, she found herself in the shade of the ranch house porch, scissors in hand. A hatless man was seated before her, and several others milled about, waiting their turns. Jess laughed at the absurdity of feeling like the sole shearer in a barn full of sheep. Fortunately, Red Deer soon joined her, and another chair and pair of scissors were brought.

Jake, Diaz, and several of the Paiute men continued to work the mustangs throughout the morning while Jess and Red Deer trimmed two dozen heads of hair. Finally, the last newly shorn man thanked Jess, jammed his hat on his head, and hurried down the steps to help set up markers for the next day's race.

Red Deer waddled off to see where Two Hands had gone, leaving Jess by herself to look out over the yard. Smiling, she leaned against the railing and watched Jake lower a saddle onto the back of a stiff-legged paint while Diaz held the reins tightly. The mustang skittered sideways at the weight of the unfamiliar object, but when Jake threaded the cinch strap through the buckle and then pulled tight, the paint bucked so violently that he nearly pulled Diaz over.

Jake stood steadily and managed to fasten the buckle.

All at once, Diaz tossed the reins to Jake and scrambled up onto the corral fence. Jake grabbed the reins and a fistful of mane, then twisted the horse's ear to distract it, giving himself a brief moment to gain the saddle.

The paint exploded in a maddened rage. Jess stared in amazement, and the many cowhands paused their various activities around the compound to watch the man hold fast to the horse.

Jake kept his seat as the horse lunged forward, rearing and bucking its way across the corral.

When it neared the other side, it made up its mind to rid itself of its burden for good, and it spun hard, throwing the rancher straight into the fence.

Jess gasped when Jake hit the ground, but Jake only snatched up his hat and put it on again, gaining his feet.

Swiftly, his manner turned to one of cool purpose. From one of the corral posts, he grabbed a coiled lariat, faced the mustang, and began moving slowly toward it.

Jess remembered all too well how Jake Bennett could use a rope.

His gaze steady on the thrashing paint, Jake uncoiled the lasso. The mustang faced him, eyes wild, nostrils flaring.

Diaz climbed down from the fence with a rope of his own. He stretched out the big loop, swinging it over his head. Once, twice, it whirred around…around. Then he threw it, encircling the animal's neck. The horse reared with a whinny of protest. Diaz dug in his heels, but the incensed horse dragged him along, plowing up dust.

Jake waited for the right moment, then began to spin his lariat. He threw it.

The rope caught the front hoof farthest from him. Jake twirled the rope, moving in. He snared the other hoof. The horse fought it. Violently.

Watching from the porch, Jess shook her head. "It's no use," she murmured with a grim smile. "No use at all."

With the horse hobbled, and with Diaz holding it by the other rope, Jake swung up into the saddle again. Diaz loosed the lariat around the horse's neck. Jake swiftly slipped it over the animal's head and tossed it to him.

Freed, the paint reacted instantaneously. It leapt straight up and tried to run, resisting the hobbles. Jake rode it out.

All at once, the mustang gave up trying to throw him. Now he tried to escape him.

The other ranch hands shifted unconsciously with the mustang's movements.

The horse bounded forward with nearly enough force to spill a man's hat, halted, then leapt again. Jake reined the pony toward the side of the corral. After rounding the fence line twice, the paint's gait slowed to a rough lope. Jake let it go around a few times more. He tugged the reins, and the pony came to a stop. Jake stepped down.

Holding the reins, he loosed the hobble, then tossed the lariat over the fence to one of the men. Once again, he twisted the mustang's ear and mounted.

The mustang tried a few wrenching leaps, kicked halfheartedly, then settled into another rough lope around the corral.

Jess smiled broadly as Jake continued to ride. Minutes later, Jake turned the horse and rode it around in the opposite direction. Gradually, its gait smoothed out.

Jake finally brought the panting horse to a stop. He stepped down, then turned to shake hands with a grinning Diaz before slipping out of the corral.

Panting himself, he responded to the hearty thwacks and admiration from onlookers, then broke away from them to make his way to a water barrel nearby.

"Care for cool drink, Miss Jessie?" Ho Chen's voice called

from inside. Jess turned and stepped into the house, gratefully accepting the mug he handed her. She headed back toward the porch but stopped at the window, lingering just inside the front door. Ho Chen came up beside her, and together they watched Diaz swing onto the back of the paint.

Jess was not oblivious to the weight of the mug in her hand, and she was aware of the presence of Ho Chen, but as Jake approached the water barrel by the porch, all her senses were hopelessly drawn to the remarkable man.

"He is not man who give up," came Ho Chen's voice.

"No, he's not," Jess agreed, almost absently. Through the window, she watched Jake toss down his hat and gloves. He scooped handfuls of water from the barrel and rinsed his face and neck. Jess tried not to stare.

"You are happy here?" Ho Chen asked.

Jess looked over and nodded, then returned her attention to the window. Still standing by the water barrel, Jake glanced around. Seeing no one but the cattlemen, he unbuttoned his shirt, shrugged out of it, and tossed it over a fence rail.

Jess's breath caught in her throat. Jake splashed handfuls of water on his head and ran his fingers through his hair. He was wearing trousers, boots, and his gun belt, but Jess saw only his muscular arms and back reflecting the gleam of the sun.

And the crescent-shaped scar of a nasty burn that stretched from his shoulder blade to his ribs.

The floor seemed to shift beneath her. Trembling, Jess reached for the windowsill to steady herself. The mug was taken from her hand just before she collapsed against the wall, slowly sagging to the floor. Ho Chen was beside her.

"Jake's scar...?" Jess managed, cringing and hugging her arm that had been burned that last horrific night in Carson City. When she'd first arrived at the ranch, Red Deer had treated her raw skin for days. She still had scars.

They were nothing like Jake's.

Jess's eyes searched Ho Chen's. "Was Jake's burn…from…?" She couldn't breathe.

Ho Chen gentled his gaze. "It was from night of fire," he confirmed softly.

Jess felt she was lost in a nightmare.

"After Lone Wolf take you away, Mr. Bennett go in house to try to save your father, but the upstairs fall in. Wood burn him. I was there. I saw."

The upstairs fell in. "You pulled him out, didn't you? You saved him."

Ho Chen humbly lifted a shoulder.

Jess's stomach twisted in remorse. "He could have died, Ho Chen. He might not—"

He squeezed her hand. "Mr. Bennett no longer hurt. Is okay."

Jess kicked her foot, angrily, as if fighting off a wolf again. "I blamed him for so long! I *blamed* him, Ho Chen!" She stared across the room, unable to focus on anything. "And he had tried to save my father." She laughed faintly in agonizing regret. Tears burned her eyes.

Jess felt as though she was floating—numb, except for a throbbing pain in her heart. She remembered things that had seemed of no real significance until now: Jake's careful movements when he'd first arrived at the ranch, his discomfort as they'd played poker with Seth, his new sheepskin coat.

Jess knew now what had happened to the old one. In her mind, she saw Jake stumbling away from the burning house and shaking off the flaming coat. The sound of fire roared in her ears. She was reliving that night. Though she hadn't been there, she was seeing what had happened.

A distant-sounding voice said, "Miss Jessie?"

Jess didn't hear it clearly, nor did she register the sound of shuffling feet hurrying down the porch steps.

She remembered the blinding orange heat on her skin,

remembered how faint she had been standing several yards away, and Jake had gone into the house...he had gone in.

There was a movement, and a large, familiar form hunkered down beside her. Jess's nightmare faded, and she could see the dark trousers, the damp, white shirt, and the concern in the handsome face beneath his hat brim.

Then he was pulling her up, up on her knees, up against him, and he was holding her.

Jess was afraid to hug him back, afraid to hurt his scar. Her hands curled into fists that grasped his shirt instead.

She was shaking, saying she was sorry, so sorry, and he gently stroked her hair.

She cried.

He let her.

∼☞⊰⟨⟩⊱☜∼

Jake rested an elbow on his knee. The mug Ho Chen had given Jess was in his other hand, and he passed it to her.

She set it on the floor. For once, it didn't matter that Jake was so close. In fact, she was glad for it.

"I didn't know...about the scar. Ho Chen never told me anything until now." Her eyes lifted. "Does it still hurt you?"

He actually chuckled. "I had a mustang out there trying to trample me a while ago." He pushed back a lock of her hair that had come loose. "The hurts always pass. No," he said, "not anymore." He pointed to the mug. "Have you tried it?"

Jess knew that he was trying to bring her around; she knew that he had forgiven her. And she also knew that there was work to be done for the party—fun work with good people. "No. What is it?"

The gold flecks in his whiskey-brown eyes sparkled. "I'm not telling."

Sighing, she gamely picked up the mug. "All right, then."

She brought it to her lips and sipped a taste. The flavor of sweet lemons flowed over her tongue. She looked up at him in surprise. "Lemonade?"

"Yes, ma'am."

Jess could hardly contain herself. She couldn't remember the last time she had tasted lemonade! She took another sip. A long sip.

"You like it, then?"

Jess finally stopped to swallow and breathe. "It's wonderful."

"Good. We have two barrels of it." He pushed himself to his feet and extended an arm out to her. "Care to see what else we've got?"

In response, Jess accepted his arm and was pulled to her feet.

Instead of escorting her out, Jake hesitated. "Are you all right now?"

"I am. Bennett?"

"Hmm?"

Despite her decision to hold herself to friendship, Jess felt her feelings for him teetering on a precipice. He was so warm, so near. If she reached out, she could touch him. But she knew what lay beyond that precipice: an inescapable love, a terrible dread, and eventual loss. Her heart threatened to tear inside her, but she knew she could bear it, as long as things between Jake and her remained as they were. She was still glad to be in his company. "Thanks."

The corners of his eyes crinkled warmly. "My shirt was wet anyway."

Jess lifted her hat from its peg and pulled it on.

"Are you ready?" he asked.

"Ready."

They walked out.

The yard was quickly filling with scampering Indian children, lighthearted adults, and the appealing scent of roasting pig. She and Jake looked on from the shade of the porch.

Jess saw Red Deer disappear into the cookhouse. Between that building and the smithy, a pig was sizzling on a giant spit; over the second fire, a side of beef was cooking. Ho Chen paused beside it to smile up at Jess, then returned to his work. Jess saw that each meat was held on a stout, iron crossbar that rested on Y-topped poles over a fire pit. She suspected Doyle had fashioned the giant iron skewers and poles.

Suddenly, she remembered that she had wanted Doyle to craft candleholders to light the cookhouse for the night of the Fourth. She went back inside, grabbed two handfuls of tapers from the candle box, and dashed down the stairs with a hasty "see you later" to Jake.

∾⌖⟨⟩⌖∾

With a grin, Jake descended the stairs, pleased to see that Miss Hale wasn't going to let a bump in the emotional road keep her down.

"Hey, Jake!"

"Jake?"

Half a dozen of his men were hurrying toward him. Were he to guess, he would bet the anticipation in their strides had something to do with the landmarks for the races. With a last look toward Jess, he went to join them.

∾⌖⟨⟩⌖∾

Supper that night was served outdoors with everyone eating day-old biscuits and beans, groaning over the tantalizing aromas of the roasting meat. Sampling would have to wait until tomorrow, however.

Afterward, Seth and Reese talked Jess into a game of poker, and before long, seven more had joined their game. Jess had just accepted a fresh deck to shuffle when Jake sat down across from her with his mug of lemonade. He glanced around at the ranch hands who were about to play against her, as if doubting their good sense.

Jess shot him a questioning look. "Shall I deal you in?"

"Not me," he said. He spoke loud enough for all to hear. "I know better. I've seen you play before."

The other conversations fell silent, and all eyes turned to Jess. She curved her lips in a sweet smile and oozed her Southern charm. "Now the only reason I win is because y'all go easy on me because I'm a lady." Her hands neatly parted the deck, and she shuffled fluidly, tapping the cards together with an abrupt snap. "You boys just play, and don't worry yourselves none about my feelin's."

Then she dealt, sending cards flying around the table, precisely, one on top of the next.

Like a dealer in a saloon.

Several pairs of eyes turned warily to Jake.

He merely smiled, shrugged, and sipped his lemonade.

Chapter Fifteen

The Fourth of July dawned as one of the hottest days that summer—and one of the best. Jess was up at daybreak to water the garden, pleased with how well the plants were growing. The watering done, she took a walk by the creek, joyfully taking in the sights of mountains, blooming sage, and wildflowers. There were not as many wildflowers as there would have been if it had rained, she knew, but they were color and life, and somehow, they would survive.

And...God had put them there.

Jess breathed in, then let out a long, delighted sigh.

When I see things like this, Lord, I feel that You can't be very far away at all. In fact, I see You everywhere. She looked off to the south. *When I see the mountains, I feel Your love, because You didn't put them there just for You to enjoy—You put them there for us! Out of Your great love for us! And these flowers...* She bent down, sat back on her heels, and thrilled over a cluster of pink-petalled bitterroot. She passed a slim finger over a soft, narrow petal, lightly touching its fiery orange center. *You made this. You decided how many petals it would have. You put it here.* She turned to look up at the house. *And You gave us the barn swallows....* Eight young ones were perched on the edge of the roof, trying their wings, impatient for their mothers to return with breakfast. *And the butterflies...* Jess smiled at the thought of her old nickname. *And each day, You give us hope.*

Jess stood up again, marveling that God had chosen these ways to show her His closeness. Through His creation. "Thank You, Lord," she murmured.

All at once, a breeze broke the stillness of the desert and swept over her, stirring the hemline of her gown. Whispering.

Jess walked into it, filled with awe. The wind streamed through her hair, brushing the skin of her arms. A few moments later, it calmed and quieted.

It seemed as though the Lord had answered her.

And whether He truly had or not, Jess knew that He had heard her.

∾⋘❖⋙∾

As the day unfolded, Jess watched the men participate in all the events they'd prepared for—the races, the "chicken" pull, the shooting—and the Paiutes even challenged the cattlemen to try their skills with bows and arrows. Ho Chen kept everyone happily fed from the pig and beef roasts, as well as with dried fruits and pies. Jess nearly teared up when she found out that he had prepared her mother's favorite berry tarts, just for her.

There was the lemonade and a barrel of whiskey to quench everyone's thirst, and sweetened pine-nut pudding for dessert, which the Paiute children especially loved.

After sundown, Seth jogged over to the bunkhouse to get his harmonica, and Taggart brought out the fiddle Jess had seen the morning she and Red Deer had removed everything from the bunkhouse. A man appeared with a banjo and another with a guitar, and together, the four musicians had the cookhouse floor trembling from the clapping hands, stomping boots, and whirling dancers.

The ranchmen had been thoughtful to remove their spurs beforehand.

Jess and the Paiute women laughed until they ached as one man after another unceremoniously grabbed them for a dance. The men were ready to cut loose, and they were full of energy.

Jess lost count of how many times she had danced, and, gasping for breath when the latest song ended, she held up a hand when not one but three men stepped up to claim her for the next dance. "I need to sit one out," she panted.

"Oh, but Miss Jess—"

"Lemonade?"

Jess glanced up just as Jake pressed a mug into her hand. She smiled gratefully and took a drink. Seeing that the three would-be dance partners were still crowding her expectantly, Jake shot them a wordless glare. They disappeared.

"Thanks," she said, laughing softly. "I needed to be rescued."

He bowed with a smile. "Glad to be of service, ma'am."

Jess savored another sip, then slowly lowered her mug. "Now what is that look for?"

Jake took a drink from his own mug. "What look?"

"That look. That's not your usual ranchman's gaze." Instead, she thought his eyes seemed warm, fervent.

Another song began. They stepped back to avoid the dancers. "Should I treat you the same as I treat the men?" he asked quietly.

"After all we've been through together, I suppose not," she answered, suddenly not wanting to continue along those lines. "This has been a good day." She sighed. "A good celebration."

Jake smiled.

❧⊶✠⊷❧

Looking down at her, Jake wished the music would slow. He wanted nothing more than to pull her close and to find a way to tell her that he loved her. He wanted her to know it was safe to love him back, to trust that he would take care of her. He wanted to tell her that he would not let anything hurt her again. But he knew that this time, this place—it wasn't apt. Those things would come, he promised himself. Soon.

"The ranch fits me," Jess said, surprising him with her admission. "I can't imagine doing any other kind of work again."

"And the folks here?"

She sipped her lemonade. "They seem to fit me, too," she said, then looked away.

Reese whirled past, doing a jig. Then Taggart appeared before Jess, handing off his fiddle to someone else. "My heart'll break, for sure," he vowed, "if ye don't dance with me just once."

Playing along, Jess fluttered an imaginary fan. "I declare, that would be simply tragic."

With that, Taggart abruptly handed her cup to a passing Seth, then pulled her into the swirling crowd.

Jake's smile faded as he turned pensive once again. He set aside his own mug and stepped out into the evening air, his thoughts preoccupied with the most desirable dance partner—and life partner.

⌘

After two dances with Taggart, Jess took a break as the musicians paused for refreshments. Suddenly, a mysterious leather bag appeared. No one, not even the cattlemen, seemed to know where it had come from. When they opened it, they found, to everyone's amazement, that it was filled with tiny playthings for the Paiute children—a multitude of animals carved from small pieces of wood.

The children's eyes grew round while their parents

exclaimed excitedly over the toys. Doyle knelt down by the bag and let each child choose an animal.

As Jess looked on, she recalled seeing Diaz carving wood in his spare time. She searched the crowd and finally saw him standing across the room, leaning his shoulder against the wall. His expression was passive as he surveyed the scene and took intermittent bites from one of Georgeanne McKinney Hale's best-recipe tarts.

Jess made her way through the crowd and came to stand beside him, seeing the scene from his perspective. Diaz glanced at her and nodded, and she smiled. For several moments, neither spoke. At last, Jess said quietly, "I'll see that your sack is returned to you."

Diaz finished his last bite of tart and wiped his hands on his shirt. Keeping his eyes on the children, he asked softly, "What sack is this, mariposa?"

Jess looked at the happy families gathered in the center of the room. Two Hands was showing Lone Wolf an open-winged hawk. "The sack you filled with joy."

Diaz moved away from the wall and turned to her. "That sack belongs to *Dios*, Jessica. It is what He gives that brings joy." He tipped his hat respectfully. "Sleep well, mariposa." Keeping to the shadows, Diaz followed the wall to the door and quietly slipped out, contented, into the night.

∞∽⊰⬥⊱∾∞

As tired as she was from dancing, the summer night was too hot for Jess to rest well. She had been in bed no more than an hour, dozing lightly, when she heard Jake's door close as he entered his room—and heard it open minutes later as he left again.

Jess gave up trying to sleep, at least for the time being,

and climbed out of bed. Mildly curious about Jake's late-night wanderings, she moved to the window to see where he was headed. The sounds of music and dancing still rolled from the cookhouse. Red Deer had told her that the party would likely last until the sun came up—which couldn't be far off, by Jess's calculation.

She looked down into the yard. Lone Wolf and Red Deer were just leaving the party. Two Hands had gone home hours ago with friends, leaving his uncle and aunt alone. As she watched, Red Deer rested her head on Lone Wolf's shoulder. Lone Wolf pulled her close and settled a loving hand against his wife's round belly. There seemed to be an unusual closeness in their manner as they walked—it was a private moment, and Jess felt like an intruder for having seen it. She shifted her eyes away from the two.

The outlying ranch was still. For several minutes, Jess watched the shadows and open places for movements. She had expected to see Jake paying a visit to the mare-and-foal corral or checking on the mustangs, but he was doing neither. Then she saw him—he was leading a saddled Cielos toward the stable, and they disappeared behind it. After a moment, Jake reappeared, now in the saddle. He rode off.

Jess made fists with her hands on the windowsill. She recalled the day she and Jake had ridden the range and walked together. He had come close to telling her about the rosebush then, but he had been evasive, and then had come the mustangs' interruption. He had never brought it up again or ventured to explain.

"No more," she muttered. When she'd first come to the ranch, she'd wondered why the cattlemen, who clearly knew about the bush, behaved as though it didn't exist...why they turned their backs whenever Jake left with the cuttings, never questioning his intent or destination. Moreover, it seemed that whenever he took cut roses and left the compound, he was troubled and in need of comfort. For a man who talked about diamonds in the desert, and who had caused her to battle her heart over him, Jake seemed of two minds about loyalty. It seemed the "honorable" ranchman kept a mistress.

Hastily, Jess pulled on her clothes and boots, not bothering to braid her hair before hurrying down the stairs, through the door, and out to the stable, where she saddled Meg. She'd heard Jake ride toward the west. As quickly as she could, she followed, taking the same direction he had gone. She was going to find out what—or who—he was keeping from her. She had been toyed with long enough.

Jake pressed Cielos into a gallop. Weeks had passed since he'd been to visit Olivia—his Livvy. He'd gone to her grave less and less often since Jess had come to the ranch, and he had been there hardly at all since he'd fallen in love again. For more than a year, he had made this journey countless times, always with roses in his hand, always holding on to his memories of Livvy. But this...this was a ride he'd never thought he would make.

He was going to tell her good-bye.

When he came to her burial place, he dismounted and, as usual, tied Cielos to the juniper tree.

Then Jake removed his hat and approached the headstone, squatting down to lay the roses on her grave.

"I need to talk to you, Olivia," he said softly. Gazing at the eastern sky, which was slowly lightening to gray, he sighed. "I expect you and I spent a hundred or more sunrises together, didn't we? When we married, I thought we were going to get all the rest of them, too, but I reckon the Almighty had other plans."

Leaning on one knee, he inched the roses closer to the base of the headstone that bore her name and that of the little daughter they had loved. As always, his heart clenched a little as he remembered holding Livvy by his side and laughing with her over their tiny daughter's sweet smiles, her giggles.

Jake cleared his throat. "After you, I never thought I could love anyone again. I guess I didn't want to, truth be told. I wanted us the way we had been." He hesitated. "But if you had lost me instead, I'd have wanted you to marry again, so you'd have someone to care for you. And I now know that if you could, you'd tell me to do the same." He turned his hat in his hands. "I never planned for such a thing to happen, but the truth is, I've fallen in love again, Livvy. I think you'd like her. Her family name is Hale, in case you meet her ma and pa. She's a lot like you—strong and determined—and she loves this land. It's a part of her, the way it's a part of me, and she's alone now, like I am. I want to take care of her, and to have her by my side. I want to grow old with her, just like you and I always talked about. I hope you understand, Livvy, because it means I won't be able to visit you as often, although I'll still come when I can."

Jake's heart was heavy. He felt he was losing her all over again, but, oddly, he also experienced a growing sense of peace—as if she had heard him and understood. As if she had given him her blessing.

When he heard a horse and rider approaching, Jake knew it was Jess. He pushed himself to his feet, sending the Lord a prayer that he might find the words to calm her wary heart.

Jess recognized the area as the place she had seen from the hilltop months ago on the day she had found the dead calf and vultures. Quite clearly now, she remembered the burial marker

Jake was standing beside. When he turned to face her, she looked down at him. There was no mistress, no romantic tryst, no one else at all.

"I apologize for intruding," she said softly, dismounting. "I saw you cutting the roses, and I followed." She tied Meg beside Cielos.

"An intruder is someone you don't want with you," Jake murmured. "You could never be that with me."

Unsettled by his tenderness, Jess crouched down beside the marker. She tried to make out the names by moonlight. Suddenly, her head shot up and her wide eyes met Jake's.

"Olivia and Sadie Bennett?" Jess searched his face. "Jake?"

"Jess, I've been meaning to tell you this, but I didn't quite know how. Olivia was my wife. She...she'd been gone about a year when you and I met."

Jess closed her eyes with regret. She finally understood the pain she'd often sensed in him. When he'd said that working horses and cattle could take one's mind away from one's troubles, he was speaking from experience. How could she have been so blind—so heartless?

Her eyes opened, and she gazed again at the stone. "And Sadie was...your daughter?"

"Yes. I met Olivia in Sacramento City in the spring of 1860." He chuckled softly. "I'd gone to buy a bull from Livvy's pa. On the way, I found this young woman up to her ankles in mud. She was tugging on her horse's halter, trying to budge that stubborn animal to get her wagon unstuck. I think she was about ready to shoot him when I pulled up and offered to help. I got the wagon unstuck. To thank me, she invited me to supper." He smiled, remembering.

Jess couldn't help smiling. "So, that was it."

"That was it," he confirmed. "We were married three weeks later."

"Three *weeks*?"

"Three weeks. We had no doubts. It was right."

Jess looked away, uncomfortable with the pointed way he was watching her. Softly, she said, "And Sadie?"

"She was born the following winter. She was a beauty. Black hair and blue eyes, just like her mama. In their last months, Sadie was walking, and it was all Olivia could do to keep her from climbing the stairs. Her bedroom was the middle one," Jake explained, "and that was where the cat liked to hide. She was always looking to find that cat." He was gazing down at Jess, awaiting her reaction.

For Jess, the last unknown details about him began to fall into place. She thought back to all the oddities she'd puzzled over since the day she'd arrived at the ranch—the feminine, floral soap, the dresses packed away in the trunk, the braided belt, which she knew now Jake must have made for Olivia. There were other things, too—the dressing table itself, which had probably had its own place in Jake's bedroom while Olivia was alive; the rose-print calico tablecloths. The ranch was marked indelibly by the touch of a woman. A woman who had loved Jake very much.

Jess stood and faced him, her manner gentle now. "And the rosebush?"

"Olivia's mother had always grown roses, so I planted one to help her feel at home. Now I take cuttings when I come to visit her and Sadie." He seemed a little embarrassed. "I even take the branches when they're bare. I guess I wanted her to know that I'm keeping her roses alive, that I won't forget her." As an afterthought, he added, "Her favorite color was yellow."

Hence the yellow roses, which he now remembered her by. A breeze stirred, billowing her skirt—also yellow, like the roses. She smiled to herself. With black hair and blue eyes, Olivia must have been a beauty, especially in yellow. "Is Olivia the 'white woman friend' Red Deer sometimes speaks of?"

"I suppose she is. I didn't want Livvy to go that day," he

went on, "but Sadie was a year old and bundled against the cold, and Olivia wanted to visit her mother. Her mother would come to Lake Tahoe to stay with Livvy's sister for a time," he explained. "The cattle were dying with the cold, and I felt Olivia and Sadie would be fine; I was needed here." His jaw tightened. He slapped his hat against his thigh. "I was wrong."

Jess had the prickly feeling she wasn't going to want to hear the rest. He clearly wanted her to know, though, so she waited patiently for him to go on. The first hint of sunrise lit the eastern sky.

"On her way to see her ma, Livvy was...waylaid...by outlaws camped in a bend of the mountain. There was nothing in the wagon worth taking, so it was she they were after. A woman." He pinched the bridge of his nose. "As that day wore on, and I worked the cattle, I felt more and more that I should have gone with her. By mid-afternoon, I could think of nothing else, so I went after them." He looked at Jess again. "I found them about twenty miles south of here."

Found them. Jess didn't know what to say. As a boy, he'd buried his mother, and as a man, he'd buried his wife and daughter. He'd buried her family, too—and her father had been a friend. All along, Jake had known exactly what she was feeling; patiently, and in subtle ways, he had worked to help her through it. Jess searched his face. When she'd asked about the roses, she had never expected this. "Did you ever find the outlaws?"

"I didn't need to. There were five of them, all lying dead not far from where they'd..." The words caught in his throat. He rephrased them. "Not far from Livvy. It seems they'd had some mighty poor intentions, and Livvy decided to fight rather than give in to them. I guess she knew they'd kill her anyway." Jake looked down at her, and from his wordless expression, Jess could tell that he hadn't spoken of it since then. "Near as I can tell, they shot her horses to stop the wagon. Knowing Olivia, she grabbed Sadie and tried to run to protect her, but they caught Livvy. Her arms were bruised and her dress was torn, but she pulled her gun and fired on them, and they fired back.

"I found them both shot, Livvy dead and Sadie lying curled in her arm like she was sleeping. I found the gun in Livvy's other hand." His deep voice was filled with pride. "She'd emptied it clean."

His revelation explained so much—why he had been so determined to keep Jess at the ranch, how upset he became whenever she tried to run, why he'd insisted she learn to shoot. He knew the dangers of the West and the importance of self-defense, lessons that had cost him his precious wife and daughter to learn.

Jake glanced skyward. "But they're with the Lord now, with my mama...and with your family, too."

Jess passed her eyes over a carpet of dried yellow roses left from other visits. "You miss them dearly."

He nodded with a reflective smile. "I can't wait to see them again."

"Again?"

"In heaven."

"That's a long wait."

"Not so long. The years have a way of slipping by, especially when you have something at the end to look forward to. Then the Lord will bring us home, and we'll all be together again." He looked over at Jess. "I thought you read the Bible."

"It's been a while," she admitted, "and I've never thought that far ahead."

"I've learned to look at things differently, I reckon. It's not as though I'll never see them again, at least not as long as I don't stray from the Almighty." He lifted his eyes to search the bluing sky. "No, we'll always have Again."

Jess looked up, as well, recalling that Ambrose had used

nearly the same words in the last letter he ever wrote. "That's why I've wanted to go to the cemetery where my family is buried, to be close to them." She glanced pointedly at the roses that dotted the grave. "Surely, you understand that need."

His steady gaze met hers. "I do. For almost a year, hardly a week went by that I didn't come out here. There were times when I came nearly every day."

"Were?" As soon as the question was out, Jess wished she could take it back. She didn't want to know what *were* meant.

Jake faced her squarely. "Jess, I came here tonight to say good-bye to her. I won't forget her or Sadie, but their time here is done. So is your family's, but I still have now, and so do you."

Jess started to shake her head and took a step back. The old, familiar fear climbed up her spine.

"We're right for each other, Jess. What we both want is here. The open land, the sky above us, the horses."

Desperate to be away, Jess turned and hurried toward Meg.

Jake caught hold of her arm and gently pulled her around to face him. He held her shoulders firmly. "No. You're not running this time."

Jess clenched her jaw and squirmed.

"Jess, listen."

"No!"

"Losing your folks was hard on you. I know, because losing my ma killed a part of me. Later, when I met Olivia, I knew she was right for me, and I was committed to her. We got married, but it still took me a long to give her my heart. Are you hearing me? I wasn't ready to chance losing it again."

Jess twisted away from his hold and started walking in no particular direction. Jake stayed put but kept talking, more fervently now.

"In time, I did love Olivia, and with all my heart. She gave me Sadie, and then I lost them. After that, I kept working the ranch, but I believed my life was over." Tears now streamed down Jess's cheeks. She turned around and looked into his eyes. "But then I met you, and I know now that no matter how much I fear losing you, it is nothing compared to my fear of never getting the chance to love you at all."

Jess stilled abruptly and stared up at him in amazement. She felt as though he'd just offered her the sun, moon, and stars—and that he was capable of delivering them. At that thought, every memory of him came rushing back—every time he'd stood between her and danger, each moment he'd been there for her. Her heart took a step forward. She wanted him, she realized—she wanted him for always.

In the next instant, that longing was swallowed by a threat so great it felt like a chasm opening beneath her, consuming her.

"Jess, what—?"

All her fear, all her rage, all her desperation erupted in one explosive shout. "I don't want to love you!"

Jake's gaze locked with hers. "Tell me why, Jess."

"I'm afraid! I'm afraid it'll be taken away…afraid you'll be taken away! I don't know how to love only a little!"

Jake took a step toward her. "I know you don't."

She was trembling. "I don't want things to change between us. I want to work the ranch together, and live here with you, and…and…"

"And what, Jess? You want me to stop loving you?"

"No!"

"You want me never to hold you?"

She shook her head, gasping for breath through her tears.

"Should I stop walking with you, caring about you, keeping you safe?" He didn't give her a chance to answer. "I want to share my life with you. I want to wake every morning with you by my side. I want to give you children to love, calves to feed, and horses to name." Jess smiled behind the wet wisps of hair clinging to her temples. "I want to see you rip buttons out of the men's johns and watch you shoot crooked." Now she was laughing. "I want to watch you cut cattle out of the herd. I want to see the firelight reflected in your hair. I want to raise horses and not be doing it alone." Jake had sobered. So had she. "I need you, Jess. I need you with me."

Her tears stopped entirely. Jess wasn't sure how he'd ended up so close to her. She wasn't sure of anything at the moment, except that she wanted him to be even closer.

Jess felt his arms embrace her, meeting at the small of her back. She burrowed against him, listening to the beat of his heart—strong and sure. It was a sound she could easily grow accustomed to.

What if you lose him? her old doubts asked. From somewhere inside came the reply: *If you walk away from what you have now, you'll lose him anyway.*

The rising sun burst upon the horizon. Jess turned her face away, suddenly realizing how tired she was. She told him so.

Briefly, Jake hugged her tighter. "Let's go back."

Neither spoke as they walked together toward the horses, Jake setting his hat on his head.

At the juniper tree, he untied Meg and gave Jess a leg up into the saddle. Once he'd settled on Cielos, his eyes found hers.

"I'll need time," she finally said.

He answered softly, "You have it."

271

Chapter Sixteen

As the days grew longer, Jess's work increased, for the heat of late summer sought to drain the life from growing vegetables and grains. She and the Paiute women worked constantly to keep the garden sufficiently watered. It was the hardest summer Jess had ever known. For more reasons than the weather.

For weeks, she had felt a growing sense of unease. She would jump at sounds and shifting shadows, and even the ranch hands kept their rifles closer than before. Jess wanted to believe that another attack would never come, but she knew as soon as the thought crossed her mind that that would not be the case. Too many fires had been set, too many cattle had been stolen, and too many watchful men had passed by to sweep out the door as of no consequence. Besides, she knew it in her gut.

Furthermore, Jake had assigned cattle-tending to the others so that he and his best horsemen could focus their efforts on breaking the mustangs. He worked longer hours than ever, and in his rare free moments, as well as at mealtimes, he casually kept his distance from Jess. She knew that it was partly to prevent the men from speculating about them and partly to give her time to think. And she quickly found that not being close to him distressed her more than she could have imagined.

In mid-August, she finally sought out her longtime confidant.

"Ho Chen?" Stepping in from the blinding outdoors, she couldn't see him in the dimness of the cookhouse.

"I am by cooking table, Miss Jessie," he called.

Jess closed the door quietly, then made her way to where Ho Chen was preparing the noon meal.

"You're welcome to leave off the 'Miss,' Ho Chen," she said. "I'd hardly be taken for the daughter of a business owner anymore."

Ho Chen returned her smile. He continued to observe her as she fitfully scrubbed her hands in the washbasin. He turned back to the cutting board. "You are hungry?"

Jess dried her hands. "No, I—" Abruptly, she fell silent. She took up a carving knife and a piece of meat, which she began cutting into cubes. "I wanted to talk to you, if I could."

Wordlessly, Ho Chen reached up for a string of onions, then began to peel off their outermost skins. He was listening.

"Jake and I have begun to care for each other, and he's asked me to marry him. I think I even love him, but since the fire, I've lived in terror of losing someone again. Now when I think of marrying..." She shook her head, sawing the meat more vigorously. "He's been patient, Ho Chen—so patient. He's never once pushed for my answer. I feel my love for him building, but as it does, so do my worries. Now I'm starting to wonder: what will it take to pull me one way or the other? How will I ever know?" She gave up all pretense of helping and slammed down the knife. Her eyes were tearing as they met his. "What am I supposed to do?"

Ho Chen set down his knife and the onions and wiped his hands on a cloth. He thought for a moment, then spoke. "I remember your father say, 'A man is never any better than he is when he is at his worst.' You need chance to see Mr. Bennett at time of great trouble to know for yourself what kind of man he truly is. Any man can show kindness when there are no troubles. It is in the trials he must face that he will show his honor or his shame. This is what you must wait for. When you see how deep his worth, love will overcome, and fear will no longer matter."

Jess reflected on his words. Then she looked up, searching his face. "You think I should marry him."

"I know you almost four years, Miss Jessie," he said. "After fire, I see you very, very sad. Then I see you grow happy with this place and these people, and I know your Mr. Bennett. I know his worth."

She thanked him and excused herself. And as she walked out of the cookhouse, his voice trailed her. "But it is not I who must be certain." He picked up his knife and began chopping again.

❧

September arrived, and still no rain had come to water the land. The grain crops failed. Most of the vegetable garden had survived, though, and Ho Chen worked with Jess and the Paiute women to harvest the plants and to store the vegetables for the coming winter.

Nearly all the mustangs had been saddle-broken. Since autumn roundup was only a month away, the men began to discuss which mustangs to sell in the weeks ahead and which to keep for breeding or for use on the ranch. Jake sent three of the cattlemen to Fort Churchill and to every town between the ranch and Carson City to search out buyers for the mustangs. He and the other cattlemen stayed behind to finish the breaking.

Whenever Jess had a few free hours, she rode to the Indian village to visit Red Deer. Her friend was terribly thin for one so far along in her pregnancy, and Jess feared for her. Though Red Deer always cheered up to see Jess, she was quieter now, and she rose less and less often when Jess arrived. She no longer spoke of the nightmares she'd had, but Jess knew by the dark shadows beneath her eyes that she was still not sleeping well. When she voiced her concern, Red Deer only assured her that such things sometimes happened when a woman was nearing the time for childbirth.

Jess continued weaving late at night, hoping to finish the blanket before the baby came. She became adept at twisting in colored yarns with consistent pressure, and her fingers bled where the woolen strands chafed them. Still, she kept at her task, no longer weaving for Red Deer's baby but for Red Deer herself. Completing it would encourage Red Deer to fight for her very life. Into the orange background, Jess had woven colorful symbols: a large gray wolf to signify the child's father and, opposite it, a circlet of the yellow flowers for which Red Deer had been named. In the very center, she wove a cradle basket like those the Paiute women fashioned for infants. Immediately beside it, with its graceful neck curved, stood a beautiful and nurturing doe, colored red.

It was on her return to the ranch after a visit in the Paiute village that the relative peacefulness Jess had come to know was shattered.

At first, only a single *crack!* echoed from the direction of the compound. Jess slowed Meg, alarmed by the odd sound. In the next instant, the entire ranch resounded with an explosion of gunfire.

The anticipation was over.

With a sharp kick, Jess sent Meg flying toward the distant buildings. She was already gripping her gun. The loss of her family might have been the start of a fanatical swath of terror, but she would allow no other settlers to be harmed, no matter their origins. This would be the end of it.

Her eyes scanned the rapidly passing landscape to see mounted ranch hands racing in from the range.

As she neared the compound, she saw several horsemen with bandanas over their faces firing on the ranch hands, who fired back. One of the cattlemen fell.

Blood pounded in her veins. Four of the outlaws headed for the gate of the farthest corral…and the mustangs.

Jess cocked the hammer of her gun as she rounded the stable. She leveled the revolver.

BOOM!

The report from her gun was lost in the roar of the others; yet one horse fled, its saddle empty.

A sound like a buzzing bee whizzed past her ear. Blinking back the fear that seized her, she aimed again and fired.

Her eyes found Jake's as he mounted Cielos. He yelled something she couldn't hear, gesturing violently with his gun.

Jess ignored him.

Several ranch hands were on foot, but most of them had gained their horses and were preparing to counter the attack.

Jess saw a renegade leap from his horse and reach for the mustang gate. She fired, splintering the wooden post near his hand.

The man jerked back, seeing a horse with an empty saddle charging toward him. He dove out of its path.

The mustangs, mares, and foals panicked, throwing themselves against the far side of their corrals in an effort to break free of the enclosures.

All at once, Taggart was riding on Jess's left, Seth on her right. The three parted ways as the outlaws rode in from every direction. Jess was determined to hold her own.

When she found herself free from pursuit for a moment, she scanned the fracas for Jake. A galloping horse suddenly reared before her, its eyes rolling white as it fell over backward, crushing its rider beneath it. She saw Jake, thirty feet away. He was holding off two renegades while a third gunman rode in, unseen, behind him. With a stab of her heels, Jess sent Meg in an arching leap over the fallen horse, barely registering the irate expression Jake was directing at her.

Holding out her gun, she sighted along her arm and focused on the curled fist of the outlaw behind Jake. She pulled the trigger. Jake's expression changed to bewilderment. He turned to see a pistol flung from the hand of the man who had been aiming at his back.

~◦≺⫤≻◦~

Jake's eyes snapped to Jess. She was moving again, firing. Another man dropped his weapon.

Her words from months earlier suddenly taunted him: *I usually hit what I aim for, Bennett, and I've never yet hit a polecat in the foot.* He had dismissed those words then. He respected them now.

Jessica Hale knew how to shoot.

A shot ripped across Jake's forearm, burning like a hot knife. With one eye on Jess, partly to admire her and partly to protect her, he rushed into the battle once again, driving Cielos into the thick of it.

~◦≺⫤≻◦~

As Jess reloaded her gun, her eyes darted about the riot of men and horses. She glimpsed Ho Chen near the smithy, brandishing fire irons with steel-eyed purpose. Paiutes with bows had positioned themselves around the corrals, and they had begun streaming arrows toward those least inclined to end the fight.

In her scrutiny, Jess hesitated a moment too long. One of the outlaws gained on her from behind and swept her from her saddle, knocking the revolver from her hand. As he reined in his horse, she looked up into the leering eyes of the skeletal, balding man from Carson City.

Jess struggled to snatch his pistol. Suddenly, Lone Wolf rode in fast. He flipped his rifle, caught it by the barrel, and swung.

The man holding her slumped in his saddle.

Jess fell to the ground, her gaze fastened on the rifle sheathed below the pommel. She pushed herself to her feet and yanked the rifle free.

Lone Wolf swung again. The man tumbled to the ground, and his horse skittered away. Immediately, Lone Wolf dismounted and knelt to bind the man with rope.

"Jessica?"

"I'm fine!"

She heard another horse coming up fast behind her, and she thrust the rifle to her shoulder, cocked it, and spun around.

In reflex, Jake pushed the rifle barrel skyward, shooting a glare at Jess as he galloped past.

Lone Wolf leapt back into his saddle and rejoined the fight. Jess smelled smoke—sure enough, flames were rolling up the walls of the smithy.

She saw Jake rein in Cielos and jump down. He dragged an unconscious Doyle up and over his shoulder, then carried him at a run to the cookhouse.

Jess pressed herself to the side of the bunkhouse. She held the rifle at the ready, eyes sweeping the yard.

Half a dozen mustangs were out, running for the open range.

Diaz ran to the gate and pushed it closed. He exchanged gunfire with a masked horseman.

Diaz went down.

Jess screamed.

Reese yelled that he was behind her, watching her back.

Jess strained to see what had happened to Diaz. The thickset man who had shot him fell from his saddle, but a second man was riding toward Diaz to finish him. Jess took aim. Fired.

The man fell backward off his horse.

Beyond him, the burly man stood up, cradling the arm she'd wounded earlier. He searched the ground for his gun. His bandana had slipped away, and his pockmarked face was visible as he yelled to one of his associates. Jess gasped in recognition, reaching for Reese's horse. "Reese!" The boy hoisted her into the saddle, and she kicked the horse into a swift run. She pulled up beside the man who had once dug his fist into her hair, leveling her rifle on him.

He had called to a mounted outlaw, who was now speeding toward them. Reese ran past her and fired a warning shot. After a brief standoff, the horseman threw down his gun.

Several moments passed. The air seemed to quiet as fewer shots were fired. Only a handful of outlaws remained, barely distinguishable in the dust stirred up by the commotion.

Knowing they were gaining the upper hand against the outlaws, those ranch hands still on foot mounted horses and pursued the retreating marauders.

Seth appeared with several lengths of rope in his hands, and he and Reese began tying the two men. The burly one stared up at Jess. "I never expected to see you again."

To Jess, that was tantamount to an admission of guilt for killing her parents—and for trying to kill her. "If I'm a surprise, you'll be simply giddy when you see the jail at Fort Churchill."

He managed a glare before Seth and Reese led him and his associate away.

Once the yard cleared, Jess shakily lowered her rifle and tried to catch her breath.

The battle was over.

A few ranch hands moved to stand guard at the perimeter. Others ran to the smithy with buckets of water to douse the flames. The wounded ones propped themselves against watering troughs or building walls and held their guns on the groaning outlaws until help arrived.

Spinning her horse around, Jess retrieved her revolver and hurried to the cookhouse, where Jake had taken Doyle. She dismounted, tossing her reins to Will.

"Jake?"

"Over here!"

Jake, Ho Chen, and Lone Wolf were crowded around Ho Chen's bunk, and Jake was pressing a clean cloth to Doyle's chest while Ho Chen uncorked a bottle of whiskey.

"I have to tell you—"

Jake cut her off. "Go find Taggart. Tell him to make sure everyone at the Paiute village is safe. Then tell him to send two men after the mustangs."

"I will," she panted, necessarily putting off the news of her attackers, "but if Doyle needs a bullet cut out of him, you'd best get him to the house. The light is better, and the main room has more space to tend him." With that, she was out.

Jess ran across the yard to where Taggart, Seth, and Reese were loading the outlaws into a wagon at gunpoint. All around her, ranch hands were tying bandanas to bleeding wounds. Those with arm injuries used their free hands and their teeth to knot the bandages. Jess was relieved to see Diaz leaning up on his elbow, in pain but managing.

Jess relayed Jake's instructions to Taggart and then raced to the house. Just as she stepped through the door, Jake and Lone Wolf lowered Doyle's limp form onto the sofa.

She glanced at Ho Chen. "What can I do?"

"Get hot water. Clean towels. Cloth for bandage."

Lone Wolf knelt to feed the fire while Jess hurried to the

kitchen for a water bucket and some empty pots. Her arms full, she ran out the door and headed for the pump.

～◦☆◉☆◦～

Jake opened the door of the linen cabinet at the end of the short hallway. He pulled out a few tablecloths and tore them into strips, just as he had done for Jess. In his mind, he could still see her shooting boldly and with stunning accuracy. From a galloping horse.

"Mr. Bennett?"

Jake spun around to face Ho Chen.

"He is awake."

In long strides, Jake crossed the room to Doyle's side. Seeing the man's jaw clenched in pain, Jake swept the whiskey bottle from the table and pressed it into Doyle's good hand. He met the man's eyes. "See what you can do to empty that bottle."

Glimpsing the steely flash of Ho Chen's blade, Doyle smiled faintly. "I think I'd better, at that." Taking the bottle, he raised it to his lips and took a swig.

In his mind, Jake saw no one but Jess.

～◦☆◉☆◦～

A few moments later, Jess hurried in through the door. She was weighed down by buckets and pots of water, and Lone Wolf rose from the fire to help her.

"I think the men saved most of the smithy," she told Jake, "and Taggart sent Seth and Reese after the mustangs. No one at the Paiute village was hurt." To stop shaking, she examined Jake's torn sleeve and the furrow of blood cutting across his forearm. It was only a graze, but it would need to be tended.

Relieved that Jake would be all right, Jess finally allowed

herself to see the severity of Doyle's wound. A jagged hole showed where the men had torn away his shirt. Unable to hide her worry, she looked in Doyle's eyes instead.

"I think..." Doyle took in several hard breaths, gesturing with the bottle of whiskey. "I think you best leave now, Jess. You're welcome to come back later, when Ho Chen here gets me stitched back together."

Struggling against the desire to help however she could, she looked at Jake.

"He'll be fine, Jess," he assured her. "See if any of the others need a hand."

On impulse, she laid her hand on Doyle's forehead and murmured a promise that she'd be back soon.

She left quickly, sending up a prayer for him as she ventured into the ranch yard.

∾❦◈❦∾

"Here, hold this." Jess placed a clean cloth in Diaz's palm and pressed his hand over the wound in his side. She already held another cloth against the exit wound. All around them, efficient Paiute women tended to the injured. Someone had started simmering a pot of medicinal herbs over a fire. A young Indian girl stirred the brew.

"Jess?"

It was Jake. Her heart twisted, knowing he had brought news of Doyle. She looked up. "How is he?"

"Weak, but he'll make it. Ho Chen did a fine job."

Jess let out a sigh of relief. "Jake, I saw two of the men who attacked me in Carson City. Taggart loaded them in a wagon with the others."

"I know. I saw them. Do you feel better now that they've been caught?"

"A little. But the others are still free."

"The others aren't the ones stealing and burning Southerners' homes. These men are."

"A few of them got away."

"They're not going to risk their skins riding into a ranchful of enraged cattlemen again, if that's your next thought, so don't fret over it."

"But if they—"

"Jess." Jake knelt down beside Diaz. "Look around you. If you were one of those outlaws, would *you* ride in here again after witnessing the fight these boys put up? No, you wouldn't, and neither will anyone else who escaped today. They're destructive and full of hate, but they aren't stupid." He remained calm, reasonable. "We'll keep an eye out, but after the losses they've suffered today, you have to know they won't be back."

Jess blew out her breath again. "I suppose you're right. And my family has been avenged. I've waited a long time for that."

Jake looked as though he wanted to take her in his arms and comfort her. He didn't. They both knew there were wounded to help. "And how's Diaz?" he asked.

The Spaniard's mouth curved into a pained, white-toothed grin. One eye squinted against the bright sun. "I think maybe, boss, the lovely mariposa here would have flown to my side sooner, if only I had not waited till now to get shot."

Sending him a quick smile, Jess answered Jake. "The bullet passed through, but he's lost blood. Hiram's the only other one who's hurt badly. Ho Chen will need to see to him. Most of the others have cuts and scratches. One of the Paiute men has a knife wound, and his wife is stitching him up." Two Hands came up beside Jess and held out a cup of steaming herb tea. She thanked the boy, taking the mug from him and handing it to Diaz. She glanced up to see Nate driving the wagon out, heading for Fort Churchill. Will and two others rode horses alongside, heavily armed. They rounded the stable and disappeared.

"Jake, that burly man said he hadn't expected to see me.

He didn't even know I was here, which means they were after something else."

"They wanted the mustangs."

Jess felt greater relief to know the outlaws' motives than to know that they had been captured. No one was looking for her with plans to kill her. Perhaps no one had seen her when Lone Wolf carried her from the fire. Her cloak hood had been covering her face. Even so... "Why did they wait until now to attack us? The ponies have been here for more than two months, and those men knew it. We started seeing them in June."

"They waited until the mustangs had been broken in. They're worth more that way. They must have figured we were getting ready to sell them ourselves."

"This was more than stealing and burning homes. They tried to kill Diaz, Doyle, and many others."

Jake pulled off a glove and rubbed his jaw with his thumb. "Do you remember I once told you that I didn't know a woman out West who didn't know how to shoot? This is why. We don't have many lawmen out here, Jess. This kind of thing happens, but now it's over. It's over," he assured her. He glanced around. "Did Red Deer stay at the village?"

At the mention of his caregiver's name, Two Hands showed worry in his gentle eyes. Meeting his gaze, Jess gave him an encouraging smile. "With the baby's arrival only a few weeks away, she's been tired, so she's keeping close to home," she explained. "I'm sure she's fine."

Jess sent Two Hands on his way and then bent down to check Diaz's bleeding. She caught Jake smiling at her. Her mood lifted a little, just as it always did when he looked at her like that. "What?"

"I guess it won't be necessary to teach you how to shoot from the saddle, after all."

Looking away, Jess busied herself cleaning Diaz's wound, chagrined she'd been found out.

"A tin is no smaller than a hand, Jess." Seeing Diaz's look of curiosity, Jake explained, "I saw her shoot the guns out of the hands of two men."

Four eyebrows rose as the two men awaited her explanation.

At the reminder of what had happened, Jess realized she had mortally wounded at least one man. She closed her eyes a moment, wishing they could talk about something else. "I was within range," she said, almost indifferently. "Either of you could have made those shots. I took away the use of their gun hands. I could do it without killing them, so I did."

"Why didn't you let on earlier that you could shoot?" Jake asked.

"Keeping that knowledge to myself amused me at the time, and it was a card I could play, in the event there was a need."

"And rifles, Jess?" he said gently. "You know your way around a rifle, too, don't you?"

Jess diligently wiped bits of dried blood from the wound. "Well enough to keep Diaz from getting shot a second time."

Diaz turned to look at her. "You are the reason I still breathe, mariposa?"

Sudden tears filled her eyes. She threw her cloth into the water bucket, then began wrapping a clean bandage around the man's middle.

"I've never had to defend my life before, or the lives of people I care about. I feel sick because of everything that happened today, but I'm glad that the two of you and the others cared enough to look out for me." She secured the bandage and wiped her nose on a sleeve. "And," she said, her voice thick with emotion, "I'm grateful that someone once loved me enough and had foresight enough to teach me to defend myself."

Jake looked at her thoughtfully. "Isaac taught you to shoot?"

Jess shook her head. Wanting to go check on Doyle, she stood up. "No. Ambrose did."

~❦~

For days, Jake noticed that Jess kept a discreet eye on the wounded men, yet she respected the cattlemen's pride and did not mother them solicitously. She glanced briefly at the men's coloring during supper and watched for signs of their pain when she passed them in the stable. And though they were healing rapidly, Jess remained quiet and pensive, even when she was with Jake.

The morning after Doyle, Diaz, and Hiram had resumed their regular chores after a hiatus, Jake stepped from the corral, having broken the last mustang at sunrise. He glanced up to see Jess leaving the house. She was wearing her hat pulled low on her head, and she had a bandana knotted at her neck. She was carrying her coat, which she had begun to wear at night, as well as a large sack of provisions and a canteen, which she filled at the pump.

They had regained a sense of ease and comfort, but it seemed to Jake that it was about to be thrown to the wind. He latched the corral gate and walked toward her. The Almighty had blessed Jessica Hale with tenacity, he reflected. She looked as though she intended to use it to the fullest.

~❦~

Jess heard Jake approach. She capped the canteen and headed for the stable, her gaze locked on her goal.

The crops had been gathered, the scattered mustangs had

been found, the men wounded during the attack had healed. With these things accomplished, Jess felt justified in leaving the ranch to do the one thing she had yet to accomplish. She had put off this trip for far too long.

Despite Jake's warnings of the dangers of travel, and despite her own promise, she had to go back to Carson City—had to go there to let go of the past. She, too, needed to say good-bye, just as Jake had.

The thieves' attack had shaken her more than she'd let on. The ranchmen and the Paiutes had become her family. Reliving the threat of loss all over again was a lashing on top of a lashing that hadn't fully healed. She had to put to rest everything that had gone before, or she'd be afraid for her own sanity if ever it happened again.

Inside the stable, Jess tossed her coat, sack, and canteen onto a shelf.

Jake followed her to the stall she entered, dropping a hand onto the open gate. "Where are you headed, Jess?"

She led Meg out and inspected her hooves. "To Carson City."

"Carson City? What happened?"

Jess pressed the lead into his hand as she passed him to reach down a bridle. "Nothing happened. I need to pay my respects to my family, and I want to get my brother's letters from the safe in the import store. They're all I have left of him."

She slipped the bridle onto Meg, her fingers deftly buckling the chin strap. She flipped the reins over her horse's head.

"You're going to put yourself in danger again," he cautioned her. "There are still men out there who are enraged over wounds we all inflicted. They could be watching the ranch."

"Are they watching the ranch?"

Jake sighed. "No, they aren't."

Taggart and Diaz stopped several paces away, not sure

whether to go or to stay. Jess nodded a greeting to them as she retrieved Meg's saddle.

"This is a little sudden, isn't it?"

"No, Jake. This is long overdue."

He secured Meg's lead to a support beam. "I'll saddle Cielos and go with you."

"I'm going alone."

The two cattlemen walked out again, wordlessly detaining the others who were on their way in to saddle mounts.

"After all that's happened, did you really think I would let you go alone?"

She raised an eyebrow as she laid the saddle over the back of her mare. "Let?"

"I'm not going to argue with you, Jess. You know it isn't safe to go alone."

"Jake, I have to do this on my own. I will be careful." More gently, she added, "Thank you for caring."

Jake laid a hand on her shoulder to still her. His deep voice softened. "There are times when the Almighty uses your friends to tell you things, Jess."

Her hands paused on the leather. She considered his point.

"I understand your need to stand on your own, to prove to yourself—and maybe to everyone else—that you're not afraid. But when someone fills your heart the way you do mine, you want to be there for that person when you believe she needs you. Losing Olivia taught me that. I know you can get by on your own just fine, but I'd sure want to be beside you if you needed me."

Jess looked up at the tall man with the steady brown eyes. Meg stirred beside her, bringing her attention back to the ranch duties that needed to be done. Yes, she had to go, but she knew that asking Jake to abandon the ranch for her sake wasn't right. He had all this to see to, and besides, she could take care of herself. "You can't just pick up and chase after me. You're needed here at the ranch."

Jake leaned over to catch her gaze. "Jess, I know well what needs to be done. Sometimes one matter has more importance than another. This time, your heart matters more than anything else. We'll be gone only a few days, at most. The boys will look after things until we get back."

Outside, the men pretended not to listen. They began wagering silently on the outcome.

Jess felt a pleasant lightness inside her. She tipped her head to the side. "You're using Paiute logic on me, aren't you?"

"Paiute logic?"

"You know, talking with me calmly until I agree with you."

"Is it working?"

The ranch hands leaned in closer.

When she didn't answer, Jake murmured, "Shall we go to Carson City?"

"Say yes!" Taggart growled.

Jess sighed, then stepped into a curtsy her mother would have applauded. "I would be grateful for your kind escort, Mr. Bennett."

A chorus of cheers went up from the ranch hands outside. With a touch to his hat, Jake responded in kind. "Your servant, ma'am."

The men burst into the stable, all of them in high spirits as they grabbed up their gear and made for the stalls. Jess shared a smile with Jake, then resumed her labors as she answered each man's jovial greeting. Jake gave instructions to the men, naming Lone Wolf as the one in charge of the ranch until they returned.

Only minutes after the building had filled, it cleared again, Jess leading Meg out alongside the other horses. She saw Cielos tied near a corral. Beside him, Jake tugged the last stirrup into place.

Reese appeared with additional provisions for them, and he tossed Jake a bedroll. The second bedroll he tied onto Jess's saddle himself.

"I thought you might want to sleep in more than just your coat," he said, too much a boy to avoid blushing, too much a man to let her tie it herself. When Jess thanked him, he nodded, then strode past the gawking cattlemen to where he had left his horse.

Jake and Jess gained their saddles.

Sensing that the men wanted a moment with their leader, Jess lifted a hand to them, then rode out at a gallop, knowing Jake would follow her.

∾⌇⛬⌇∾

It was Diaz who stepped forward first. "What's happening, boss?" He nodded to the shrinking figure of Jess. "The señorita have trouble?"

Some of the men around him were mounted up; others stood near their horses. All awaited his answer.

"No trouble," Jake replied. "Only something she needs to settle for herself. We'll be back within the week."

"Hey, boss."

Jake found Doyle's gaze on him.

"You keep her safe, now."

"I intend to." He turned Cielos around and nudged him into a trot. After a brief pause at the rosebush, he applied his spurs and rode out onto the range.

Chapter Seventeen

As they neared the cemetery, located north of Carson City, passing men gave Jess curious looks that prompted her to pull her hat lower. She began to realize that this trip was going to be more troubling than she'd expected. Though she knew the chance of meeting them was remote, she couldn't help but watch for the remaining men who had attacked her, as well as for anyone else who might recognize her and be startled to find her alive. She was relieved that Jake had come with her—with his forbidding presence, few men, if any, would be apt to cause trouble.

As a group of headstones came into focus before them, Jess's longing to be near her family began to battle again with her reluctance to see the actual place where they were buried. She saw Jake glance at her with his characteristic probing, concerned look. Giving him a brief smile, she pushed aside her disquietude as best she could.

There was no one else in sight when they dismounted at the cemetery. The place was peaceful and quiet, though nothing like the family plot at Greenbriar, she mused. Her pace quickened at the thought. They should have been buried together. They should have been buried with Broderick.

Jake came up beside her. "Shall I wait here?"

Jess looked up at him, not bothering to hold back her tears. "Thank you." He pointed out the area where she would find their grave.

Taking her time, she wandered for several trying minutes before finally mustering the courage to approach the plot Jake had indicated. She paused and let out a long, shaky breath. After a moment, her eyes searched out the Hale stone.

It was there, two stones away.

As if on puppet strings, she slid off her hat and moved forward. The stone became larger in her eyes. Choking on tears, she fell to her knees before the marker.

"Hale," it read:

Isaac Donelson
Georgeanne McKinney
Ambrose Irwin
Jessica Annelise
Emily Frances

Jess took in each of their names, sobbing harder until she pressed her fists to her temples to shut the pain of it from her mind. She was deeply touched that Jake and Edmund had included Ambrose's name with the others, and they had ordered her own name added for her safety. But her friend Elsie was buried in her place with no recognition whatsoever.

Wanting to picture her family in her mind, Jess closed her eyes. They were there.

Jess could see her mother's delight as she cradled a lilac blossom in the formal garden at Greenbriar. She could hear Emma's giggles as they sat together and played. She smelled once more the fragrant pipe smoke that clung, as an aura, to her father. Ambrose stood near a paddock waiting for her, his smile brotherly and proud. Then there was Elsie...

Jess dropped her gaze to the earth that lay between her and the ones she loved, pressing her hand to the dry, rocky mound. It was bare except for a few shriveled weeds. She wiped her face on the shoulder of her cloak.

"I told you I'd come to visit you, Elsie," she murmured, then smiled. "Dat's vat goot friends do."

Jess stared at the tombstone, her thoughts naturally flowing to the Almighty. *Lord, I know You have a plan for each of us. Whatever plans You had for my family and for Elsie must have been completed, but continuing on without them is so painful, Lord. I don't understand why You took everyone away, and I know I'm not meant to understand, at least for now.* She stroked the grave. *But I'm glad they're with You...and I'm glad You're with me.*

Jess sat quietly for a long time. After a while, she heard Jake approach. He crouched down beside her.

Jess laid her head against his shoulder—the one that had been scarred when he'd tried to save her family. Finally, she met his gaze. The wind ruffled the dark locks of his hair. His hat rested in the dirt beside him.

Tentatively, she reached up and smoothed her hand along the firmness of his cheek. He appeared not at all surprised by the touch, nor was she surprised when his head lowered and his lips met hers tenderly.

After a moment, she rested against him again. His leathery scent comforted her, as always. There, in his arms, her inner wounds finally began to fade. Her family was safe with the Lord. With Him walking on one side of her, and with Jake on the other, she knew she would weather any storm life sent her way.

She paused at that thought, not nearly as troubled as she expected to be by the direction in which her heart was pulling her. "We'd best get over to the import store if we want to be on our way home by nightfall," she said.

Jake agreed, but he made no move to rise until she did. When they were on their feet, Jess stared thoughtfully at the marker once more.

Jake didn't rush her. When she did turn to him, he simply dusted off their hats, handing Jess hers and placing his own on his head. Jess noticed the bundle near his boot. It looked like a bundle of rags.

"What is that?"

Jake picked it up and handed it to her. "It's something I brought from the ranch."

It was slightly heavier than a pair of moccasins, and it felt damp. Curious, she unrolled the layers. When she pulled the last one away, her eyes fell on six yellow roses.

"Oh, Jake." For a moment, she couldn't speak. Then she managed, "I'm so glad you brought them." She smoothed the delicate petals, then frowned. "Six roses? One for each would be five—oh. You brought one for Broderick."

"Yes, ma'am."

Jess smiled to stave off the threat of new tears, shaking her head to think of how stubborn she had been at the ranch. "I'm glad you came with me."

Jake nodded but didn't answer. She didn't expect him to.

Once she'd laid the roses at the base of the tombstone, they left the grave with its spray of yellow.

Neither of them said anything more until they had mounted their horses. "I need to order a new tombstone," Jess announced.

Jake glanced at her. He clearly hadn't expected that.

"I want my name taken off and Elsie's name engraved with the others."

"Why?"

"I'm not dead, and I don't intend to be anytime soon. Elsie was my dearest friend. She deserves to be remembered."

Jake considered that. "Is anyone likely to visit the grave?"

"Just the Van Dorns."

"Then that shouldn't be a problem. If Miriam sees the stone changed, Edmund will know how to explain, but I'd best be the one to talk to the stonecutter and order it."

"What will you tell him?"

"That when I ordered the first one I was mistaken about the name of the girl."

"Will that cause a problem?"

"As I recall, the man likes his whiskey. I don't think he'll remember the first grave marker, nor will he care." He patted the pocket holding his coin pouch. "Besides, an extra twenty in gold goes a long way to keeping a man forgetful."

Jess reached for her own coin purse. "I intend to pay for this, Bennett."

He hesitated a moment over the "Bennett." "We'll settle up later," he said.

When they entered the bustle of town and found the place, Jake pulled out his notebook and pencil. Jess wrote down the spelling of Elsie Scheuer's name, then waited outside with the horses.

When Jake came out, he showed her the facing page in the small book. "He sketched how the new stone will look."

"Hale," it read, like the last one:

> Isaac Donelson
> Georgeanne McKinney
> Ambrooc Irwin
> Emily Frances
> and dear friend
> Elsie Scheuer

"It's just right," she said.

Jake put away the book and mounted up. "He said he'll have it out there by the end of the week."

"Were there any problems?"

"No."

They turned their horses, Jess careful to avoid looking in the direction of the burned-out Hale house. Then, thinking of the import store, her heart leapt in anticipation. This was what she'd been waiting for—finally having her brother's letters with her. To keep.

It was all she could think of as they joined the traffic. Suddenly, the store was standing, tall, before them. Jess's eyes moved over the shimmering window glass where sweeping emerald letters revealed the name of her father's store: HALE IMPORTS.

At Jake's prompting, they crossed the road.

As the new primary owner, Edmund could have changed the name of the business if he had chosen to. *How like him that he had left it just as it was,* she reflected—a tribute to his friends. They dismounted near the door.

She had often stood on this very spot with her father, talking of business, of her mother. Once, they'd even argued about Ambrose here.

Jake tied the horses to a hitching post nearby. "Are you ready?"

"More than ready."

Jess entered with Jake close behind. Nothing had changed. The walls were bedecked with the same gilt-framed mirrors and paintings, familiar European furnishings covered the floor, and the same corner desk was loaded down with papers, books, and inkwells. All of it was exactly as it had been—even the frazzled yet good-hearted man seated at the desk. Jess smiled broadly as her father's friend and business partner glanced up.

"Jess!" A tired-looking Edmund stood up and came directly to her, his relief apparent as he enfolded her in his arms. With a plain, clean-shaven face and a sparse but frantic head of hair, he wasn't handsome, the dear man, but he had a keen mind for business, and he had always done all he could for her family. Edmund pulled away and smiled down at her. "You look more beautiful than ever. The time at the ranch appears to have been just what you needed."

"It's so good to see you. Is Miriam well?"

"That she is, that she is." He waved a hand absently. "She

keeps herself busy with her charity functions, hosting benefit after benefit. Before long, I expect even Carson City's ale hounds will feel compelled to dress like diplomats and bring a donation." Jess smiled. "Jake!" Edmund shook his hand, sincerely grateful to the rancher. "I am indebted to you, sir, for seeing Jess through."

"It's been my pleasure. In truth, I don't know how we managed so long without her."

Jess told Edmund about the attack at the ranch, and that two of the men were in jail. "Edmund, the other seven...were any of them found?"

"No, Jess. I spoke with the sheriff every day for weeks. No one seems to know anyone who matches Jake's description of those men. I don't think we'll ever figure out who they were. Although," he brightened, "since they've undoubtedly moved on, you can return to Carson City for good, and..."

Jess was already shaking her head.

Edmund frowned. "I gather you don't intend to stay."

Jess took in the overstuffed room that, although familiar, felt more confining than ever. "This was never for me, Edmund."

His shoulders slumped. Behind him stood a monstrosity of paperwork. She didn't envy him.

"But you were so good at what you did, Jess."

"She's also good at what she does now," Jake said.

Jess smiled up at Jake in gratitude, then returned her attention to Edmund. "I've finally found my place. All that social calling, fancy-dressed balls, trussing myself up like a holiday cake...that's not who I am."

Edmund took her hands in his and smiled sadly, as though he was saying good-bye to his own daughter. "Edmund, I need to feel the wind in my face. I need to work hard so that I can see the rewarding results of my efforts. Out at the ranch, there are so many of the Lord's creatures... Oh, Edmund, you should see it! I was there this spring when the calves and foals were born! They were the sweetest things you ever saw. This life…here…" She shook her head. "I wasn't meant to be walled in."

Edmund bowed his head reflectively. When he looked up again, the tiredness remained in his eyes, but with it was the hint of a smile. "You're a Hale, there's no denying that." With an exaggerated sigh, he looked over at the desk just as two papers slid from the stack to the floor. "Well, I could always throw the lot of it in the dustbin and start over."

Jess leaned up and kissed his cheek. "Thank you for understanding, Edmund."

He cleared his throat. "What are you going to do now?"

"I'll stay on at the ranch, at least until the war is over. Greenbriar is mine now, so I'll likely want to go see it afterward…maybe stay a while to rebuild any damage these years of neglect and war have caused."

Edmund glanced up at her hat, which she hadn't removed. "I suppose you came to retrieve your brother's letters, then."

Jess bit her lip. She stood only feet away from the longed-for keepsakes. "Yes, Edmund. Are they still in the safe?" She was already rounding the corner into the stockroom where it waited.

Edmund bent over to pick up the papers. "They are. Do you remember the combination?" He sat down at the desk.

Jess's heart trembled. She felt as if she had walked a long, long road and was finally nearing the end of it. Waiting for her were the last tangible memories of her brother. They were only letters, but they were all hers. "I remember it, Edmund," she heard herself say.

Jess knelt down and slid her palms smoothly down the cool, painted surface of the safe, shutting out everything else. Jake and Edmund disappeared; the world went away. For her, the safe's contents were everything. She lifted trembling fingers to the dial and spun it. From far off, Edmund murmured sadly that one last letter had found its way since the fire. To Jess, his words felt like the thrust of a bayonet, though she didn't blame him for the unfairness of it; she blamed the war. Firming her grip on the handle, she pulled open the thick metal door.

Stacked in the bottom were the old account books she had once kept for the store. On a shelf above them sat four pouches of gold coins, earnings her father had paid her that she had set aside long ago for a future need.

To one side, just as she had left them, lay the bundles of letters Ambrose had written, letters she had been forced to hide from her father in the bookkeeping safe. She reached in and pulled the bundles out onto her lap.

She paged through them, finding that all the envelopes were there, along with all the letters. Some she had bundled with string, others with ribbons. When each stack had grown too large, she had begun another.

With a brief frown at the dimness of the back room, Jess pushed off her hat, letting it hang on its strings down her back. She pulled out a few letters at random and opened them to see the words Ambrose had written to her. She smiled over this letter, grew pensive over that, and skimmed over the progress of the war, long outdated, as he had lived it. Finally, Jess checked the safe one last time before standing up. As she did so, a few of the letters slipped from the stack and scattered on the floor.

Jake stepped in. "I'll get those, Jess." He picked them up and tapped them together, then pulled one to the top. "I think this is the one that hasn't been opened yet."

With a glance at the hopelessly cluttered desk, Jess handed the larger bundle of letters to Jake. She took the letter from him, allowing her gaze to pass over her brother's handwriting on the envelope.

"Edmund, the postmark says Chicago," she murmured

in confusion, holding it closer, "but the rest of the markings are smudged."

"Chicago?" Jake eyed the older man. "When did this arrive?"

Edmund was distracted, frowning at some numbers. "A week or more ago, I think."

Jess shrugged at Jake, then patiently dug for a letter opener on the desk. Finally, she slit the envelope and unfolded the letter.

My dearest Jessica, it began, as always. She smiled and read on. All at once, her heart quickened, and her world grew dark, except for three beautiful words: *I am alive.*

Chapter Eighteen

J ess!" Jake dropped the letters and grabbed hold of her. "Jess!"

Edmund abandoned his stool and came to her side. "What is it?"

Jess's vision cleared and filled with a brown hat, piercing brown eyes, and bristly cheeks that needed a shave. She raised a soft hand to his face. Never had he looked so precious.

"Talk to me," he urged her.

"Ambrose...is...alive," she breathed, then started to laugh. Joyous tears trickled from the corners of her eyes, and all at once, she firmly gained her feet, laughing to the skies in pure elation. "Ambrose is alive!" she shouted, then grabbed Jake's shoulders and shook him. "Do you hear me, Bennett?"

Stunned, Edmund wrenched the letter from her hand, not caring whose name was on the envelope.

Jess threw herself into Jake's arms. "I told you, Bennett, Hales don't die easy!"

Jake smiled at her, but when he looked over her head at Edmund, his smile slowly faded. Jess glanced between the two men, her heart sinking.

"Listen to this," Edmund said. "Ambrose writes that he was captured by Union forces during a cavalry raid in Ohio. He and his men were taken to a prison called Camp Douglas, in Chicago."

Jess felt herself transformed from butterfly to badger in a matter of seconds. "How long, Edmund? How long has my brother been in prison?"

Edmund looked worriedly at her, then scanned the lines. "He arrived August twenty-seventh. Three weeks ago."

"What happened that he didn't write Jess since last October?" Jake asked.

"He says that he was ill for quite some time."

"No, he wasn't. He's just protecting me. Ambrose doesn't get ill."

Edmund frowned. "Conditions during wartime are very hard. He may have been ill."

Jess knew better. "Ambrose was shot, Edmund."

"He seems fully recovered now," Edmund offered.

"Yes," she said distractedly, "he does."

Jake stepped directly in front of her. "What are you thinking, Jess?"

"I'm...just overwhelmed," she lied, and not very well. Then she arrived at a decision. "Excuse me a moment."

She hurried out to where the horses were tied and returned with her saddlebags. Without a word, she stuffed all of Ambrose's letters into one of the two side pouches. Going behind the door of the safe, she added leather pouches to the other. Slinging the bags over her arm, she closed the safe with a final spin of the dial.

Jake was watching her. "Would you like to wire the prison, Jess? Ask if they'll give Ambrose a message for you?"

"Thank you, no. I'll communicate with Ambrose in my own way. Edmund?" She gave Edmund a parting kiss on the cheek. "Thank you for everything. I'll come to see you again in the spring."

She didn't mention whether she would come back to stay. She didn't know herself, and for now, future decisions had ceased to matter.

Ambrose was alive.

"Edmund." Jake extended his hand and shook the ink-stained hand of the other. He turned to follow Jess out.

"Jake?"

He faced the man again.

"I'd like to tell Miriam about Jess...maybe come for a visit."

"You'd both be welcome, Edmund, but I think it would be best to keep Jess's whereabouts between you and Miriam, for now. Only two of the nine men who attacked her were caught."

Edmund held up a hand. "Enough said, my friend. Miriam is as gabby as ever, and if she finds out that Jess is alive, she'll tell the whole town. I'll keep this to myself until Jess returns."

"I'm obliged."

"Take care of her, Jake. She's very dear to me."

"And to me," Jake assured him, then stepped out into the sun.

∞⬦∞

Within minutes, Jake and Jess had left Carson City, Cielos and Meg stretching their legs and quickly covering the miles. Jake didn't try to slow down, didn't ask Jess her thoughts. Apparently, he knew she needed to run out her emotions, and she was grateful.

They were two-thirds of the way back to the ranch when it became too dark to ride any further. The horses needed to rest, Jake told her—they'd been running them hard. Determined to press on, she didn't answer. It took the threat of the rope in Jake's hand to convince her to camp for the night.

The next morning, they were on their way before sunrise. Jess hardly spoke a word. She was so intent on her goal of getting to the ranch that the horses began to foam from her pushing them. Jake had to warn her to slow the pace. Twice.

It was still early—about nine, by Jess's calculation—when they finally approached the ranch. She glanced east, gauging the distance she could cover by nightfall.

Several men called out greetings when they dismounted in front of the stable. Jake answered them, but Jess merely waved, then quickly unsaddled Meg.

The entire ride home, she had thought of Ambrose, rejoicing that he was alive, even if he was in prison. While she had stood listening to Edmund read the letter, her mind had locked on the fact that Union generals were no longer allowing prisoner exchanges. Then she recalled from newspaper articles that conditions at most prisons, in the North and the South alike, were deplorable—little or no food, bad water, rampant disease. Men died by the thousands. She had known before she left the store what she had to do. It was the reason she had left Jake and Edmund staring at her while she fetched her saddlebags, and it was the reason she had returned to the safe.

Jess untied her saddlebags and laid them to the side with her bedroll. In the worst prisons, she knew, the armed guards were little more than a deathwatch, and the war raged on. Ambrose's starving or freezing, therefore, was not to be tolerated.

Jake approached her with an inquiry on his face, but before he could speak, a mustang galloped around the corner of the stable and halted abruptly. Lone Wolf reined it in dangerously close, and Jess started as the Indian man said emphatically, "Friend of Red Deer, come!"

By the intensity in the man's face and the urgency in his voice, Jess could tell that Red Deer's time had come. Lone Wolf reached down and pulled her up onto the palomino's back, holding the reins from behind her.

"Reese!" Jess cried. "Bring the orange blanket from my room to Red Deer's lodge, please!"

Jake was looking up at them in alarm. "What happened?"

"It is Red Deer," the Indian said.

No sooner had Lone Wolf spoken than the two of them were flying out of the yard.

Jess felt her heart breaking all over again. For weeks, she had prayed that Red Deer would live through the birthing, along with the child, but she realized that God's will could very well be different from her own. The agony she had glimpsed in Lone Wolf's face told her that he knew just what she had feared—that his wife would not survive.

As great as the urge was to cry, Jess held it back. Red Deer needed Jess's strength in her last hours—she needed the comfort of knowing that she was in the Lord's hands, even in death.

They were in the village and then the lodge before Jess realized it. She paused to let her eyes adjust to the shadows. There was an odd, smoky smell, and several women were singing quietly or speaking softly to Red Deer in Paiute, encouraging her to bring the baby.

Red Deer wore a short tunic and knelt weakly on a mat between two women who were holding her. She was alarmingly pale. Suddenly, Jess saw that her friend didn't have hours left. She had arrived just in time to be with her in her final minutes.

"Red Deer?" Jess said softly, sinking to her knees in front of her. She touched a hand to Red Deer's damp cheek. Her eyelids parted.

When she saw Jess, her eyes closed again in a smile of gratitude. Red Deer pulled away from her supportive friends to hold instead to Jess. "Oh, my friend," she breathed, "my friend. So glad...you are here. What would I have done these past months without you?" She drew in her breath, then groaned horribly as birthing pains raked her.

To keep her from falling, Jess shifted her own position and

held Red Deer tightly. When Jess laid her cheek on her friend's black hair, she noticed a large pool of blood soaking into the mat beneath Red Deer.

"Do you remember, Jessica, the first day...we went to the creek?" Jess sensed a smile in Red Deer's voice. "You told me... of your beloved Kentucky, and I told you I would have a son."

Jess spoke past the tightness in her throat. "I remember." She recalled the time they had spent playing in the creek, splashing each other and reliving the joys of youth.

"You...became my friend that day. That was the happiest day I remember."

"It was for me, as well," Jess whispered. It was true. Jess recalled Red Deer's laughter and the water running from her hair. It would be how she would always remember her.

When Red Deer said nothing more, Lone Wolf knelt beside his wife to share Jess's burden. Red Deer laid her head against his shoulder.

Several more spasms came, each more brutal than the one before. Helplessly, Jess stroked the short, black hair, agonizing that Red Deer's nightmares were coming true. She would be taken from her son.

Red Deer shuddered. All at once, Jess looked around wildly, desperate for a way to save her. They were losing her.

"Bring your child," Lone Wolf bade his wife softly. "Let your eyes rest on him and his on you. Let me tell him how strong you were for him. Let me tell him of your great love."

It was all Red Deer needed. When the next pain came, she pulled together her strength and, with a terrible, anguished cry, brought forth her child.

One of the women received him.

"It's a son," Jess cried shakily. "You have a son!"

With joyous tears in her eyes, Red Deer collapsed against her. Lone Wolf pulled his wife into his arms, held her close against him, and laid his big hand alongside her face. After a seemingly endless moment, he gently laid Red Deer down.

Jake's low voice drifted in from outside. Another woman entered the lodge. She brought the orange blanket Jess had spent months weaving for her friend. The woman handed it to Jess, then quietly ducked out again.

As her own tears began to run, Jess hugged it against her, wishing she could cling instead to Jake. But she knew he would leave Red Deer with her family and friends now and would wait outside for her.

Jess sat down beside Red Deer just as the boy was laid in her friend's unmoving arms. He was sweet with his tiny, round face and silky, black hair. He yawned, his mouth impossibly little.

Blinking to hold back death, Red Deer turned her head to memorize his face. "He is red." She smiled softly to Jess. Seeing her need, Lone Wolf moved the infant against her.

The beautiful mother this child would never know kissed his brow. Red Deer's damp eyes moved to Jess. "Is he healthy?" she asked.

Jess bent over him and nodded, unable to answer. She felt like she herself was dying inside. "He's perfect," she finally managed. Knowing her friend was fading, Jess leaned forward and kissed her cheek. Then she unfolded the blanket.

Red Deer saw it but could not speak. Though the Paiute women had used many cloths to try to stop it, the blood beneath her was spreading beyond them. Jess held the blanket so her friend could see it better.

Both she and her husband looked at the woven pictures in admiration. Jess gazed at the friend she loved. "I made it for you, so that you would remember the day of your son's birth." Jess spread it over Red Deer and the quiet baby lying in her arms.

"It will...have to be for my son now," she said. "So that he... will remember me." Red Deer looked at Jess once more. "I love you...my sister," she said. Then, with a final smile, she said, "Weep not for your dead, but sing and be joyful, for the soul is happy in the Spirit-land."

Jess kept herself from crying out. "I'll see you there," she whispered.

Red Deer nodded faintly, turning her eyes to Lone Wolf, whose face was streaked with two lines of tears. He bent down and spoke tenderly to his wife in Paiute, then kissed her. When he sat up again, he kept one hand on her shoulder, the other on their child.

Seeing the life slip out of her, Jess reached under the blanket and held Red Deer's hand, determined not to let go until her friend had passed to where the Great Spirit Father was waiting.

Red Deer's eyes fell closed. The baby began to cry, as though he knew he was losing someone, and Red Deer exhaled long and deep. Jess felt Red Deer's hand cease its trembling, and only a moment before it stilled, she felt a gentle squeeze. Then she was gone.

Around them, the women started to wail. Jess was sobbing now, too, but she kept holding Red Deer's hand, knowing this would be the last time she would see her until she joined her in heaven. *Thank You, Lord*, she prayed, *for every moment she and I spent together. Never did I meet a more beautiful person, a more loving example of You.*

A small shadow fell across the still form of Red Deer as Two Hands came to stand beside Lone Wolf. His eyes were sad as he quietly mourned his second mother who had died. Then he studied the baby. He sat down next to the boy and gently took one tiny hand in both of his.

The sight stole Jess's breath from her. She had seen that protective look before, many times—in the eyes of Ambrose.

Beginning to feel like an intruder among Red Deer's family, Jess quietly left the dwelling. Jake was standing outside, gripping his hat in his hand. Without words, Jess leaned against him, welcoming his warm embrace.

∽౿⚜౿∾

The following day, at sunrise, Red Deer was buried beside Olivia and Sadie Bennett. The Paiutes and the ranch hands gathered around her grave, Jake and Jess among them. Many women, including Jess, cried to see Red Deer's dresses, ornaments, and baskets—all her possessions—buried alongside her. To her surprise, Jess saw the cattlemen were as moved as the Paiutes. Not one of them had dry eyes, and, for once, none of them wore his hat. Taggart's hair stood out in a blaze of orange. The Indian people had all cut their hair in mourning.

When the dirt had been shoveled and smoothed over Red Deer's grave, Two Hands and the other Indian children each brought forward a small mud animal to leave with her. One by one, the children laid their gifts atop the slight mound of earth. Then Two Hands looked at Jess and held up three fingers. Jess wasn't certain what he meant until he touched her hand.

Jess looked down and saw the three roses she had forgotten that she was holding. She smiled softly at the boy and held up three fingers in agreement. Then she stepped forward and laid down the blossoms—one for Olivia, one for Sadie, and one for the sister of her heart, Red Deer.

Jake looked on, touched that she had thought of his wife and daughter.

When Jess stepped back, her eyes met those of Lone Wolf, then focused on the sweet child he held in his arms. She walked over to him and kissed the babe on the forehead. He nodded once, thanking her without words for her friendship to his wife.

Finally, the old man, Standing Bear, spoke to them all of Red Deer's strength and courage. He said the words first in Paiute and then in English so that everyone could understand.

The sun was fully up and the sky's band of color had vanished when the mourners headed back to the ranch, many of them on horseback. The Paiute mothers had come with their children in the wagons. The group left the graveside in silence. Jess and Jake mounted up, as well, Jess pausing to look back at the peaceful mounds dotted with tiny animals and roses.

⧫

While they rode back to the ranch, Jake kept a close eye on Jess, prepared to battle any new fears that might have surfaced after the loss of Red Deer—fears that might threaten their newfound closeness. But as they entered the ranch yard with the others, he concluded that though she was sad, she was also collected. What was more, she had been content to ride beside him all the way back.

That made him uneasy.

⧫

Shaking back her hair, Jess dismounted apart from the others and fixed her gaze on the sun, still rising to its zenith. Her sadness for Red Deer lay heavy in her, but a sense of purposefulness had settled there, as well. Ambrose was out there somewhere, and she was not going to let one more person she loved die. She had already decided to go to Camp Douglas prison to see Ambrose and to take him food and clothing. But her conviction had just changed.

She was going there to get him out.

Jess held up her skirts and hurried to the house, promising

herself the sun wouldn't set on her until she was somewhere on the other side of Nevada Territory, well on her way to the States.

In her room, Jess tossed aside her gown and pulled on one of two pairs of trousers that Reese had outgrown months ago. She'd planned to alter them to fit a couple of the Paiute boys, but now she needed them herself. After flattening out the second pair on her bed, she rolled into it two shirts—one cotton, one flannel—which she had borrowed unashamedly from Jake's room. These she rolled into her bedroll. She pulled on a third shirt, also flannel, and shoved the buttons through their holes. Immediately, she rolled back the sleeves that hung well past her hands; the shirttails fell to her knees. At the softness of the fabric, an image of Jake filled her mind, threatening to deter her conviction. One part of her ached to stay at the ranch with Bennett. The other part knew that she had to go to Ambrose.

Half sighing, half groaning, Jess stuffed the unwieldy shirttails into her pantlegs. She buttoned the waist of the trousers, then gathered it in with the braided leather belt that had been Olivia's.

She retrieved her saddlebags from the doorway, making sure that the four pouches of gold coins she had brought from the store's safe were still there. She withdrew Ambrose's letters, still bound with ribbons, and tucked them next to the jewelry box Jake had made for her in a drawer of her dressing table. She *would* be back, and, Lord willing, so would Ambrose.

Jess buckled the gun belt around her waist, threw a few items into the empty saddlebag, and hurried downstairs. From the water bucket in the kitchen, she filled two canteens, then stuffed a sack with dried fruit, jerky, beans, and the fresh biscuits Ho Chen had left. She grabbed up her things, pulled her hat from its peg, and headed out into the sun.

Though the horses had been put away, the cattlemen and

311

many of the Paiutes were still milling about the yard. They stood in groups, talking quietly. Jess realized as she passed them that Jake must have given the men the day to themselves out of respect for Red Deer. She was touched by the gesture.

She would miss them. Snow would soon block the roads over the Rockies, so it would be spring before she could get through to see them again. Yes, she would miss them all, but she had to go.

Jess strode over to the mustang corral, stopping near the gate and swinging the saddlebags over the top rail. She laid the rest of her gear on the dusty ground. The men's conversations trailed off, and they started to gather near the corral, openly observing her.

Jess ignored them except for saying a quick word of thanks when they stepped out of her way. She walked past them into the stable, then returned with saddle and bridle, which she set up beside the saddlebags. Inside the corral, she caught one of the mustangs and brought him out. Several minutes later, the horse was fully saddled and impatient to stretch his legs.

Jake stepped through the crowd and came to stand beside her. "And where are you off to now, Jess?"

"Chicago, to my brother."

Jake stared at her. She didn't flinch.

"He's in a Union prison, Jess."

The cattlemen silently exchanged glances.

"Yes, he is, and if I don't help him, he could die there. I'm not going to let that happen."

Diaz took a tentative step forward. "Your brother is not dead? I thought la mariposa mourned him."

"I did. He was missing and presumed dead, and I mourned him, but I've just received word that he's alive."

Her voice wavered. She felt in awe of the Almighty's love… and despair at the look she saw spreading through the ranch hands' eyes. To her, it resembled withdrawal, contempt, and a sense of betrayal.

Jess hadn't expected that. Her mouth went dry. She had become a traitor, leaving them—and their apparent Union sympathies—to go to her Confederate brother. But hadn't Jake once said that most people know honest men stand on both sides of the conflict, and that the worst trouble comes from the fanatics? Still, she saw that gleam in their eyes, that hatred. Unable to confront it, she completed her task with her face averted. Then she addressed Jake, though all could hear what she said.

"I'm taking the mustang and saddle. I believe my three horses should be a fair enough trade." She untied the lead and gathered up the reins.

Jake's hand stopped her. "No, Jess. We need to discuss this."

Jess lifted her face, letting him see the score of emotions there. "I wish you could feel what I'm feeling. It's as if the Lord has raised Ambrose from the dead. Do you have any notion what it is to lose everyone you love and then gain one precious person back again? You lost your wife and daughter. Imagine if you walked through the door of your house and they were standing there waiting for you." She could tell by his expression and by the tilt of his head that he meant to stop her from going. "Jake, if that really happened, if Olivia and Sadie were really there, you'd go to them, and nothing would stop you."

"Ambrose is in the middle of a war."

Her stubbornness flared. "You'd still go to *them* even if *they* were."

"Ambrose is in prison. He isn't getting shot at anymore." His voice remained calm.

Hers didn't. "Ambrose wrote to me about men he knew who had been in prison camps. *Knew.* Do you know what that means? It means they didn't survive it. Ambrose isn't safer in prison. The conditions there are horrible! And now there are no prisoner exchanges! Jake, I refuse to have my brother returned to me only to have him die in prison!"

Jake didn't budge. "There are outlaws out there other than the ones who attacked the ranch, and the Plains Indians are warriors who are angry with the white men. Whether you fool them dressed as a man or get found out as a woman, things could go badly for you."

"I heard the men say that a federal colonel and eight companies of soldiers are guarding the Oregon Trail along the Sweetwater River and the North Platte now. From what I've heard, there hasn't been any trouble with the Plains Indians since he's been there."

"It's not possible, Jess."

"It *is* possible."

"It's two thousand miles. You'll get snowed in before you get there."

"The Pony could have ridden it in two weeks."

"Pony Express riders changed horses every ten miles, and they rode all night. Don't you see why I can't let you do this?"

"I'm not asking your permission. I only wanted you to understand why I have to go."

Jake stared at Jess. "Ambrose doesn't know that your parents are gone," he said.

Jess blinked. "I'll have to tell him."

The broad shoulders stiffened. "Jess, what will Ambrose's life be like if you die on your way east? Have you considered that? He would have no one, just like you had no one. Would you want that for him? He would spend the rest of his days knowing he might have had a sister to grow old with, if only she hadn't died trying to help him. He's been in a war, Jess. How much more loss do you think he can take?"

Jess understood what he was saying, and she didn't try to deny the logic of it, but neither did she believe that Ambrose had much of a chance at having a life if she didn't get him out of prison. "I've thought of all these things, Jake, and I know the challenges I'll face, but the end of the war is nowhere in sight. Ho Chen said his country has been at war for twelve years now. Twelve years! I can't just wait for the war to end and hope Ambrose is still alive then." Saddened by the cool way he regarded her, she lowered her voice. "I believe the danger in traveling there will be minimal. The difficulty will come in getting him out."

"Getting him out? Jess…"

Not wanting to leave matters like this between her and Jake, she tried once more. "The day you and I met in Carson City, I told you that if a telegraph operator didn't help me, I'd go east and track Ambrose down myself."

Jake grunted and looked away.

"You knew then that's what I meant to do, if all other options failed. That's what I intend to do now. If I'm not able to get him out, I'll at least see to his needs." Jess shifted her gaze to the others. Every one of the cattlemen had heard her, and the Paiutes, if they hadn't comprehended, at least had gotten the drift of it. Not one of them had moved from where he was standing.

She couldn't leave without explaining—or at least trying to. Turning in a circle to face each of them directly, she took in their familiar faces, one by one. "I've lost my family, my home, and yesterday, my dearest friend. Two days ago, in Carson City, I learned that my brother is alive. He is in prison, as you heard. He's in a Northern prison."

The ranch hands watched her, their expressions inscrutable. Jess mustered her courage and went on. "Since I arrived here, not one of you has treated me unkindly, despite my origins. I came to feel like I was a part of you, a part of the ranch. I felt like I belonged." Her eyes settled on Doyle, who towered above the others. "My family never owned another human being, nor did they condone slavery. But when my brother joined with the local militiamen to protect our homes, the Union army ordered a surrender and demanded they send the Federals their guns. Only then did his militia join the South." Still, the men held back from her. "I only told you so I could apologize. If you're going to think of me as a traitor after today, I thought you'd best know why."

Jess led the mustang around. She looked once more at these people she had come to love, wondering when she would see them again. After her departure, she didn't much expect she'd be welcomed back.

Her eyes touched on Taggart and Reese. Beside Reese stood Seth, who could neither read nor write, yet who sent frequent letters home. Next to him was Diaz, with his love for horses. There was little Two Hands, who appeared uncertain but brave. Beside him stood Lone Wolf, holding his newborn son.

They were tough, rugged men who carved toy animals for Indian children, loaned a frayed woolen scarf to a hapless bookkeeper, and helped a couple of women hang a clothesline. They were men who found pleasure in a good game of cards, who risked their lives to look after some cows, and who had inspired and captured her heart.

Standing Bear had been listening nearby. Now the gray-haired man walked up to Jess and laid an ancient hand on her shoulder.

"*'Greater love hath no man than this, that a man lay down his life for his friends,'*" he quoted John 15:13 with a gentle smile. "I see you have this great love for your brother. I will pray that the Good Spirit Father keeps you safe on your journey, friend of Red Deer."

Jess lifted her eyes to his wrinkled face. "Thank you."

She turned and pulled at the reins, and the horse followed her. The ranch hands slowly parted, making a path for her. She had nearly reached the edge of the crowd when Ho Chen stepped in front of her. Jess smiled, glad for this man who had brought so much joy and wisdom to her life. When he didn't move aside, she looked at him wonderingly.

"What is it?"

Ho Chen bowed slightly. "You will see."

Jess wasn't certain what he meant, but he said nothing more. She led the horse on.

"Reese?" Jake's deep voice broke the silence behind her. "Go saddle the roan for me."

Jess's feet stilled, her rigid back to the men. She drew a few shaky breaths, afraid to hope what Jake had meant by that.

"I'll do it, boss," Reese said. "If it's all the same to you, I'll be going on the gray."

Jess spun.

"*I* will ride the gray, *cabrito*," Diaz told Reese. "You take the buckskin, and don' whine none. We keep la mariposa waiting." He winked at Jess and followed the boy into the stable.

Jess stared at Jake in amazement. He held her gaze boldly.

Taggart tugged the waistband of his trousers more securely over his paunch. "Why are ye surprised? Ye are part of this ranch, and ranch folk do for one another, just as ye have done for us since ye came here. Ye should know by now it's our way. Maybe it is how the good Lord meant for us to be."

"But—"

Taggart stepped closer. "We are not at war in this place, but that's not saying we don't sympathize plenty with those who are." With that declaration, he huffed after the others.

Jess's small smile spread larger as the men hurried to ready mounts for the journey east.

Ho Chen remained just as he had been, except that now a mild, enigmatic grin curved on his mouth. Jake was going with her, and Ho Chen had known that he would.

Jess shared his smile. Her heart soared.

Jake walked up beside her, lifting his eyebrows. "Olivia wasn't nearly this much trouble."

Jess laughed out loud. "Neither is a cattle stampede."

Jake smiled at that. "The boys and I need to get some things together."

Within five minutes, Jake returned from the house. Their three other companions hurried over from the bunkhouse by way of Ho Chen's kitchen. They added guns, clothes, bedrolls, and provisions to their saddles.

Diaz, Taggart, and Reese mounted up, and with the freedom of britches, Jess easily gained her saddle. Jake turned to the others. He shook hands with several of them, then clasped wrists with Lone Wolf.

"I will watch after your ranch, as always," Lone Wolf said. "The work will be good."

Jake considered this, then nodded. "Doyle will be your right hand, if you have a need." He thought a moment. "Sell the mustang stallions. Breed the mares with the Morgans, come March. After roundup, deliver the beeves we're contracted for. The contracts are in my desk. Sell all but a hundred of the rest." He smiled at Jess. "We're going to turn this place into a horse ranch next year."

While the two clasped wrists again, Jess nudged her horse over to Doyle. She reached her gloved hand toward him.

For a moment, Doyle ignored her hand as he met her gaze. Then slowly, he lifted his hand and shook hers. "You keep yourself safe, Jess. This ranch needs you."

Seeing a mixture of acceptance and understanding reflected in the faces of the others, Jess smiled tremulously at Doyle. She had mistaken their sharp attention for anger. She guided her horse to join the others, her thoughts turning to another matter. "I'm not certain you should come," she told Jake, meaning it. "You're needed here."

His mouth quirked. "Well, ma'am, I'm not asking your permission."

Jess rolled her eyes. His amusement was beyond her. "Don't you see that you could lose everything?"

He sobered. "How can I lose everything if I still have you? I love you, Jess. Let's go get your brother."

Taggart's voice boomed out. "Which way do we point the beasts?"

Jake met Jess's frown with a calm smile. "To Chicago."

Reese spoke up. "Where are we gonna stay for the winter, boss?"

"My pa's farm is in Illinois. We'll stay there."

Diaz drew her gaze. "Your brother waits, mariposa."

Exasperated from her own conflicting emotions, Jess put a fist on her hip and glared at him. "What does that word mean, anyway, Diaz?"

Taking no offense at her tone, the Spaniard answered gently. "*Mariposa*, señorita, means 'butterfly.'"

Butterfly.

Impatient for the adventure to begin, Taggart and Reese whipped their horses into a run, and Diaz took off behind them.

Jake lifted his hat to his men, then set it back on his head.

Side by side, Jake and Jess kicked their horses into a gallop, leaving the ranch in many capable hands. They headed east toward Chicago—and Ambrose.

Chapter Nineteen

The afternoon sun was at their backs when the prairie ended at the outskirts of Chicago. Jess sighed as she counted the days since she had stood in the front room of Hale Imports with Ambrose's letter in her hand. Twenty-six days. Twenty-six days since her world had fallen out from under her. Ambrose was brought back, Red Deer taken.

The journey over the Rockies and across the Plains had been longer and harder than she could have imagined, and yet she had seen some indescribably beautiful country. Like the Pony Express riders, they had switched mounts as often as possible. Nearly all the ranch owners in the western territories had honorably refused additional coin for taking perfectly good mounts in trade. It must be a cattlemen's code, she mused, and Jake had been no different. From the first time that Jake pulled out a heavy pouch of coins, Jess had insisted she pay for their expenses. Jake hadn't argued with her, but neither had he taken her money. Each time he returned to camp with supplies, she asked him to name an amount, but he waved her question away, telling her they'd figure it out some other time.

Now Jess was speechless as she gazed at the crowds and the maze of mud-hole streets. As they neared Lake Michigan, entire city blocks of buildings, as well as individual businesses, stood high on thousands of scissors jacks five feet or more above the ground. Even on horseback, she could see straight under them. Stairs led up to the businesses overhead, and customers came and went as if all cities hovered in the air. Beyond, the land flowed virtually straight out to the lake, explaining the necessity of raising the low-lying city to a higher grade. Dozens of huge wagons rolled by, hauling ponderous loads of dirt that were undoubtedly destined to fill in space beneath one of the raised buildings. Above the steady rumble of city noise, a train whistle screeched. The air was ripe with the stench of raw fish. They dismounted in front of a hotel, the entrance of which was at the top of a stairway, above their heads.

Though Jess wanted nothing more than to continue on to where Ambrose was being held, Jake checked her into a room, adhering to the plan they had devised. There, she made wise use of her time, bathing and then trying her hair this way and that until she was satisfied that she looked the part she would need to play. Jake returned with a blue and white striped taffeta day dress and all its accoutrements, which he had purchased for Jess, surprising her with his eye for fashion.

But then, she reminded herself, the man paid attention.

Jake also told her that Tom Rawlins had left a message at the telegraph office in response to the wire Jake had sent him from Fort Laramie. Tom had successfully obtained permission on their behalf, authorizing their visit with the Confederate prisoner Ambrose Hale at Camp Douglas.

After three long years of being apart from her brother, Jess would see him tomorrow—if he was still alive.

For the remainder of the evening, Jake, Diaz, Taggart, and Reese spread out over the city, visiting taverns and asking idle questions over games of cards.

When they gathered in Jake's room late that night, they had learned plenty about the city—and unfortunate details about Camp Douglas prison.

"All of you, stop coddling me. What else did you hear?" Jess demanded, casting a worried glance at the bandaged knife wound on Reese's arm. "Jake, you wouldn't want me to keep anything from you. Don't you keep anything from me."

Jake leaned an elbow on the small, serviceable desk he sat beside and rubbed his eyes. "You're right, Jess. No secrets." He nodded his approval for his men to tell all.

Jess turned to Reese, who was fidgeting beside her on the couch. "You first."

"Well, uh, Miss Jess, ma'am? Folks around here don't dislike Southerners. They hate us. More than I've ever known anybody to hate anything. I'm not even from what most folks consider the South. I'm from Missouri." He looked to Jake, reluctant to continue.

"Go on," Jess ordered.

"I…I think if the boss hadn't stopped those men, I'd have been a goner. They didn't just see me as an enemy. The man with the knife said my kind had betrayed everything our fathers and forefathers had lived for and fought for since they first arrived on this continent. He said secessionists were traitors."

Jess eyed Diaz and Taggart, who stood near Jake. "What else?"

Diaz hadn't budged, and his arms were crossed angrily. "The colonel of Camp Douglas is a bad *hombre* named De Land. One barkeeper said De Land was held in a prisoner of war camp in the South, maybe treated badly. Now he thinks up ways to torture the prisoners. He had his soldiers raise a level two-by-four high off the ground, and he makes men sit on the narrow edge with bags of sand tied to their ankles for hours—until they pass out from pain. Many of the men's feet break and they are crippled. They call it 'the mule.'"

Jess's head felt sickeningly light. She could taste bile.

"Ye wouldn't believe this man, De Land, I'm telling ye,"

322

Taggart agreed. "His men beat prisoners' naked backs with sticks or shoot them for sport, and he promotes them. He starves the Confederates, as well, and diseases spread, like dysentery and typhoid and smallpox. On Sundays, people from town ride the streetcar to a platform near the camp and pay ten cents to see the prisoners. I heard they see dead men carried out nearly one an hour. Reese is right. Since the prison guards see the Confederates as traitors, they feel justified in brutalizing them and letting them die."

Jess slumped against the back of the sofa, her arms limp. Her face felt feverish, and the room suddenly grew dark. The odd sound filling her ears was like bubbles breaking in a hundred glasses of champagne. "How many have died?"

"It's hard to say," Taggart's voice responded, sounding distant. "I thought it wise to speak to a grave digger to find out all I could, and he knows a great deal, though I wouldn't say he's always honest in business. He said the camp stopped keeping a record of the dead months ago, and universities that teach doctorin' pay him to dig up corpses for them to study. When there are too many to bury, he throws the bodies into the lake out there. They sometimes wash up on shore. I asked him to guess, and he said between two and three thousand."

Jess felt herself being pulled gently against a solid chest. "That may be," Jake's voice said above her, "but some guards are corrupt and are known to accept payoffs. A lot of men have escaped."

With a weak hand, Jess squeezed his arm. "Then the men are found, right?"

"Not all of them."

"But some are found and taken back," she probed, inwardly begging him to disagree with her.

"Yeah, some are taken back."

Jess trembled as she clipped sapphire earrings to her lobes. She stepped back to assess her overall appearance in the mirror. The blue and white gown hinted at wealth; the wide-brimmed straw hat and the cascade of curls falling to her waist lent her a touch of youthful innocence.

When Jake knocked on her door moments later, she opened it to see the striking figure of a dark-suited businessman who had to duck his head to step through the door. There was nothing Jess could do to mask her admiration of Jake Bennett. She took in his appearance with astonishment, not bothering to shut her mouth. Her eyes flitted from his polished black boots to the gray felt hat pulled low over his eyes.

"That should do," she managed. Flustered for the first time since she'd met him, Jess found her white gloves and tugged them on.

"The clothes…they won't work well on the ranch," Jake reminded her.

Jess preceded him out of the room, her cheeks warm. "I know. I just like seeing you this way for once."

Jake gazed down at her. "I know just what you mean."

As they descended the stairs toward the main floor, her fingers played with the folds of her skirt, clenching and smoothing them with her hand.

"If I'd known you wanted wrinkles in your dress," Jake teased, "I wouldn't have asked the dressmaker to press it."

Feeling her panic rise, Jess bit the inside of her cheek. Hard. "Either I'm going to see my brother today or I'm going to learn that he's dead."

Jake glanced at her expression and said nothing more. She was too scared to be lifted out of her fears by humor, and he knew it.

Jess hardly noticed when Jake helped her into the rented

buggy. Her awareness swiftly returned as he started the horses. They rolled toward the prison—and toward six hundred Union sharpshooters.

A violent convulsion shook Jess's frame.

Jake drove the pair of grays out of the town, heading south. To the east, sailing ships and barges lumbered up and down Lake Michigan. Somewhere, a church bell rang. A few carriages passed by, probably driving to Sunday services in Chicago.

The prison camp was only four miles from the city, Jake had learned. All too soon, a sprawling stockade fence appeared on the horizon. Pulling her gaze away, Jess looked out over the prairie instead. To the west, she glimpsed three horsemen heading south along another road at a leisurely canter, seeming to have no plan other than enjoying the autumn day. Diaz, Taggart, and Reese.

A large hand settled over hers and held it tight. Forcing herself to remain calm, Jess let out her breath, then released Jake's hand.

Her gaze drifted ahead to the prison. It was less than a mile away now. A few houses were scattered about the area, some close to the stockade. They seemed totally out of place—symbols of contentment and warmth located a stone's throw from a tall pine fence enclosing prisoners of war suffering calculated torture.

"My father and brothers and I came here when I was a boy," Jake commented, as if hearing her thoughts. "His farm is about a day's ride from here. This used to be the Fairgrounds before the war."

It had also been a training camp for soldiers, she'd once read. The wind shifted, bringing with it the stench of human waste. Jess nearly gagged. How could anyone stand to live near such squalid conditions?

The prison loomed ahead. Its massive fence stretched

skyward, equaling the approximate height of three men, and it ran perhaps two-thirds of a mile across. Along the western wall of the fence, armed sentinels looked down from high sentry boxes spaced seventy-five feet apart. That was, Jess knew, where the prisoners were. Taggart had learned that wooden stakes protruded from the ground a hundred feet from the fence, along its perimeter, to form the martial law zone. Anyone crossing it from either side could be killed. Jess clenched her hands in painful fists, as if holding tight to a last strand of hope. Overall, the stockade was imposing, solid, and, as the good men of Chicago had revealed, *nearly* complete.

"Ambrose is in there," she said. *Along with six thousand Southern men*, Jake had told her the night before. She glanced at him. "I feel so close to the war, I almost expect to hear cannon fire."

The wall rose high beside them, too high to scale, appearing unbroken by any entrance but the main one, facing Lake Michigan. Jake found a place for the horse and buggy in the shade of a towering oak, and he set the brake. He gave Jess a hand down, then retrieved a package from beneath the seat. "Are you ready?"

She dipped the straw brim of her hat once. They entered beneath a massive entryway that bore the name of the prison in big black letters: Camp Douglas.

The large headquarters building stood at a distance to the right, flanked by smaller yet equally foreboding structures. Beyond those, a parade ground was partly visible, the United States flag flying boldly high above. Barracks for the Union soldiers enclosed the parade on at least two sides, as far as Jess could see. More of the stockade separated that field from the prisoners with nearly enough fencing to enclose a city, she thought.

When she hesitated, Jake merely drew her arm through his and led her into the headquarters building.

A well-fed Yankee with thick brows, a sergeant by his chevrons, slowly looked up from his desk. "Can I help you?" he asked, his tone surly.

Jake stated their business and presented their authorization to visit Confederate prisoner Ambrose Hale.

The sergeant called for a pair of guards who, amid snorted chuckles and tomfoolery, managed to escort them down a series of hallways to a small room. Still snorting, they told Jake and Jess to wait, then shut the door behind them.

Jess stared at the wooden table and chairs in the cell, hardly daring to breathe.

Jake moved to the window to see Federal soldiers passing outside. He glanced back. "Jess?"

She laid her hat on the table and wiped the sweat from her forehead. "I'm all right."

Minutes crawled by. Then a quarter of an hour passed. Though Jess heard no sound from the hall, she knew a guard had taken up position on the other side of the door. She stood uneasily near the window when Jake moved away, her eyes fixed on the solid plank fence across the parade ground. She waited in suspense for word from the guard.

There are six thousand prisoners, Jess reminded herself. It would take time to locate Ambrose and bring him here. *But this long?* another part of her argued. The camp had stopped keeping a record of the dead, according to Taggart's report. Corpses were sold to medical schools. Bodies were thrown into the lake. Sometimes, they washed up onshore.

Her nerves raw, Jess kept glancing at the door, then turning her head to search the grounds outside the window. Something must have gone wrong. What if Diaz, Taggart, and Reese had been caught spying? What if...what if Ambrose *was* dead? Then the guards would find someone who had known Ambrose—someone whom they would bring to verify that fact. Yes, that was exactly what they would do. Cold now, Jess hugged herself and let that idea sink in. This was the fear she had struggled against every moment of the two-thousand-mile trek across the continent.

Another hour passed. Jess wiped dampness from her eyes and willed herself to hope that she was wrong. When she looked up, Jake was leaning against the wall, watching her somberly.

Boot heels clicked in the hallway, approaching. An order was called out. The posted guard entered through the door, then stepped to the side.

Jess watched a tall, painfully thin man enter. The man wore rakish but unkempt civilian clothing, and his sandy hair and mustache were styled long. He slowed to a stop, barely paying Jake any notice. His gaze fixed on Jess.

She lowered trembling hands, tears running freely down her face. She felt no more than a breath away from shattering.

Slowly yet steadily, the man continued toward her.

Jess saw years of fatigue in his dirty face, the deep lines the war had carved there. None of it mattered. She tipped back her head and looked up into her brother's blue eyes.

Ambrose took her hand, his mustache lifting with a smile. "Hello, butterfly."

Jess's tears had subsided, but she wasn't ready to let go of her brother. She'd waited too long, been through too much.

And she still had to tell him that it was only the two of them now. The rest of their family was gone.

Jake thanked the corporal who had brought Ambrose to the cell. The corporal responded with a brief touch to his hat, then left. The guard who'd entered ahead of Ambrose shut the door and took up position inside it to watch the prisoner.

Ambrose sought to disentangle himself gently as he pulled out a chair. "Here, Jessica, sit down." Not ready for the moment to end, she only tightened her hold. Ambrose held out his free hand to Jake.

"Ambrose Hale. You must have brought Jess. I'm grateful to you."

"Jake Bennett. I've heard a lot about you."

Jess raised her eyes as the two men she loved shook hands. She didn't care that they saw her cry. Her heart was full. Ambrose was alive.

At her brother's insistence, Jess finally accepted the seat, but she kept clinging to his hand. "I thought you were dead," she said.

Ambrose pulled another chair closer and sat facing his sister. He took in a breath to answer, then grinned as he searched her face. "Now why would you think that? You know it takes a lot to do in a Hale."

Jess wasn't ready for banter. Especially since the fire had shown her otherwise.

"Ambrose, your letters stopped. The last one came a year ago. After four months of waiting for another, I asked that a telegram be sent east. The reply said you'd been killed in a battle in Kentucky."

Jake went quietly to the window and gazed outside, giving the siblings some privacy.

Ambrose studied his hands. "I was shot at Perryville, Jess—in the chest and again in my leg. I scarcely remember the horse carrying me away from the battle. I must have fallen eventually, because some Shaker men found me lying in the woods near Harrodsburg."

Jess wiped her cheeks. "Shakers found you?"

"They were passing by when the horse I'd been riding came out of the woods with an empty saddle. They found me and took me to their village. I spent four months healing and one more working to get my strength back."

"So, you stayed with them five months." Jess knew little about the Shaker people, other than that they were members of an industrious religious order who lived apart from others.

Ambrose patted her hand. "The women know herbs and healing. With their help, I came through just fine."

There was appreciation for them in his smile, and Jess wanted to ask about the people and their way of life. Before she could, however, her eyes were drawn to his forehead. With a small frown, she reached out and pushed aside his hair to reveal a thin, white scar that angled across his temple and disappeared into his hairline.

"Saber?"

Ambrose looked surprised. "You recognize the wound?"

"I've had occasion to see an injury or two," Jess said evasively. She glanced up. The guard near the door searched her face. After a moment, he pulled his gaze away.

"Yes, it came from a saber," Ambrose said. "A month or so before I was captured."

Jess sighed, relieved at last to know what had happened to him yet regretting what he'd been through. "You still didn't write after you were well again."

"I returned to my post to scout for John Morgan. There was no getting the mail through, Jess. The Federals kept us busy in Tennessee until July. By then, Vicksburg was under siege, so Bragg sent us on a raid up to Louisville to try to lure some of the Yankees away." He shook his head with a smile. "Instead of stopping at Louisville, Morgan just kept going."

"To Ohio, your letter said."

"We were captured near New Lisbon."

"New Lisbon! How did you get that far north?"

"You know Morgan."

"Yes, I suppose I do." Fearless, audacious. A thorn in the side of the North. Legendary in the South.

"Is he here at Camp Douglas?"

"No, I believe he was imprisoned in Columbus." He chuckled. "Whether he's still there or not depends on how long that prison can hold him."

Jess eased back in her chair. At some point, she would need to reveal her own intent to free him come nightfall, but with the guard watching her so closely, she knew she had to wait.

She was just starting to recover from the stresses of the morning when Ambrose carefully cleared his throat.

"Father would never have let you come here if he was alive. What happened, Jess?"

∽⊶⊰⊱⊷∾

Telling Ambrose about the fire came hard.

In his letters, he had written of battles in which he had lost neighbors, old schoolmates, and friends. Yet Jess saw that losing his family, especially their mother, was a terrible blow, and he had never even met Emma. Even so, Ambrose's eyes never left hers as she related the details about the fire. In them, Jess saw grief over his own loss, together with anger that she had been forced to survive it alone.

At least two of the arsonists were in jail, she assured him.

Afterward, she spoke for a long time about the ranch and the people there, being careful to avoid revealing its location with the guard in earshot. She told him that she had found her place, had found herself. That she was happy. And she told him about her struggles trying to find the Lord, only to discover that He had never left her. "I thought He would reveal Himself through His power, perhaps send a violent thunderstorm, but He didn't. He was subtle, like a whisper," she said, remembering the morning of July fourth, when she'd heard a sound like a gentle voice in the breeze. "He didn't leave me at all."

"He never does," Ambrose agreed. "A lot of folks need something like a war to see that, but it's true."

Jess felt the guard's eyes on her again. This time, she kept her gaze on Ambrose.

"I suppose Southerners and Yankees are none too fond of each other anymore," Ambrose said, "but the fact is, many of us will be side by side in heaven one day." He gazed out the window at the Union parade ground. "Well, some of us will. The ones who still care. It doesn't make much sense, does it?" he reflected. "We share the same Father, and we all pray for His protection. Then we go out as soldiers and shoot men who we would call our brothers in faith. But does one man's faith allow him to burn homes and destroy lives? Does the faith of another allow him to force a race of people into perpetual slavery? Every man in this war prays for God's rescue, but I've often wondered how many have had the faith to pray for His help to stop doing wrong. Maybe when we strive to see matters through God's eyes instead of our own, we'll see more clearly." He sighed. "I don't know. It's difficult to reason out much of anything anymore." Wearily, he combed his fingers through his hair, giving Jess another glimpse of his scar. "But we were raised knowing duty and loyalty to our families and our homes, so until those wrongs are stopped, we're honor-bound to go on—to finish what's been started."

Patting his breast pocket, he said, "I still carry your ribbon with me."

Jess smiled. She could see Ambrose was deeply troubled by the news she had brought, yet, for her sake, he forced himself to set the pain aside.

"Now then," he said, crossing his legs, "when were you planning to tell me that you found someone to love you?"

Thinking he was accusing her of accepting a suitor without familial consent, Jess opened her mouth to defend herself. But then she saw the light of approval in her brother's face—all the love he'd ever felt for her.

She heard Jake turn away from the window.

Needing a moment to collect herself, she rose and went to unpack the fruit and bread they'd wrapped among the new clothes for Ambrose.

She paused, gazing down at her brother.

"How do you know he loves me?"

Ambrose smiled. "How could he not, butterfly?"

∞⋘∰⋙∞

While the three of them savored the repast they'd brought, Jake and Ambrose talked about ranching, cattle, and horses.

Seeing that the guard was looking away, Jess considered him briefly. He was young—young enough to be away from home for the first time. With his pale hair askew beneath his forage cap, he reminded her of Reese or Seth. Feeling her scrutiny, he met her gaze. His eyes were green, like hers, and they seemed to hold a measure of sympathy.

Before Jake and Ambrose had finished eating, the guard was replaced with another. This man looked like he'd rather shoot the three of them than guard them.

Jess saw her chance.

"Ambrose, you haven't told me a thing about the house. The last time you wrote, you said those mean ol' Yankees had stopped up all the wells with everything they could lay their hands on."

Bemused, her brother stared at her.

"Tell me, did they really close off every last well? Surely

there must be one left open. Digging another would take an impossibly long time."

Already bored with what he probably considered bumpkin chatter, the guard rocked on his heels and glared at the opposite wall.

Comprehension dawning, Ambrose gave her a hard look. Jess met him, glare for glare. She meant to do it. She would get him out. For a moment, Ambrose debated, then shifted his gaze to the formidable rancher beside her. Slowly, Ambrose nodded. "There is one well left. I think it'll be enough to give us a new start."

"I'm so relieved! Tell me, is it the one near the southernmost paddock? I do so love to go there and watch the foals and their mamas run."

"No, it's the one by the northwest paddock, but the fences there have been burned, and though some neighbors are working to repair it, it isn't safe yet to contain new foals."

"Then there truly is a great deal of work to be done."

"Indeed, there is." Ambrose studied them both. "We would do better to hire some good men to help us get that new start."

Jake leaned forward. "I'm acquainted with three besides myself who could lend a hand. They'd be willing—and are more than able—to see to those fences for you."

Ambrose thought for a moment. "That should do."

While the men exchanged a meaningful nod, Jess glanced around the room and gave a dramatic shiver.

"Oh, Ambrose! How long have you been in this dreadful place?"

"I've heard that there are prisons worse than this, and it's been only two months."

"Oh, brave Ambrose." Jess patted his arm. "If I were here, I'd be terrified to sleep at night."

For the rest of the afternoon, Ambrose, Jake, and Jess reflected over the course of the war until the guard finally stated that it was time for the visitors to leave.

Jess stood up, her heart beginning to pound. The simpler part of their plan was over. From here, their lives would be at stake. Wordlessly, she took her straw hat from Jake.

In the hallway, flanked again by a pair of guards, Ambrose quietly accepted the gift of clothing from his sister. The new trousers and coat were coal-gray and black—colors that would help him blend into the night.

Jess stared up at her brother, struggling not to show her fear. Like a dutiful sister, she kissed his cheek, but she couldn't convince herself to let him go.

After a moment, she felt a hand on her arm. Gently but firmly, Jake drew her away from Ambrose. "He has to go now, Jess," he murmured.

Jess took Jake's arm absently, letting him guide her back the way they had come, but she turned back before Ambrose was out of sight.

At the far door, Ambrose was standing between the guards, looking back at her.

He raised his voice so she could hear him. "The Lord has a plan, Jess," he called, just as he had years ago from the stagecoach that carried him away from Carson City. "Remember that."

❧

Jess's tenacity, Jake thought, had returned with a vengeance. He walked her to the buggy, certain his arm bore indelible nail marks.

Jake watched her expression as he helped her into the seat and then climbed in beside her. All traces of worry had vanished. She looked like a loaded cannon, primed to fire.

It was about time.

∞⊰⧉⊱∞

When they gathered in Jake's room that night, Taggart confirmed what Ambrose had said about the fence. "There are lads workin' to board up the holes—twenty or more comin' and goin', nice as ye please. A man can walk right out."

"Holes?" Jess considered that. "How many places are there to come through the fence?"

"Three remain, mariposa," Diaz said. "The fence burned and was torn down. It is only now that they build it again."

Jake and Jess exchanged a look, and Jake nodded once. "Ambrose told us the same. That's our way in. Taggart?"

"Southern lads are not the only ones taken ill with smallpox. Fewer than five hundred guards are well enough to stand their posts. Of those, many are off searchin' for their own deserters. I figure a dozen or less'll be patrollin' the fence tonight, beside those in the sentry boxes above."

Jess glanced around. Reese frowned thoughtfully.

"With all the prisoners," Diaz said, "one of us may get in, but how will we find the one man we're looking for?"

"Jess's brother knows we're coming. He'll find us," Jake answered. "The moon's a mere crescent, so once we get there, it'll be hard for us to see one another."

Diaz grinned. "It will be even harder for the soldiers to see us."

"That, boys, is our advantage." Jake glanced at Jess. "We'll go in slow and quiet. I don't want any gunfire if we can avoid it."

"Why look at me when you say that, Bennett?" Jess asked, batting her eyelashes innocently.

The corner of his mouth lifted. "I don't want you going down in history as the woman who started a battle at Camp Douglas prison."

Jess heard the underlying warning through his tease, and she took it to heart. She did not want to be the cause of any injuries—or deaths.

Jake turned to the others. "Before we leave, we'll need to wrap strips of cloth through the horses' bit rings, the links of the harnesses—anything that makes even the slightest noise. No one wears spurs, and we'll have to cover up silver buckles and ornaments that might catch the light. Anything else?"

When no one answered, Jess pushed herself to her feet. "Well, it's settled, then. I'll go in and get Ambrose."

"What?" The question came from every man in the room.

Jess was not put out. After all this time, she had learned from Jake how to reason calmly. "It makes sense. I know what he looks like, and I can pass as a young man."

"No." Jake's face had turned to stone. "I'm going in."

Jess gave a derisive laugh. "You'd stand out like Gulliver among the Lilliputians."

A small argument erupted. Taggart announced he'd shave his flame-hued beard and go in. Diaz denied the significance of his skin color. And Jake declared over the clamor that he would slip through the fence.

A quiet voice broke through the debate. "I'll go in and get your brother for you, Miss Jess."

There was a stunned silence. All eyes swung to Reese.

"I don't know what Lilliputians are," Reese said, "but I do

know this. The boss there would stand out for certain, like you said. It don't matter none how much orange Taggart parts with; if he had to run, those Yankees'd hear him huffing like a steam train and find him. Diaz…Diaz don't look like no Southerner I ever saw, and there ain't no way a one of us is going to let you go through that fence, Miss Jess. The folks at the ranch would never forgive us if we came back without you."

Jess sat back down, her expression intentionally blank. She was grateful for his loyalty, but she alone bore the weight of responsibility for them all. *She* had wanted to come east, *she* had wanted to break Ambrose out. She would not send anyone else inside a military prison. The boy had already been knifed.

Reese continued. "Now I ain't too tall, I don't stand out, and Diaz there has taken to calling me Sticks, which means I'm skinny enough to look like one of them fellers who've been living on army food for the past couple of years." The other men considered his point. His eyes cut to Jake.

"Diaz and Taggart and I are the ones who spent the day studyin' the fence line and the lay of the land around. Any one of us knows better than either of you how to go about getting in and out, and Miss Jess can tell me what her brother looks like." His gaze fell on both Jake and Jess. "And I'll feel a whole lot better knowing the two of you are watching my back. There ain't nobody what can shoot better."

Jake stared at Reese. "Reese is right," he finally admitted, acknowledging the wisdom of his plan.

Jess looked away, refusing to comment.

"He's the only one who might blend in among the prisoners without drawing notice," Jake went on. "He knows the dangers. He's steady. He pays attention, and he speaks a little like a Southerner. If he's questioned by a guard, he could pass as a Confederate." He faced Reese. "You've done the job of a man too long to be treated like a boy now. Your decision takes guts, and it's the right one. We'll all make sure you come out safely."

That decided, Jake leaned forward and pulled out his notebook. He opened it to a blank page, on which he sketched out the prison walls. The men discussed where each of them would take position.

Jess sat back from the others, mentally spinning out a plan of her own.

At last, Jake recommended they all break to get a few hours' rest before starting out. Jess felt his eyes on her as she rose with the others, and she forced herself to make appropriate chatter as everyone left his room.

In her own room again, Jess locked the door, then stripped off her gown and petticoats. Instead of resting, she pulled on a flannel shirt, britches, and a pair of boots. Combing the curls from her hair, she then braided it and gathered every last strand under her hat.

Suddenly, Jess paused, alert. She had heard a noise in the hall that sounded like a floorboard creaking. For several minutes, she stood motionless. All was silent.

Jess collected her saddlebags and laid them on the bed, tossing the dress aside. She was going to get her brother, and she didn't need any extra weight slowing down the horse.

Finally, she pulled on her gun belt and checked the loading of her revolver.

When enough time had passed for Jake and the others to fall asleep, Jess shouldered her saddlebags and left the room. She tread lightly past Jake's closed door, listening for sounds of stirring within. None.

Jess stole down the stairs.

At the livery stable, she went immediately to the corral, where a dozen or so horses stood resting. She moved along the fence, looking from one animal to the next, searching for the markings that would identify her horse. It wasn't there.

Realizing that it had been put in a stall, Jess went around to the front of the barn, lifted the latch, and pushed open the giant door.

Shadows vanished as starlight spread over the floor of the barn—and over its occupants.

There before her, looking as vengeful as the four horsemen of the Apocalypse, stood Jake and the cattlemen.

Jess glared at them, unable to hide her anger. "How did you know?"

Diaz crossed his arms as if contemplating a creature of great interest. "*La mandíbula.*"

"What?" She was seething.

Jake's handsome face softened with a smile. "Your jaw, Miss Hale. It stiffens only when you're digging in your heels about something. You looked exactly like that when you and the others left my room."

Diaz said, "You think we would let you go by yourself, mariposa? Never. We will let no harm come to you."

Jess attempted the glare again. It fell markedly short. "I'm responsible for your being here. *I* don't intend to let any of *you* come to harm."

"Ye hardly made us come, Jess," Taggart pointed out. "As I recall it, ye had—how did ye say it, boss? Little choice in the matter."

Reese grinned. "And I don't see as how you have any say now."

Her resistance failing, her eyes searched their faces, finally resting on Jake.

The other three discreetly stepped back.

"So, now what?" she asked Jake softly.

"Now we go get your brother."

Jess let out a combination of a chuckle and a sob. Jake pulled her gently against him.

"I love you, Jess," he said.

She smiled into his shoulder. "I know. And I love you—"

"Wait!" He took a step back. "Look at me when you say that, or it seems like you're talking to my shirt."

She laughed, fastening her eyes on his. "I love you, Jake Bennett."

Though his face spoke his delight, his hands settled sternly on his hips. "You know, it's taken you long enough to say it."

"I should have, long before now."

With these confessions behind them, they quietly prepared their horses to ride. Jess could sense the men's tension in addition to her own as they mentally prepared themselves for the next few hours and the challenges they would bring.

The horses picked up on the heightened emotions of the group. They shifted about as bits were slid over teeth, bridles were buckled, and cinches were pulled tight. The cavernous barn echoed with the whir of cylinders and the rasp of leather as the men checked their loading and holstered their guns. Finally, hat cords were tightened and stirrups creaked as the riders stepped into their saddles.

Outside, Jake pushed the barn door closed.

"Which way we headin' out afterward?" Reese asked.

"Straight back the way we came," Jake said. "When we leave the prison, head west. We won't be returning to Chicago. I want Ambrose to ride with either Jess or Reese. They're the lightest. After we have him, there's no telling how things will unravel. We'll have to cover one another, and no one rides out alone. We stay in twos, at the very least. My pa's farm is a ten-hour ride at a lope, just north of that red bridge we passed coming here. His is the only drive lined with oak trees. Get back there anyway you have to. Just don't let anyone follow you there."

Jake moved his horse alongside Jess's. "I'll be watching you closely, Jess. Dressed like one of us, the soldiers will be aiming at you just as much as at anyone else here. If things turn bad, I want your promise you'll get yourself on a horse and get out of there as fast as you can."

Jess was already shaking her head.

Jake grabbed her horse's headstall suddenly. "You don't promise, you don't go."

Jess snapped her mouth shut. She had never seen him so adamant—so determined. Still, she bristled at his threat. "You think you're going to stop me?"

He nodded sharply. "I'll tie you so tight you'll wish Diaz had done it, and I'll leave you to spend the night on the barn floor."

Looking at him, Jess knew that he meant what he said. Yet she grudgingly acknowledged to herself that, whether she went along or was left behind, he only intended to keep her safe. "I promise to get away if things turn bad."

Some of the steeliness left his eyes. "Good." Though his horse snorted and pulled, Jake held it beside Jess's. "Reese goes in?"

After a silent, fervent prayer for the young man, Jess finally agreed. "Reese goes in."

Chapter Twenty

Huge clouds rolled in from the west as the five sped south toward Camp Douglas prison. Jess looked up to see pinprick stars disappear and then reemerge above, the clouds alternately plunging them into inky blackness and moving aside to cast the land in a hazy gray.

Jake was no more than a shadow ahead of her, and when she glanced around, the men behind practically vanished like bats in the night.

Despite the coolness of the late hour, droplets of sweat broke out on Jess's forehead. Her heart thrummed unsteadily as she pushed her horse to keep up with Jake. She knew the intermittent cloud cover would help shield them from the eyes of the Union sharpshooters. The danger was that it would equally frustrate their own attempts to distinguish the movements of the guards.

Within minutes, the smattering of houses became familiar, then the dark shapes of the prison walls emerged. Without a word, they slowed their horses to a quiet walk so they wouldn't wake any civilians. They moved off the road to further muffle the sound of the hooves with the prairie earth.

Though no lamplight shone from the homes, Jake led them in a wide circle around the residences to avoid being seen in the event that someone stepped outdoors en route to an outhouse.

As they came within view of the sentries, they dismounted and began to use the moments of greater darkness to their advantage. They waited patiently behind clusters of trees or lone carriage houses, stealthily slipping closer to the western wall each time a cloud cover fell.

When they were perhaps four hundred yards from the stockade, they entered a small grove of oak trees. There, they split up. Diaz and Taggart wended their way south, pulling their horses after them.

Leaving their own horses tied to a tree in the grove, Jake, Jess, and Reese took their rifles and continued on foot, then on their hands and knees, and finally on their stomachs, keeping as low as possible.

When they reached the last cluster of bushes large enough to conceal them, they stopped to study the perimeter of the stockade and the sentry box high atop it. Here and there, soldiers looked down, silhouetted starkly against the night sky, with rifles gleaming against their shoulders. Below them, other guards patrolled the fence line, several hundred feet separating one man from the next. All was quiet inside the camp.

Ten minutes of tense silence passed. Then they heard the distant hoot of an owl.

Diaz and Taggart had taken their position.

It was time.

Jake unrolled a tattered gray coat he'd purchased in town and handed it to Reese. It would be his only disguise. Reese gave Jess his hat for safekeeping and shrugged into the coat. Then he unbuckled his gun belt and passed his weapons to Jake. At this, Jess nearly protested out loud, but Jake silenced her with a solid hand on her wrist. She suddenly realized that if Reese were found by the guards, he might be able to talk his way out of trouble; if they found him armed, however, they could shoot him as the enemy.

The two men inched forward on their elbows through knee-high prairie grass. Jess deeply wished she had never agreed to let Reese go in to get Ambrose.

While Jake and Reese kept watch on a passing guard, Jess slowly crept up to Jake's side. She placed a hand on his arm, and he turned his face to look at her. "Can you see any of the openings in the stockade?" she whispered.

By way of an answer, he pointed to three stacks of lumber she hadn't noticed—two just to the south and another much further down, nearer where Diaz and Taggart were waiting. A cloud drifted overhead, draping the camp in black. When it passed, Jess realized that the lumber lay where the wall had yet to be finished. She figured that the gap the men had found that afternoon must be behind the stacks. The shifting shadows made the openings nearly impossible to see.

A guard rounded the corner of the stockade and headed away from them. Jake and Reese inched toward the lumber, crawling like cats on the prowl.

Jess followed until she was within range of the first sentry box. A half-buried wooden stake was protruding from the ground before her. She was one hundred feet from the wall, no more than fifty from the roaming guards. The dead zone.

If she moved suddenly, the sentry in the box would see her.

Without a sound, she laid her rifle on the ground in front of her. She lifted the brim of her hat slightly and wiped the sweat trickling from her hairline with her sleeve.

Ambrose, she thought, *only a little while longer. Only a little while and you'll be out of there for good. Oh, please don't let anything happen to you now.*

The instant the words lighted in her mind, she knew she was sending her wishes in the wrong direction. *Almighty Father,* she prayed, *I don't know of anything in Your Word that tells me whether freeing Ambrose is right or wrong. Perhaps, during a war, there are no answers to that. I only know that while David hid from King Saul in a cave, he prayed, 'Bring my soul out of prison, that I may praise thy name.' Over the past months, You've blessed me with*

345

countless reasons to praise Your name. Above all, You've given me hope of a future with Jake, and You've brought Ambrose back to me. You've given me the faith to praise Your name, no matter what comes. Now I ask that in Your mercy and in Your love, You would enable us to free Ambrose tonight and You would grant that none of us is harmed.

Jess pressed her cheek to the ground as another guard strolled by. Then when he had passed, she carefully looked about for Jake and Reese. She saw nothing but the tops of the grasses blowing in the breeze.

Her gut wrenched with the realization of just how deeply she loved Jake. What if he were discovered? A picture flashed through her mind of him lying, shot, in a circle of Federals, his eyes staring dully at the stars. Jess had to fight the urge to go to him. She wanted to know what it was to be his wife. She wanted Jake to hold her close on long winter nights. She wanted to swim with him in the creek on balmy summer evenings. She wanted to continue working the ranch together and to give him children to fill the emptiness left by Sadie's absence. Jake Bennett brightened her life and brought her joy, and he loved her. Jess sent one more prayer heavenward, asking the Lord to protect them for one reason more: she wanted to be with Jake, and she wanted forever.

Silently letting out her breath, she searched again for signs of Jake and Reese. Another guard passed. There was a movement in the grass about twenty feet away. She gasped when Reese's head emerged. He and Jake were too near the opening—they might be seen! Yet Reese looked first to one side and then to the other, noting the positions and distances of the guards. Jake leaned close to the boy and whispered something as Reese nodded, listening. Then, flat on his belly, Reese moved forward.

Jess was breathing hard now, trying to stifle her gasps.

It had all come down to this.

She watched him go. Forward, forward. Another hoot sounded—Jake signaling to Diaz and Taggart that Reese was going in.

A shadow spread over the land. She saw Reese crouch down, hidden by darkness. When the clouds slid by, the place where Reese had been was empty. He was in.

Jess breathed a tentative sigh of relief. The first goal had been achieved.

Keeping her eyes level with the grass, Jess reached back, pulled open her holster, and slid the revolver free. Bringing it up in front of her, she waited, heart pounding against the ground.

Minutes passed, turning into a half hour. Then another half hour. Two of the guards stopped to chat directly in front of the opening. Her nerves stretched as tight as banjo strings.

The six of them would need to be well away from here by daybreak, her mind screamed, or the guards would be able to see them and follow them. They were running out of time.

In the next instant, Jess watched in horror as the two guards readied their rifles and swung the stocks to their shoulders.

They were moving in Jake's direction.

Jess nearly cried out. She stifled her panic and forced herself to think.

Diaz and Taggart were positioned hundreds of yards away near the second break in the wall. They were nowhere near enough to help Jake. She was much closer and fully able to help him.

The two Yankee guards began to sweep the grass with their rifle barrels as they moved along. Using her elbows, Jess turned herself until she faced them head-on. Carefully, she drew back the hammer, grimacing when it clicked loudly in place.

The guards didn't appear to have heard.

Jess laid her finger along the trigger guard, bracing her gun hand firmly on the palm of her other hand.

One of the soldiers called up to the sentry above, who moved to the outside edge of his box and looked down where the other man was pointing. While he scanned the field from his vantage point, the two on the ground moved further apart.

Jess sighted along her barrel. One of the guards motioned to the other. Suddenly, both rifles swung into position to fire.

Jess took aim at the gun hand of the soldier nearest her. She curled her finger over the trigger.

One of the Federals shouted and kicked at something with his boot. He stared down at the grass, but the other muttered something and then burst out laughing, apparently teasing his alarmed partner. Both of them moved away. The laughing one shouldered his rifle in unconcern, but the other persisted in searching the ground until he had almost reached the wall. After they exchanged a few more words, they waved up to the sentry and resumed their rounds.

Jess lowered her revolver with a sigh far shakier than the last. Jake had been no more than a body's length from those guards, she knew. That they hadn't seen him was nothing short of a miracle.

Jess uncocked the revolver and rested her head on her arm.

The air felt cooler now, and damp, as if a storm were rolling in. She raised her head, then nearly jumped out of her skin to see Jake beside her.

"Shh, it's me."

Unable to stop herself, she grasped his shirt and leaned over, embracing him as best she could from a horizontal position. "I thought they'd found you! I thought that was the end of it!"

He hugged her close. "We're not out of this yet," he reminded her.

Steeling her nerves, she let him go and moved slightly away. "The guards found something," she said. "I saw one of them kicking at the ground. What was it?"

Jake looked around. "A few pages of newsprint the wind had blown in. I found them in the grass and took them with me, thinking they might come in handy. The pages fluttered just enough to keep the guards' attention away from me."

Jess nodded, still battling her fright. *The newspaper might not have worked*, she thought. *The soldiers might have captured him.*

"I have to get back now. I just wanted to be sure you were all right."

All right? Jess searched his face, noting the steadiness in his eyes. Jake Bennett was a man calm of purpose. He was undaunted by fears, even now, and he was watching out for her. How, she wondered, could she ever be afraid with this man by her side?

"I'm fine, Bennett," she said, her tone confident again.

Jake leaned forward and kissed her. Then he looked toward the opening where Reese had entered the camp. "They're ready."

Jess turned her head to see two shadows emerge through the fence—the slender form of Reese and the taller silhouette of her brother. Hope collided with tension inside her as she resumed her place.

Jake was already moving away.

Jess scanned the dead zone for the enemy. Unexpectedly, a single guard rounded the corner, patrolling in the direction opposite of that in which the other guards had been walking all night. Stranger still, Jess thought she recognized something familiar in the way he moved. Her eyes flew to the guard box. It was empty. The sentry!

Desperate to call to Jake, she maintained silence and clamped her jaw shut. With the rifle in one hand and the revolver in the other, she began pushing herself away from the man.

He was coming straight for her.

Jess shook her head, denying what was happening. Obviously, he had seen her from the sentry box. Why hadn't he simply alerted the guards on the ground? Why had he come after her himself? Earning points toward a higher rank? Going for his big chance to be promoted to paper shuffler?

Not at her expense.

He was less than ten feet away. Eight feet. Six.

Jess dropped her rifle. She rose up on one knee, pulling up her revolver.

His rifle was aimed at her heart.

In the next second, she envisioned Jake, her brother, and the other three men whose lives would be affected forever by the choice she would make in the next moment. She recalled Jake saying, "We'll go in slow and quiet," and she remembered Reese going in without his guns.

Jess took a deep breath.

And threw her revolver away.

The man lifted his boot to her stomach and forced her back down in the grass.

Jess avoided glancing toward her rifle. She hoped he didn't see it—hoped he no longer saw her as a threat.

The guard was searching her face. His own was hidden in the shadow of his forage cap, but she thought she saw a frown. He lifted his rifle and pushed her hat off her head.

Her braid tumbled free.

To her surprise, the man immediately withdrew his boot. She saw amusement on his face when his head turned to scan the area.

What was more, she recognized the pale hair and the lines

of sympathy around his eyes. He was the young soldier who had first stood guard in the room in the headquarters building.

"I'm sorry, ma'am," he said softly. "I thought you was that big feller."

There was a loud double click beside Jess. "Shoulder your gun."

At the tone of Jake's command, the soldier swiftly obeyed. In the open space beyond him, Jess saw Ambrose, Reese, and several other shadowy forms hurrying away from the prison wall. Evidently, the Yanks would be missing not one but nearly a dozen of their prisoners come morning.

The young soldier dropped his gaze to the bore of Jake's gun. Doing his best to ignore it, he turned his attention back to Jess.

"I couldn't help but hear what you told your brother today, ma'am. I sure am sorry for you, losing your family and all, and if you'll allow me to say so, ma'am, I haven't heard a voice as pretty as yours since my mama died when I was a boy. My pa's family is from Michigan, and I'm nothing more than a farm boy, ma'am, so I don't much know if what I'm about to do here is right or wrong. All I know is, it seems right to me."

Jake eyed him. "What do you mean?"

He pulled off his cap. "I'm seein' to it her brother leaves with her." He looked again to Jess. "I sure don't want you losin' nobody else."

Jess was stunned. She could see no trace of duplicity in his eyes; she heard nothing but kindness in his voice. His stance was that of a man worthy of respect.

She could hardly believe what was happening. After Yankee sympathizers had destroyed her family, another Yankee was making certain that its remnants were put back together again.

The young man nervously followed the movement of Jake's gun. He calmed a little as it was uncocked and lowered.

Jake kept his voice quiet. "You just happen to be on duty tonight?"

"No, sir. I took another man's post so's I could see that you and that Kentucky feller got away safe."

"How did you know we'd come back to get him out?"

He smiled a little. "Well, sir, I didn't exactly figure that the lady here would be comin' with you, but I surely saw how much she cared for her brother. She, uh, she also looked as though her mind was good and set on something, and neither of you seemed like the kind of folks who'd leave a good man here to die."

Jake rose up on an elbow. Another guard came into view. The escaping Confederates dove to the ground. "I'm much obliged to you," Jake said.

The soldier nodded, pulling his cap on again. He began to back away. "Ma'am, I hope I didn't hurt you none, but I thought I was going to have to take a gun away from your gentleman there to get him to listen to what I had to say." He gave Jake a salute. "Godspeed."

Jess halted him with an urgent whisper. "Please, you said helping us seemed right. How can that be when my brother and I are from the South?"

He kept his back to her, his eyes on the other guard. "Like I said, ma'am, I don't want you losin' no one else." He rubbed his nose with a knuckle. "And my mama was from Lexington."

"Sergeant!"

Their rescuer casually started toward the oncoming guard.

Jess found Jake's hand in the grass as the youth led the other guard away. "I feel like a durn fool," she heard him telling his fellow Yankee. "I come all the way down here only to scare up a rabbit."

Jake squeezed Jess's hand, bringing her attention around. "Ambrose and the boys already made it to the horses. Now it's our turn."

Jess glanced skyward. "The clouds are gone!" she whispered anxiously. "They'll see us from the sentry boxes!"

"We'll go slowly," he assured her. "Besides, we have a friend up there."

Jess met his gaze, and Jake smiled the crooked smile she loved.

Painstakingly, they retrieved her hat and Reese's handgun and rifle, stopping frequently to wait for a guard to pass. They moved as fast as they dared, concerned that one of the other prisoners would be seen and thereby alert the sentries to their escape.

Gradually, they made their way to the copse of trees where they'd tied their horses. Diaz, Taggart, Reese, and Ambrose were waiting for them. The moment they were relatively safe from view, Jess left Jake's side and rushed to Ambrose, embracing him fiercely.

"I love you, Jessica."

She hugged him tighter. Then, knowing that they were still near enough to be discovered, she pulled back, turning to thank Diaz, Taggart, and especially Reese. They had risked their lives for her, as well as for her brother, a stranger they had never met.

Jake handed Reese his hat and guns. Without a word, they walked out, careful to keep buildings and trees between them and the sentries. When they had reached a safe distance, they stepped into their saddles. Ambrose swung onto Jess's horse and pulled her up behind him. They left at a lope, and within minutes, Camp Douglas prison had faded into the night.

They rode for several miles, keeping a cautious eye out behind them. But the road remained clear—no Federals were on their tail.

Feelings of triumph ran high, and Jess almost laughed aloud in joy. She held onto Ambrose, thinking about how much had changed since they last were together. Then she glanced heavenward, where thin wisps of clouds were floating high above. Beyond them glistened stars that a young Jake had believed were the walls of heaven. Jess searched the sky, more sure than ever that heaven existed. In the next moment, she was sending God a tearful prayer of thanks, praising Him that, after all the hard times that had fallen on her and Ambrose both, freeing Ambrose from prison had been smooth and successful.

Jess also prayed His blessing on an enemy soldier whose name she didn't even know.

∾⚬⊰⬥⊱⚬∾

Two hours west of Chicago, they reined in their horses and prepared to split up.

Jake looked at the cattlemen. "You three ride north. After an hour, turn west. From what the folks said in Chicago, the Federals at Camp Douglas rarely ride the four miles to town to look for escaped prisoners, since they usually find them much closer to the camp. So, the farther away we get, the less likely we'll have trouble. But watch your backs, just the same. Jess and Ambrose and I will go straight to my father's farm. We'll meet you there."

The ranch hands murmured their agreement, but Ambrose turned to look over his shoulder at Jess, his eyes filled with regret.

"What is it?" she asked.

Ambrose glanced at the others. "I'll be forever grateful to you for what you've done for Jessica and me. You've interrupted your lives out of kindness to Jess and traveled across the country to free me, and I look forward to the day I can repay you for that." He looked at his sister again. "But I can't go with you."

The ranchmen were careful not to react, but Jess pulled her hand away from her brother. "What do you mean, you can't go with us?"

Ambrose dismounted, then lifted her down. Jake took the reins from him.

"Walk with me a little, Jess." Ambrose led her away from the others. Finally, he stopped and faced her.

"Please tell me you're not leaving," she begged. This couldn't be happening—not again.

"I have to, Jess. I have to find my way back South. The war isn't over."

"It can be! The war can be over for us! Please, Ambrose— please come with us. Jake already said that his family will let us stay with them until you're strong again. Next spring, we're going back to the ranch. There are horses, Ambrose—more horses than Father ever owned. And there's land just waiting to be built on—miles of it! We could be a family again!"

Lovingly, Ambrose studied her face. "You look like mother," he murmured. He said nothing more.

Jess's shoulders fell. She knew she had her answer. "I thought you would stay with us."

"I can't, Jess. Jake was kind to offer his father's home to a Southerner, but the man's neighbors might like nothing more than to shoot me on sight. I won't allow trouble to come to his family on my account." He gave her braid a brotherly tug. "You be careful, too, as long as you're here. Stay close to Jake until you go back west. He's a good man. He'll keep you from harm."

Jess was desperate to keep him there. After discovering he was alive, she'd had only a few precious hours with him. "You can't travel south! You'll never get past the Federals! And if you do, the Confederacy will only think you turned traitor in the Yankee prison. They'll hang you just as surely as the Federals will if they capture you!"

"No, Jessica, they won't. John Morgan knows me. He knows I'd never betray him or Kentucky." He smiled softly. "Your heart pulls you west, but me...my roots are elsewhere. The South is where I belong."

Jess's moan of frustration dwindled away. She knew he was right. Even when he'd moved west, his heart had remained in Lexington. "You've always wanted to rebuild Greenbriar."

"Yes, I have," he said. "I once heard Grandmother say that if ever a blessing had been spoken on a place that anyone who stood on its lands would forever remember its warmth, its belonging, and its sureness of home, then that place was Kentucky."

"And you believe that," she said softly.

"I believe it."

A small smile formed on her lips. "I think that same blessing was spoken on Honey Lake Valley."

So much had changed for them both since the beginning of the war, she mused. In many ways, they had missed a large part of each other's lives. It pained her that, as they continued on from here in their own directions, nearly a whole continent would remain between them. But she knew they would always be close in heart.

"Send me a letter with the Bennetts' address as soon as you settle, okay?"

She smiled past the tightness in her throat. "You write back, too, or I'll come looking for you again."

"I don't doubt that," he said. He glanced over her head, then met her gaze again.

Jess took a long breath. "You have to go, don't you?"

"I'm afraid so. Only a couple of hours left until sunrise."

Jess stepped closer to him. His sandy hair and mustache were just as she remembered them, his blue eyes glowing with a brother's love. She reached up and touched the tiny wrinkles in his brow that were new to her, placed there by the war.

"Will you be able to tell me good-bye, Jess?"

"There really are no good-byes, if you think about it. Since the Lord will eventually bring us to heaven, we'll see each other again, one way or another. I hope it will be here, and I pray that it'll be here. I'll pray He keeps you safe, and that He brings an end to the war, but I'll be able to let you go."

Ambrose took her hand, his eyes beaming. "I'll be so glad when the war is finally over and I can come visit." He shifted his weight restlessly. "I'd better go, Jess."

Jess smiled up at him. He was every inch a Kentucky gentleman, so straight and tall. "Don't let the war take you from me. I've seen your name on a gravestone once. I don't want to see it again—not until you've lived a long, long life."

"Nothing could take me from you, little butterfly. We'll always have each other."

Jess smiled through her tears.

Ambrose turned and approached the cattlemen to shake their hands and thank them. Finally, he walked up to Jake's horse and reached out his hand. Jake leaned down and shook it heartily.

Ambrose glanced over at Jess, who was waiting quietly. "Take good care of her," he said.

"You'd be surprised how many people have made that request on her behalf," Jake said, shaking his hand once more. "You can depend on it."

Jess smiled at Ambrose as he walked toward her, leading her horse. He was dressed in civilian clothes rather than a uniform, and he looked more like a businessman than a cavalry scout or courier. Inwardly, she agreed with him that he had every chance of making it safely home. "Send me lilac blossoms from mother's old hedge when you return to Greenbriar."

"I will. But it will take time to rebuild the house and grounds as they once were."

"Maybe not as long as you think."

"Maybe," he said. Jess hugged him, then stepped aside.

He climbed up into the saddle.

"Ambrose," she said, "even if you have to give up the horse, keep the saddlebags."

He glanced back. "Why? What's in them?"

"Something that belonged to Father. Something that now belongs to you."

Moments later, Ambrose Hale was riding south with a thousand dollars of Hale Imports gold.

"It's for Greenbriar," she murmured with a smile.

"Are you tired?" Dawn was approaching when Jake spoke over his shoulder to Jess, who was riding behind him, arms wrapped around his chest.

The rhythm of the easy gallop lulled her, but the beauty of the sights they passed kept her awake. She pulled her gaze from waving willow branches and smiled up at him.

"I'll sleep later. There's too much to see now."

"I understand that right enough," Jake said, pressing her hand warmly. "You know, if we're going to stay here for the winter, we might as well look for Thoroughbreds to buy to take to the ranch with us come spring."

She smiled. "Thinking of adding on to the ranch, Jake?"

"I might be."

Her heart taking flight, Jess rested her head against the soft flannel over his shoulder blade. Beneath it was the long crescent scar, left there when he had tried to save her father.

What a good man Jake Bennett was—a man of faith who lived according to an honor code shared only by the rarest of men. How blessed she was to have him in her life.

She thought back to the terrifying precipice her heart had hovered above just months ago. The precipice was gone. *Ho Chen was right,* she thought. Time and again, Jake Bennett had shown his true character—his honor, his courage, his very great worth. She reflected on the countless times when he had refused to back down in the face of hardship, when he had maintained his character and his trust in the Lord. In her mind, in her heart, and in her soul, there were no more doubts. Not about Jake, and not about the Lord's presence in her life.

Jess lifted her gaze. Above them, streaks of pink and violet clouds brightened the sky. "Look, Jake. Sunrise."

Jake reined in his horse, and together, they watched as pink lightened to peach and yellow hues.

"The Lord is telling us good morning," Jess said.

"That He is," Jake agreed. "I want all the rest of our sunrises to be like this, Jess." He turned in the saddle to look at her. "You and me. Watching them together." His dark eyes searched her face, speaking silently yet plainly of his love. "You've never given me an answer, little lady."

Jess lifted her hand to his cheek. "Jake Bennett, I would be honored to be your wife."

A breeze stirred, sounding ever so much like a whisper among the grasses.

Epilogue

November 1863

D oyle and Seth threw down their shovels and wiped the sweat from their brows. Hot in their coats despite the wintry cold in Carson City, they stepped back to study the placement of the new tombstone Jess had requested.

Seth had raised his eyebrows when Doyle had read him the instructions printed on the telegram, and they had looked at each other with growing smiles when Doyle had read her name.

Jessica Bennett.

Seth gathered up the shovels, and Doyle pulled out the telegram again, comparing the specifications with the markings on the new tombstone.

Satisfied that the wording was correct, Doyle put the paper back in his pocket and followed Seth to the wagon, marveling at the faith of the tenacious young woman he had come to respect.

"Hale," the marker read:

Isaac Donelson
Georgeanne McKinney
Emily Frances
and dear friend
Elsie Scheuer

And beneath the names read the epitaph:
I can't wait to see you again.

About the Author

Tammy Barley's roots run deep and wide across the United States. With Cherokee heritage and such ancestors as James Butler "Wild Bill" Hickok, Ralph Waldo Emerson, and Henry David Thoreau, she essentially inherited her literary vocation and her preferred setting: the Wild West. An avid equestrian, Tammy has ridden horseback over western mountains and rugged trails in Arizona.

Tammy excelled in her writing studies at a local college, where she explored prose, novel writing, and nonverbal communication. She even enrolled in acting classes to master character development. In 2006, she published two series of devotionals in *Beautiful Feet: Meditations for Missionary Women* for the Lutheran Women's Missionary Society. She won second place in the Golden Rose Contest in the category of inspiration romance, and she serves as a judge for various fiction contests.

In addition to writing, Tammy makes a career of editing manuscripts, ghostwriting, and mentoring other writers. She also homeschools three children. Tammy has lived in twenty-eight towns in eight different states, but her family currently makes its home in Crystal Lake, Illinois.

Coming Soon:
HOPE'S PROMISE
Book Two in The Sierra Chronicles
By Tammy Barley

Chapter One

Western Nevada Territory
May 1864

W ould you care to rest a while, Jess?"
Withholding a smile, Jess leaned forward in
the saddle as her horse clambered up beside Jake's
to the top of the rocky bank. When the ground leveled out,
she glanced at the progress of the small herd of Thoroughbred
stallions close behind, then tossed a lightly accusing gaze to her
husband.

"Rest a while? Are you coddling me, Bennett?"

In the shadow of his hat brim, Jake's whiskey-brown eyes
sparkled at her as he grinned. "No, ma'am, I wouldn't dare." He
nodded sagely to Taggart and Diaz, who were wrangling on the
opposite side of the herd. "But the boys haven't stood on their
own feet twice since sunup, and they're looking piqued."

"Piqued?" Jess looked to the burly, orange-haired Irishman
and the sinewy, born-in-the-saddle Spaniard, and she burst out
laughing. "Those two wouldn't walk to their dinner plates if they
could ride!"

The sleek, long-limbed Thoroughbreds continued towards
the mountains, heads bobbing. From her position riding flank,
Jess took in the beauty of white noses and white socks flashing
amid the bays, chestnuts, and blacks, framed by the red earth
and green pines of the Sierra Nevadas.

They were going home.

Jess quieted, but her smile remained. "I couldn't stop now,
Jake. We have only ten miles before we reach the ranch."

Ten out of seventeen hundred, she mused, *and eight months since*

I've seen this part of the country. When they had left the ranch, they hadn't been married, and she hadn't been certain she'd ever come back. Even so, she hadn't forgotten the beauty of the mountains, her love of the ranch in Honey Lake Valley, and her dream to raise horses with the good man beside her.

Amid the scattered rocks and fragrant clusters of gray-green sage around them, desert flowers added brilliant splashes of purple, red, and orange. When they had left, the land had been brown, dry from a year of heat and draught. Clearly, the winter snows and spring rains had come, for now, life bloomed everywhere.

Well, almost everywhere. With a twinge of sadness, Jess pressed a gloved hand to the flatness of her stomach.

She and Jake had married in the fall, on one of the most beautiful autumn days God had ever created. As a wedding gift, Jake had given her the herd of Thoroughbreds, which were grazing in the Bennetts' paddock even as the pastor stood with them beneath an arch of trees and joined them as husband and wife.

All she had wanted was to give Jake a child in return. And now, it seemed, she was barren.

"What do you suppose they're thinking, your horses?"

Jess dropped her hand and smiled. "*Our* horses," she corrected him. "They're probably wishing they had taken a train instead."

Jake chuckled, his broad shoulders stretching the seams of his white cotton shirt. "Is that what you wish, Jess? That the transcontinental was nearly finished instead of only beginning?"

"No, I wouldn't want to be packed into a noisy passenger car anymore than you would. I'd rather see the land—be a part of it."

"Well, this land looks as though it's seen some rain this year."

"I was just thinking the same."

The Bennett Mountain Ranch—our ranch. Tickled by the thought,

Jess laughed out loud. "We're going home," she said, a pleasant tightness in her chest. "I feel...." She lifted a hand, uncertain how to describe her feeling. "I feel like a young falcon, about to soar into the wind for the first time."

He smiled in understanding, then suddenly turned tense, alert. He drew his Remington. An instant later, Taggart and Diaz did the same.

"What—?"

A rock burst on the ground beside Jess. The sharp report of rifle fire echoed across the desert. All at once, shots exploded, pelting the road around them with shattered stones and dust plumes. Drawing her own revolver, Jess whipped her mare around and looked past Jake to an outcropping of rocks, where rifles barked and gun smoke curled away.

The mare abruptly jerked, then reared high, spilling Jess's hat and causing her long braid of hair to tumble free. The horse teetered on its hind legs, then fell over backward.

Pain exploded through Jess's back and lungs.

Then, darkness.